Alex Palmer is a Canberra-based novelist who took up writing full time when she was made redundant from the Australian Public Service. With *Blood Redemption*, she won the Ned Kelly Award for Best First Crime Novel, and shared the Sisters in Crime Davitt Award for best crime novel by a woman with Gabrielle Lord. She is currently completing her third novel, *The Labyrinth of Drowning*.

Also by Alex Palmer

Blood Redemption

THE TATTOOED MAN

ALEX PALMER

HarperCollins*Publishers*

Supported by the ACT government

www.arts.act.gov.au

Author's Note
All events, places and individuals depicted in this novel are wholly fictional. Any resemblance to any actual event, place or individual, whether existing or historical, is purely coincidental and unintentional.

HarperCollins*Publishers*

First published in Australia in 2008
by HarperCollins*Publishers* Australia Pty Limited
ABN 36 009 913 517
www.harpercollins.com.au

HarperCollins*Publishers*
25 Ryde Road, Pymble, Sydney, NSW 2073, Australia
31 View Road, Glenfield, Auckland 10, New Zealand
1–A, Hamilton House, Connaught Place, New Delhi – 110 001, India
77–85 Fulham Palace Road, London, W6 8JB, United Kingdom
2 Bloor Street East, 20th floor, Toronto, Ontario M4W 1A8, Canada
10 East 53rd Street, New York NY 10022, USA

National Library of Australia Cataloguing-in-Publication data:

Palmer, Alex, 1952– .
  Tattooed man.
  ISBN: 978 0 7322 8572 2 (pbk.).
  I. Title.
A823.4

Cover design by Natalie Winter
Cover image by Shutterstock
Typeset in 11/15 Sabon by Kirby Jones
Printed and bound in Australia by Griffin Press
70gsm Bulky Book Ivory used by HarperCollins*Publishers* is a natural, recyclable product made from wood grown in sustainable forests. The manufacturing processes conform to the environmental regulations in the country of origin, Finland.

5 4 3 2 1   08 09 10 11

For John Lacey

What is the price of Experience do men buy it for a song?
Or Wisdom for a dance in the street? No, it is bought with the price
Of all that a man hath his house his wife his children
Wisdom is sold in the desolate market where none come to buy
And in the wither'd field where the farmer plows for bread in vain.

William Blake, *Vala*, or
The Four Zoas, 'Night the Second'

1

The dead sat at the table like those who are about to eat but never
will. Dinner plates set before them contained a meal left
untouched. Their rested mouths, their closed eyes, the unshifting
weight of their bodies, had a finality beyond waking. A middle-aged
woman sat between an older man and a teenage boy. She wore a
diamond pendant that caught the glittering rays of the sun. Her
sideways-tilted head, its artificial honey curls, leaned towards the
teenage boy across a short but unreachable distance. The boy looked
the most peaceful of them all. His head hung downwards and his black
hair shone in the sun. His stained T-shirt was emblazoned with the
word *Nature* in letters formed out of intertwined trees. In contrast, the
older man had been caught out in the most unexpected surprise. He
leaned backwards, mouth open, arms loose at his sides, his glasses
opaque in the white light.

The fourth guest, seated at the head of the table, was naked. This
corpse was mummified, its skin wrinkled, its face and body withered
almost past recognition. One of its dry hands rested on a thick bound
document placed beside its table setting, the blue cover stained with
blood like the white cloth beneath.

Paul Harrigan thought he must be the only living person left in
existence. Somehow he had walked unaided into the land of the dead,
a stony landscape that gave no relief from the heat. With a movement
that might have seemed an act of grieving, he squatted down beside the

fourth and naked body. In the white glare of the sunlight, it grinned nothingness at him. Gently Harrigan reached forward and with his gloved hand extracted the bound booklet from beneath the dead man's hand.

He stood up. These motionless figures created a pool of silence, but there was no quietness, only the anticipation of further violence waiting its turn. Whichever way he turned, they drained his energy out of him. They seemed to reach up and tug at his sleeve, to draw him down to sit at their table in their permanent stillness. The air carried the stench of a powerful insect repellent; he could not breathe. This was breaking point. The job did not call for more than this, not even from him.

'Get on with it,' he said, and stepped out of the way of the watching forensic team. They moved past him in a small crowd to resume their jobs, their footsteps clattering on the paving stones. Blue police ribbons hung lifeless in the hot air.

Harrigan turned to his 2IC who had come to stand beside him. Trevor Gabriel was a big man, round-headed and broad-shouldered with almost no neck. Harrigan was as tall but without Trevor's bulk.

'How long have they been here?' he asked.

'A bit less than twenty-four hours,' Trevor replied. 'That's exactly how we found them, down to the last detail.'

'Jesus,' Harrigan said softly, feeling the impact rock him. 'Come to dinner, pay with your life, and you don't even get to eat. Take me through it one more time. Who are they?'

Trevor ran his hand over his close-cut black hair, a gesture that was the equivalent of a shrug.

'The body at the end. Who knows? It's got no ID, nothing. According to his credit cards, the man with the glasses is Jerome Beck. He's not known to us. The woman is Natalie Edwards. Definitely known to us and this is her house. The boy is her son, Julian. He's nineteen. I doubt he was an intended target. I'm told he came home early from a camping trip. Poor bloody kid. It was wrong place, wrong time for him.'

Harrigan said nothing at first. He hated this, walking in on scenes where all he could do was clean up afterwards. When did he ever stop anything like this from happening?

'Who gave you that information?' he asked.

'His father. He's sitting in the government car outside. Senator Allan Edwards, the federal Minister for Science and Technology. He's the one who called us.'

Harrigan drew on his extensive store of Sydney scuttlebutt. The senator and Natalie Edwards, a well-known businesswoman with a dubious reputation as a money launderer, had been divorced for more than fifteen years after a short, stormy marriage. Back then, the senator had been Allan Edwards, businessman. His political ambitions had been realised only after his marriage had died.

'I saw him when I went out to talk to the press just now,' Harrigan said. 'What was he doing here? His ex-wife didn't pick up the phone and say drop by and see me.'

'He had an appointment. It's in her diary. He says he wants to tell us why he was here but so far he can't put two sentences together. Can't say I blame him.'

Harrigan looked around. This was a private place for a killing: a large house in the leafy, far northern waterside suburbs of Sydney. The patio was a contained circle surrounded by the thick barrier of a tall silver-green hedge. A narrow archway gave a view onto Pittwater, dotted with yachts and pleasure craft on this hot Sunday afternoon in early December. The place would not stay so self-contained for long. The dead had become a public exhibit to be dissected with a painstaking scrutiny. An enthusiastic audience in the shape of the media was already outside on the street, beating at the front gate.

'How did they die?' he asked.

'Leaving out our man on the end there, one shot only to the back of the head for each of them sometime between eight and eleven last night. It was very clean shooting by somebody who knew how to do it. It was all over in a few seconds.'

Clean wasn't a word Harrigan would have used just then. He had been dragged out here during the first days of his summer leave, travelling the distance across greater Sydney to see this grotesquery.

'How many killers? One, or more than one?' he asked.

'Impossible to say. Could be just one person. We're looking at a teenage boy and two middle-aged people, all soft targets.'

'Is this a ritual killing, or an execution, or both?'

'Whatever it is, it's professional and they must have used silencers. Otherwise they'd have woken up the neighbours.'

'Considerate bunch, aren't they?' Harrigan grinned blackly. 'And they brought the mummy at the head of the table with them?'

'Had to have. He wasn't lying around the house for them to use.'

Harrigan couldn't prevent a harsh, short laugh. 'Who are these people? Why do this?'

He became aware that he still held the bloodstained booklet in his hand. He began to leaf through the thick bound document. It was a detailed and complex scientific specification fronted by an equally complex-looking contract. Each page, the cover included, was marked with the same identifying number.

'Is this the only copy? When you're signing a contract like this, aren't there usually two of them?'

'That's the only one we've found so far. You'd have to say they wanted us to find it. It couldn't have been more obvious if they'd nailed it to the fucking front door.'

Harrigan read over the preamble. Agricultural produce grown according to the attached scientific specification was to be supplied by the International Agricultural Research Consortium to an organisation called World Food and Crop Providers. The address on the contract placed the latter's offices in Johannesburg, South Africa. Their CEO had already signed; a name unknown to Harrigan. In contrast, the spaces beside the printed names of the three principals for the Consortium were blank. Two of the unsigned names were only too well known to him.

'Jerome Beck, Natalie Edwards and Stuart Morrissey, all directors of this consortium,' he said. 'Head offices, York Street, Sydney. That's Morrissey's business address. What would Edwards and Morrissey be doing involved in agricultural research?'

'Old Stewie did grow up on a farm,' Trevor replied.

'That was decades ago. As far as I know, he hasn't been home for years.' Harrigan located the sums specified for payment on delivery and whistled. 'There's enough money on offer. What was this consortium supplying? Wheat, tobacco, rice, white yam. Why are they so expensive? Why send them to Johannesburg?'

'It's whatever's set down in that specification. We've had a quick look at it. None of us can understand the science, boss. We're going to have to get someone in to tell us what it means. But if you want my opinion, that contract says it all. Two of the biggest scam merchants around, Morrissey and Edwards, in business together. Whatever this consortium is, it's got to be bent. Which means that whoever Beck is, he's got to be bent as well.'

Harrigan considered that if Stuart Morrissey had been sitting at the table with Natalie Edwards right now, two of the major players in the money-laundering business in his bailiwick would have been out of business permanently. A sour, if effective, way to shut down their extensive criminal and financial networks. As it was, Nattie Edwards' death would create a gap that any number of questionable individuals would want to fill. She'd had a finger in a large number of pies, had been the source of an almost bottomless bucket of dirty money that somehow always managed to come out clean.

'Where's Morrissey?' he asked. 'Was he supposed to be here last night? Is there another body lying around the house you haven't found yet?'

'Come and listen to this. We think it's him. Looks like last night's dinner was turned on for them to celebrate signing that contract. It didn't work out that way.'

Harrigan handed the contract to one of the forensic officers for bagging and followed Trevor through open double doors into a lounge room. An answering machine stood on a telephone table just inside.

'*Nattie. It's me. Look, I'm sorry I couldn't get there, I'll tell you why when I see you. Did you sign without me? If you did, just call me. I'll come up there today and sign whenever you want.*'

'That's him,' Harrigan said. 'How come his lottery numbers came up last night of all nights?'

'We'll ask him. But he's a little rat. People like him always survive.'

Not like that poor kid sitting out there. Harrigan shook away a pervasive revulsion. He looked around at the large and opulent room, the state-of-the-art sound and entertainment system, the original artworks hanging on the walls.

'They took nothing? There's enough here to make it worth your while.'

'They didn't touch a thing. You saw the stone Edwards is wearing. It's genuine. Why not take it with you? Call it a fringe benefit. Whoever these people are, they haven't left us a trace.'

In his mind's eye, Harrigan saw Natalie Edwards seated at the table, her diamond gleaming in the white light. He looked back outside at the scene, unable to prevent himself from staring at the dead surrounded by their living attendants. His gaze was drawn to the naked figure at the end of the table. The ghost of a nagging possibility had entered his mind.

'Do you want to talk to the minister now, boss?' Trevor asked. 'I don't think we should keep him waiting much longer.'

'Give me a moment,' Harrigan replied, moving out through the doors onto the patio again.

'Harrigan,' a voice boomed. 'I didn't recognise you in your civvies. Weren't you born wearing a suit?' Kenneth McMichael, the pathologist, a huge and untidy man with a legendary foul temper, had buttonholed him. 'Quite a sight, isn't it? Makes me think of musical chairs. The music's stopped and while there are enough chairs to go around, I'm sorry, ladies and gentlemen, it's endgame.'

He spoke like a satirical game-show host. Harrigan felt his patience thinning dangerously.

'It always makes me feel warm all over to see you, Ken. Do we know how that man at the end died?'

'No. It's impossible to tell in that state. I can tell you he took a shot to the right shoulder sometime ante-mortem but it's hardly a mortal wound. You'll have to wait for the autopsy if you want to know anything else.'

'Can you get one of your technicians to give me a hand? I need to look at his left shoulder.'

'As always, your wish is our command,' McMichael replied with his usual glacial sarcasm.

At the pathologist's direction, the technician stretched the shrunken skin on one arm for Harrigan to look at. It was like fine yellowed leather, ingrained with coarse sand. A small tattoo came into view, an aged caricature of Marilyn Monroe as a golden-haired smiling skeleton in a red dress and matching high heels. Two updraughts of air raised her voluminous skirts above her bony legs. There was a signature just visible beneath it: AMBRO.

Trevor was standing behind Harrigan, watching. 'Oh, fuck me,' he said, as soon as the tattoo came into sight. 'Tell me it isn't true.'

'No one else, mate,' Harrigan replied. 'That's Ambrosine's signature. She only ever does one of any tattoo she signs. Look on the bright side. We know what's happened to him now. We're not chasing shadows any more.'

'I'm guessing we have an identification,' the pathologist said dryly.

Harrigan moved back. 'For your information, Ken, we've just found the body we've all been looking for the last three months. That's former Detective Senior Sergeant Michael Cassatt sitting there, otherwise known as the Ice Cream Man. Fuck knows how he ended up here.'

'Full of surprises, Harrigan,' McMichael said, writing down the name in his notebook. 'I've often wondered what you've got tucked away in that head of yours. All right, we'll chase up his dental records. Can we take him now?'

'Be my guest.'

McMichael's careful technicians surrounded the dead man. Watching them, Harrigan's mind was filled with the memory of his father's funeral, twelve years ago. He had been standing at the church door greeting the mourners as they arrived. When he turned to go inside, Mike Cassatt had come from behind and taken him by the shoulder.

'Don't be frightened, Paulie,' he'd said. 'I'm not here to hurt you. I want to show you this. Ambro put it there. I got it for old Jimbo.' He meant Harrigan's father. He'd pushed up the sleeve of his red polo shirt to show off the bony tattoo. 'Like my dream girl? Isn't she beautiful? *Come dance with me...*' he'd sung while eyeballing Harrigan. 'See you, mate.' Then he'd walked away.

There was another echo in Harrigan's mind: Cassatt's voice again, just ten days after the funeral, at night-time in an alleyway in Marrickville. Joyfully vicious words uttered close into Harrigan's face: *You're dead, mate.* But not before you, Mike, he retorted down the years of wasted time. In reply, Cassatt's death mask grinned at him across the table. Then the body was lifted away.

'Boss? Boss, are you listening to me?' Trevor was talking in his ear. 'We've got a fucking federal government minister sitting in his car on the other side of the hedge. Cassatt's the last thing we need here. What do we do?'

Harrigan suppressed a caustic smile. Anything to avoid the taint of the Ice Cream Man. Two months ago, he himself had signed off on the decision to declare the notoriously corrupt ex-detective missing, presumed murdered. It had started with Cassatt's wife found shot dead in their home at Oyster Bay with the house left ransacked. Next Harrigan had received a visit from Cassatt's solicitor, the greasiest man he'd ever dealt with. After Leanne Cassatt's murder, the solicitor had gone to check his client's safety deposit box and found it emptied out. Then Cassatt's car was located burnt-out and cannibalised at a derelict factory site near Parramatta. In the boot were the charred remains of bloodstained clothing. When it was finally confirmed as the Ice Cream Man's own blood, Harrigan was forced to conclude he must be dead. Until then, the only blood Cassatt had left behind him was always somebody else's.

'Boss? Talk to me.'

'You do what you'd normally do,' Harrigan snapped back. 'You find out how Cassatt died and what he was doing here in the first place. What difference does it make who he is?'

'Because it's not going to be that straightforward. Anything about the Ice Cream Man gives the commissioner a coronary. When he hears about this, he's going to want to put his oar in. God knows how much he'll fuck us around. Then there's you, boss.' Trevor spoke more quietly. 'There's all those rumours out there about you and Cassatt. You've told me they're shit and I accept that. But people are going to talk. The commissioner's going to wonder what's behind them, the way he always does. Every move we make, he's going to be looking over our shoulders.'

'Let him,' Harrigan replied savagely. 'You can handle it. That's what you're paid for.'

He peeled off his gloves. Sweat prickled across his forehead. He felt a growing impatience needling at his self-control. 'Let's go talk to the minister. It's time I introduced myself.'

They found Senator Allan Edwards at the front of the house, sitting at a garden table and stroking a pedigree Rottweiler that sat with its head on his knees. Not far from his feet, a flock of tiny fairy wrens, their feathers satin-purple and bright powder-blue in the sunlight, picked their quick, indifferent way through the garden beds. Parked on the gravel, Harrigan saw the minister's white government car, his driver standing beside it, smoking a cigarette and staring at the ground. The high walls surrounding the house and garden had turned this space near the garages into an artificial oasis, creating a sense not so much of calm as of stretched and tense inaction.

'Senator Edwards? I'm Commander Paul Harrigan. New South Wales Police. I'm in charge of the Homicide and Violent Crime Command. My people are running this investigation. You've met my inspector, Trevor Gabriel. I'd like to give you our deepest sympathy for what's happened here. I want to assure you we'll do everything we possibly can to find whoever is responsible for this outrage and put them away.'

Harrigan's professional etiquette, his passionless voice, were doing the talking for him. In this job, detachment was his protection. While he spoke, he watched the politician watch him. Edwards must have been close to sixty. His cheeks were a mat of broken veins while his eyes had an aged, liquid white glaze to them. He might have accumulated an extra ten years in the last few hours. He didn't offer his hand. Harrigan could see that it was trembling. The dog looked up with innocent eyes and then sat at the senator's feet.

'This is Matilda,' Edwards said. 'She was Julian's dog. She was locked in his room. You're going to solve this, are you? Are you going to bring my son back to life as well?'

If only we could, Harrigan thought.

'Did you come here to see him, Minister?'

'No, I came to see Nattie. Julian wasn't supposed to be back until tonight. She was expecting me, we'd organised this appointment a week ago. Check her diary, it'll be there. Someone else must have checked it because they knew I was going to be here today. You can keep this. It's not an official phone, it's my personal one.'

Edwards gave Harrigan his mobile phone. An SMS message was on display, a string of numbers and letters with the words: *This will get you in the gate.*

'I received that message while I was on my way here,' Edwards said. 'When we arrived, no one answered the intercom. I told my driver to try the numbers like the message said. They opened the gate so we drove in. I could hear Matilda barking from somewhere inside. I didn't know why she'd be here. I heard flies. I went through to the patio —' He stopped. 'I'll never forget that sight. Not until the day I die.'

After this, he couldn't speak. Harrigan gave the phone to Trevor and waited for the senator to become calm.

'We'll trace that call, Minister, wherever it might have come from,' he said. 'Who would have the number for that phone?'

'A dozen people at the most. Julian was one. There are things I need to tell you about this. They're important but I can't get a grip on the facts —'

Again, he was about to break down. Harrigan signalled to a uniformed police officer.

'I think you should go home now, Minister. My people will be in touch and arrange to see you at another time. This is my card. You can call me on any of those numbers any time you need to. This officer will help you to your car.'

Edwards dumbly pushed the card into his pocket and stood up. The dog got to her feet as well.

'I'm taking Matilda with me. She needs a home now. I'm not usually like this, I can assure you.'

'It's not a problem,' Harrigan replied. 'I have a son myself.'

'Is he your only child?'

'Yes, he is.'

'How old is he?'

'He turned eighteen today,' Harrigan said, restraining his usual reluctance at voicing anything personal.

'Maybe you do know. I'll never understand how anyone could do this.'

After seventeen years on the job, Harrigan was forced to admit, if only to himself, that he didn't always understand either. Even after he'd joined the dots of how and why, some fundamental motivation continued to escape him. They watched the senator being driven away, caught a glimpse of the waiting media on the other side of the high metal gates, the cameras flashing and the TV crews running in pursuit of the white car after it had turned into the street.

'Our killers wanted him to see that,' Trevor said. 'Why would you do that? It's fucking cruel.'

'Our killers believe in shock value,' Harrigan replied, dispassionate as always. 'All right, I'll leave you to it. You've got it under control. But from now on, you forget I'm on leave. If the Ice Cream Man's involved in this, I need to know where it's going. At all times, I want you to keep me briefed.'

'I can do that, boss, but there's one other thing before you disappear. Ambrosine. Is she alive? And where is she? If the Ice Cream Man's dead in there, we should be talking to her.'

'You want to know where Ambro is?' Harrigan said. 'Walls have ears, mate. Is that information going to travel?'

'I would have thought you'd know you could trust me by now,' Trevor replied, with a quiet touch of anger.

'I told you she was alive. I must trust you.' Harrigan gathered his thoughts. 'Yes, I know where she is. I spoke to her when we upgraded Cassatt's disappearance to murder but she was freaked over something. She wouldn't talk to me. She said she hadn't seen him for months.'

'Did you believe her?'

'No, but she wasn't going to tell me any different.'

'Can't she come out of hiding now?' Trevor asked. 'Tell me where she is and I'll send a team to talk to her.'

'No. There's still one very angry bikie out there waiting to blow her away. I'll have to talk to her myself. I need time for that to happen. As soon as I get anything out of her, I'll talk to you. Right now, I've got places I should be.'

'Okay, boss. Thanks for coming all the way up here. Say hello to Gracie for me when you see her. I haven't caught up with her much since she started working for that joint agencies task force, whatever it is.'

'I'll pass it on,' he said. If she's still talking to me.

Harrigan had given his spiel to the media scrum on the front street not long after he'd first arrived, as usual stonewalling them before he'd gone to take in the murder scene in more detail. Tonight his image would be broadcast on the evening news bulletins whether he liked it or not. Avoiding a second encounter, he made his escape through a rear gate out to the laneway where he'd parked his car. He stopped to look back at the house, a flamboyant architectural vision of curved sandstone walls and wide windows offering panoramic views. As a mausoleum, it was more ornate than most he visited in his line of work. Harrigan let himself out, hoping he would never have to come back here.

2

Outside on the street, under the hard blue sky, the trees shivered in the extreme heat. A hot wind gusted around Harrigan with a low roar. It carried the promise of bushfire, a warning to watch for thick plumes of smoke above the expensive houses built onto these steep, forested hillsides. He had left his car deeply shaded by the laneway's trees. When he walked towards it, he saw a Harley-Davidson parked in front, blocking his exit. A woman dressed in a white T-shirt and motorbike leathers was sitting on the hog side on, seemingly waiting for him.

'Paul Harrigan? Commander Harrigan?' she called out. 'Do you have a moment? I do have a reason for being here.'

The voice was clear and caught his attention. Harrigan hesitated. The woman stepped lightly to the ground and moved towards him.

'Why don't you take this?' she said with a smile, offering her card. 'Then you won't have to wonder who I am.'

Sam Jonas. Personal Security Manager. Life Patent Strategies Inc.

Harrigan studied the card and its owner. She was tall, close to six feet. The set of her shoulders under her T-shirt and her tight, muscular body said she worked out regularly. She was in her mid, possibly late thirties. Her hair was black, braided at the back of her head with a thick fringe over the forehead. A longish face, smoothly and finely carved. Her tanned skin was flawless, her eyes almost green, her mouth dark red without lipstick. In this catalogue of perfection, there was no semblance — at least to him — of sensuality. His immediate instinct towards her was distrust.

'Sam Jonas. Is that your real name?'

'Why wouldn't it be?'

'It's just a question. I ask them in my business. What are you doing here? How come you know who I am?'

'Isn't Paul Harrigan well known? You often get your picture in the paper. Aren't you touted as commissioner material? That means something in this town.'

'But you knew this was my car.'

'No, I didn't. They wouldn't help me at the front gate so I came back here. When I saw the car, I thought it might belong to someone who's involved in whatever's going on in there.'

This explanation, faintly plausible, left Harrigan wondering why any knowledge about him should be of interest to someone who, so far as he knew, had no connection to him. He noted her accent: Australian overlaid with an English intonation. Someone who had spent a lot of time in Britain.

'Why are you so interested?' he asked.

'I'm here for my employer. Do you know the name Dr Elena Calvo? She's the CEO for Life Patent Strategies. Senator Edwards is Elena's connection to the Australian government. He was supposed to be at a meeting with her today, but he didn't turn up and he's not answering his phone.' Sam glanced at the house with a turn of her strong and graceful neck. 'His PA said he was up here. Then we heard there'd been a multiple shooting. We only want to know if the senator is okay.'

Sam's words brought back the blackness of the scene inside the house. The faces of the dead became masks mirrored in Harrigan's mind, looking out through his own eyes. For a moment, the outside world disappeared.

'So is he?' Sam's voice, harder this time, interrupted his thoughts. 'Is the senator still on his feet? Did you talk to him?'

'I've talked to him. If your concern is for his welfare, you're better off leaving him alone.'

'Is there something on your mind, Commander? Did you see something in there you didn't like? I'd have thought someone with your background would be used to dealing with the dead. Isn't it all straightforward enough once you face up to what it means? You must have done that by now.'

Throughout, there had been a hard edge to her voice. She stood with her arms folded, watching him with her sharp green eyes.

'How would you know? Dr Calvo knows the senator, does she? Why send you up here? Why not come herself if she's so concerned?'

'Because that's my job. That's what I do for Elena. I check things out.'

'Do you? Why are you introducing yourself to me like this?'

'I told you. I'm trying to find out if a good friend of ours is in one piece. You've just told me he is. Now I can go back and tell Elena the same thing. She worries. There are people she cares about.'

'Tell her to wait for the senator to contact her next time. Can you move your bike? I've got to get going.'

'You're running this investigation, aren't you? You'll be the one who decides what does and doesn't happen,' she said without shifting.

'Why do you want to know that?'

'I want to tell Elena that everything's under control.'

'Yes, I'm the one who makes the decisions. You can tell her that if you want to. I'm the only one who makes the decisions. You can tell her that too.'

She stepped closer, looking him directly in the eyes.

'Everything I read about you, Commander, tells me you're on the way up,' she said softly. 'I can make you an offer worth your while. If you like the good things in life, this is the way to get them. If you want influence where it counts, a positive answer now will get it for you. All you have to do is tell me you're interested. After that, it'll be very straightforward.'

'You can go back to your boss and tell her I don't do business with anyone.' He spoke sharply enough for there to be a deeper silence in the air. 'Say something like that to me again and I'll charge you. Now leave.'

'It's your word against mine, Commander. You'd have to prove I said it first,' she replied, unfazed. 'That might be embarrassing to you. But at least I know which way you'd jump.'

She walked away. He looked at her strong, muscular shoulders and arms, the tautness of her body from her waist to her ankles. Her movements were quick and assured.

'Wait,' he called.

'What?' She turned back sharply.

'You look strong to me. Are you? You work out, don't you?'

'I can look after myself if that's what you mean. Do you approve or disapprove?'

'It's just a question.'

'I know. You ask them in your business.' She smiled mockingly. 'See you.'

Speedily she was helmeted up. She disappeared out of the lane, the sound of the Harley's engine reverberating over the distance. Harrigan got into his car and sat tapping the steering wheel for a few seconds. Then he reached over and picked up his diary, his book of life, from the seat beside him. This A4-sized book came with him wherever he went, plotting out the details of his allotted time. He took out a glossy brochure he'd placed inside its back cover. It announced that the corporation Life Patent Strategies would be floated on the Australian Stock Exchange in the near future. Selected investors were invited to the black-tie occasion in the function rooms of the Museum of Contemporary Art at Circular Quay. A champagne buffet would be served. It was an opportunity to be a part of the latest developments in biotechnological research, a venture with the full backing of the Australian government.

Harrigan's invitation had come by means of an old school friend who was now a stockbroker. His eighteen-year-old son was the reason for his interest. Born crippled with cerebral palsy, Toby had a clear mind that was locked in a twisted body. Barely able to speak, he had lived his life in a wheelchair and needed twenty-four-hour care. The biotechnology corporation, its scientific program focusing on the regeneration of the human body, had offered the possibility there might one day be a cure for him. Harrigan had accepted his invitation to the launch even though he knew that any help for his son was most likely decades away.

He studied the brochure for several moments. The photographs of two individuals smiled out at him: the minister he had just met, and

Dr Elena Calvo, an attractive, fair-haired woman in her mid-thirties. Her biography gave an impressive list of achievements. It identified her as born in Switzerland and having lived in various countries in Europe and the United States before making London her home. Now she intended to establish her business in Australia. A habitual questioner, Harrigan's first thought was, why come here, all the way to the other side of the world? Aren't we out of the way? What do we have that you want?

He read further. The brochure highlighted LPS's signature project: wide-ranging research into the regeneration of the human body following major burns, carried out under the direction of an English-born scientist, Dr Daniel Brinsmead. Harrigan glanced over Brinsmead's résumé, an imposing list of academic qualifications including a stint at the British army officer-training academy at Sandhurst. There was no picture of Brinsmead but judging from the dates attached to his qualifications he must have been in his early forties. Harrigan closed the brochure, returned it to his diary and put both back on the passenger seat.

Knowing that she was genuine didn't dispel the sense of unease Sam Jonas had left him with. Unwillingly, he found himself comparing her to Grace. Grace Riordan was ten years younger than he was and, to Harrigan's mind, an unlikely woman to find in his profession. A trained police officer, she had walked into his life eighteen months ago when she had briefly worked for him on his homicide squad. Usually he was too ruthless to become involved with someone in these circumstances; it could have meant death for his ambitions. But fate was kind to him, giving him an out, removing them both from each other's workplaces. At almost the same time, he had been elevated into his current position and she had got a job working in a joint state-federal task force called Orion, supposedly dealing with intelligence coordination. In reality, Harrigan was fairly certain it was an anti-terrorism unit although he had never asked Grace if this was so. Their occupations built walls of secrecy into their relationship whether they liked it or not.

With no disrespect to Grace's talents, which he admired, he had wondered if it had been her father's name that had swung that job in her favour. She was the daughter of a retired brigadier, a man who had fought in the Vietnam war and been awarded the Military Cross. In the present, Kep Riordan was best known for writing sharply perceptive columns on defence matters for various newspapers and magazines. He was more a dove than a hawk these days but it was still the type of pedigree people in the intelligence business valued.

It had taken Harrigan some time to get past Grace's particular armours — the face paint, the dull suits she wore to work — to find the other woman, the one who liked to dress up in party frocks and go out and enjoy herself. The one he had just left standing once again to come up here. This time, even he knew he was pushing it.

With her guard on, Grace was calm. Without the guard, her emotions were powerful. In contrast, Sam Jonas seemed cold; she had brushed off his questions, and him, as if both were small, blind flies. 'I'll check you out,' he said to her absent presence. 'I'll find out who you really are and what you really want.'

He drove away, noticing from the gauge on the car's dashboard that the temperature outside was 37° C. It needn't concern him; secure in his air-conditioned car, he could discount the weather as an irrelevancy. He reached the main road south quickly, merging into the stream of traffic. The grey bitumen had become silver, the colour of solidified water. Around him, burnished car bodies glinted in the sunlight.

Sam Jonas couldn't stay in his head; neither could Grace. The Ice Cream Man erased them both. Rumour had it that when Cassatt had joined the force back in the early seventies, his first commanding officer had ridiculed both his background (said to be French, from New Caledonia, a generation or two back) and his wog name, and had introduced the new boy to everyone as the Cassata. Over time, the Cassata became the Ice Cream Man, the man who gave out the sweets. By then, people had stopped laughing at him for any reason.

Harrigan turned off his mobile phone. White external light burned the road ahead. The scene in his mind was night-time in a back alleyway in Marrickville those ten days after his father's funeral, where he had gone supposedly to meet an informant. The arrangement had been a trap. Around him, out of the dark, three other policemen had appeared: Jerry Freeman, Joe Saba (dead years ago, found shot, slumped over his steering wheel one Sunday morning early) and Mike Cassatt.

Their punches hit home into his ribcage, knocking the air out of his lungs. With a crack to his head with a nightstick, Saba sent him to the roadway barely conscious. His attackers pitched into him with ferocious, incessant kicks, all three laughing, high as kites. Cassatt was almost choking with glee. He spoke: 'Get him up.' Saba and Freeman dragged Harrigan onto his knees, standing either side to hold him upright. He swayed in their grip, wondering why he kept blinking, only later understanding that his blood had been pouring down his face. Cassatt pulled his head up by the hair.

'The joke's on you this time, Paulie. You've fucked me around once too often. You're going to do this to yourself. You're going to paint your brains on a paling fence.'

There was shrill laughter from one of the men holding him, he still didn't know who. Cassatt squeezed Harrigan's hands around his own gun and pushed it against Harrigan's clenched mouth, his clenched teeth, with all the obscenity of a cock.

'You're dead, mate.'

Words spoken with utter joy. Through his blinking eyes, he had seen Cassatt's face up close. His eyes were half-closed, his mouth was set in a strange half-smile. Transfigured with ecstasy on the edge of the single moment when he would see the back of Harrigan's head shatter.

There had been a glitch in time in which Harrigan felt his body dissolve and a black pit open underneath him. Then all at once they were dazzled by car headlights turned on them at high beam. For whatever reason, pinned in this light, Cassatt had not forced a shot from Harrigan's own hand. He smashed his jaw with the gun instead. 'Run!' he shouted. They threw him forwards onto the laneway and were gone, all three, while he lay there in atrocious pain, astonished to be alive.

Harrigan, driving through the strip of shops fronting Collaroy beach, found himself in slow traffic. He turned into the parking area next to the surf club, fluking a spot vacated by someone else. Leaving his car there, he walked the short distance to the beach. It was crowded with sunbakers in luminous costumes. The hot wind carried the sound of their laughter, of people's small screams when they ran into the water. Swimmers dotted a blue sea too flat for surfers; mothers held their tiny naked children by the hand on the edge of the immense Pacific. With pink plastic bubbles wrapped around their arms, the toddlers danced in the docile waves. The sea and the sky had the shining sticky liquidity of melted ice cream.

Harrigan sat down in the sand. With his index finger, he traced the slightly uneven line of his reconstructed jaw, feeling the old ache come to life like a twist of hot wire in the bone. His life had teetered in a fragment of time, perhaps no longer than the blink of his eye. In that instant, his fear had peeled him to the bone. Bare-headed in the heat of the late sun, he was cold with the memory. Handfuls of hot sand slid through his fingers. He thought of Cassatt's death mask. The man's preserved skin, his shrunken face, merged into one with the colour of the sand.

Harrigan had always seen the occasion of his near murder as a fixed point to which one day, in the event of his real death, he would be forced to return. A gunshot was a final sound. In his dreams, he waited to hear the single shot that in life had never been fired. He knew that as soon as it was, nothing would save him and he would die. Each time he had this nightmare he fought his way out of it, feeling that he was surfacing from his grave.

Cassatt's capacity to corrupt his life spread further than his nightmares. Harrigan was one of a number of people (so he guessed) who would have lain awake these last two months wondering who had their hands on the contents of Cassatt's safety deposit box; questioning what would happen to their lives if those contents were ever made public. He grinned sardonically. He was stuck on the same old carousel. After all these years he was still running after his old enemy.

The pervasive heat broke through his thoughts. His shirt clung to his back with sweat. He stood up, catching a faint breeze from the sea, the promise of some coolness from an easterly wind. Its cleanness was a good medicine after a long and bizarre few hours but he'd still had enough. He drove back out onto Pittwater Road under an evening sky that was softening to an infinite blue, thinking of home and sanctuary.

3

Harrigan stopped off at Cotswold House, the private facility near the water's edge at Drummoyne where his son lived. Toby's mother had abandoned him to Harrigan when he was a baby and then walked out of both their lives. One way or another, Harrigan had cared for his son ever since. As a father, he had learnt that each child has its own particular smell, something in the skin. He thought that blindfolded he would know his son by his smell and the touch of his hair. Toby was a part of himself, fundamental to his happiness and the holder of possibilities he couldn't have let die at any time.

Susie, the manager, was outside at the barbecue. Toby had lived in places like this all his life. This was the best of them; Harrigan had made sure of that.

'I guess I'm too late,' he said. 'Looks like the party's over.'

'I'm afraid it is. A while ago now.'

'I'll go in and see Toby in that case.'

'He's asleep, Paul. Today really took it out of him. I don't think we should wake him, I'm sorry. He had a great time though. He said to say good night if you came back.'

'When did Grace leave?'

'Half an hour ago. She was sitting with Toby before he went to sleep. They're very fond of each other.'

'I've missed everybody. Thanks, Susie. I'll see you. I'll be round tomorrow.'

'I'll tell Toby. Good night.'

He walked out into the warm night air. There could have been few worse times to have received a call like today's than at this afternoon's barbecue. The entire extended Harrigan family had been there to celebrate Toby's eighteenth birthday, a milestone he was never expected to reach. Harrigan's two formidable older sisters had arrived in convoy with their numerous noisy offspring and partners. Grace had spent most of her time deftly sidestepping their shamelessly intrusive enquiries about her relationship with him. 'Thanks for throwing me to the wolves,' she had said to him *sotto voce* when he left. Toby, who couldn't speak easily, had signed to him, *You always do this*. Harrigan had felt their mutually accusing gaze follow his every step to his car.

You always do this. Always walk away. After a while, people got tired of it and walked away from him. It was an old story.

He drove home under the glitter of the streetlights, reaching his two-storeyed terrace in Birchgrove not so long afterwards. The upstairs iron-lace veranda shone like a piece of silver trim; the pale, almost ash-pink frontage offered shelter from the night's heat. From time to time, usually at parties, he was asked how he could afford to live in a waterfront house on the Balmain peninsula on a policeman's wage. He could have told his questioners he was no blow-in. He had been born in the district in the early sixties, down near White Bay. Maybe it was just over the hill from where he lived now, but it might as well have been another universe. Even today, where he had lived as a boy was one of the less desirable parts of the neighbourhood. At that time, the peninsula had been a rough place known for its poverty. Its graceful, decaying nineteenth-century terraces sold for almost nothing; its forgotten waterside mansions were more often knocked down and blocks of ugly red-brick units built in their place. Their views of the harbour, the bridge and the city were like gifts thrown away. Those same terraces and mansions sold now for sums unimaginable back then.

The real reason for his silence was the house itself, an inheritance from his paternal aunt while he was still a teenager. No easy endowment, instead a down payment on her interference in his life. A church-ridden, unmarried woman, she had been fiercely ambitious where his future was concerned, nagging and meddling. After her death, his parents had lived in the house with him. Their arguments were ingrained into the walls like some porous inner skin; their deaths had happened here. Even his ancient cat was buried here. Menzies, a ferocious, ragged tom inherited unwillingly from his father, was peacefully snoozing the big sleep in a sunny spot in the garden. It was all too close to the bone for chitchat.

He let himself inside. The house was dark and silent. Grace had said she would meet him here after she left Toby's barbecue. She had her own key; she could have let herself in. Maybe she'd changed her mind and left him high and dry. Stood him up in exchange for his leaving her marooned once again. Why wouldn't she? He had done it often enough to her.

He went through to the kitchen where he poured himself a whisky and felt the silence of the house wrap itself around him. He caught sight of his face in an oval-shaped mirror set in a cedar sideboard that had belonged to his aunt. At the age of forty-one, his darkish fair hair was beginning to thin and the strain in his face was obvious. He looked away.

He remembered he had a phone call to make. The name Stuart Morrissey had rung warning bells for Harrigan from the time he'd first read it in that bloodstained contract. One complication led to another. Stuart led to his brother, Harold, who lived out in the sticks, on a property called Yaralla near a town called Coolemon on the edge of the Riverina.

After Harrigan's near murder at Cassatt's hands, the senior ranks in the police force, embarrassed by the scandal, had sent him out to Coolemon to get him out of the way. He'd stayed there on and off for seven years, often working on secondment to the Australian Federal Police and in the end spending more time out of the town than in it. Discovering that Stuart Morrissey's younger brother lived out there had been something unscripted. Harrigan met Harold for the first time when he had some stock stolen. Expecting another scam merchant, he found himself dealing with a man almost too honest to protect himself. Harold had proved more than once that he was someone you could trust. Just eight months ago he'd given shelter to Ambrosine, a tattooist with three children who had taken one too many risks as Harrigan's informant. There was no phone in the cottage Harold had let Ambrosine have, and out there the signal for her mobile could be unreliable and it was unsafe to use it. The best way of reaching her was through Harold's landline.

Harrigan put down his glass and picked up the phone. His call went unanswered, the phone ringing until it cut out. Harold was the only person Harrigan knew who didn't own an answering machine. He called again, with the same result. Feeling marooned himself, he put the handset back in its cradle.

'Paul? Are you here? You left the front door open.'

Grace's voice startled him. There was the sound of the door shutting, then her heels clicking along the hallway. She walked into the kitchen carrying a bunch of Oriental lilies, a rich iridescent pink in the light. Flowers were something she often brought into his house. She was slender in her summer dress. The sight of her face, framed by her long dark hair and beautiful like the Madonna's, occupied his mind for some moments.

'Hi,' she said, smiling.

Usually he would have kissed her. Tonight he was pinned in his chair by an invisible weight.

'Where have you been? I thought you'd be here by now.'

Grace put the flowers on the table. She gave him a quick, sharp-eyed look, one that got under his skin like itching powder.

'I was buying these flowers. How did it go up there? Not too good.'

'Do I look that bad?'

'You look like death. Your face is like white rubber.'

'Did you cope okay after I'd gone?' he asked, avoiding this.

'Your sleazy nephew made a grotesque pass at me. His wife was standing right beside him. I couldn't believe it.'

'That's Phil. He'd have a hard time finding shame in a dictionary.' Harrigan tried to joke but the humour died in the air. He breathed deeply. 'They said Toby had no brain when he was born. They said I should let him die. Look at him now. He'll be at university next year. What did they know?'

'You're not talking about your sisters. They're not like that. Who's "they"?'

Cassatt with his jabbing voice, each word like a fist in your face. *Put him away, he'll die soon.*

'It doesn't matter.'

'It does matter. It matters to you, that's pretty clear.'

There was silence.

'What's going on?' Grace asked.

'Nothing.'

'Nothing,' she repeated with exasperation. 'Don't tell me that. When you're like this, it's like being locked in a room with no light and air. I can't deal with it. Tell me what's going on.'

'Don't drag this stuff out of my head. Leave it where it can't do anybody any harm.'

He was back there at Pittwater in the unending sunlight with the seated dead. They were staring at him, willing him to sit down with them. Cassatt's shrunken face and his living voice joined them in a mix of savage memories. *You're dead, mate.*

'I'm not dead,' he shouted.

'What?'

'Get out of my head!'

He turned and threw his whisky glass at the opposite wall with all the strength he had. It exploded, spraying glass around the kitchen. Grace jerked around, bending away, shielding her face from the fallout.

'I can't breathe. I've got to get out of here.'

Harrigan was gone, outside to his yard, stumbling onto the thin grass. He turned on the garden tap, squatted beside it and tossed cupped handfuls of water into his face, trying to get some coolness into his brain. He stood up and drew in breath, stared down at the bay, all the connecting pieces of land and buildings on the opposite shore, everything that had been familiar to him since his boyhood. The scene settled into place; he had a grip on the present again. Wiping his face with his handkerchief, he heard Grace behind him. She was turning off the tap which he'd left running.

'You haven't walked out on me,' he said. 'Did I hurt you?'

She looked him in the eye.

'No, you didn't but you could have. Who did you throw that glass at?'

'I didn't throw it at you. I'd never do that. It was at ghosts in my head. I did hurt you. Look at your arm. I'm sorry,'

He'd seen a sudden splash of blood on her arm. A shard from the glass must have glanced her skin. In the shadows, the blood was almost black. She lightly touched the thin, moist trickle and then stared back at him. In the mix of darkness and reflected light, her face had taken on a blue tinge. He placed his damp handkerchief gently onto the scratch. She reached to take hold of it, her hand touching his briefly. After a few moments, she took the handkerchief away. The scratch had stopped bleeding. She looked at the cloth with its small concentration of blood and then at him.

'Why did you do that?'

He slipped his arms around her. She leaned against him, shivering despite the heat. He put his hand on her hair.

'I'm not sure myself. Don't tell anyone you saw me lose it like this.'

'No,' she said, moving back and looking at him. 'You tell me. Why did you do that?'

'It's what I saw up at Pittwater,' he said finally. 'I walked in on a massacre. Four people dead at a table out on a patio. Three of them had been shot. One of them was a nineteen-year-old kid.'

'Then we find a way to deal with that. But you can't do this again,' she said softly.

'It's not going to happen again. I'm not going to let myself down like that. I don't want to do that to you and I don't want to be like that to myself.'

She was still standing back, looking at him.

'In there, you said "I'm not dead". Who were you talking to? I can't deal with you when you're like this if I don't know what's going on.'

The noise of the night insects, the distant sound of music, filled the air around them. He heard a fainter sound, waves breaking against the weathered sandstone retaining wall at the end of his garden, ripples generated by a boat passing the mouth of the bay.

'Come inside and I'll tell you,' he said. 'I need to clean myself up first.'

In the bathroom, she washed her cut and dressed it. He showered and changed. They came downstairs. He swept up the scattered glass. She arranged the lilies in one of his aunt's vases.

'Thanks for the flowers,' he said, considering that in the scheme of things he was supposed to give such things to her.

'Do you like them?'

'I do. I always do.'

'Good. It's all part of having a bit of fun and sparkle in your life,' she said, looking at him with a glint in her eye.

'Maybe you should have bought white lilies instead of pink. White lilies in a wreath with a sash that reads *Harrigan's Career, Rest in Peace.*'

'What are you talking about?'

He shut the kitchen door.

'I'm going upstairs to get something out my safe. It's a tape and I need privacy to play it. Do you want to smoke? Go ahead. I'm having another whisky.'

He got her an ashtray. They exercised this unspoken tolerance towards each other's vices. He had once smoked heavily and now loathed the taint of cigarette smoke. She had once had the choice between drinking alcohol and staying alive. These days just the smell of it made her ill. She kept beer in her fridge for him; he supplied her with ashtrays that had been unused for years. When he came back downstairs, he put a small audio tape on the table and poured himself a second whisky. She looked at the tape but didn't touch it. He sat opposite her and watched her light up. No one else smoked in his house.

'Have you heard any of the news coverage?' he asked.

'I was listening to it in the car. Four dead. Two were men but they didn't give any names. The other two were Natalie and Julian Edwards. They said the minister found them. I thought Edwards didn't have anything to do with his ex-wife. He didn't want her reputation damaging his.'

'He was seeing her about their son. One of those bodies was someone called Jerome Beck. I've never heard of him before. But I can tell you the other one was Mike Cassatt, dead as a dodo. Almost mummified. We couldn't even tell how he died.'

'You're joking! What would he be doing there?'

Harrigan sat over his drink for a few moments without touching it.

'Throwing a time bomb into my life,' he said. 'You see this tape? Mike gave it to me about a year ago. I came home one day and found him sitting in my backyard.'

'Why would he come here?'

'That's another story,' Harrigan replied. 'When I saw him, I thought he was going to kill me. He laughed instead. Said he had cancer of the liver. He was going to die and he was taking me with him. Then he left that tape and walked away. Except he wasn't dying. It was a misdiagnosis. He rang to tell me he hadn't forgotten me or the tape and I could wait to find out what he was going to do with it. Meanwhile, it was in his safety deposit box. If you want to know why I did what I did tonight, you need to listen to this tape. But it's dangerous to know. I don't want to put you in danger. If you want to go there, you have to make that choice yourself. If you say no, it won't matter.'

'Who are we going to be listening to?'

'The Ice Cream Man himself.'

'Tell me why you have this connection to him first,' she said carefully. 'Everything I've heard about you, he's always there somewhere. Why?'

'You tell me what you've heard first.'

She tapped ash gently into the ashtray.

'Basically two stories. One says you took him on and he almost killed you for it. The other says you were in his pocket from the time you started. But you fell out over money and he went after you and put you in hospital. After that you went straight and you were slick. No one could prove anything against you. I've heard another story as well. The one about Eddie Lee where everyone's careful not to mention any names too directly.'

'You've heard about him?'

'Oh, yes. It's all old gossip.'

Old gossip never seemed to die. Harrigan remembered the press conference where he'd announced they were upgrading Cassatt's disappearance to a murder inquiry. A crime reporter from a national daily had got to her feet. 'I've got three questions for you, Commander,' she said. 'Is it true you started your career in NSW Police under the auspices of the Ice Cream Man? Do you have any information that ties him to the still unsolved murder of Edward Lee? And instead of the unknown assailants you've always claimed were responsible, was Cassatt behind the incident twelve years ago that put you in hospital on life support?'

28

'There's a one-word answer to those three questions,' Harrigan had replied. 'No. Does anyone want to ask me a question about the case at hand?'

The journalist had printed all three questions in the paper the next day. Grace must have read that story, heard all these things said, and still never talked to him about them.

'I didn't believe any of those stories.' She spoke suddenly, breaking into his thoughts. 'I don't believe you'd ever take money from someone like Cassatt. And I don't believe you could ever be involved in anyone's murder.'

'I've never taken money and I haven't killed anyone,' he said. 'But Mike did almost kill me. One night in a back alley in Marrickville. There were three of them. You've met one, Jerry Freeman. Mike wanted me to eat my gun. He said, "You're dead, mate." Now you know who I was throwing that glass at.'

'How come you're still alive?'

'Some brave person I never got to thank shone their headlights on us at high beam. Mike never fired the shot, I'll never know why. He smashed my jaw instead and ran.'

Grace shook her head, her eyes glistening.

'That's too close. I don't want to think about that. Did you take him on?'

'Like a fool, yes. I kept baiting him. I'd sabotage his operations. I'd let journalists know what he was up to. I'd tip off crims who had it in for him. Once I arrested one of his couriers and flushed his stash of heroin down the toilet. I can't believe what I used to do. I must have had a death wish.'

'Why? Did you want to be a hero? A totally dead one.'

'I was high on the adrenaline. I knew how dangerous it was and I was getting a kick out of it. Mad.'

'That doesn't explain why you took Cassatt on in the first place,' she said.

'Because every time I look in a mirror, I'm supposed to see him looking back at me. I was supposed to be him; he was supposed to be the older brother I never had. Cassatt's been there since I was born. His father and mine were old mates, they were in Korea together. After his dad died, he was always around at our house. Dad wanted me to be just like Mike. He used to say to me, "He's someone you should look up to. He makes his own luck. You follow him and he'll take you places."'

'Didn't your father know what sort of a man he was?'

'Dad knew everything about him. My father was a petty crim. He wasn't always like that but that's how he ended up. He got into pilfering when he worked on the docks. Then he started working for Mike's mates — they had a machinery repair business down near the container wharves. They were importing heroin. Mike was greenlighting them, Dad was their cockatoo. I didn't want to be like either of them.'

She had a habit of flicking the end of her carefully manicured fingernails with her thumb when she was thinking. Today, they were a yin and yang of light and dark red. He noticed these things about her, the small pieces of her body language he had learnt to read.

'Play the tape then. I don't want to live in the dark about something like this.'

'It's about a murder, Grace. Are you sure you want to take that on?'

'You said it was my choice. Play it.'

4

'When you listen to this, Paulie, tell yourself one thing. You owe your dad your life. You kept giving me grief but I waited till old Jimbo died before I did anything about it. You're so high and mighty now, but remember I got you your job as a favour to him. You owe me but you've always been disloyal. Even when you first came out of the Academy and you went to Dave McKenzie in Robbery when you were supposed to be with me.

'Took me a while to get you over to my squad. You didn't help any. The day I watched you walk through the door, I thought, I'm going to break you. Me, Joe and Jerry were there to meet you. I've still got the tie I had made for you, with New Boy on the nametag. "Put it on," I told you. "Everyone here's got one and you're one of us now." You closed up and I wondered if you were going to walk out on me. But you couldn't throw your job away. You had that spastic kid to support.

'I let it go a fortnight. Then I told you, "You don't leave tonight, you're driving for me." It was just me and Joe, but you stayed, you got the message. You were twenty-three. Way past time for you to get blooded. I watched you drive us to Double Bay. Were you going to see it through, I wondered. But you kept driving and you parked where I told you to.

'It's dark there, in that corner of the street back from the shopping centre. People don't see you. Finally the man we're waiting for turns up. *Mr Edward Lee. Merchant banker. He'd been out to dinner and was heading for his car. The last meal he ever had. I got him out of some bad stuff and he thought he could renege on me. I warned him: "You can't not pay me, mate. You like fucking little boys too much and I can prove it." Bold as brass, he came back: "You can get away with anything in this town if you know the right people. I know enough to protect myself but you'll go down." Bad mistake, Eddie. If people knew I'd let that happen, they'd walk all over me.*

'He was on the floor in the back of the car before he knew what hit him. Joe put the cuffs on him and stuck a bit of tape over his mouth. His face, the way he looked. I laughed. I said, "I thought you liked this sort of thing, mate." I told you we were taking Eddie home. You must have known what was going to happen. I saw your hands shaking. I thought, you fucking coward. I'm going to make you do this.

'We got into his house through the garage. I had Eddie by the hair. "You're going to be sorry for what you said, mate. You're not bringing me down." Joe and me, we let him have it. Put the boot right in. Here's your chance, Paulie. Prove yourself. No way. You ran for the fucking door. It took the two of us to drag you back. "You shoot him," I told you. "You do it now." I shoved that gun in your hand but you dropped it. You shouted at me: "No!" I smacked you in the face for that. You had blood coming out of your mouth, on your shirt, your tie. You were a mess. I did it myself. Twice in Eddie's head. Finished. Then I rubbed some of Eddie's blood on your tie. "Welcome to the club," I said. "This is how it is. Get used to it."'*

Harrigan hit the stop button. He sat there, caught in the memory in his head. Grace had forgotten to smoke; her cigarette was dead in the ashtray.

'Unsolved Sydney mysteries,' she said, her face pale in the light. 'Who killed Eddie Lee? Is that really what happened?'

'Word for word. They took the house apart after that looking for money. They found it. Mike knew where to look. Then he said I needed fortifying and we went somewhere else. I drove. My hands were shaking but I got there.'

'Where?'

'Some flea-bitten dump in South Sydney called the Sportsman Club. It's not there any more. Mike had an arrangement with the owner. Free beer and free roots in exchange for not bothering him too much about his other activities.'

Grace raised an elegant eyebrow ever so slightly. 'Daggy décor. Saggy sex workers in G-strings pulling the beers,' she said with a kind of wry gloominess.

'I don't remember much about it. I was twenty-three. I'd just seen someone shot dead. I wanted to get out of there. They were laughing themselves sick. They wanted to get pissed.'

He pressed play again. '*We always had the back room to ourselves. The girl turned up and I asked for a jug. I took out a little money and tucked it into your top pocket. You looked sick, I thought you needed cheering up. "What's that for?" you said. I give you money and you say that to me. It sure as fuck wasn't anything you'd earned. "Buy something for that spastic kid of yours," I said. "In case you don't know it, Joe, Paulie here has a kid. No, he's got a vegetable." I looked you right in the eyes. "Put him away. He'll never know who you are. He'll die soon." The beer arrived. You got up, said you needed a piss. I told the girl, "Get us another jug. Then you can make yourself useful to my young friend here. He needs a fuck."*

'*When you came back, you weren't wearing your tie. You threw it on the table with the money I gave you and the car keys. "I'm leaving," you said. "I've got better things to do with my life than run after you." Joe went dead quiet. I told you, "You say that to me. You cunt." Then you walked away, right into the girl carrying the beer. You were soaked. I shouted, "You've pissed yourself, Paulie." Me and Joe, we laughed. I thought, you're finished.*

'*We got to your place before you did. Old Jimbo was in hospital at the time, otherwise I would have done it somewhere else. That was the night we let you know what we could do to you if we wanted to. I told you, "Keep your mouth shut or you're dead." You knew I meant it. About three weeks later, Dave's got you back on the job. Then I find out why you're back. You start giving me grief. You think you can take me on. You paid for that, mate, big time.*

'*This is the final payoff, Paulie. I've got your tie. It's got your blood on it along with Eddie's. I've got the gun that shot him, it's got your prints on it. I've got this tape. They're all in my safety deposit box. When the time comes, they're all going to Marvin Tooth. Special assistant commissioner, the man who spends half his life up the commissioner's arsehole. Good old Fang. The man who wants to be commissioner way ahead of you. When I'm gone, you go too. Look forward to it, mate.'*

Cassatt's voice stopped, the tape continued in silence. Harrigan rewound it and took it out. Grace sipped warm soda water.

'That's a voice from the grave,' she said, her own voice shaking a little. 'Is everything on that tape true?'

'Every word. And now someone out there has everything that was in Mike's safety deposit box. They've got their hands on my life and there's no way I can know who they are. Until they ring me up and tell me they want something from me.'

She shook another cigarette out of the packet and lit it. He watched her gathering calm. She was like this, never clingy or brimming with overdone sympathy.

'Whoever has it, it's not the Tooth,' she said. 'If he had any of that evidence in his possession, let alone this tape, you'd be out of a job right now.'

Harrigan smiled dryly. Grace had her own unpleasant memories of encounters not only with Marvin but with his son as well, including an attempt by the two of them to drive her out of her job while she'd still been with the police. Baby Tooth, as Marvin's boy, Sean, was known, was also a serving police officer. On a fast track through the ranks, he owed his promotions solely to his father's patronage.

'What evidence is there left from Eddie Lee's murder?' she asked. 'Any DNA? Can they tie you in?'

'There'd be enough. We've still got the clothes he was wearing. It wouldn't be hard to get a match.'

'How would you protect yourself if any of this did get out?'

'Do what everyone does. Deny everything. Get a good lawyer.'

'It wouldn't save you,' she said. 'Maybe you wouldn't go to gaol for being an accessory but the publicity would finish your career for good. Did you say anything to anyone at the time?'

'No. If I had, it wouldn't have mattered who my father was. Right now, I'd be a little pile of bones for the fishes somewhere off South Head.'

Grace shivered. 'Don't say that, not even as a joke. Why didn't you go after them later when they almost killed you? Why not accuse them? Take them to trial.'

'Because no one would have supported me. My reputation would have been dragged through the mud. I'd have been hounded out of the force and put under so much personal pressure it would have wrecked my life. I'd walked away alive. That was as much as I could expect and I knew it.'

'But why stay in the job? You could have done something else. Didn't you have your law degree by then?'

This was a question Harrigan wasn't prepared to answer, even to himself.

'Why should I let them chase me out?'

She drew on her cigarette and didn't reply. They sat in silence for a few moments. Her smoke curled in the air.

'What a story,' she said. 'The Ice Cream Man invites you into his life. Drinking bucketloads of beer in stinky clubs and fucking bored sex workers who couldn't care less whether you're alive, dead or a rubber dick. Why would you want to live like that? It's *so* nowhere.'

Harrigan had never heard the feared Ice Cream Man brushed aside with so much uncompromising female disdain. It made him laugh from deep inside until the tears came down his cheeks. A nagging tension was resolved; his personal nightmares might have disappeared into the air with the grey wisps of her cigarette smoke.

'Was it really so funny?' she asked.

'Yes, it was.' He grew serious. 'That's not the end of it. I've asked Trev to keep me briefed on what's happening with this investigation. I have to, Grace. If the Ice Cream Man's involved, I have to know where this job is going.'

Suddenly there was a hint of tears in her own eyes, angry ones.

'Do you? I knew when you went up there today, it wasn't just going to be for one afternoon. What did you say? We'll be on leave together. Nothing will get in the way.'

'You heard the news. There's a federal government minister involved. I can't just walk away.'

'But you can walk away from us.'

'No, it's not like that.' Harrigan took Sam Jonas's card out of his wallet and handed it to Grace. 'Something else happened today. She was waiting for me when I left the house at Pittwater. She works for a company with a connection to the minister. She asked if I'd be prepared to take a bribe.'

'Did she? Personal security manager. Doesn't that mean bodyguard?'

'She talked like she was more into intelligence gathering.'

'For who?' Grace asked.

'The CEO of that company. This is who they are.'

He took the LPS brochure out of his diary and handed it to her. Grace flicked through the pages.

'This is very high powered. I can see why this Elena Calvo would have guard dogs. She's got a lot to protect. Why is she worried about these murders? How do they affect her?'

'That's a question worth asking. Meanwhile, her guard dog can go home and tell her she's wasting her time.'

'What were you doing with this brochure?' Grace asked.

'I was thinking of investing. Maybe it could help Toby. Maybe not.'

'It's always worth trying,' she replied with a touch of gentleness. She handed it back. 'Here we are again. A week into our holiday and you're already back at work. Why am I here with you when you've always got something better to do?'

'Don't say that.'

'Why not? Where are we going with this? Between your past and your work, there's never any space for us.'

'There's no other person in the world I could have told that story to. Not even Toby. I can't be myself with anyone else the way I can be with you. I know you, Grace. You don't drop your guard with anyone else the way you do with me.'

'But you still can't make more time for us even when you say you will.' She stubbed out her cigarette angrily. 'God, this is all so messy, so dangerous. You could lose everything over this.'

'That doesn't have to include us. Let me put this tape back in my safe. Then we can call it a night. We don't get much time together. Let's take the times we can. They're the best part of my life.'

'Then why do you ration them?' she asked, raising that eyebrow again. 'You can promise me something before we do anything, Paul.'

'What's that?'

'Don't lock me out of this. You said it yourself, this information is dangerous to know. Well, I do know it now and you're right, it is dangerous. You can tell me what's going on from now on. Especially if you're in there watching it.'

'Grace, I can't give you the details of a confidential investigation. You know that. You can't tell me about your work either.'

'I'm not asking for anything you have to keep confidential. Just enough information so I know where you are and what's going on. That way I can protect myself.'

'You can rely on me to protect you. Don't forget that.'

'I still want you to make me this promise. If I'm going to deal with this, I need to know what's happening.'

'Then you've got my word. I promise.'

It had always been like this. She wrung things out of him no one else could; their relationship kept surviving by a whisker. Harrigan thought that survival in these terms must have been his particular gift. It was the story of his life.

Later, in the quietness, she lay in bed beside him with her head against his shoulder.

'How did you get away from them?' she suddenly asked. 'Your twin nightmares. Your father and the Ice Cream Man. You escaped. How?'

'Why do you want to know?'

'I'm putting you together in my head. Am I allowed to do that?'

'It was my aunt,' he replied after a short silence. 'She was my father's sister. She hated him. She used to tell my mother there was no way I was going to end up like Jim. I always did well at school without trying too hard so she decided I was going to St Ignatius Riverview whether I wanted to or not.'

'Why there?'

'Because she thought it was the only school in Sydney. She paid the fees to get me in, which was pretty much all the money she had. Then my mother worked two jobs day and night for the next six years to keep me there. She was a pantry maid at Balmain Hospital in the morning and a cleaner in the city at night. She started work at 6 a.m. every day. She got up at four in the morning. It didn't matter what else she had to do, she always left me a clean uniform, ironed to an inch of its life, waiting for me to wear.'

'Oh my God,' Grace said. 'You had to succeed under that kind of pressure, didn't you?'

'I had no choice.'

She lay there without speaking.

'Have you put me together?' he asked.

'Maybe a little,' she said, her voice drifting in the soft light. 'It's time to sleep on it.'

She curled up and slipped away. He turned out the light and lay awake a little longer. In the dead hours of the night, he woke. Some dream was troubling him, some half-remembered image that faded from his mind as soon as he opened his eyes. *Nothing. Nada.* His first whispered thought while he stared into the shadows. Instinctively, he touched Grace to see if she was still there or whether he had washed up on some blank shore in the land of the dead. He felt her ribcage rising and falling with her breathing, imagined he could hear the sound of her heart. He slept again.

5

In the partial darkness of his kitchen, Harold Morrissey picked up his telephone and dialled a number he rarely called unless he had to. While he listened to it ring, he glanced out of the window. Dawn was beginning to break along the low undulating skyline, a clean transparency edging against a darker, fading blue. Once more it would be a clear, fine day. Finally his call was answered.

'Yeah?'

'Stewie. It's Harry. You're still alive.'

'Of course I'm fucking alive. What the hell is this? Don't you know what time it is?'

'I just heard on the radio there's been a shooting up at Pittwater. Four people dead. They didn't say who they all were, just that one of them was Natalie Edwards. I wondered if maybe one of the others was you. Wasn't she the woman who was here with you and that other bloke last week?'

'Let me tell you something, Harry. If anyone asks, none of us were there including Nattie. If you tell anyone we were, I'll say you're fucking hallucinating. I'll take you to the law. Then you'll lose everything you've got. So keep your mouth shut.' Stuart put the phone down.

Harold hung up, thinking that he should have expected as much. In its own way, the early morning call had summed up the relationship of the two brothers to perfection.

Harold left his farmhouse to start the day's work, stepping into a still faintly cool air. An oleander bush bloomed a hot summer pink near the back door, while the house fence was covered with gnarled wisteria and thick-trunked grape vines planted by his grandmother eighty years ago. These days, the vines were almost leafless, some of them already dead. Like the land around him, they had been stripped bare by the drought and the heat. The only green came from a stand of old well-grown pepper trees stretching along the south-western side of the rambling wooden farmhouse, their bright foliage almost shocking in the dryness. On the north-eastern side, the sole shade was given by a self-sown sugar gum growing too close to the veranda, its white trunk arching over the bull-nosed roof.

In the pale light, Harold walked out the gate into the main yard, heading towards the kennel where his dog, Rosie, had spent the night chained up. Her enclosure was sheltered by an old moonah bush that was still holding out in the drought. Some twelve years ago his father had walked this same distance, unexpectedly falling into infinity when his heart had stopped mid-step. Since then Harold had supposedly shared the management of their property, Yaralla, with his older brother, Stuart. Almost as soon their father's will was read and they were pronounced joint owners, Stewie had said, 'We can mortgage the place now.' 'Like fuck we will,' Harold had replied instantly, knowing through bitter experience that whatever money they raised jointly, Stewie would never repay his share of it. Instead the money would disappear on one of his scams. It would make money; Stewie's scams always did. It was just that neither Harold nor the farm would see a cent of it.

Since that first day, he and his brother had grappled each other to immobility. Nothing could be done on the property without the agreement of the other. There had been no improvements other than those Harold had been able to pay for out of his own cash flow or smaller personal loans. Without sufficient credit, no substantial work could be done. Everything cried out for repair but now, in the drought, there was no money at all.

Harold opened the gate to Rosie's enclosure and unchained her. She didn't need feeding, there was still some dried food in her bowl. Meat she got in the evenings. Right now, she was anxious to stretch her legs.

She trotted after him to the machinery shed where he parked his ancient white ute and leapt up into the cabin beside him.

Harold started the engine and drove out onto his property, some ten thousand acres on the edge of the Riverina. The landscape was so stripped of its vegetation, it had become an X-ray of itself. Out on the horizon, scattered trees shimmered in a dark line between the soil and the immense sky. This morning, Harold was following his routine of hand-feeding his stock. He was heading towards his north-eastern boundary across the paddocks that stretched around him as a barren patchwork. There was still water in the dams in that part of his property and he was pasturing his stock there before he faced the question of what to do when even this water ran out. The tray of the ute, where Rosie usually rode, was loaded with feed he could barely afford to buy. When worked, the red soil on his property broke down into dusty clumps; it varied in colour across the landscape from a pale dirt-pink to a dark and hot iron-red. For three years, he'd had no crops out of any of it. The future was as bleak and unending as the blue skies that rolled above him every day. He had stopped believing it would ever rain again.

After Harold had been driving for a short while, a structure came into view. It was the Cage, as he called it, a construction built by his brother six months ago along their most distant boundary. Its alien glass and steel glittered in the early light for some time before its outline hardened against the sky. The Cage was Harold's sole failure to keep Stewie at bay. This singularity didn't count for much. There could have been few failures more significant or more heartbreaking to him than this one.

On impulse, Harold drove over for a closer look. Always when he came out here, he hoped that somehow the Cage might have miraculously disappeared overnight. Always it was still there. With this woman's death, maybe something had changed. The trees Stuart had cleared to build the thing still lay in heaps next to the high steel fence enclosing the broad acreage where they had once stood. Their dry leaves rattled in the early morning breeze. Other than the raucous calling of the crows, it was the only sound in the landscape. Harold came to a stop outside the locked gate and got out of the cabin. Rosie followed him and began to nose along the base of the steel fence. As always, there was no way in for either of them. He had no key to the gate. From the beginning, he had been locked out.

Harold remembered vividly the day six months ago when he had arrived here to see the bulldozers clearing the old-growth grey box eucalyptus trees that had once covered this low slope. When he'd tried to stop them, the drivers had ignored him. The man in charge had threatened him if he didn't get out of their way. 'This is my property, mate!' Harold had shouted. 'That's not what we've been told,' the man had said. 'I'm taking my orders from Stuart Morrissey.' He told his workers to keep going; the trees crashed down.

Harold had driven back to the farmhouse and rung Stuart. They had argued furiously. By the time Harold hung up, he'd realised he could only stop the bulldozers by going back with his shotgun and taking the law into his own hands. He wished he had. Daily he'd watched while the fences went up, the greenhouses were built, and then the water tanks had arrived and were filled with water trucked in from outside the district. Who had pockets deep enough to finance this? Not Stewie. Stewie's own money was never spent on anyone except himself.

Once the Cage was finished, they had planted one crop in the open, which they had covered with netting, and presumably others in the greenhouses. Unlike his desolate harvest, these unnaturally irrigated crops had flourished. Away to Harold's right was the wide access road the bulldozers had cut the first day they had come in. It ran along his fence line, connecting the Cage to the Coolemon Road, an all-weather gravel road that served as one of Yaralla's boundaries. The gate between this private road and the public highway was always kept locked. It was something else for which Harold had no key. Despite this, other people came and went along this private road regularly. He often saw them late in the evenings, speeding against the horizon in their four-wheel-drives. Stewie had never told him what they did inside. When Harold asked his brother questions, he received threats in reply.

The little Harold knew about what went on inside the Cage he had found out by eavesdropping. Once this would have disturbed him, but Stewie had given him no other choice. These days he was glad to find out any little detail however he did it. It was this subterfuge that had allowed him to link Natalie Edwards to Stuart in the first place.

Less than a week ago, he had looked into his living room to see three unannounced visitors sitting there: Stuart, an older man with glasses and a middle-aged woman with artificially fair hair. Both these people had been strangers to him. All three were drinking his whisky, talking. It was late afternoon and the curtains had been drawn against the western sun. Seated in the shadows, they hadn't noticed him, had kept talking.

'Well, Jerome,' the woman said, 'from what we've seen today, we're all ready to go. Everything's come along nicely. Mind you, it's a god-forsaken spot. Why would anyone want to live here?'

'It's the best place for it, Nattie,' Stuart said. 'How many people are going to see it on that boundary? The property next door's run by a manager for some agribusiness. He won't care.'

'Stuart's right. It's a good spot. It's working better than I'd hoped.' Jerome spoke with a guttural accent Harold didn't recognise. 'We'll sign the contracts in the next few days at the latest and then I'll send the staff out to harvest. I want it all shipped to Jo'burg before the end of the month. They'll find a location for the testing over there. Once we've signed, I'll courier them their copy of the contract. But first I have to let the old man know we're on schedule.'

'Your people will have to get a wriggle on, mate, if we're going to meet that deadline,' Stuart said.

'I've already got the shipping lined up,' Nattie said. 'When I told them they were dealing with Natalie Edwards, they sat up and paid attention. They'll move quickly.'

'My people will do it anyway, don't you worry,' Jerome replied. 'I want to replant with a new round of crops as soon as we can. We have to move this program along. The whole setup here took too much time.'

'Who's that?'

Nattie spoke. She had seen Harold standing in the doorway.

'That's Harry,' Stuart had replied, frowning.

'How long has he been there?' Jerome asked.

'Don't know. How long have you been standing there, Harry?'

'I just got here. How long have you been here?'

Stuart ignored him.

'Don't worry about Harry,' he said to the others. 'He's harmless. He never does anything.'

Rather than be shut out of his own living room, Harold walked in and sat down. 'Good afternoon,' he said.

This was greeted with silence. Stuart made no introductions. All three had stared at Harold as if he was the intruder. The wind was shaking at the curtains while heat and dust hung in the air. Jerome glanced at Natalie and Stuart and then got to his feet.

'Time to get out of this dump. We've got a plane waiting on the airstrip.'

'Don't forget your keys, Jerome,' Stuart said. 'You don't want to leave those behind.'

Jerome laughed. He picked up a complicated set of keys attached to a keyring in the shape of a heavy bronze football. Nattie and Stuart stood up too, also collecting their wallets and keys.

'Dinner at Pittwater for the contract-signing, people,' Nattie said. 'I'll get it catered. I think we should celebrate.'

'Turn on the champagne,' Stuart said. 'It'll be worth it.'

'You can pay for that, Stewie. Your share will stretch to it.'

After pocketing his keys, Jerome had picked up the whisky bottle and screwed the lid back on. He made to walk out with it. Harold reached over and pulled it out of his hand.

'That's my whisky, mate. I'll keep it, thanks.'

'Keep it,' Jerome said. 'It's rotgut.'

'You're a possessive little man considering all you own is dirt,' Nattie said in passing.

Now, some six days later, this woman was dead but for what reason Harold couldn't know. He looked at the Cage's high fences, strung along the top with electrified wires marked by signs that read *Danger*. There were no strangers here to warn off, just the birds who couldn't read and whose bodies lay scattered at intervals along either side of the fence. There was nothing he could do about this. He called Rosie to him and drove away.

6

The sound of Harrigan's mobile penetrated his sleep. He woke to the sense of Grace's body curled next to his. Otherwise, the room was airless, oppressive. Already it had started to grow hot. He fumbled for the phone.

'Commander Harrigan?' He recognised the voice of Chloe, the commissioner's personal assistant. 'The commissioner has sent you an email, one that's been generally distributed to the public. He would like you to look at it and call him back.'

Harrigan glanced at the clock. It was later than he normally slept; the room was bright with morning sunlight. Grace turned towards him, smiling, sleepy-eyed, her hair falling in thick, dark strands across her bare shoulder.

'I'll call within the hour,' he said.

'The commissioner said as soon as possible.'

'Wait for the call.'

'What is it?' Grace asked.

Harrigan lay back on his pillows. 'The commissioner's sent me an email. He wants me to look at it.'

'You'd better do what he wants in that case,' she said dryly.

That was the worst of mobile telephones. They let people like the commissioner invade the privacy of your bedroom. If Harrigan had still been a smoker, he would have lit a cigarette. Instead, he pulled on a pair of shorts and went down to his study. Grace appeared in the doorway behind him while his laptop was firing up, wrapped in her red kimono.

'Why don't you come in and have a look?' he said. 'I don't think this is just "Good morning, how are you?"'

'I've never been in here before,' she said. 'It's always looked too private.'

'This is where I keep myself to myself. Come in. Take the weight off your feet.'

'Do you mind if I open the window?'

'Go ahead.'

The morning air carried into the stuffy room the sweet smell of jasmine from an ancient vine that covered the length of the garden fence. Harrigan's study was upstairs at the back of the house. At night, from the window, he could see the lights of Louisa Road reflected in the water across the bay. His study was a bare room, the furniture spare and the floorboards covered with a worn imitation Persian rug. His bookcases lined one wall; his safe, two chairs and his desk, which was made of old dark wood and had come with the house, made up the rest.

Grace sat in his spare chair. In the morning light, her skin was shadowed to a soft pearl. She studied the contents of his bookcases. Journals on law and policing, digests on forensic medicine and psychology, mixed with Norman Mailer's *The Fight* and *The Executioner's Song*. Truman Capote's *In Cold Blood* and Ellroy's *My Dark Places* shared space with *Crime and Punishment*, *The Devils*. Histories of racing and boxing stood next to them. On a shelf not completely full were a pair of Harrigan's own boxing gloves, from a time when, as a twenty year old, he had tried unsuccessfully to make a career as a boxer. Even if the attempt had been a failure, he still remembered it as a gap in his life when his time had been his own.

'Do you only ever read books on crime?' she asked.

'Of course not. I read the form guide as well.'

He saw her looking at the wall above his desk. His law degree hung beside a collection of prints, reproductions of works by the Spanish artist Francisco Goya that Harrigan had bought overseas years ago. Savage satire from *The Caprichos* mixed with horrors from *The Disasters of War*. He watched her look at these representations of bizarre human folly hung alongside those showing useless fighting, massacre and the dead. Facsimiles of the original nineteenth-century Spanish publications of Goya's collected series of prints were visible on the shelf beside his desk. Beside them was an outsized book titled simply *Goya*.

'You're a fan,' she said.

'He's an obsession of mine. I'm like that. Once I decide I want something, I hang on to it.'

She got up from the chair and went to look at the prints. '*And still they won't go!*' she said aloud, reading the title of one. Misshapen yet human creatures desperately held up a monolith about to crush them while nonetheless staying huddled beneath where it would fall.

'Don't you think people are like that?' he said.

'It's grotesque.'

'It's people who are grotesque. He's showing us what we are.'

'What about this one?' she asked.

One can't look. Unseen soldiers thrust bayonets in from the right of the print, towards huddled people waiting in terror on their summary and bloody massacre. Pity had been expunged from the etched shadows.

'You have to look,' Harrigan said. 'That's the point.'

'You don't think it's sadistic?'

'No. It's about sadism. It's a voice for all the people who die like that. The man who drew that is bringing them back to life. That's an accusation.'

'It's a fine line. Why did he draw things like this?'

'It's what he saw in his own life. He lived through a civil war. He put it down on paper.'

'They're all so bleak,' she said. 'Except when you get to her. What's she? Rest and recreation?'

Separated out from the rest was a print of one of Goya's paintings, *The Naked Maja*. She seemed to smile out of the picture, looking directly at the watcher, both an enigma and a challenge.

'I like her,' he said. 'She's beautiful. Like you.'

She gave him a half-smile that was slightly self-deprecating. He often thought Grace didn't seem to know how lovely she was. When they had first met, he'd been harsh towards her, too harsh. At the time, he'd said it was the fault of the pressure of his work. He regretted it now and hoped he had made up for it since, even given the time his job took out of their relationship. What do you see in me? A question he wasn't going to ask her. Just keep seeing it.

'Why do you have these on the wall? Why do you need to look at them?' she asked.

'I don't look at them all the time. Sometimes I take them down and put them away because I don't want to see them for a while. I just need to know they're there. They take the pressure out of my head.'

'Why?'

'Because I see things like this all the time in my job and I can't pretend I don't. This is what we do to each other every day. I know what that means. Someone else knew that as well. They knew enough to put it down on paper like this so it has some meaning.'

'Someone else knew how we get a real thrill out of hurting each other,' she said softly. 'That won't ever change.'

He wondered what lay behind her words. Perhaps, since he was opening himself up to her like this, he should have asked her. He knew that she had grown up in New Guinea, a childhood that was still a vivid and beautiful dream in her mind. The dream had been shattered when her mother had died suddenly of cerebral malaria when Grace was fourteen. Her father had brought them all back to Australia where Grace had spun off into a cycle of wildness that hadn't ended until she was in her twenties. For a few years she had been an alcoholic, although no one would have ever guessed that now. Somewhere along the way she had also acquired a faint scar that ran like a silken thread down the length of her neck. He had never asked her and she had never told him who had put it there or why. All the times they had made love, he'd never once intentionally touched it or put his mouth to it.

'I'd better see what the commissioner wants.'

She looked over his shoulder as he opened his inbox. Three emails, all with the same subject line and attachments, were waiting for him. Two had been forwarded: one from his son, the second from the commissioner. The third had been sent directly to his personal address from an unknown source. The time identified them as being sent sometime after midnight. The subject line read: *They gather for the feast*. Harrigan opened the one addressed to him first. The message consisted of a URL followed by the words: *Ex-Detective Senior Sergeant Michael Cassatt leaves his grave and arrives at Natalie Edwards' table at Pittwater for dinner.*

Three pictures had been attached to the email. Harrigan didn't look at these immediately but went to the website. The words *They gather for the feast* flashed on screen again. The first image took his breath away. In sharp colour, the dead sat at the table on the patio at Pittwater, assembled for a meal they would never eat, Cassatt at the head as if presiding over them. He heard Grace draw her breath in sharply.

'Oh my God,' she said. 'Is that what you saw? How did you recognise him?'

'Intuition. We looked at his left shoulder, he had a tattoo there. Why send this out? What's the point?'

'Is that man with the glasses Jerome Beck?'

'Yeah, that's him. Will anyone else recognise him now? Is that the point?'

He went to the next photograph. Cassatt lay in his unidentified grave, recently dead. In the narrow trench, his face and body, just recognisable, were shockingly marked.

'Someone worked him over before he died and they weren't gentle,' Harrigan said. 'What did they want? And why tell the world like this? If you're going to splash it all over the net, why not tell us where his grave was as well?'

'They can't want you to know. It's like advertising,' she said. 'Or reality TV. They want us to think it's real life. Except that it's artificial from the beginning.'

'Whoever did that to Mike must have buried him as well. They have to know where his grave was. Whoever that person is, they'll know someone was looking over their shoulder while they were doing it.'

'Why wouldn't this be from the person who killed him?' Grace asked.

'I think it's more likely it's not,' he said after a few moments' thought. 'This is someone telling us what they want us to know. Someone wants us to see a connection between the killings at Pittwater and Mike's murder. Killers usually keep things secret. These people want this out there.'

'Then it's also a message for Cassatt's killers, whoever they are. Someone's on to them.'

The third photograph showed Cassatt in this same grave in the mummified state he'd been in at the table at Pittwater. The narrow confines cradled him like a child.

'Before and after,' Harrigan said. 'We saw you bury him and now we've dug him up and taken him to Sydney for a meal with the dead. Who are these people?'

'Twisted,' Grace said. 'You'd have to be. I'm going to have a shower. I need to wash seeing that away.'

Harrigan opened the other two emails. Each was identical to the first. The commissioner's came with the concise message: *Please phone.* His son had written: *Isn't this where you went yesterday, Dad? These pix are everywhere, they've been posted all over the place. People are putting them up on their own websites. Sicko.*

Thanks, mate, Harrigan typed in return. *Sorry about yesterday, see you today if I possibly can.*

He picked up the phone and made his call.

'Paul,' the commissioner said, dispensing with greetings. 'Have you seen the email?'

'Yes.'

'It's gone to every media outlet in the country. Some newspapers have managed to get those pictures out on the street already. That's bad enough. But if you check the *Sydney Morning Herald* online, you'll find there's media speculation this investigation may already be compromised as a result of Cassatt's body being found at the scene.'

'How is that possible?'

'According to them, the Ice Cream Man may have had evidence implicating a serving senior police officer in the Edward Lee murder. This senior officer may wish to protect himself by impeding the investigation.'

'Is this alleged senior serving police officer named?'

'Of course not. The paper isn't planning on being sued. The journalist is very clearly referring to the various rumours connecting you to Cassatt —'

'There is no truth whatsoever in those rumours,' Harrigan snapped, wondering why fate had to do this to him.

'I didn't say there was. But I won't have it said that, under my command, this service is subject to the same degree of corruption that existed with Cassatt.'

'I'm not aware anyone is saying that.'

'I don't intend to give them the chance. I discussed the matter with the special assistant commissioner. Marvin advises that you should stand down from your position as commander during this investigation. However …' The commissioner drew breath. Harrigan, awaiting the axe, sensed a reprieve. 'Senator Edwards phoned a short while ago. He wants to meet with the senior officers managing this investigation, including you. You impressed him yesterday. He was very insistent that you be involved. Can you be here in an hour?'

Harrigan smiled mordantly to consider that, purely by circumstance, he'd managed to avoid one of Marvin's more outrageous gambits.

'I'll be there,' he replied. 'Are you asking me to break my leave?'

'Not as such. I'm asking you to make yourself available as needed. I would expect that from all my executive officers. You will be conducting yourself as though you have nothing to hide.'

'I have no reason to do otherwise, Commissioner.'

There was a pause. 'There's something else you need to know. I received an anonymous parcel this morning. It contains a dossier that appears to be from an intelligence-gathering organisation. It's relevant to this case.'

'Someone sent this to you?'

'With a note that says: *Read this and it will explain who Jerome Beck is.* I've discussed it with Marvin. He thinks it's a hoax. I don't share that opinion. It appears the senator also received a copy of this same dossier but a day sooner than we did. That's what he wants to discuss with us.'

'Strange happenings, Commissioner,' Harrigan replied.

'Yes, unfortunately. In an hour.'

Harrigan put the phone down, reflecting that there was no mistaking the commissioner's priorities. He went and found Grace in the bathroom where she had finished showering and was brushing out her hair.

'They want you to go in, don't they?' she said.

51

'In an hour. They want me to talk to the minister. I don't have a choice. I have to go.'

'Of course you don't have a choice. You can't ring them up and say I'm not coming in, my girlfriend won't let me.'

'You're a lot more to me than just a girlfriend.'

She put her hairbrush back down on the vanity. Small items indicating her presence had begun to appear in his house. A bottle of her perfume on the dressing table in his bedroom; a cream silk chemise tossed over a chair; a brightly coloured packet of tampons in his bathroom cabinet.

'But you're still going in. You still don't have a choice. It's not whether either of us likes it. It's the fact that you don't have a choice.'

He didn't like where she was taking this.

'According to God, those pictures are everywhere,' he said, changing the subject. 'They've even made it to some of the newspapers this morning. It's too much for his sensibilities.'

'I'll get dressed and go and get them. We should see this.'

By the time Grace came back from the corner store, he had showered, shaved and dressed and was eating a quick breakfast. She spread the papers out on the table. The headlines were ghoulish enough: *Ice Cream Man's body found in House of Death*. There were photographs of Harrigan as the head of the task force together with colour pictures of Nattie Edwards' gaudy house at Pittwater. A school photograph of Julian Edwards when he could have been no more than thirteen covered the *Daily Telegraph*'s front page. Harrigan could almost hear the sub-editors salivating.

'The *Australian* talks about Stuart Morrissey,' Grace said. 'They say he had a number of business connections with Natalie Edwards. Is he involved in this?'

'He had a deal going with Edwards and Beck. The three of them were meeting to sign a contract on the night of the murders. He didn't turn up. I'm waiting to find out why.'

'Beck's just an unidentified body in these reports. No one's even speculated about him. They're all more interested in the Ice Cream Man.'

Harrigan glanced at his watch.

'I have to go. What are you going to do today?'

'What am I going to do?' Suddenly, she couldn't hide her disappointment. 'I think I'll go over to Bondi, go for a swim. I was going to cook dinner for us tonight. Is that still going to happen?'

Grace was a very good cook. It relaxed her, she said, to put food together at the end of a working day. The kitchen in her tiny flat, small as it was, was packed with cooking utensils and foodstuffs whose existence had previously been unknown to him. She did this kind of thing, took care with how they ate and drank. With her, he had dressed himself up and gone to restaurants he would otherwise never have looked inside, found himself at films, cabaret nights and concerts. He thought she was trying to civilise him. He enjoyed this, it relaxed him. Whether it was having the intended effect was another question. On the rare nights when his time was his own, he still went to the boxing. When the fighting was good, he came home feeling clean.

'I'll be there, if that's what you want.'

'Then I'll see you.'

He tried to take her in his arms but she shrugged away from him. He went after her anyway and held on to her. They leaned against each other.

'You don't have to put distance between us,' he said.

'You don't have time for us. You have to see the commissioner. That's the way it always is.'

'Just for now. You don't have to look so sad.'

'For now and always. You have to go. I'll see you tonight,' she said, this time slipping away and succeeding in putting air between them.

I'll be there. He had said it to her, he had said it the commissioner. Always, people demanded things from him.

At his father's funeral, Jim Harrigan's mates had agreed there was something to be said for going out the way old Jimbo had. Propped up against the bar of the William Wallace with a half-drunk schooner of Tooheys New in front of him. As usual, Harrigan the son had different ambitions. He had no wish to live out his old age in an empty house with only a bottle of whisky for company or to be like the other men he saw in pubs, watching Fox Sports and eating alone. He had hoped Grace might be persuaded to move in one day. So far, things could not have gone worse.

Always careful with his appearance, Harrigan dressed smart casual, eschewing a tie. There had to be some benefit to supposedly being on leave. In the clear sunlight, he drove to Victoria Road and joined the city-bound traffic. Is this what I want? He had always avoided giving much time to this question. This morning it forced its way into his mind. Vehicles flowed slowly across the Anzac Bridge; traffic fumes shimmered against the concrete bulwarks lining the roadway. Through the bridge's steel web, the sky rolled above him in a blue curve.

He felt a sense of revulsion, he couldn't help it. Everything in him wanted to stop his car, to get out and leave it where it was; to start to walk and to keep walking; to disappear into the fabric of the city as if he had never existed, to sleep in the open with the derelicts where no one knew him. It was an instant as powerful as it was brief. He kept driving.

7

In the commissioner's office, four men were waiting for him. Rumpled in a suit and tie, the minister had the same shell-shocked look as yesterday. He fidgeted with sharp and jerky movements, causing Harrigan to think of the walking wounded. Why don't you scream at the walls? Howl? His adviser sat with him, a nondescript man who listened intently and didn't say a word.

Opposite them was the commissioner, his thoughts impenetrable as always, his agenda beyond anyone's surmise. An older man with an unreliable temper, he had survived the countless scandals that had plagued the force over the last thirty-five years to reach this pinnacle. Noted for being without much mercy, he had a long memory for perceived insults and past injuries, real or imaginary. Harrigan looked at his unhealthy face, his balding hair, and wondered if he would look like this when he was sixty.

The fourth man was Marvin Tooth. Unlike the others, Marvin smiled at Harrigan when he walked into the room. It was the assassin's smile. At the sight of it, the skin between Harrigan's shoulderblades began to itch. The media were inclined to present Marvin as a friendly grandfather, silver-haired and avuncular. Godfather would have been the more accurate description. There was nothing coy about the Tooth's ambitions. Barring earthquake, floods or acts of God, he would be sitting in the commissioner's chair almost as soon as it was vacated. It was fair to say he had never wanted anything else so much.

'Commander Harrigan,' Edwards said, getting to his feet and extending his hand. 'I understand you're on leave. I didn't realise that. Thank you for coming in like this.'

'It's not a problem, Minister. Thank you for taking the trouble, given what happened yesterday.'

'This is life and death to me now. I will do everything I possibly can to find out who is responsible.'

'You can be assured we will put every resource we have into this, Minister,' the commissioner said, unsmiling. 'In case you're wondering why Marvin is here, Paul, he'll be managing the budget for this investigation. You'll remain the ultimate arbiter of operational decisions, though presumably you'll delegate that authority to your 2IC while you're on leave. If any negotiation proves necessary, I'm sure you can work it out.'

The commissioner at work, Harrigan thought. Divide the minions while protecting your backside at the same time. The golden rules for corporate success.

'Shall we start?' Marvin said.

'Before we do, where's Inspector Gabriel? I asked for him to be here,' Edwards said.

'He's busy at the moment, Minister,' Marvin replied. 'I'm not convinced he should continue as the operational officer in charge of this job. That's something I wanted us to discuss. I have a very well-qualified officer I can recommend.'

'As far as I could tell, he did a good job yesterday. Why are you replacing him?'

'We're not.' Harrigan shut down the possibility ruthlessly. 'Personnel is my responsibility, Marvin. You don't need to concern yourself with it. For your information, I have complete confidence in Trevor.'

'Then get him. I want him here,' Edwards said.

They sat in awkward silence while Chloe located Trevor Gabriel. Harrigan contemplated Marvin's attempted removal of both himself and Trevor, all before the morning tea break. Why waste time? Shortly afterwards, Trevor arrived.

'Sorry about this. No one told me I was supposed to be up here.'

'You're here now,' the commissioner replied with an acidic glance in Marvin's direction.

'Let's get on with the reason why I was visiting Nattie yesterday,' Edwards said impatiently. 'I understand you received your own copy of this document this morning but there's no point in wasting these. You can thank my staff for working most of the night to get them ready for you.'

Edwards' adviser handed to each of those present a high-quality copy of a thick dossier. The top of each page was marked with a series of file references, then the name *Beck, Jerome*. Harrigan leafed through detailed notes, surveillance photographs, maps tracking the subject's movements, emails, lists of associates, known aliases. Each page was stamped *Top Secret*.

'This was hand-delivered to my electorate office sometime on the night my son and ex-wife were shot.' Edwards' voice shook. Barely, he recovered himself. 'My office has a mailbox for those constituents who prefer to deliver documents in person. This was left there.'

'Do you have any surveillance cameras, Minister?' Harrigan asked.

'No, unfortunately we don't. This is the envelope it came in but there's no information on it. There was this note too.'

The envelope and a note identical to the one received by the commissioner were sheathed in a plastic sleeve. As Edwards had said, there was nothing to identify where either had come from.

'It's my belief,' Edwards continued, '— and this is based on experience, I have been a cabinet minister for the last five years — that this is a surveillance dossier from a British intelligence agency. You'll note that all the pages have the British government seal in the lower right-hand corner. Before you say it could still be a fake, the nature of the information contained in that document tells me it's almost certainly genuine. Whatever this agency is, it's been on this man's trail for years. My adviser will sum up the contents for you. He had the pleasure of reading it last night. It runs to several hundred pages.'

The adviser blinked exhausted eyes. 'It's a very detailed document. I've only been able to skim it so far. It tells us that Jerome Beck was born in 1946 in Dresden, in what became East Germany. Father unknown. His mother died in 1997 in Berlin. There's no record of any other close family. He fled from East Berlin when he was eighteen. He applied for political asylum in Britain and was granted it. He's a British citizen but he's not based in any single country. Until he came here, his address could have been any number of different locations in Europe and Africa. He was identified as an illegal arms dealer from the 1960s onwards, working mainly in South East Asia. In the late seventies and eighties, he was attached to the South African special security forces under the apartheid regime, working mainly as an *agent provocateur*. In the nineties, his name was linked to an international arms-smuggling syndicate known to deal in arms sourced from the former Soviet Union. He was also questioned in relation to the murder of a Russian journalist who was investigating that syndicate. Then around 1997, about when his mother died, he disappeared for a while. In a more recent incarnation, he worked in a scientific research facility in north London. He seems to have been an administrator of some kind. By all accounts, this employment was above board. However, during that time, he was also associating with individuals who may have been involved in the illegal diamond trade out of Africa. Then about four years ago, the dossier was closed and that is the end of the information. All in all, he's had a very comprehensive criminal career.'

'A busy boy,' Trevor said.

'Very. He was a career criminal and a murderer,' Edwards replied. In an instant transformation, his body tightened up like a clenched fist. 'Julian's dead just because he was in the same room as a man who was nothing but a piece of rubbish.'

'Do you need anything, Minister?' Harrigan asked after a short pause. 'Can we get you some coffee?'

'Let's just get on with it.'

Marvin looked up from his copy. 'Why send this to you, Minister?'

'I assumed I was being warned off Beck. But given what's happened since, that can hardly be the case. I've a question for you, Trevor. You're the operational officer. Why do you think these murderers sent those pictures out on the net this morning?'

Harrigan watched Marvin stare coldly at his 2IC.

'The killers' motives are their own, Minister,' Trevor replied. 'From our perspective, it's blown the investigation wide open and put it squarely in the public eye. The publicity will just keep on going. My judgement is, that's what they wanted to achieve. Also, they couldn't have known we'd already identified the Ice Cream Man. They were making sure we did.'

'Had you? How did you do that?'

'Cassatt had a unique and distinctive tattoo on his left arm. Given the state of the body, it wasn't immediately visible. The commander here checked it on instinct.'

'Well done,' Edwards said.

'You obviously knew the Ice Cream Man well, Paul,' Marvin said.

'It's a very well-known tattoo,' Harrigan said, and noticed Edwards glance quickly at Marvin, summing him up.

'I agree with you, Trevor,' Edwards said, 'but I also think my son's killers wanted us to be each other's insurance. If you weren't prepared to act on this information, then I certainly would be.'

'We would always act on information of this significance, Minister,' the commissioner responded coldly.

'I'd expect so,' Edwards replied. 'Now, to get to the point. I'm not so ill informed that I don't know my ex-wife's business. She knew exactly who Beck was. Julian told me he was given her name by an associate in London. You need some background. It's a complicated story and it starts with Julian. He was a troubled young man. We had joint custody but I was never there and he always lived with his mother. He had bad influences, he never finished high school. He experimented with anything he could ingest and he drank heavily. I let him down in other words. But recently he'd started to get involved in green politics. He'd joined an organisation and was working for them. It gave him a sense of purpose. I used to listen to him talk about it. He had real capacity, maybe he could have been a leader. Then just last week he told me he had something on his mind. Among other things, it had to do with your ex-Detective Cassatt.'

'Was your ex-wife involved with Cassatt's activities in any way?' Harrigan asked.

'She certainly was. It's also true to say that Cassatt was angling to be involved in hers and Beck's,' Edwards replied. 'My ex-wife's house is very big. Julian had his own self-contained flat. Nattie didn't always know when he was there. One day, she was entertaining Beck, Stuart Morrissey and your Ice Cream Man in her lounge room. There's a mezzanine floor just above it. Julian had had a hard night. He'd gone up there to look at the view and recover. They were just below him, talking. He heard every word they said.'

'You're telling us your ex-wife and those three individuals were in business together.'

'It's exactly what's in the dossier. According to Julian, they were importing diamonds. Blood diamonds, conflict diamonds, diamonds mined illegally in places like the Congo or Angola. It's a filthy business. This meeting was about landing their first shipment. Beck had organised supply from the Democratic Republic of the Congo, although he didn't say exactly where in that nation. Nattie and Stuart said they had arrangements in place for the diamonds to be marketed here. Cassatt said — and I'm sorry to have to say this to you — he and another policeman named Jerry Freeman had organised protection for the couriers. Does anyone here know that name?'

There was a heavy silence while Edwards' listeners stared at him.

'The name Jerry Freeman is known to us but he's no longer a serving police officer,' Harrigan replied. 'You're saying that both he and Cassatt were involved in this diamond-smuggling scheme.'

'That's my information. They had people onside in both customs and the police. What they needed now was the money to make payments to those corrupt officers.'

The commissioner had gone white with shock. He sat forward so quickly he surprised the other listeners.

'That's a most serious allegation, Minister. I hope you have solid information to back that up. I don't intend to have my officers' integrity slurred on the basis of rumour.'

'I'm only telling you what I was told. I would suggest to you that the information is solid as it stands.'

'You should realise that Cassatt was a liar, Minister.' Marvin spoke more sharply than was usual. 'He could have been boasting.'

'This is hardly my field,' Edwards replied, 'but at a gathering like that, how could he be lying? He'd have to deliver. Evidently he did deliver. I don't remember any reports of your people seizing shipments of contraband diamonds in the last few months. Unless you want to correct me now.'

His listeners responded with silence. The commissioner sat back, his eyes bright with anger, outrage written on his poker face for those who knew how to read it. Marvin's face had a watching expression, half-shrewd, half-fearful.

'When did this meeting happen, Minister?' Harrigan asked.

'Four months ago.'

'Why didn't your son tell you this earlier?'

'Put yourself in his shoes. He'd be dobbing in his own mother. Later he heard in the media that Cassatt was most likely murdered. He decided to leave it where it was.'

'Why tell you about it now?'

'It was mainly to do with Beck. The key to this whole story is this. Beck had another venture going with Nattie and Stuart Morrissey that was altogether separate to this diamond business. A consortium that was involved in researching some kind of experimental crop lines. That sounds ordinary but apparently it wasn't, not according to Julian. Nattie stumped up the money to get this agricultural consortium off the ground. She was repaid later out of the profits from the diamond-trading scheme. The whole point of that venture had been to finance the consortium. Evidently, the start-up costs alone were huge. Just recently Beck seemed to be suggesting to Nattie that I might like to be involved as well. They were close to signing a contract, it was going to lead to a new phase in the business. With my contacts in government, I could be useful to everyone. If need be, I could protect their interests. That's when Julian came to me. He said he knew it was the last thing I'd want to do.'

Harrigan decided not to ask the minister why Beck would be so sure of his cooperation in the first place.

'You'd want to protect your son in that situation, Minister.' Marvin was still flicking through his copy of the dossier. He spoke in a neutral voice without looking up.

'Of course I would. He was getting his life on track, I wanted it to stay that way. I told Julian I'd talk to Nattie and we'd sort things out. I'd tell her and Beck to go jump in other words. Julian could live with me from then on. He said he was planning a quick trip to Tasmania in the meantime, they were mounting a blockade. I think he came home early because he knew I'd be talking to Nattie the next day. Now they're both dead.'

They waited for some moments while Edwards again controlled himself.

'We found the contract you've just referred to at the scene yesterday. The shootings prevented it from being signed. It's a complex scientific document, it'll need analysis before we can say what it's about,' Harrigan said carefully. 'It identifies their venture as the International Agricultural Research Consortium. The amount of money specified for payment on delivery is extremely large, inconsistent with what they were producing. Do you have any information on that?'

'None at all. Julian said they were very close-mouthed about the details.'

'So, as I understand it, Cassatt wasn't involved in the consortium, just the diamond-trading business. Did he know anything about this consortium?'

'He certainly knew about its existence and, according to Julian's account of that meeting, he was angling to become involved in it. Presumably he was murdered before that was possible.'

Speedily removed, Harrigan translated to himself.

'Beck was a strange man by Julian's account,' Edwards continued. 'He kept trying to impress people. He gave Nattie the diamond she was wearing when I found her. He gave Stuart diamonds as well. I can only assume they were examples of his blood diamonds. They were rough diamonds, they needed to be cut.'

'Were they cut here, Minister?' Trevor asked.

'Yes, they were. Unfortunately, I can't tell you who did it.'

'Do you know what sort of visa Beck had?'

'He had an Australian passport. It was thoroughly legitimate. Julian said he boasted about getting it. He said the officials were stupid.'

'I can see his point,' Harrigan said. 'Assuming that dossier to be authentic, in coming here Beck could only have had the aim of involving himself in more illegal activity. The entire history you've given us shows that to be the case from the moment he arrived. How thorough were the character checks?'

Edwards could only shrug. His face was haggard. 'Clearly, not good enough,' he replied in an exhausted tone.

'Excuse me, Minister,' Marvin interrupted urgently. 'There's something very significant we have to consider ahead of anything. It's imperative this dossier be assessed under the utmost secrecy. If this is from a secret service agency, there will be important matters of national security to consider. We could be endangering any personnel who might be identified by it. I think it's vital that knowledge of this dossier does not go out of this room.'

'What are you talking about?' Edwards replied sharply. 'How can it be assessed if it doesn't go out of this room? Don't you trust your own people?' Suddenly he laughed loudly, without humour. 'Special Assistant Commissioner Tooth, isn't it? Well, Special Assistant Commissioner, I've been in politics for a long time and I know exactly what you're up to. I don't intend to have this information buried by you or anyone else.'

'Minister, that wasn't my suggestion.'

'Yes, it was. Why are you doing this? Is there something in that dossier that frightens you? Are you avoiding the simple truth there may be corrupt officers in your service? Are you frightened what the publicity will be if that story gets out? What's your angle?'

In a rare sight, Marvin could barely frame a sentence. His face went deep red and he threw his copy of the dossier onto the coffee table as if throwing it away. The commissioner stared at him with surprise and anger.

'I hope you're not implying what I think you're implying, Minister.' Marvin's own voice was distorted by anger. 'In my entire career, twenty-seven years, I've never accepted so much as a cup of coffee as an inducement. To say otherwise is a gross insult.'

Harrigan found himself almost gaping at Marvin, usually so meticulously calculating. Even Edwards looked startled.

'I have no idea how you can interpret what I just said as a personal accusation,' he said sharply. 'All I was doing was talking the politics.'

The commissioner intervened before anyone else could speak.

'The special assistant commissioner has clearly misunderstood you, Minister. Let me assure you that if any of my officers were compromised, they would only have time to clear their desks before they left this building for good. Then they'd be subject to the full force of the law.'

'I don't doubt that's true. Which brings me to my next question. I've just given you information that indicates there are corrupt police in this force. What are you going to do about it?'

'I will be contacting the Police Integrity Commission immediately this meeting is over,' the commissioner replied, clearly stung. 'I will direct all my officers to cooperate fully with their investigation. But, before they can act, they'll need to interview you. They'll need access to all the information you have.'

'I'm available whenever they want to talk to me. Which brings me back to the dossier. What do you intend to do with that?'

'We will assess this information comprehensively, including verifying its authenticity. We will also put every effort into finding its original owners. They have a right to know it's been stolen. But if it is from an intelligence organisation, then we do have to maintain a strict confidentiality. We may endanger the lives of the agents involved if we don't.'

'I'm not a fool, Commissioner. I'm aware that's necessary. So far I've told no one else about that dossier except your people and my own staff, who I know I can trust. But let me tell you, I will not tolerate having this information ignored or suppressed. I'll put it up on the web if I have to. I'll blank out the names of any innocent parties but I will still put it up there. I'll investigate it myself. I've told you. It's my son with a bullet in the back of his head. I want his murderers found. End of story!'

Edwards spoke with extraordinary control, intensely and ferociously angry. The weight of his grief was balanced on the finest edge. Everyone waited, almost as if they weren't breathing. Harrigan glanced at the commissioner who nodded.

'Perhaps we should take this information down to the task force, Minister,' Harrigan said in his detached voice. 'Let them get started on it.'

'I think that's a very good idea. Yes, let's go and meet the workers. Yesterday you wanted me to make a statement. I can do that now. Do you mind, gentlemen? Are we finished?'

'Thank you for your time and information, Minister. It's clearly very valuable.' The commissioner spoke smoothly, rising from his seat and extending his hand. 'We'll be doing everything we can to solve this appalling crime. You have my word on that.'

'Thank you, Commissioner. I'll hold you to it.'

'You have my word as well, Minister,' Marvin said, also extending his hand. Edwards shook it with a sardonic smile but did not speak. Marvin didn't miss a beat. 'Let me show you downstairs. I can introduce you to the members of the task force.'

'No, Marvin. I want to speak to you first,' the commissioner said. 'Paul can do the introductions if any need doing. Thank you.'

'Before I go, Commissioner, I'd like to say that I was very impressed by the way Commander Harrigan and Inspector Gabriel handled the scene yesterday. I have confidence in them. I hope you see it that way as well.'

'Thank you, Minister. I can assure you I will keep in mind everything you've said this morning,' the commissioner replied, as always sphinx-like when receiving a compliment on behalf of someone else.

Walking out behind Edwards and Trevor, Harrigan hadn't quite pulled the door shut when he heard the commissioner say, 'Marvin. I want to discuss the way you handled yourself in that meeting. I expect better than that from my executive officers.'

The tone of voice didn't bode well. Harrigan walked away quickly, any residual pleasure at seeing Marvin slapped down expunged by the strangeness of his behaviour. The commissioner's pervasive paranoia might simmer close to the surface but Marvin was usually as cold-blooded as they came.

The complexities of this investigation were becoming hazardous. All Harrigan could do was protect himself and his people; anticipate what other people would feel, how they would act and, if need be, forestall them. He was a professional watcher, after all. What else was there for him to do with his life?

8

Outside in the corridor, Harrigan waited for the lift with Trevor and Edwards. Edwards' adviser stood in the background, the invisible man.

'Let me give you some free advice,' Edwards said. 'You should both watch your backs. Your special assistant commissioner has got it in for the two of you for some reason.'

Trevor looked like he didn't want to reply to this.

'If I could ask you a question myself, Minister,' Harrigan said quickly.

'Go ahead.'

'I understand you know a Dr Elena Calvo.'

'I do. I consider her a friend. I was talking to her on the phone only this morning. She made me feel almost human. Why do you want to know?'

'An employee of hers, a Sam Jonas, was waiting outside at Pittwater when I left yesterday. She was asking after you. Apparently, Dr Calvo was concerned for your welfare when you failed to appear at a meeting.'

The elevator arrived and they stepped inside.

'I don't know that name,' Edwards replied, frowning. 'Did this person have a card?'

'Yes, she did.'

'Then she could easily be one of Elena's security people. She's a very security-conscious woman. I don't think you need worry about that.

We did have a meeting scheduled and I wasn't there. Elena's the CEO of a company I was instrumental in getting onshore here. A biotechnology corporation: Life Patent Strategies. Exactly the sort of thing we need in my opinion. What am I talking about? Of course, she mentioned you this morning. She saw you on TV last night. I told her I hoped to talk to you today. Apparently you're on her list of investors.'

'I requested some information. I haven't made up my mind whether I intend to invest. It might look like a conflict of interest.'

'Don't be so scrupulous,' Edwards replied. 'You should invest, it's a very fine company. I opened their facility at Campbelltown eight months ago myself. It's an extraordinary building. At the time, it was one of the achievements of my career. If it burned down tomorrow, I don't think I'd be able to care now.'

'What kind of a woman is Dr Calvo?' Harrigan asked after a pause.

They had left the elevator. Edwards stopped to collect his thoughts.

'She's remarkable. Very competent, very intelligent, very attractive. And very, very driven. She has immense energy. I could use some of that now.'

He looked exhausted, trying to draw out useful information from things that had ceased to have meaning for him. They were approaching the door to the incident room. Harrigan could hear the buzz.

'I don't think we need to go into the incident room, Minister,' Trevor said. 'There's a conference room down here. You'll be more comfortable there.'

'What do you think I'm going to see in there that I won't like?' Edwards asked. 'Why don't I go and have a look?'

With his adviser behind him, he walked quickly inside the room. Harrigan and Trevor followed. The room was crowded. Telephones rang, paper was accumulating in ever-growing piles on everyone's desk, there was a sense of hurried activity. Edwards and his adviser walked over to the room's whiteboard. There, as Harrigan had known it would be, was pinned a large, full-colour photograph of the Pittwater murder scene. The room became silent, people watched.

'Were you afraid of me seeing this?' Edwards asked. 'You forget, I've seen it in real life. It was the first thing that came into my mind

67

when I woke up this morning. I'll probably die seeing it, whether I want to or not. Let me tell you, it can't do anything to me on paper. It's time for me to talk to your people. Who have you got organised?'

'I'll take you over and introduce you to them, Minister,' Trevor said. 'Can we get you some coffee? Maybe something to eat?'

'Thank you. My adviser too. We've both been working most of the night. Thank you for your time, Commander. I'm sure I'll speak to you again.'

Edwards walked away with Trevor, his faithful adviser behind him. Not more than a few moments later, Marvin entered the room and came up to Harrigan.

'Why did you bring the minister in here? Can't you find him some better accommodation?'

'He came in of his own accord. What are you doing here?'

The level of noise in the room had increased as the members of the task force returned to their work. Marvin's arrival quietened them again. Harrigan could see people staring in surprise at the arrival of so many heavyweights in their space. It would fuel the gossip for days.

'I've come down here to see how your people are spending my money. Why wouldn't I want to know that?'

He turned and walked away quickly, going into Trevor's office. Harrigan followed, angry at having to walk in Marvin's footsteps. When he reached the office door, he saw Marvin flicking through the papers that covered Trevor's desk.

'What do you think you're doing?'

'I'm your inspector's senior officer. I can look through his desk if I want to. I'm paying for this and I want to be fully informed about what's going on.'

Trevor appeared in the doorway, still carrying the dossier the minister had given him in the commissioner's office. At the sight of Marvin, blood rushed into his cheeks.

'You'd better sit down, mate,' Harrigan said. 'It's your office.'

Before anyone could move, Marvin sat at Trevor's desk.

'Couldn't you find somewhere better for the minister than a small room at the back of this badly ventilated mess of a place?' he asked Trevor abruptly. 'Who's that you've got talking to him?'

'Frankie's dealing with him.'

'Looking at her will put him off his lunch. Couldn't you get someone more senior than her? Didn't you recruit her? How do I know she's any good?'

'Frankie knows what she's doing.'

'It's not whether you think that. It's whether I do.'

'No, that's a question for me, Marvin,' Harrigan intervened angrily. 'What do you think you're doing, talking to my inspector like this? Get up from that desk. Did God rip into you because you made a fool of yourself just now? Now you're taking it out on us. Don't bother. We've got work to do.'

'The commissioner doesn't rip into me. He listens to what I have to say. But he will rip into your inspector if he doesn't do his job properly.' Marvin turned back to Trevor, ignoring Harrigan. 'The money's mine. I expect you to run your operational decisions past me for my countersigning. If you want God on your side, you'd better start doing that today.'

'No, mate,' Harrigan interrupted. 'You don't make operational decisions. God said that was my responsibility and I'm not sharing it with you.'

'You're not here. You're on leave.'

'Nothing is going to happen on this job without me knowing about it. You can get that through your head right now.'

Marvin looked at him silently for a few moments. Then he glanced around at the pictures of home and family on Trevor's desk, at the Sydney Roosters football club scarf draped over the filing cabinet. In a relaxed way, he got up from behind the desk.

'How do you know you can trust your inspector?' he suddenly asked. 'I've often heard it said that he's an embarrassment to you.'

'What did you say?'

Trevor's voice made it clear that he was close to losing it. Urgently, Harrigan signalled to him to stay silent.

'You've never heard that from me, Marvin. You be very careful saying things like that.'

'How do you know he's not a security risk as well? Did he leak any of the information that's in today's papers? Was he paid for it? How much?'

'You look me in the face when you say that kind of thing!' Trevor almost shouted.

'Quiet!' Harrigan ordered. 'You keep your scuttlebutt to yourself, Marvin. I have complete confidence in Trevor. I'll say so to God whenever I'm asked to. But I don't have to, do I? The minister said it himself.'

'Aren't you two golden-haired boys?' Marvin spoke very softly. He moved closer to Harrigan. 'It's your career down the toilet if this goes belly up. You should be careful what you do and who you rely on.'

'You know, Marvin, you never come down here to get your hands dirty. Why are you so interested all of a sudden? You must have a reason. Come on. Share it with me. I'd like to know.'

'I told you. The money's mine. I want to know how it's spent.'

Marvin walked out, the rest of the incident room silently watching him go. Trevor sat down at his desk and put his head in his hands. Unlike other offices in the building, Trevor's office walls weren't made of glass. People couldn't see inside. Harrigan shut the door.

'Don't let him bait you like that again!'

'Jesus, boss.' Trevor rubbed his large forehead. His face and neck had turned a deep, dangerous red. 'He's getting to me. He's been on my fucking back ever since I got here this morning. Where are we up to? What are we doing? He was down here bending my ear when his PA rang to tell him Edwards was here. I never saw anyone run out of here so fast in my life. Fucked if I know where that "security risk" stuff came from. I'm not letting him get away with saying that sort of thing about me.'

'No, I told you. Don't let him bait you. If you do, you'll end up hanging yourself. That's how he works. Take this and put it away with yours. Then get your head together. Tell me exactly what you told Marvin this morning.'

Trevor locked both copies of the dossier away in his filing cabinet. Then he took a packet of tablets out of his desk drawer and swallowed one of them. Slowly the red flush faded from his face and neck. The big man suffered from hypertension. Too much pressure could put him in a hospital bed or worse. Did Marvin know this? Was it all part of the plan? Harrigan glanced at one of the photographs on the desk, just visible side on. Taken at a party sometime somewhere, it showed Trevor with his partner of eighteen years, Vincent, an accountant who had his own business at Randwick Junction. They were sitting side by side on a sofa, laughing. Harrigan reflected how pictures of the people who mattered to him were always hidden in his wallet. Trevor had never had any such qualms. He'd always said he was big enough and ugly enough to look after himself. Not if the Tooth had him in his sights.

'What did I tell him?' Trevor said. 'It hasn't even been twenty-four hours. I'm still trying to put a game plan together. I've got a forensic scientist coming in later in the week to have a look at the contract and tell us what it all means. I've got Stuart Morrissey coming in today, that's something. I'm going to talk to him myself.'

'Morrissey?'

'He volunteered, would you believe? His lawyer rang the hotline just after the news broke last night. He wanted to see us as soon as we could fit him in.'

'What are you going to ask him?'

'We're giving him a light dusting over. We'll get serious when we've got our information sorted out. He's due about now if you want to watch.'

'I think I will.'

'That's it so far. I don't even know how much money I've got. Marvin hasn't fucking told me. He's still working it out, he says.'

'Can I use your phone?' Harrigan reached over and rang the commissioner's personal assistant. 'It's Paul Harrigan here, Chloe. The special assistant commissioner's neglected to send a copy of the preliminary budget to the task force. Has he given anything to the commissioner yet? Can you email a copy to Inspector Gabriel? If you could keep him informed as well. Thanks.' He hung up. 'She's not stupid. She'll keep you up to speed if Marvin wants to play games. You've got that dossier to get started on now.'

'I'll get a team on it,' Trevor said. 'We'll have to work fast. If that is a secret service dossier, they'll take it off us as soon as they know we've got it. Meantime, God is calling in the PIC. What else can happen?'

'If the PIC do find anything, all hell will break loose,' Harrigan said. 'The hares are running, mate. I don't know where they'll finish up.'

71

'This feels fucking dirty. I hate it when you don't know who you can trust and who you can't.'

'We walk through the minefields carefully. Here's something else I want you to look into.' Harrigan handed over Sam Jonas's card. 'This is the woman who was waiting for me when I left Pittwater yesterday. She was asking far too many questions.'

'This is the one who works for this Elena Calvo?'

'That's right. Find out what you can about Jonas and Calvo and check out Calvo's connection to the minister. See if it's got anything to do with this job or not.'

'Sure thing. What's this about you investing in Calvo's company?'

'I'm not investing in her company. I got them to send me some information. That's it.'

'It was just a question, boss.'

'Don't get any funny ideas, mate.'

Trevor held up his hands in a gesture of appeasement. There was a knock on the door. At Trevor's call it was opened by one of his senior people, Ralph, looking cadaverous in his cheap suit.

'Old Stewie's here with his lawyer. Are you ready to go?'

'Ready and willing. I got a bit of extra info this morning, mate, so if I drop it into the questioning, can you go with it?'

'Sure. What's the source?'

'I'll be briefing people about that later. Meanwhile, the boss will be watching this morning.'

'No worries,' Ralph said, only the blink of an eye indicating he was presumably always pleased to have Harrigan breathing down his neck whenever he was at work.

Stuart Morrissey was in the interview room standing with his hands in his pockets and his back to the door. When Trevor and Ralph walked in, he turned round, his eyes sharp in his deeply lined face. Through the one-way glass, Harrigan saw a shortish, thin man in his mid-fifties with greying hair. Stuart's expensive clothes settled onto his narrow frame as if they were slightly too large for him. Knowing Morrissey as he did, Harrigan could only guess that one way or another some other poor sod had ended up paying for them.

Trevor had just got through the preliminaries when a man Harrigan knew to be one of Marvin's sidekicks opened the door to the viewing area and walked in. Other members of Trevor's team who were watching turned to look at him. One of them glanced at Harrigan who shook his head. Throwing him out would only up the ante. Better to give Marvin no ammunition at all.

Stuart's solicitor was clearing his throat. Harrigan had encountered this man a number of times before with a similar type of client. Groomed to perfection, Lawrence was as sharp as they came with the law. As sharp as whatever had skimmed his perfectly shaven chin that morning without leaving a nick. Baby smooth. Nothing would stick.

'There are a few points I'd like to make clear before we start,' he said. 'We're here voluntarily. Anything that's said today will be without prejudice to my client. Also, we won't be answering any questions about ex-Detective Senior Sergeant Michael Cassatt. For the record, we have no information that could assist you with anything to do with him.'

'I'm not entirely certain what you mean by "without prejudice",' Trevor said.

'My client has come here offering information of his own free will. We expect that willingness to assist will be reciprocated.'

'We can discuss that later if you wish,' Trevor said, 'but we have a few questions first. Stuart, two nights ago you were supposed to be at a dinner at Natalie Edwards' house in Pittwater with her and a Jerome Beck. What was that dinner about and why weren't you there?'

'I've got a question of my own,' Stuart replied. 'Why haven't you released Jerome's name yet?'

'We're still trying to find out if he has family anywhere,' Trevor said. 'Looks like you and Nattie Edwards were all the contacts he had out here.'

'I don't know anything about that. I hardly knew him. Lawrence told you that on the phone last night. I can't help you there.'

'The question we've asked you, Stuart. Could you answer it?'

'I had a visitor as I was leaving to go up there.' Stuart spoke unwillingly. 'He wanted to go for a drive. By the time we got back, it was after midnight. It was too late to go anywhere. I got home to a message from Nattie asking me where I was.'

'What time did she leave it?' Trevor asked.

'8:05. I rang back but no one answered. I rang the next morning as well. I left a message, you should have found it. They must've all been dead. I can't believe it.'

'Has this visitor of yours got a name?' Trevor asked, unmoved.

'Ray Foster.'

Harrigan noted the name without surprise. Foster was a well-known debt collector with a nasty reputation as an enforcer. This was the Stuart they knew, after all.

'You owe someone money and Foster took you for a drive to let you know exactly what was going to happen if you didn't pay up. Is that the story?' Trevor asked.

'I told him there was no need for this carry-on. If he'd just let me go where I was going, I'd be able to pay him. He wasn't listening.'

'Lucky for you he wasn't,' Ralph said.

'What is that supposed to mean?' The solicitor leapt in.

'Your client is lucky to be alive. That's a statement of the obvious.'

'Jesus Christ,' Stuart said. His face was stripped of all its masks. He looked sick with shock and fear. 'I saw that picture on the net this morning. I've known Nattie for years. She was my friend. Why shoot Julian like that? He was just a kid. I had nothing to do with it. I couldn't do anything like that.'

For possibly the only time in his dealings with Stuart Morrissey, Harrigan believed him. His grief and his terror were too real.

'What was the dinner about?' Trevor asked.

'If I could interrupt here,' the solicitor said. 'You would have found two copies of a contract at the scene. Am I right?'

Trevor glanced at Ralph.

'I can show one of them,' Ralph said. 'This is it.'

He placed the bagged contract on the table. The dried bloodstains were dark against the blue cover.

'Christ,' Stuart said softly and looked away.

'Only one?' the solicitor said. 'Where's the other one?'

'You only need to see one in this context,' Trevor replied. 'Was this dinner put on to celebrate signing this contract?'

'Yeah,' Stuart replied, still looking away.

'It's a very complex document,' Trevor said. 'What exactly is the

International Agricultural Research Consortium? How would you describe your mission statement?'

'My client wishes me to advise you that he had only an investor's role in that consortium,' Lawrence said. 'He went into it on the advice of his good friend Natalie Edwards and took no part in its management. He has no detailed knowledge of its activities other than a general understanding that it was involved in the development of protein-enriched crop lines for Third World countries.'

'Can he tell us where this consortium is based? Where it does its research? Where it grows its crops? Presumably it does do all those things.'

'I'm afraid my client has no information on any of those matters.'

'Stuart, aren't you the joint owner of a property with your brother, Harold? It's somewhere out west,' Ralph said. 'What about out there?'

'That dump! Nothing would grow out there. There's no water.'

'Anything relating to my client's property near the Riverina has to be decided jointly by both brothers, including access.' The solicitor spoke quickly and sharply. 'You cannot go onto that property without my client's permission and he sees no reason to give it. If you do go there without his permission, your actions will be illegal and your evidence tainted.'

'You're telling us you were prepared to put money into a business you knew nothing about?' Ralph said.

'Jerome was the one with all the details. Nattie told me to put some money in because it would be worth it. I trusted her.'

'You're the sole principal left, Stuart. Are you going to continue with the business?'

'I don't see how I can do that. I don't know enough. No, it's finished as far as I'm concerned.'

'Where'd you get your diamonds from, Stuart?' Trevor asked.

'What does that have to do with this interview?' the solicitor asked.

'My information is that those diamonds were a gift from Jerome Beck. The stone Mrs Edwards was wearing when she was found was also a gift from Beck. Do you know where he got them from?'

'Who told you that?' Stuart asked.

'A rock solid source, Stuart.'

Harrigan watched Stuart look from Trevor to Ralph. He hesitated. 'He was like that. Generous.'

'Very generous, you'd have to say. How much are they worth?' Trevor asked.

'I don't know.'

'Don't you have them insured?' Ralph asked. 'Or don't you have enough information regarding their provenance to find an insurer? Do you know where they came from?'

'Out of his safe. No, I don't know where they came from. Why would I ask?'

'A man you barely know asks you to put money into a scheme you know nothing about. At the same time, he gives you diamonds because he feels like it,' Ralph said. 'I wish I knew someone like that.'

'This whole line of questioning is grossly insulting to my client,' the solicitor said.

'One thing about this contract,' Ralph said, moving on. 'It's got very strict provisions relating to the protection of intellectual property. Violate any of those provisions and you stand to lose everything you own. Why is that necessary?'

'Isn't it standard?' Stuart said.

'This contract is anything but standard,' Trevor said. 'If you were going to sign it, you must have looked it over. You must have realised that for yourself.'

'My client has answered your question,' the lawyer replied. 'He considers the contract standard. There's no need to pursue the point further.'

'What about the money you were going to get for what you were selling?' Trevor asked. 'That's a lot of money for very ordinary-looking produce. Why send it to Johannesburg?'

Stuart glanced at his solicitor before answering.

'We were signing the contract because it was ready for harvest. It was just seed stock. It was being sent over there because that's where it'd be used and they wanted to test it out first. That's all I know.'

'Was the contract going with it?' Ralph asked.

'As far as I know. I guess we'd have to exchange. Can we talk about something important? Nattie and Jerome are dead. What if these people come after me? I'm here helping you out. What are you going to do for me?'

'Why would they come after you, Stuart?' Ralph asked.

'Someone may have a vendetta relating to Jerome Beck's business, concerned with issues we possibly know nothing about,' the solicitor said. 'Two of my client's business colleagues are dead. It's feasible he may be on a death list.'

Remembering the scene on the patio, Harrigan looked at Morrissey through the window. The glass seemed to distort the man's face. He had one hand stretched out on the table. In the artificial light, Harrigan saw the glimmer of his diamonds.

'If we're going to get you protection, we'll need to justify it. You haven't given us any reason why you're in danger from anyone except maybe Ray Foster,' Trevor said.

'Nattie and Jerome are dead and you're asking me to prove why I need protection?'

'If you saw those pictures on the net, Stuart, you must have seen your old friend the Ice Cream Man up there,' Trevor said.

'Ex-Detective Cassatt is not an acquaintance of my client.'

'Our intelligence tells us otherwise. Someone really worked him over before he died, by the look of it. He must have had information someone else wanted pretty badly. Do you also have information that someone else may want to get their hands on just as badly? Is that what you're telling us?'

Stuart looked from Ralph to Trevor. His face was grey with fear.

'Anything's possible,' he replied.

'You haven't told us enough, Stuart,' Trevor said. 'If you want protection, you're going to have to tell us more about the consortium. What is there about it that could put you in so much danger? If you can answer that question for us, then yes, we can help you.'

Stuart looked at his solicitor who gave him the faintest of shrugs. Then he looked from Trevor to Ralph, calculating and frightened in one. With a movement so sudden it startled everyone, he slapped both hands on the table.

'Then fuck it! This interview's over. I'm getting out of this dump!'

'You can watch your language first,' Ralph said.

The lawyer stood too. 'If you had treated my client with more sympathy and less sarcasm, he would not be reacting like this.'

'Before he storms out of here,' Trevor said, 'let me say we'll want to talk to him again.'

'You'll be lucky,' Stuart said viciously.

'Before we do anything,' the solicitor said, 'we'd like to know the source of some of the information you presented here today. I think my client has a right to know that.'

'At the moment, it's confidential,' Trevor said.

'It won't be if we get to court. However, there's another very important matter we have to address. That contract on the table is my client's property. I will be going to court as soon as possible for an injunction to have both copies returned to him immediately. You have no business holding on to them and you have no business examining them.'

'I think you'll find we do,' Trevor said. 'Why does your client want the contract back if he's decided against continuing with the business?'

'The information in that contract is still commercial-in-confidence. It relates to my client's personal business affairs and is of no concern to anyone else,' the solicitor said.

'You can go to court if you want,' Trevor said. 'I don't like your chances but it's your client's money. Meanwhile, this is evidence from a murder scene and it'll be examined thoroughly by a forensic scientist as soon as possible. She'll go through it in detail and tell us what it means.'

'How soon is that?' Stuart asked sharply.

'I expect to have her on deck about four days from now. It's the earliest she could make time for us.'

'We'll see about that,' the solicitor said. 'You'll be hearing from me. Good morning.'

Trevor let them out of the room. They walked outside to see the small group of watchers.

'I didn't know we had an audience. This isn't a sideshow,' the solicitor said with irritation.

Stuart zeroed in on Harrigan.

'Commander Paul Harrigan,' he said, just short of being mocking. 'You've come up in the world. You were just a sergeant when you blew into my home town all those years ago. None of that baggage weighed you down, did it?'

'Time's moved on even if you haven't changed,' Harrigan replied.

Almost, Harrigan asked if Stuart had seen his brother lately. As Ralph had suggested, Yaralla would be a good place to base a company that dealt in experimental crops. But with Ambrosine and her children in hiding down there, it was better for now to keep his mouth shut.

'Let's go. We don't have the time to waste here,' the solicitor said.

Silently, the two men were escorted out. After a single glance at Harrigan, Marvin's sidekick followed them.

'What was he doing here?' Trevor asked.

'Marvin's eyes and ears,' Harrigan replied. 'I think you'll see a lot of him.'

Ralph had joined them. 'I thought we had him there. It was bad luck he jumped the wrong way.'

'Maybe someone's threatened him. See if you can find out who's been in touch with him in the last forty-eight hours or so. Other than Ray Foster.'

'We'll get the dogs on him.'

'It's a good idea keeping it quiet that we only have one copy of that contract,' Harrigan said. 'It won't do any harm to keep them guessing for a while.'

'Boss,' Trevor said, 'I had the rare and strange experience of actually believing some of the things old Stewie said in there. I don't think he's involved in this shooting.'

'No, he can't be. If he'd been there at the time, he'd have been sitting at the table with everyone else. Someone wanted to remove all the signatories to that contract before they signed it.'

'According to Stewie, they were ready to harvest,' Ralph said. 'It looks like someone wanted to put the brakes on the whole thing before it got started. Maybe this is about industrial espionage.'

'Maybe. If they did want to stop it happening, they succeeded. The venture died that night on the patio even if old Stewie's still with us,' Harrigan said. 'Next time you talk to him, put more pressure on him. Find out what this consortium really did. Check the contract first. It'd be nice to know why he's so anxious to stop us from looking at it.'

'He didn't want us checking his farm either, boss,' Trevor said.

'No, he didn't, did he? Look into the legalities of getting on that property without his consent. Be very careful that you've got them sorted out before you go down there.'

They had reached the incident room. Ralph disappeared inside. Harrigan stopped at the door. He looked at the people crowded inside the busy room and felt he couldn't breathe. He decided he wouldn't go in there a second time that day.

'I'm finished here, mate,' he said to Trevor, who had stopped with him. 'I'll go now.'

'Boss,' Trevor said, 'are you running this investigation? Or are you on leave? Because if you're not here, it's Marvin in charge.'

Grace couldn't have asked the question better herself. The way things were, the commissioner had left it to Harrigan and Marvin to fight it out in the mud.

'Consider me in charge,' Harrigan said. 'I may not be here all the time but when I said nothing is going to happen I don't know about, I meant it. You map out your main lines of investigation and then we work out where this investigation goes together. You take direction from me, not Marvin. If he gives you grief, you call me. I'll put him back in his coffin with a stake through his heart.'

Trevor laughed. 'No worries. It'll be good to have you on board. Did you get on to Ambro?'

'I couldn't make contact last night. I'll try again today. You'll hear from me as soon as I do. A word of friendly advice before I go. Edwards was right. Watch your back. I don't know what's Marvin's up to but be very careful what you say to him from now on.'

'He's just an arsehole. For all I know, he wants to big-note himself in front of a federal government minister.'

'Maybe. Just don't let him bait you.'

There was more to this than Marvin's ego, unbridled as it was, but Harrigan kept this judgement to himself. The tension and strain about Trevor was deepening. The Tooth was good at pressuring people; the ultimate aim always being to drive them out of their jobs. In Harrigan's opinion, this time it was personal as well as political. Marvin was indulging in a very private antagonism towards Trevor. Probably it added spice to the exercise.

Driving out of the car park, Harrigan contemplated a world that existed outside of his job. Maybe one day he would discover how to inhabit it. He should try to contact Ambrosine but right now he needed to feel human. He rang Cotswold House to see what Toby was doing.

'Come over,' Susie said. 'Have a late lunch.'

Harrigan had turned off his phone just before he had gone into the commissioner's office to meet the minister. There were messages waiting for him but he ignored them. He turned the phone off again. He needed an hour in which no demands were made of him. Like Grace, Toby was someone he could talk to. A relief from being always locked inside that dark enclosure in his head. There were times when his own thoughts were the worst kind of solitary confinement.

9

In the clear late morning, Harold could see the courier coming from a distance. Glinting in the sun, the van crossed the bridge over Naradhan Creek and drove across the Creek Lane into his open gate directly opposite where the bridge met the lane. It sped up the track that led to the farmhouse drawing a plume of red dust behind it.

Harold's weatherboard house had been built almost a century ago on a low rise where it had a view of the country for miles around. From the house, a long, low slope led down to the Creek Lane, a dry-weather dirt road which, like a length of discarded snake skin, followed the path of Naradhan Creek, a now dry watercourse that made up Harold's southern boundary. Here, the old Creek Bridge formed a junction between the Creek Lane and the Coolemon Road, which didn't cross the creek bed there but continued along on the opposite bank, crossing at a wider and newer bridge several kilometres away. After crossing this bridge, the road did a dog's leg around the back of Yaralla before heading across country. When the strangers who visited the Cage trespassed on Harold's property, they always drove in via the Coolemon Road to Stuart's locked gate. Other people, like the approaching courier, came in through the open front gate to the house.

Harold was sitting out on his front veranda having a late morning tea after feeding his stock. As well as its view of the landscape, the front veranda looked directly onto the ruins of the gardens Harold's mother had cultivated when he was a boy. Once these gardens had bloomed in a profusion of roses and exotic flowers. All that remained of them now was a sundial, stretches of subsiding, ant-ridden paving and stands of well-grown red flowering coral gums, one of the few native plants his mother had liked. They had self-seeded and spread, and were now encroaching into the pepper trees on the south-western side of the house. The other plants were either dead or dying and stood as bare sentinels between the farmhouse and the house paddock. Even if Harold had had the time for a garden, these days there was no water to spare for it.

Rosie was beside him; as usual she sat up and started to bark as soon as she heard the van coming up the track. 'Quiet, girl,' he said, and got to his feet. With Rosie trotting after him, he walked down the side of the house to meet the courier. It was cooler here in this broad avenue shaded by the pepper trees. They stretched in a line down to the main yard, forming a barrier against the sun and wind. This avenue had once been intended as a driveway. Now it was partially blocked by the house water tank, which stood as an obstacle to be skirted between the pepper trees and laundry. Harold reached the yard just as the van came bumping into sight over the uneven ground. It was a private firm he'd not heard of before: Everyday Express.

'Harold Morrissey,' the courier said. 'Sign here.'

Harold took the small square parcel into the kitchen and opened it. Nestled on a piece of paper was a set of keys attached to a heavy bronze keyring, a football with *Juventus* written across it. The last time he had seen these keys, they'd been sitting on the coffee table in his living room; the man called Jerome had picked them up and put them in his pocket. Harold took the piece of paper out of the small box and unfolded it.

Go and see what's inside your brother's fence. Take some specimens. Get them tested at a laboratory. Tell the police. Find out what's really growing on your property.

Harold looked at the parcel again. There was a return address along with a telephone number. He rang it only to hear a recorded message telling him the number he had dialled was not connected. The return address must be equally false. After a few moments' thought, he searched around for his Stanley knife and a number of plastic bags.

Then he picked up his own keys and walked outside, disturbing Rosie where she had settled on her blanket on the back veranda.

'Come on, girl. We're going for a drive.'

When he reached the Cage, it looked no different from how it had always been. He tried the keys in turn until one fitted. The gate swung open easily on well-balanced hinges. Rosie came up behind, about to follow him inside. 'Stay,' he ordered. 'I don't want you in here. Stay out!' She sat for a few moments, then got to her feet and nosed off in another direction.

As soon as he was inside, Harold searched until he found the enclosure's generator, the squat node of a locked steel cabinet. Once he had unlocked it, he turned the switch from *On* to *Off*. If nothing else, no more birds would electrocute themselves on the high fences. Then he looked around more carefully. Once inside the fence, there was an odd stillness to this place, a more profound silence and a sense of detachment from everything else around it.

A snaking complexity of irrigation hoses reached every plant in the enclosure. He walked up to the metal hut that housed the automatic watering system and unlocked this door as well. Nothing so sophisticated watered his pastures. Underfoot, the red ground was still dusty. This dust stained the windows of the three greenhouses built in a row. Inside the tightly sealed glass structures nothing seemed to be living except the plants. Each greenhouse was dedicated to a single crop and each crop was labelled. Two, he had recognised immediately: *Nicotiana tabacum*, tobacco; and *Oryza sativa,* rice. The third crop was unknown to him: *Dioscorea rotundata,* white yam. The tobacco had a faintly moist, almost slimy touch on his hands. He took specimens from each and dropped them into the plastic bags he had brought with him. All the greenhouses had showers and protective overalls hanging from pegs. One contained a set of basic living quarters: bed, hot plate, an alcove with a composting toilet. The bed had been used recently but there was no indication of who had been there.

The fourth crop, growing in the open under white netting, was one he had used to grow himself before the drought. *Triticum aestivum,* common bread wheat. Other than for small tears here and there caused by the wind, the netting covered the crop like a tent. He took out his knife and slit it open.

Inside, there was a faint residual dampness on the ground from a recent watering. Walking along a pathway cut through the centre of the field, he saw on the ground birds — parrots, corellas — which had escaped the fence and got in through the tears in the netting. They were starved images of themselves, heaps of pale bones dully shining through dirty feathers. He knelt to look at them. Around about, the heads of the wheat were well grown and heavy, ready for harvest. He stood up and crushed some of the wheat in his hand. There seemed to be nothing out of the ordinary about it. It should have been good feed for any stray birds. Still, he decided against tasting it. Halfway along, he found a small mouse, its tiny feet curled up to its chest in a tight circle of dried fur and bone. He picked it up, caught by its dead perfection. It came apart in his hands, the pieces falling to dust. Harold decided it was to time to leave.

He locked the gate behind him and called to Rosie. She came to him, jumping up onto the tray of the ute. He tossed the plastic bags on the passenger seat in the cabin and then drove back across his pastures to the farmhouse. At a distance, he stopped and let Rosie jump down from the tray. 'Off you go,' he said. As thin and swift as a greyhound, she raced him back home across the dry fields, her black coat shining in the sun.

Following her, he passed the shearers' quarters on the edge of his yard. Inside this unused building, wasps built their chambered nests out of red dirt. Outside, welcome swallows nested under the roof line. He drove past the machinery sheds, then the broken-down poultry yards, empty now except for his few chickens. By the time he reached the house gate, he felt a prickling sensation in the skin of his hands. When he got out and looked at them, he saw they were tinged red. He collected his specimens and went inside the farmhouse. Rosie followed him to the back door where she stopped to drink from an old ice cream container before settling down on her blanket once again.

By now, the prickling sensation in Harold's hands had begun to feel like a slow, deep burn. He dumped the crop specimens on his kitchen table and went to wash his hands in cold water. It made no difference. His skin had turned a dark and inflamed red while the pain continued to grow. He walked slowly back to the kitchen staring at them. The burning sensation grew to such an intensity he believed he wouldn't be able to stand the pain. Then as mysteriously as it had started, it began to fade. By this time, his work-hardened hands were badly blistered and covered with weeping inflammations. Even though the surface sensation was less strong, he still felt the deep burn in his skin so powerfully he didn't think he'd be able to drive.

'Jesus,' he said softly, staring at them. His gaze moved from his hands to the crop specimens that lay on his table where he'd thrown them. He remembered the touch of the tobacco, that faint oiliness. Nothing else came to mind as a possible cause.

As carefully as he could, he took the keys to the Cage out of his pocket and threw them on the table. They landed on the note they had come with. They were a dead man's keys, surely. If the woman, Natalie Edwards, had been shot dead, then one of those unnamed bodies up at Pittwater must be the man who had been here with her, Jerome. For whatever reason, Stuart hadn't been with them when they were shot. That was Stuart. A survivor.

Don't tell Stewie you have these keys or these specimens. That was an imperative. Harold got to his feet and went to ring a neighbour to ask if someone could drive him to the local hospital. For the first time in years, he would have to see a doctor. *Go to the police*, the note had said. There was someone he could call on but he needed time to think the matter through and make that decision. Always Harold needed time, even when it felt like life and death.

10

On Bondi beach, swimmers body-surfed the bright water, sunbathers gleamed with lotion on the sand. Grace sat on her beach towel. She thought about her life, her own happiness (whether such a thing was possible), and Harrigan, his moods, the way they made love. His mouth on hers, the impression of each of their bodies to the other's. Grace cradled her arms about herself in the hot sun, reliving last night's memory, balanced on the tightrope between joy and heartbreak.

She had decided years ago there was only a thread between life and death. Live with this belief on a daily basis and happiness becomes a possibility you respect. A conundrum for you, Gracie. Are happiness and Harrigan each other's contrariety or are they indivisible? Or both, a paradox?

Gently, she touched the dressing on her arm where the splinter of broken glass had nicked her skin. All that violence trapped in your head, Paul. Those black moods you have. The way you wake up thrashing at night. All those nightmares hung on the wall of your study where you sit in solitude and think. How do I deal with it? How do I stop it hurting me?

Even before she had met him, people had told her he was driven. In the short time that she worked for him, she had seen how he drove everyone else just as hard. He was still consumed by his work. She had thought it was an addiction, now she was sure. Stop working and he would die because he had nothing else to do. Where did she fit in? In the margins of exhaustion at the end of the day, a space between midnight and dawn. It was no place to live.

'Gracie. I was hoping I might see you down here today. Mind if I sit down?'

Grace looked up to see Jerry Freeman, a pale figure in a yellow shirt patterned with huge orange and green pineapples, lowering himself down beside her on the sand. He dropped a worn sports bag between them and adjusted a scrappy straw hat. His shapeless polyester trousers and plastic sandals were grey against the sand.

'What do you want? Get away from me.'

The words came out as a softly spoken visceral rejection. Her aversion and anger at his intrusion were equally mixed. The sole time Grace had met Freeman had been one morning eighteen months ago in a side street near Central station where a young sex worker, Gina Farrugia, and her petty dealer boyfriend had been found murdered. The girl had been Grace's informant; they had met only the night before. In the grey wash of the winter dawn the two had lain against the alleyway wall while Freeman, one of the investigating officers, had grinned at Grace and quizzed her. Harrigan, waiting impatiently in the background, had later spoken to her with unconscious intensity. Leave it alone, he'd said. Whatever else she did, she should stay away from Freeman. The implication had been that he wasn't just involved but responsible. But if that was true, he wasn't only their murderer. As Harrigan himself had told her, Freeman had almost been his killer as well.

'Jesus, mate, don't look at me like that. I just want to talk to you. You can't be frightened of me. Look at me. I'm too fucking sick!'

Fear was the last thing on Grace's mind, her anger was stronger. But she knew he had been sick. About a year ago, Freeman had been invalided out of the force with heart disease. Frenzied rumours about his activities had followed him out the door. Three months ago, he had been hospitalised again. Grace remembered a bulky man. He had lost weight, his skin was translucent in the sun. It was a body like a curtain barely in place. He seemed so frail you could push him over with a single touch. It was hard to fear someone who looked so broken-down.

'I don't care if you are or you aren't,' she said. 'Why should I talk to you?'

Freeman glanced around at the sunbakers, then leaned forward and spoke in a low, gravelly voice.

'Because if you don't, Paulie's going to be in shit up to his neck. He'll be out on the street looking for a new job. Unless you want that to happen, you'll listen. If you care, that is.'

There were few hooks more effective than this one. She did care, more than she remembered caring for anyone else. However much she read her heart, there was no way around it. She and Harrigan were too entangled. He mattered to her too much. She felt the same sharp fear she had felt last night, that something could happen to wreck his life.

'Talk to him yourself.'

'You think he wants to talk to me? You think he wants to sit in the same room as me and listen to what I've got to say?'

She understood Harrigan well enough to know this would make him sick in mind and body. If Harrigan was back on the job, Grace decided she could be as well, at least for as long as it took to find out what Freeman had to say. He could be any other slimebag she might have to deal with in her usual line of work. The field work she had done for the organisation she worked for, Orion, had brought her into contact with people just as bad as Freeman. Like him, they all had information you needed even if they were dangerous.

'How did you know I'd be down here?' she asked.

'I didn't. But after I watched the news on TV this morning, I thought maybe I'll go down to Bondi on the off chance. You're usually around this stretch of the beach somewhere sometime.' Freeman squinted in the sun. 'Did you know I used to see you here pretty often before I went into hospital? Don't worry, I wasn't watching you. I've lived around here all my life. I've come down here whenever I could this last year. Just to be here. I'm dying, you see. I'm supposed to be in a hospice but I came home a few days ago. I'm not going to die in a place like that. I'm going to die in the house I was born in. Now look at this. Not the front page. Open it to where it's folded.'

He handed her a copy of the *Sydney Morning Herald*. A small photograph was pinned to the inside page. The angle showed it had been taken with a secret camera. A group of men were sitting around a table in a house somewhere. Grace recognised Marvin Tooth's son, Baby Tooth; the Ice Cream Man himself; Stuart Morrissey; and the man she had seen on the net that morning, Jerome Beck. The table was covered with the remains of a meal. The used plates and empty wine glasses had been pushed out of the way and what looked like a marketable quantity of tablets had been placed in the centre. Ecstasy, she assumed. There was a time and date stamp in the right-hand bottom corner from about five months ago.

'That's our syndicate, mine and Mike's,' Freeman said quietly. 'You know, peddling the usual shit. Ice, E, a bit of coke, all that. Baby Tooth was our man on the job. Stewie used to clean the money for us. Him and Nattie Edwards. The man with the glasses is some arsehole Stewie brought along called Jerome Beck. Maybe you know the name, maybe you don't. But I bet you've seen him before. A man who looks an awful lot like him just had his picture splashed all over the net, dead as a dodo.'

'Why aren't you in the picture?' Grace asked.

'I was too busy taking it. You can keep that. I've got the disk in my bag here. There's a lot more where that came from, let me tell you.'

Grace refolded the paper and dropped it in her beach bag.

'What's this got to do with me or Harrigan?'

'It's the icing on the cake, mate. I've got tapes of all our meetings tucked away back home. He didn't know it but Baby Tooth was our fish. We had him by the balls. So when Marvin got to be commissioner, we'd have him by the balls too. With what I've got, Paulie can hang Baby Tooth out to dry and take old Fang with him as a bonus. That's an offer you don't get every fucking day.'

'That's a bribe,' she said. 'You want Harrigan to do your dirty work for you. You don't want to do it yourself.'

'I'd look at it this way if I were you. If Fang gets to be commissioner, Paulie's going to be fucked for good and all. He knows that. Now it's going to work the other way around. You can make a choice which way you want it to go.' He spoke lower. 'And it's not just Baby Tooth on those tapes, mate. Paulie's there as well. You've heard about Eddie Lee? Well, Mike talks about him on my tapes. Him and Paulie and everything that happened that night Eddie got shot. You want that to go public? Up to you. But if it does, Paulie's fucked.'

'Why are you doing this? What's in it for you?'

'This is about Mike, Gracie. Who worked him over like that and why. Because I've got good information that'll help you find that out.' Freeman looked out to sea like someone waiting for the angel of death. 'Paulie found Mike's body yesterday in that house up at Pittwater. I'm glad. He'll get a decent burial now. You might hate him but he was my mate. That's why.'

'What do you want me to do?' she asked.

'First off, come back to my place.'

'I'm not doing that.'

'Fucking Christ, mate, I'm not going to hurt you. There's nothing there waiting for you but a bunch of tapes. I want to talk about things I can't talk about here.'

'No.'

'Look.' He leaned forward again, talking as softly as possible. 'I've got a gun, okay? A .38. You can have it to protect yourself. I know you can shoot. It's in my bag right here. I'll give it to you.'

'Not on Bondi beach!'

'No, take the bag. It's got the disk in it. Take it all.' He shoved it into her hands. 'There's no one left but me, Gracie. I'm going to tell you what I've got to say and die. That's it.'

'I'll ring Harrigan.'

'What do you think he's going to say? Yeah, just hop in the car with Jerry, I don't mind. If you don't come back with me, I'm sending everything I've got to the papers. If I do, Paulie's gone.'

'Why aren't you doing that anyway? Why should you care what happens to Harrigan?'

Freeman looked down at the sand almost as if he was embarrassed.

'Because Paulie will get the fuckers who killed Mike. I wouldn't trust any other copper but he knows what he's doing. He'll want to know who they are if only so he can piss on Mike's grave about it. He'll keep going till he finds out, he'll have to. If you don't know that, you don't know him.'

This was too true for an argument. At another time, Grace might have laughed that even Freeman respected Harrigan as much as this. She looked in the cheap bag he had pushed into her hands. Just as he'd said, she saw the dull glint of gun metal.

'I'm ringing Harrigan anyway.'

The phone rang through to his voicemail as it so often did when he was working. 'It's Grace,' she said uselessly. 'Call me as soon as you can.'

'There's nothing at my house, Gracie,' Freeman said, when she shut her phone. 'Just the tapes. Do this. It'll help us both. Then I can die easy.'

Freeman's face, a stark mask, matched his words. She didn't believe he was lying. If he did have tapes back at his house, she couldn't let them end up in the media's hands. There was something else at work too. Taking risks when she was under pressure was an old habit of Grace's. If life and death were only a breath apart, there were times when all she wanted to do was walk the tightrope between them. When the emotional impress got too much — the way it almost always did when Harrigan was involved — the adrenaline, the sheer risk, relieved the tension. The way it was now. Doing something so perilous as trusting Freeman was like a drug. As dangerous as it was, it eased away a worse anxiety.

'Did you drive here?' she asked.

'No, I got a cab. They took my licence away. Said I'd be fucking lethal if I was out there driving.'

'Can you make it to the road? My flat's not that far away. I'll get my car and I'll drive you.'

'I'll wait for you at the bus stop. I can get that far.'

At home in her tiny flat, Grace looked at Freeman's gun more closely. It was a Smith & Wesson .38, the kind that used to be standard police issue. It was in good condition and fully loaded. Grace had her own gun, one that lived in a bottom locked drawer. She had acquired it illegally several years ago when an old and dangerous lover had started stalking her. The lover had disappeared when Harrigan had arrived on the scene and these days he was in gaol. The work she did now allowed her to carry firearms legally. Still, she held on to the gun. Nothing was reliable. Harrigan might walk out on her; she might walk out on him. The stalker could get his freedom. She might no longer have a job. Freeman's gun was more powerful. The compact disk was in the sports bag as well, in an unmarked case just as he'd said. Am I really going to do something as crazy as this, she thought. Again she rang Harrigan and again his phone was switched off. She took the photograph Freeman had given her on the beach and, together with the CD and the gun, put all three into her own shoulder bag. Then she left her flat. She was going to do something as crazy as this.

Freeman was a strange figure waiting for her in the hot summer wind among the tanned and slender bodies of the young backpackers with their fashion haircuts and wash-away designer tattoos. He sat heavily in the passenger seat, breathing strangely.

'Are we going to make it?' she asked.

'I dunno. Lucky it's not far.'

'Where to?'

'Round the back of Waverley Cemetery. I'll tell you where to go.'

She drove for a short while in silence. His breathing seemed to settle and become more regular. She glanced at him.

'I've got a question to ask you since I'm doing you a favour,' she said.

'Yeah?'

'Did you kill Gina Farrugia and her boyfriend?'

'You're like Paulie, aren't you? You don't let things go. Yeah, I did kill them. They owed me money. Tell you what, though — that little girl. It was a fucking awful thing to have to do. *I got the money, I got the money.* She just kept on. I —'

'You can stop right there.' Grace changed gears viciously. 'I'm not interested in hearing that. Tell me something else. Gina was raped. Did you do that too?'

'No, that wasn't me. I couldn't by then. I was too sick.'

'Who did?'

'What do you want to know for?'

'I want to send whoever did it a Christmas card. What do you think?'

Freeman laughed. It was a hangman's cackle, one of the strangest sounds Grace had ever heard.

'I can see what Paulie sees in you past your looks. Fuck 'em, they ripped me off. It'll be something for them to remember me by. A couple of mongrels. Dougie Ferry and Rob Sinclair. Dougie's in gaol already. You don't have to go after him.'

Oh but I will, Grace thought. You can bet I will. If you weren't dying, I'd go after you too.

The houses in Freeman's street were built up on the rock close to Waverley Cemetery where the graves had a view out to the Pacific Ocean. A smattering of cars were parked on the road.

'I'm the house on the corner of that lane,' Freeman said. 'Go up the side, Gracie. I can't climb the steps any more.'

Halfway along the street a narrow lane dissected the roadway. Freeman's house was elevated at the front and side, with the bulge of the original sandstone edging the street. A steep set of steps cut into the rock led to up to his porch. It was the only house in the block still in its original condition. All the others had been renovated to luxury, becoming images of tunnel vision with blank walls on either side and glass fronts set rigidly towards the view. Grace drove to the end of the lane, did a turn in the next cross street and then came back down to park beside Freeman's side gate. On the way up the lane, she had seen bars on all his windows.

He got out of the car wheezing. 'Fucking useless,' he said.

She followed him in the gate to the backyard, a small square of couch grass sporting a rusty rotary clothes hoist. The space was surrounded by high fences and the brick wall of the house next door. As soon as the gate closed behind him, she took out the gun he'd given her. He turned and laughed.

'Don't worry,' he said. 'You won't need that.'

She noticed that the back door had a new lock. Freeman deadlocked it behind them as soon they'd stepped inside.

'Why are you doing that?' she asked.

'I've told you, Gracie. It's nothing for you to be frightened of. You'll see why when we walk through.'

In the kitchen, the smell of blocked plumbing hit her like a wall. The cupboards had been left open, their contents pulled out; the fridge, already empty, had been dragged away from the wall. Even the stove and the ancient, greasy ceiling fan had been pulled out. She followed him down the hallway that ran the length of the house. Every room had been torn apart. The carpets were pulled up, cupboards and sets of drawers had been emptied. The manhole cover had been removed, junk pulled from the roof cavity and tossed onto the floor.

In one room, a bedroom, a mattress had been straightened and a bed made up. It was one of the few signs of habitation. They reached the living room at the front of the house where the sunlight was a bright gilding on the dusty windows. Freeman sat heavily in a chair. The air was musty, the room also disordered.

'Open the front door, would you, Gracie? I need some air. I don't mind that door being open because I can see people coming.'

He tossed her his keys. She opened the door but left it on the deadlock in case she had to shut it in a hurry. Hot air rushed in from the outside. Freeman had his eyes closed.

'Who turned your place over like this?' she asked. 'What did they want?'

'At a guess, Gracie, it's what I've got to give you. Those tapes. There's nothing else here anyone would want. They got in through the back door. Happened while I was in hospital. I ask myself, what if I'd been here at the time? Would I already be outside in the cemetery with my mum and dad?'

'Where are these tapes?'

'In a moment. I've got to tell you something else. Whoever did it, they did find something. That CD I gave you on the beach. I used to have prints of all those pictures. There's a few where everyone's having a real good time and I wanted them to look at, you know, to have a laugh. They were in the top drawer of that sideboard over there when I got carted off to hospital. They're gone now. As far as I can tell, they're the only thing that is gone. So whoever broke in here, they wanted my tapes and my pictures.'

'How could anyone know you had all this information here?'

'That's it, you see. Mike. Apart from me, he's the only fucking person who knew any of it even existed! It's the same thing with his safety deposit box. He's the only one who knew how to open it.' Almost to her shock, Freeman looked distressed, even horrified. 'You saw that fucking picture of Mike on the net this morning. He'd been put through the wringer. They must have done that to him to make him tell them all that. Whoever broke in here, he's the one who did that to Mike and then killed him. He must be. He's the one I want you to get.'

'Why would they want to do that to begin with?'

'You listen to the tape. It'll tell you why. It's about people with a lot to protect.'

There was silence. Grace thought how she was isolated in the silent suburban wilderness where anything could happen and no one cared.

'You've set me up. You could have given me the tape on Bondi beach.'

'No, mate. I want you to walk away from here and go back to your boyfriend in one piece. It was too fucking dangerous to carry them around. I've got to tell you something else. You see that door over there in the hallway. That's where that little girl and her boyfriend died. I wish I hadn't done that. It bothers me.'

Opening the thick, white wooden door, Grace looked at a set of stairs leading down into a black pit. There was an uprush of cold and mouldy air. The light revealed a cellar under the living room floor with walls dug out of the original rock. A single fluorescent tube lit the gloom. She moved forward but the first step shifted dangerously under her foot.

'Don't go down there,' Freeman called out urgently. 'I'm superstitious about it. People don't always come out alive. Anyway, the steps are too fucking shaky now.'

Grace put her gun away and stepped back from the door tormented by the question: how could you do that to someone else? Harrigan had his own demons pursuing him in his work; this was the one that drove her. She left the door open and the light on. A place like that needed to be cleaned out with light and air.

There was a knock on the front door. 'Good morning.' It was a female voice.

Grace turned sharply to see a tall figure outlined in the doorway. Immediately, Freeman got to his feet, if shakily. Grace rested her hand on her bag, the gun within reach.

'Who are you?' she asked.

'Can I come in?'

'No, stay out on the fucking porch,' Freeman said.

Undeterred, the woman walked into the room, her tall figure dwarfing his. Too weak to stand, Freeman had to sit down again.

'Why don't you take my card,' she said, handing it to Grace.

'Sam Jonas,' Grace read, recognising the name from the card Harrigan had shown her the night before. 'Have you got a reason for being here?'

'I was about to ask you that.'

Grace looked her over. She was strong-looking. Even in this weather, she was wearing a leather jacket. Grace wondered if there was a shoulder holster underneath it. She stood watching the two of them with a stance that said whatever was going on here, she was in control.

'Who do you think you are, walking in here like this?' Grace asked, less out of anger than curiosity.

Sam smiled. 'I go where I like and I do what I like. That's a decision I made some time ago. But you haven't come here just to pass the time of day. You're Grace Riordan, aren't you?'

'How do you know that?'

'Like a lot of people, you're on the net. I met a friend of yours yesterday. Paul Harrigan. Did he tell you that? There are pictures of the two of you together out there in cyberspace. You must know that.'

Grace could say she possessed a very minor degree of fame. Harrigan was written up in the papers often enough, usually in the crime wrap but sometimes in the gossip columns. She had been photographed with him more than once and was usually described as the ex-policewoman who was his companion.

'Why should you be interested in anything to do with me?'

'I wasn't particularly until now. Did Harrigan send you here?' Sam asked.

Grace smiled back. 'If you're not going to answer my question, I'm not going to answer yours.'

Sam looked around, taking in the mess.

'Looks like someone turned this place over pretty thoroughly,' she said. 'What would they be looking for? Did they find it? Or maybe they didn't. Is that what you're doing here? You've come to collect it.'

'Jesus, lady. Why don't you fucking get out of here? I don't have the time left for you.'

Sam looked at Freeman in his chair.

'You don't look like you've got any time left at all. You two didn't answer my question. Did they find what they were looking for?'

'Why do you want to know?' Grace asked.

'It's my job to keep an eye on things. This is an interesting set of circumstances. Whatever this is about, I think I'm going to leave you to it and see what happens. My guess is, none of us has the time to hang around here.'

She walked out, Grace followed her.

'What do you mean, none of us has the time? How dangerous is it to be here?'

'Ask him. He should know.' Sam nodded towards the open door and Freeman.

'But you don't care what happens to anyone here,' Grace said. 'Is that it?'

Sam turned sharply. Her gaze seemed to pin Grace to a square of paper with her name written across it.

'You wouldn't know what I care about or what I don't. I don't believe in getting in people's way. I let them do what they want to do and then see what happens afterwards. To me, it's the old story of the butterfly flapping its wings in the jungle somewhere. Who knows what the outcome will be? You've got a gun in that bag, haven't you?'

'What about you? Are you wearing one?'

'Will you use yours? If you do, what will happen? Those are the real questions. Bye now.' She grinned. 'See you when I see you. If I do.'

Sam walked down the steps, across to the opposite corner of the lane and got into a blue Mazda with tinted windows. She drove away quickly. Grace watched her turn out of the street. It was otherwise empty. Not even the joggers or the dog-walkers had come out in this heat. The road tar shimmered thick and metallic, semi-fluid under the hot sun. She went back inside.

'Is she gone?'

'She just drove away. What's going on? How dangerous is it to be here?'

'I'll try and make this fast. Give me my keys, mate. I'll get you those tapes.' He levered himself out of his chair. 'They pulled up all my fucking carpets but they missed this. My mate put this in. I reckon it's pretty fucking nifty.'

He knelt down by the fireplace. She watched him insert a needle-like rod into a tiny gap between the floorboards and the ornate Art

Nouveau tiles. There was a click and a square of tiles flicked up like a jack-in-a-box. Freeman took out a clear plastic bag containing a collection of miniature audio cassette tapes. Then he shut the square of tiles and put his keys back in his pocket.

'Help me up, mate.'

She gripped him under his arm, feeling the slack muscles, helping him to his feet and then into the chair.

'This is the tape you want. The rest are just deals and money.'

He handed her the single tape, marked with a white sticker, then put the plastic bag on the arm of the chair. Leaning his head back, he closed his eyes again. Grace put the tape into her bag.

'What's on this tape that's different?'

'First off, that's the one where Mike shoots his mouth off about Paulie and Eddie Lee. But mostly it's about Jerome Beck.'

'Who was he?' she asked.

'Good fucking question. Six, seven months ago, Stewie says he's got someone who wants in with us. Someone with money. Ta-di-dah, Beck turns up. Nasty piece of shit. From the first I thought, what the fuck are you really up to, mate? He wasn't that interested in our syndicate, he wanted our contacts. He was importing diamonds and he didn't want anyone giving his couriers shit. Stewie was in on that deal. He had a couple of diamonds Beck had given him. Why the fuck was he throwing those things around? It was stupid, drawing attention to himself. I didn't trust him. I started taping him along with Baby Tooth. Anyway, it all happened. Beck got his shipment of rocks in, we got our payoff. Trouble was, Mike got curious. You see, Beck had another deal going with Stewie and Nattie Edwards, the diamonds were paying for it. Beck kept saying he was going to make a shitload of money out of that deal, like a real shitload. It'd make the diamonds look like crap. That was a red rag to Mike. He wanted in, wanted to know what it was all about.'

'You said Beck was nasty.'

'He had a chip on his shoulder. He drank like a fucking fish, and when he did he got vicious. You could see he thought we were nothing. He used to talk all the time like he was somebody special and we were living in a garbage dump. Anyway, by the time he got his rocks here, Beck had worked out that Stewie was pretty fucking useless except when it came to ripping a dollar off his mates. But Mike had contacts, good contacts. Some of them went all the way to the Bearpit. That was useful, Beck wanted those. So he made out he was going to sideline Stewie and bring in Mike. What he was really doing was playing them off one against the other. I told Mike that. He wouldn't listen, of course. He kept pushing at Beck, saying, come on, count me in. Then one day, out of the blue, Beck takes Mike to this place down south. Some bright, new, shiny laboratory that's just been built out at Campbelltown. Fancy name. Life Patent Strategies.' Freeman put a sarcastic edge on the words. 'Beck takes Mike on a tour, says to him, you want be in on this other deal I've got going with Stewie and Nattie? Then you need to see this place because this is where it all happens. Funny thing was, that place really put the wind up Mike. He came back and said no way. Started talking about cutting Beck out. He didn't want anything to do with him any more.'

'What would Beck have to do with a place like that?' Grace asked.

'Fucked if I know. I didn't get a chance to find out either. Because right after that, things started to happen. You know Ambro? Mike found out where Paulie had hidden her.'

'I've heard of her. She's a tattooist.'

'Yeah, and Paulie's informant till she did the dirty on Mike once too often. She blew the whistle on a couple of bikies who were supplying him with ice. Paulie put them in the can. Their mate's still out there looking for her.'

Grace hadn't heard any of this before but it wasn't surprising. Neither she nor Harrigan were able to talk in any detail to each other about their work.

'I thought she used to work for Cassatt,' she said.

'Mike did too. He wasn't a happy man when he found out the opposite. With Paulie of all people. Paulie had this safe house lined up for her. This is where you can hang Marvin, mate. He leaked to Baby Tooth where it was. Little Fang says so on that tape I gave you.'

'How could Marvin know that?'

'Because he controls the money. He reads the money trail. Paulie wants money for a safe house, Marvin's got to okay it. He calls in a favour, gets the address. No problems. Now someone, we never found out who, must have tipped off Paulie that Ambro's cover was blown because he took her somewhere else quick smart. But Ambro's got this funny kind of psoriasis. She gets a special ointment for it on the government, not many people use it. Mike paid someone in the health department for a list of every chemist in New South Wales that was selling that ointment for the government. He read it through once and said, I know where she is. He went out to hunt her down. The night before he went, he rang me to say he was leaving the next day. I never saw him again. I reckon wherever Ambro is, that's where Mike's grave was.'

'Didn't you know where he was going?'

'He wouldn't tell me. Next thing, I'm in hospital. When I wake up, I hear Leanne's dead and someone's cleaned out Mike's safety deposit box. Next I hear Baby Tooth is off to Perth with his wife and kids. His dad got him some job with the local coppers over there on their anti-corruption squad. I ring Stewie. He hangs up without talking to me. Next thing, I hear on the radio Paulie's calling Mike's disappearance murder. When I finally get home, my house is like this.

'Put it together, mate. I've had a lot of time to think this out these last few months. Whatever deal Beck had going with Stewie and Nattie, when he took Mike down to that place in Campbelltown, he pushed someone too far and too hard. And he *knew* that's what he was fucking doing!' Suddenly Freeman was angry. 'You listen to that fucking tape. It's like he was fucking saying to whoever was watching him, *Come on! Get me!* And they fucking did. Someone came down on him hard and they swatted us along the way. They put the screws on Mike to find out what Beck had let slip. And he told them, he must have done. 'Cause that's why they're knocking on my door now. They want my tapes. They're cleaning up, protecting their arse.'

He stopped. His mouth was blue. 'I'm going outside now. I'm feeling cold. I reckon you should get out of here now, Gracie. Take those other tapes too. Paulie'll want 'em.'

The plastic bag holding the rest of the tapes was still sitting on the arm of his chair. Grace left them there and followed him out onto the porch. She had one more question to ask before she left. He sat down in a shredding cane chair, labouring with his breathing. Out here, the sky was an endless blue above the marble angels in the cemetery. The sea matched the sky, curling out towards the horizon where both blended together in a hazy line.

'Why didn't Cassatt kill Harrigan that night in Marrickville?' she asked. 'Or even at some other time?'

'Fucked if I know, mate. It's a mystery to me. Because of old Jimbo, I suppose.'

The straightforward casualness of this chilled Grace almost more than anything she had heard that morning. Freeman's breathing was becoming harsher.

'Let me call an ambulance,' she said.

'No, mate. I just want to sit here in the sun. It's not going to be long. I'll give you my keys and you can let yourself out the back. Don't bother to —'

He stopped. In the sudden silence, Grace heard the sound of a motorcycle coming speedily down the lane, then saw it stop at the foot of the steps leading up to Freeman's porch. With a final effort, Freeman pulled himself to his feet. 'Get inside,' he said, his voice squeezed for breath. At once, Grace stepped back inside the doorway.

The rider dismounted and came up the front steps at a run. Dressed in black leathers and wearing a helmet, he was unidentifiable. He reached inside his jacket and took out a gun. Seconds only had passed.

In the instant the gun was fired, Freeman pushed himself between Grace and the shooter. There was a series of dull, muted cracks. Grace leapt backwards into the house, slamming the door so hard and so quickly she fell to the floor. A bullet thudded into the wood at almost the same instant the door slammed shut. She remembered at once that it was on a deadlock. The keys were in Freeman's pocket where whoever was out there with a gun could get them. There was no way out through the back door, which was locked, or the windows, which were barred. She was trapped.

She ran for the cellar, the only possible shelter, shutting the door behind her. There was a bolt on the inside of the door; she slid it into place. Moving as quickly as she could, she went down the stairs. As Freeman had said, they were dangerous. They kept shifting under her feet, once almost catapulting her forward. Down in the cellar itself, there was no place to hide. With the light on, she was like a rat in a trap; it would be like shooting into a fishbowl.

Grace had trophies to prove she could shoot straight. With no other choice, she took Freeman's gun out of her bag and shot the fluorescent tube in half, dropping to the floor to avoid the racket and the ricochet, hoping the bullet would bury itself in the wooden floor above. The tube's broken pieces fell like a faint iridescent rain before disappearing into blackness. I'm burying myself in another person's grave, she thought, shivering in the cold, dead air. The silence was greedy, like something waiting. Along with their breath, it had absorbed the final sounds of the last people to be killed in here. The smell was vile. It was a terrible place to die.

She felt her way along the side of the stairs, until there was enough space underneath them for her to hide there. Even by touch, she could tell they were held up by an unstable scaffold. She heard the door handle above being rattled by someone. Then, with a crash, the door was kicked open. She looked up. Daylight illuminated the cracks in the underside of the top step. She pressed herself into a niche in the wall, holding Freeman's gun, waiting. Her teeth had been chattering. With her left hand, she forced her mouth closed. Whoever it was turned the light switch off and on several times. When nothing happened, they stepped forward in the dark. The first stair moved under their feet and they stepped back. From where she was, Grace could see nothing of them.

'Are you down there, man?' said a soft, male South African voice. 'I'll find you. I'll hear you breathe.'

Grace, barely breathing, had her hand over her nose and mouth. He would be able to smell that a gun had been fired in here, even if he hadn't heard it. If he walked into the dark down those dangerous steps, he would know that she had a better chance of getting him before he got her.

'Let me tell you something, man,' the gunman said. 'That little trick of yours didn't fool me for one second. I saw that bag of tapes on the chair. But I can count. I know there should be five tapes and one CD. You give me the tape you're holding and you can walk away. You don't know me, I don't know you. Easy. That's all I want, that tape. I'm taking the rest with me anyway. Just give me the one to make up the whole.'

He stopped. They both waited.

'You're not fooling me. I know you're down there. You don't want me coming after you, Auntie. You give me that tape and you're safe.'

There was another pause. 'Let me tell you something, man. It doesn't mean anything that you've got that CD. I've already got all the pictures on it. If they hit the media, they'll take people down. Maybe it's someone you know. Someone you care about. You can stop that happening.'

Again, silence.

'Look, man, if it's money you want, we can talk about that. You give me that tape. There could be more money in this for you than you can dream about. You think about that.'

She could hear growing agitation in his voice. Then all at once he was gone, shutting the door behind him. The tension snapped, she leaned back against the rock, breathing deeply. After some moments, she took out her mobile phone. The illuminated screen said no signal. Pressed into the rubble, she was in too much of a cave. If she moved into the centre of the cellar it might be possible to make a call. She waited for more long, terrible minutes, wondering if he would come back.

Suddenly, the door was pushed open again and brilliant torchlight flashed down the stairs, its beam raking across the cold room. Grace froze where she was. Then a broad Australian voice called out, 'Police. Is anyone down there? Walk into the light. Keep your hands where we can see them. Come out now.'

In the dark, Grace leaned back against the icy rock, breathing the filthy air too deeply. She wouldn't die in here after all.

'I'm down here,' she called. 'I'm holding a gun but I'm not going to fire it. Also, I'm on the job. Okay? I'm one of you.'

'Then come out where we can see you. Keep your gun in sight at all times,' the voice came back.

'I'm coming out now,' Grace called, and moved towards the light illuminating the stairs, light-headed to be alive.

11

When Harrigan reached Cotswold House, he found Toby sitting in the sun poolside in his wheelchair, having lunch with his therapist, Tim Masson. Performing an old ritual, Harrigan and Tim took turns in helping Toby eat. In front of them, the convergence of the Lane Cove and Parramatta Rivers created a wide expanse of water flowing around the industrial rocks of Cockatoo and Spectacle Islands. On the further shore, townhouses encroached on the green waterline. At the end of the meal, Tim left father and son together, wheeling the mobile table back to the kitchen.

'How are you?' Harrigan asked. 'I'm sorry I had to leave like that yesterday. Believe me, I wish I'd been here instead.'

Toby could speak, and sometimes did, but usually found it too hard to get out an individual word. With his good hand, he typed a text message onto a miniature display device he kept with him, in this case attached to his wheelchair. Harrigan thought of his son's words living and dying in the soft darkness of his thoughts, caught there like moths trying to find their way out to the light. The glossy and sophisticated brochure from Life Patent Strategies with its promises of bodily regeneration flashed into his mind. Could they untie his son's disabilities, at least help him speak? The hope was too sharp to think about. He watched Toby's deft movements across the keyboard. His silent speech was quick, a mix of electronic words and his own private sign language, rejigged from the signing of the deaf.

Grace was madder at you than I was. I'm good but how are you?
They're all over the net those pictures that got emailed out this
morning. Real sicko stuff. Are you okay?

'I'm fine, mate. I'm keeping it at arm's length.'

You look like you've been run over by something.

Harrigan smiled. For the first time that day, he let his backbone
relax.

'I feel like it,' he said, a rare admission. 'Everyone wants too much
from me today. It's like being drained dry.'

Why do you have to keep doing it?

'I've been on the job for seventeen years. I don't know what else I
could do.'

You could do something else if you wanted to.

'I could change my life, you mean? I think about it sometimes. I
wonder what it'd be like if I did. But I don't know how to do it.'

You still don't have to be a policeman forever.

'Don't talk about me, let's talk about you. Why are you all dressed
up? Are you expecting someone?'

Toby was wearing a shirt he'd received as a birthday present, a soft
blue cotton, light and cool. His crooked legs were bare in the sun. The
summer heat relaxed his body, loosening its muscular tightness.

Emma's coming to see me. Hypatia are having a BBQ for me at her
place. It's going to be a hookup all around the country. We're going to
talk about it today.

Hypatia was an all-girl online mathematicians club that had found
Toby through his website and taken him under their collective wing as
an honorary member. His son, who had scored perfect marks in
mathematics throughout his final school year, exchanged complex
equations with them across the net. Harrigan had met them smiling at
the other end of the webcam. Five brilliant girls, both attractive and
ordinary, who lived across the continent from as far away as Perth.
Emma was the Sydney-sider. Toby's shirt, expensive and carefully
chosen, was her gift, bought on behalf of all five girls. *For Toby,* her
card had read. *Love from us all.* Harrigan hesitated. His son had had
his heart broken before.

'Don't let her hurt you,' he said.

I'm not stupid. I know she's never going to want to have sex with me. I don't care. She talks to me. I just want to be with her. Emma's going to enrol in the same course as me next year. We're going to be at uni together.

'That's great. You'll have someone to study with.'

If that's what she wants to do. It's okay. She might find someone else she wants to talk to when she gets there.

Toby began to drool, something he did from time to time. Harrigan took out his handkerchief and wiped his son's mouth, the spittle soaking into the fabric. Could a seventeen-year-old girl deal with this? Out on the water, boats and ferries plied their way. Close by, the water in the swimming pool was an inviting turquoise. Toby liked to swim in the pool, kicking out with his one good leg. These were the constraints of his son's world; perhaps they hurt him more than they hurt Toby. Harrigan thought of his son's website where Toby had drawn a precise representation of his crippled body for other people to look at. He had written: *This is how my body is twisted.* Harrigan had made that twisted body; it should have matched his own. It would have done if there hadn't been a glitch somewhere in Toby's otherwise clear brain, some short circuit that had cramped his muscles permanently.

'Toby,' he said, 'if you just ask, there are women I can get for you. I can organise whatever you want. I can set things up for you at home. You can have all the privacy you want. You just have to let me know.'

Not someone who cares about me. Just something paid for. I don't want that. I don't want to talk about it now.

'Just remember. You're only human. Think about it like that.'

I do think about it. But it's not what I want just now. I'll tell you when I change my mind. It's like you. You don't have to be a policeman forever. One day you'll change your mind.

'I'll still have to find a way to earn a living.'

You're only human. Maybe you could think about it like that.

Harrigan laughed. At the same time, his beeper went.

'Wait a second, mate. I've got to make a call,' he said. Walking towards the pool, he turned on his phone. 'Tell me that again,' he said after some moments, his tone almost incredulous. There was a lengthy silence. 'No, I'm still here. I'm just taking it in. I'm on my way right now.'

What is it?

'Mate, I've got to go. I always do, don't I? Let me know how things work out for your barbecue. Am I invited?'

Yeah, you and Grace. But if you come, you have to stay.

'I'll do my best.'

No, Dad. If you want to come along, you have to stay.

'If that's what you want, then I'll stay.'

Harrigan was about to drive out of the car park when he saw a dark brown Holden station wagon pull into one of the visitor spots. A teenage girl got out, slender in jeans and a T-shirt. Her hair was a bounce of dark curls streaked with iridescent pink and she had a piercing in her nose. Emma. She was followed by an older woman whom he guessed to be her mother. He should have stopped to introduce himself but he didn't have the time. Just think about my son, he thought as he drove away. Don't go breaking his heart or driving him to distraction.

He drove over to Waverley Cemetery as fast as the traffic would allow. When he reached Freeman's house, the street was full of police cars. Freeman's neighbours crowded the tall windows of their houses, watching. Harrigan ducked under the blue ribbons. Freeman lay where he had fallen. He was surrounded by the pathologist's team who were photographing him. For the second time in two days, Harrigan saw the huge figure of McMichael bending over another of what he sarcastically described as his clients.

Harrigan walked along the side lane. He saw Grace's car, Rosebud, a lovingly polished 1972 red Datsun 240Z, parked beside the gate. She called it her piece of retro culture on wheels and had done out the interior in seventies kitsch, right down to the zebra-striped seat covers. A uniformed officer let him into the backyard. Trevor was standing beside the back door, talking to two of his people. Harrigan walked up to him and the two officers went inside the house.

'Where's Grace?'

'She's inside taking Frankie through what happened,' Trevor said. 'Do you want to talk to her?'

'When she's finished. What was she doing here in the first place?'

'She says Freeman came up to her on Bondi beach. You'll remember the Firewall investigation — Gina Farrugia and her boyfriend? Freeman killed the both of them here in his cellar. It was on his mind.'

'Are you telling me Jerry Freeman had something on his conscience?'

'Apparently. He was dying of heart failure. He wanted to share it with someone before he carked it.'

Harrigan believed this no more than if he'd been offered a three-dollar note and assured it was legal tender. 'Show me where it happened,' he said.

He followed Trevor through Freeman's squalid house, wondering why anyone would want to live like this.

'What happened in here?' he asked.

'According to Gracie, Freeman told her the place was turned over while he was in hospital. He didn't know why. But that's why I'm here, boss, when I've got other things to do. If the Ice Cream Man's dead up at Pittwater and someone's taking pot shots at Freeman down here, it'd be nice to know if there's any connection. Especially when someone's done over the place like this.'

'Why did Grace come back here if all Freeman wanted to do was unburden himself? Did he have something he wanted to give her? Maybe something connected to the Ice Cream Man?'

'You'd think that but she says no. She says she drove him home because he was too sick to get here by himself.'

Harrigan perceived that Trevor had as many doubts about the story as he did. If Grace had been anyone else, Trevor would have found a way to search her bag and her car, even her person if necessary. Harrigan would have expected him to. But because of who she was, Trevor wouldn't lay a finger on her. He'd accept what she had to say and wait for her to decide to tell him the whole story.

Out on the porch, Freeman lay face down on the steps. The bulk of his body and his blood covered them. When Harrigan appeared, McMichael straightened up, raising his bushy eyebrows.

'Harrigan. We meet again after less than twenty-four hours. You could be stalking me. Not a good idea. I only go where the dead people are.'

'That thought had crossed my mind before today. Just tell me how he died.'

'He took three bullets to the chest. One went straight through the heart. I'd suggest it probably shortened his life by about half an hour. He was a very sick man. He appears to have saved your lovely lady friend's life by making himself the target instead of her. Maybe you should thank him posthumously.'

'I'd watch what you say, Ken. You're not sacrosanct,' Harrigan said in the very calm voice he used only when he was genuinely angry. McMichael took the meaning and went back to work without another word.

Harrigan thought how all three of the men who had once tried to kill him were now dead. The last of them, Freeman, had just fallen through that small, immense crack between here and nowhere, pushed out by someone who wasn't so very different from Freeman himself. Harrigan could ask himself why he'd built his life around men like this. He went back inside with Trevor.

'Is what old Slice and Dice just said true?' he asked.

'Pretty much. According to Gracie, Freeman put himself between her and the gun. The gunman was riding a motorbike and he was helmeted up. All she could tell us about him was that he wasn't a very big man. The patrol saw him turning into the lane when they were coming in the other end of the street. We're looking for him now.'

'Who phoned in?'

'A woman two doors down. She didn't hear anything. She went out to check her mail and saw Freeman all over the steps. Gracie said the gun was pretty quiet.'

'Where is she now?'

'Down in the cellar with Frankie. She was pretty cool, boss,' Trevor added admiringly. 'Anyone else would have been dead by now.'

'Yeah,' Harrigan replied, feeling ice all the way down his spine.

He looked down into Freeman's filthy private graveyard, now glaringly lit. Broken rock and grey dust covered a packed earthen floor, turned almost monochrome under the white light. Grace hadn't seen him. She had her hair tied back and was holding herself too straight. He could see the tension in her shoulders. Trevor's senior sergeant, a sharp-tongued, sharp-minded woman, was with her. As frumpy as an unfashionable primary school teacher in her paisley blouse and ugly navy slacks, Frankie was as cynical as they came.

'I was standing there,' Grace was saying. Harrigan watched her point to a place under the stairs. 'He had a South African accent. Soft voice. His exact words were: "Are you in there, man? I'll find you. I'll hear you breathe." He tried to come down the stairs but they were too shaky and he couldn't see in the dark. He would have known I had a gun and that I'd used it just a short time ago. Then he left.'

'This was Freeman's gun?'

'Yes, he took it out when I got here. He was worried for his safety. He told me to hold on to it.'

'You didn't think that was strange?'

'No. It fitted the man he was,' Grace replied.

'And you think this killer was a professional?'

'I'd say he's done this before. I couldn't tell what make his gun was but it wasn't something you'd buy cheaply. He shot left-handed as well.' Grace folded her arms protectively about herself. 'Is that it? Can we get out of here now?'

'Just a few more questions. Let's go back to when you were standing on the front step.'

Harrigan turned away. 'I want to see Grace's car,' he said to Trevor.

Outside in the hot sun, Harrigan looked at the Datsun parked in the laneway.

'This hasn't been moved, has it? Our gunman would have seen it when he came up here. He'd have to guess this was Grace's car. There's no other reason why it'd be parked here.'

'That's so.'

'Have you checked it?'

'We haven't had the time yet.'

Harrigan walked around the car, turning to look down to where the lane met the road. What would you have time to do? Where would you stop? He looked at the polished bodywork. Gloved hands don't leave a mark. He took out a handkerchief and felt under the back wheel arch. Something hard and rectangular was attached at the top of the arc. It came away with a sharp tug.

'What do you think this is?' he said, showing it to Trevor.

'At a guess, a tracking device. Maybe we can put it on another car and sting him.'

Grace had appeared at the back gate. She came up to them.

'This was under your car's wheel arch,' Harrigan said. 'We think it's a tracking device. Trevor's suggested we put it on another car and sting the man who tried to kill you.'

'Can I see it?' she asked

He handed it to her, still wrapped in his handkerchief. At times like this he wondered what her work really involved. Probably she knew about this kind of technology, who had it and what they did with it.

'It depends on how sophisticated the device is,' she said, giving it back. 'These days, some of them are made to send out a warning if they're disturbed. That means he'll already know you've found it. That device is very new. You might want to test it out first or you'll just be telling him where you are.'

'Whoever shot at you,' Harrigan said, 'wasn't going to wait to check your rego before he came after you again. He was coming after you as soon as you drove away from here. Why would he want to do that?'

'I don't know. Maybe he thinks I can ID him by his voice.'

'Gracie,' Trevor said, 'are you sure Freeman didn't give you something this person would want?'

'No, but the gunman might have thought that he did.'

'You're saying he may know we've found this device. Is he still going to come after you? Do you need protection? Tell me and we'll organise it now,' Harrigan said.

'That's my choice, isn't it? No, I don't need it. I don't see why he'd come after me now.'

'If you don't want protection, do you want to be armed?' Trevor asked. 'We can organise that, no worries.'

'I can organise it myself. I've got a licence to carry a personal firearm.'

'Mate,' Trevor said, 'it's possible this person is our Pittwater killer. Maybe he started with Cassatt and those three other people and now he's ended up here with Freeman. If you know anything that ties this killer to anyone who got shot up at Pittwater, I need to know about it. Believe me, I don't want to come and clean you up the way I'm cleaning up Freeman right now.'

'That's not going to happen.'

Both Harrigan and Trevor looked at her in silence.

'We're going to have to impound your car,' Harrigan said.

'What?'

'We have to, Grace. I'm taking it in.'

'No, you're not. You've found that device. Why do you need my car?'

'It has to be checked by Forensics.'

'Paul, you are not taking my car.'

'Grace, we're not having a private conversation.'

She looked around to see everyone, including Trevor, staring open-mouthed at the boss's orders being countermanded.

'All right, take it,' she said, and walked away to the other side of the lane where she lit a cigarette.

'Right,' Trevor said, looking the other way. 'I'll get this thing bagged.'

He walked off with the tracking device. Once he'd gone, Harrigan crossed the road to speak to Grace.

'What are you holding back?' he asked very softly. 'What have you got that someone wants to track you down like this to get it?'

'I can't tell you that here. I need to get home. Have they finished with me?'

'Do you want me to check?'

'No, I'll wait for them to come and tell me.'

'Grace, just tell me. Do you need protection? I'll get it for you right now.'

'I don't know.'

'*You don't know —*'

'Trevor's coming,' she said.

Trevor joined them and handed Harrigan back his handkerchief.

'Okay, Gracie,' he said, 'do you want to go home now? We don't need you any more. Just for your info, we're keeping your name out of the media. You were brave, mate. Really brave. If there's anything else you remember, anything you want to talk about, just pick up the phone. We can talk privately. It's no big deal. If you do decide you want protection, if the boss here can't fix it up, then you ring me day or night.'

'Thanks, Trev,' she said, barely able to frame the words.

'I'll drive you home,' Harrigan said. Then to Trevor: 'You don't need me any more, do you?'

'No, boss. We've got it in hand. I'll call you with an update tomorrow.'

'Do that.'

* * *

In the car, Harrigan saw tears rolling silently down Grace's cheeks.

'Are you all right?'

'I'll be fine. I just need to sit here and cry a little.'

'I'll get you home.'

Out of the corner of his eye, he watched her cry for the duration of the short journey. His mind went back to the cellar under Freeman's house and then to the front steps. Images of her shot dead in either place were vivid in his mind. He snuffed them out ruthlessly. He looked at her staring out of the window. Don't ever do this to me again, whatever else you do.

Reaching her building, he drove down the ramp into the secure garage in the basement, the security door rolling shut behind them. In the late afternoon no one else was down there, only rows of vacant cars in the cool, concrete cavern. She got out of the car first and stood there wiping her eyes with a tissue.

'Grace.' Harrigan had to ask, not even stopping to close the car door. 'What were you doing going to Freeman's place? He's scum. Anything could have been waiting for you there. Half a dozen of his mates! Why didn't you ring me?'

'I did. Your phone was off. He gave me his gun on Bondi beach. He said if I didn't trust him, I could use it to protect myself.'

'On the beach!'

'It was in a bag.'

'Well, that's all right then. How did you know he wasn't setting you up? If you get shot with a gun in your hand, it's self-defence. Then I live with you dead while Freeman gets his revenge.'

'It wasn't like that!' She turned towards him so abruptly he stepped back. 'I work in this field too. I was there. I made a judgement and it was the right one. You've got no business talking to me like this. He gave me these. They're for you. Take them.'

One after the other, she took the tape, the CD and the photograph out of her shoulder bag and handed them to him. He took them, pushing the tape into his pocket, tossing the CD onto the driver's seat through the open door. Then he looked at the photograph.

'Shit,' he said softly.

'According to Freeman there's more where that came from, on the CD,' she said. 'That tape is from a series of syndicate meetings with him, Cassatt, Morrissey, Baby Tooth and Beck. They met regularly.'

'Beck?'

'That's right. The tape connects Beck to Life Patent Strategies. Freeman believed that whoever worked Cassatt over did so to find out how much he knew about that connection. Beck took Cassatt down to their laboratory at Campbelltown earlier this year. After that, all hell broke loose.'

'The gunman thinks you have this tape,' Harrigan said.

'No, he knows I do. It's one of five. The other four were in a bag on the chair. He took them with him.'

'Grace, you're in real danger.'

'Wait,' she said. 'There are other things you need to know. Today's gunman is the same person who turned over Freeman's house. He didn't find the tape but he did find copies of the photos on the CD. He told me that today when I was in the cellar. He was trying to cajole me into coming out.'

'You shouldn't have been there.'

'It's okay. I handled it. According to Freeman, this man must have killed the Ice Cream Man because Cassatt was the only other person who knew this information existed. Also, Sam Jonas was there today. She must have been watching the house and seen me arrive with Freeman. She walked up to ask me what I was doing there. She knew who I was and that something was going to happen. She drove away and left us there to get shot.'

'Christ,' Harrigan said, still staring at the photograph. 'You've got to have protection.'

'No. I don't want people breathing down my neck. Look, for all the gunman knows, I've given this tape to the police or to you. Which I have. Why would he think I've kept it? If he was going to try and get to me, it would be to ask that single question: where is it?'

Harrigan tossed the picture onto the car seat and almost slammed the door. 'Why did you put yourself in danger like that? Why didn't you tell Freeman to wait until you could get in touch with me?'

'He was dying.'

'He was scum!'

'I can't call him scum, not now. He saved my life,' she said.

'I'm supposed to feel grateful to the man who almost killed me! Grace, you have to come back to my place. If you won't have protection, I've got to keep you safe.'

'I can look after myself here.'

'You don't have a gun. I've got one I can give you,' he said, his tone heated.

'I don't need a gun from you.'

'Why? Have you got one? I didn't think you did.'

'No, I don't,' she said angrily, looking away.

Harrigan hated guns; he always had, despite the fact that his work revolved around them and he had carried them often enough. Nothing filled him with more contempt than the sight of new officers — men or women — whose egos swelled as soon as they put on their firearms for the first time. It disturbed him to think she might have a gun when he didn't know about it.

'I've got to listen to this tape,' he said. 'Come back with me. We'll be safer together.'

'Then I'll be stranded. I don't have my car. You've taken it in. The police garage will keep it from here till eternity.'

'I had to do that. You know that.' Suddenly Harrigan was angry as well. 'You shouldn't have spoken to me like that in front of my people. It looked bad.'

'Can't you handle it? Not everyone jumps when you say jump.' She turned to him. He couldn't recall the last time she'd looked so angry. 'I knew what I was doing today. I'm a professional. I trusted my judgement and I was right to do so. I have the training to deal with that situation and I did deal with it.'

'No, Grace. I know you. You like to take risks. You take them whenever you're upset. That's what you were doing today and you almost got shot! It doesn't matter how professional you are, one day your judgement's going to be wrong. It has to be. I've got a reconstructed jaw to prove it.'

'I did what I did because I thought it would help you. You can't say it won't. All that information is invaluable and you know it.'

'I'd never ask you to do anything like that for me.'

'Then maybe I won't in future. See you.'

She walked off quickly. Exasperated, he went after her.

'That wasn't an insult. I know how valuable this information is. That goes without saying. All I meant is that you don't have to risk your life for me.'

She was at the door to the stairs, opened it. 'I need to think. I'll talk to you later.'

'All right, whatever you want.' He'd had enough. 'My door is open if you want to come and see me tonight. If you don't, fine, but that's your decision. I want you there. If you don't want to be there, that's up to you. I'll see you.'

The door to the stairs slammed shut. She was gone. He drove out of the garage into the late afternoon with a sense of finality, of leaving and never coming back. She could come to him if she wanted him this time. There were times when there was nothing else to do but leave it to her. He drove towards the city feeling drained of any emotion.

12

The television blared at the crowded waiting room in Coolemon District Hospital, a news update being broadcast during a break in the one-day cricket match. A smiling blonde-haired woman appeared sitting at the desk.

'Police have released no further details concerning the second unnamed man found dead in the house of businesswoman Natalie Edwards, despite the release on the internet of photographs of the victims earlier today. John Makaris begins our exclusive coverage at the scene. A warning that some viewers may find the following scenes disturbing.'

It was the first time Harold had seen the photograph. He had no computer and hadn't turned on his television that day. It shocked him so much he forgot briefly the pain of his burned hands. Jerome, a dead man at the table, stared out at him from the television screen. The name of the other dead man, ex-Detective Senior Sergeant Michael Cassatt, was repeated with endless close-ups of his mummified body.

'Harold Morrissey.'

The doctor was calling him in his impenetrable accent. Originally from Glasgow, William Campbell had been despatched to the isolated confines of Coolemon District Hospital for four years by the Department of Immigration as a condition of his permanent residence in Australia. It had been said that when he first arrived, people needed subtitles to understand his dialect. Still, they'd found him to be a good doctor and trusted him.

He swabbed Harold's hands clean and examined them.

'How did you do this? Did you touch any kind of acid or corrosive substance today?'

'I don't know what caused it, Doc. Something out on the farm I picked up.'

'Didn't you notice at the time?'

'No.'

'That's hard to believe. Whatever it was, it's burned through the skin almost down to the flesh. You'd have very hard hands normally, wouldn't you?'

'I've been a farmer all my life. They're not soft.'

'I don't know what state your hands would be in now if they were. I've not seen anything like this before. It's beyond the treatment I can give you here. You need to see a burns specialist.'

'I can't leave my farm,' Harold said.

'You'll have to,' the young man replied firmly. 'I'll make the arrangements. In the meantime, I'll prescribe you painkillers and we'll get those wounds dressed. I'll give you some sleeping tablets as well. The pain might keep you awake tonight.'

It was a lengthy process. Harold's hands were photographed and samples taken of the burnt skin. When he was finished, the doctor handed him a letter with the details of his appointment at the burns unit at Concord Hospital within the week. Harold could barely thank him. A trip to Sydney was the last thing he had time for right now.

'You have to go,' the doctor reiterated. 'How did you get here today?'

'My neighbours. She drove me in their car and he drove my ute for me.'

'You're not going to drive home!'

'I have to, Doc. I can't live where I do and not drive. You've just shot me full of painkillers and I've got a whole packet here. I've got to use my hands.'

The doctor admitted defeat. 'If you need more, ring me. Try to be as careful as you can. And keep that appointment.'

Harold left the hospital and drove back to Yaralla. His progress was slow; even with painkillers it was difficult to drive. Eventually

Naradhan Creek came into view, marked by a thick line of old red gums and low scrub. He crossed the creek, but instead of going straight ahead through his main gate, he turned left onto the Creek Lane. He was visiting Ambrosine.

It hadn't been a problem for Harold when Harrigan had rung him late one night to ask if he could give Ambro and her children shelter. He had a cottage on the Creek Lane, about two kilometres along from the Coolemon Bridge, he'd been happy to let them have. They had arrived first thing the next morning, sleepy-eyed and exhausted, Harrigan delivering them to Yaralla in person. It was lonely out here for a woman with three children. The cottage had no landline phone, and while there was a mobile phone signal it was unreliable. Supposedly it was only temporary until Harrigan could sort out something else. That was months ago now.

Harold had checked the electricity and the water, then poisoned the white ants, making the cottage as liveable as he could. Through winter, he supplied Ambrosine with firewood. Her children spent days glueing bright papier-mâché figures onto the doors and window frames, covering the filigreed tunnels the ants had eaten out of the wood. The shapes were small pieces of radiance in the drab house.

He drove into Ambrosine's yard. In the early evening light, the moon was visible as a huge orange globe low to the horizon behind the house. At the door, a voice yelled at him to come inside.

Ambrosine was in her frowsy kitchen stacking dirty dishes next to the sink. He heard the blare of the television set from the room her three children shared.

'I was wondering when you were going to get here,' she said, reaching for a burning cigarette perched on an ashtray. 'Want a drink first? I'll finish up here and then we'll get started.'

She poured a generous measure of whisky and handed him the glass. 'Jesus, mate,' she said. 'What happened to your fucking hands?'

The doctor had covered his hands with clear, plastic-like dressings which he'd said would give greater protection. The burns were clearly visible.

'Something on the farm today. I wasn't being careful enough. It makes it hard to touch the steering wheel.'

'I fucking bet it does. That's nasty. Are you okay for this with those hands?'

'Yeah, the doc gave me enough painkillers for an elephant.'

She grinned. 'You won't feel a thing then.'

He sat at her table drinking while she finished her cursory cleanup. Her paintings covered the walls in the sour-smelling room, scraps of paper as short-lived as her tattoos were permanent. They closed in on you, each one crowded with obsessive details. He looked at them: vistas of her kitchen with its unhinged cupboards, scraps of old food covering the table, piles of unwashed dishes scoured by mice, cockroaches and ants; her three children perched on disintegrating chairs on the front veranda, staring at the watcher; a disarray of broken toys, bones and debris covering the bare ground in front of a tiny house that was isolated under a huge blue sky. Harold had once asked her why she painted things this way. 'It's my life,' she'd said. 'What else is there? I want us to know where we are when we eat. Nowhere.'

'Did you hear the news?' he asked, finishing his whisky.

'About the killings up at Pittwater? Yeah, it was on TV.' She frowned. 'It doesn't make any fucking difference to us whether Mike's dead or not. We're still stuck here. If we got in my van and drove away somewhere else, I'd open the front door one day and there'd be someone standing there with a shotgun. But what if we do stay here? How safe are we then? I know this place is your home, but every day I think we're going to die. I wake up at night and I feel like I'm at the end of the world.'

'Don't think like that. You won't be able to get up in the morning.'

'There's no chance of that. The kids get me up, no matter what. They like it here better than I do. Come on, mate. You're late enough as it is. It's time we got going.'

'There's something I want to ask you first.'

She sat down at the table with him. 'What?'

'Do you know anything about this Natalie Edwards?'

'Why do you want to know about her?'

'She was up at my property about a week ago. Her, old Stewie and the other bloke who got shot with her. Jerome. He's the one they haven't named yet. I saw him on the TV at the hospital.'

'Shit, mate. I'm glad they didn't know I was here. You want to know about Nattie Edwards? She was a bitch. A fucking ruthless bitch who didn't care who she walked over for a dollar. What were they doing here?'

'I don't want to tell you. It's too dangerous. It's to do with this.' He opened his hands for her to look at once again.

'Jesus, mate. Ring Harrigan. He's running that show. I saw him on the TV. Fucking talk to him.'

'You think I should?'

'Yeah, I do.'

'I've lived here all my life,' he said. 'I'm frightened. I've never been frightened before.'

'Harry, ring him. Go home and call him now. You can come back tomorrow.'

'No, we'll do a bit first. Just half an hour. I need the time to work out what I want to say. It'll settle me down. Then I'll go home and call.'

'If that's what we're going to do, get in the front room and strip for me.'

Ambrosine called the lounge room her studio even though Harold was her only canvas. He stripped in front of a dark mirror, becoming both naked and dressed. His thin, strong body was webbed with her gorgeous tattoos — an image of his property as it used to be when there was rain. His torso was a waistcoat of brightly coloured birds, and the trunks of eucalyptus trees curled around the hard muscles of his legs. The topography of his ten thousand acres was compressed into an imprint etched onto the stretch of his back. Ambrosine had left her signature — AMBRO — drawn in a spider's trace of blue ink beneath his ribcage.

She appeared beside him in the mirror. Her body was large in her loose black dress, her long dark hair spilled over an array of stars tattooed on her neck. She ran a finger around an image on his shoulders and he shivered. She had done all these tattoos for nothing because she needed to. She had to work, she said, otherwise she wouldn't survive.

'I don't ever want you to die. That way, there'll always be these tattoos. It'll be something I'll have done with my life. Apart from my kids.'

'I don't know how possible that is,' he said, half-smiling.

He lay down on her table, willing his body to relax.

'I'll do a bit more work on the owl,' she said, speaking of a tattoo she was working on across his torso.

'Yeah.'

She rolled up her sleeves and began to mark his skin to guide her needle. He could see the psoriatic lesions covering her forearms. Where she hadn't covered them with tattoos, the lesions marked much of her body. She called them her personal tattoo, one worked from the inside through the genes that made up her skin.

Tonight, his own tattoo would be missing one of its strange and necessary accompaniments, one that was as fundamental to the ritual as the permanent markings left behind. The thin rivers of pain that followed her needle would be dulled by the doctor's painkillers. There were times Ambrosine worked on him when the world disappeared and there was only him, his tattooist and his pain. It was worth it to him. He was this property, every bit of red dirt that made it. Nothing would shift him from here, including death, even if they were the deaths of others and not his own.

He lay there while Ambrosine worked, in his mind forming the words he would use to persuade Harrigan to come all the way out here. They came down to a simple sentence. I need your help.

13

Harrigan sat at his desk listening to the voices of the dead. They did not whisper but spoke in ordinary tones, spinning off his miniature cassette player thin and low. The first was a voice Harrigan hadn't heard before. It had a guttural intonation: Beck's. The other two, Freeman and Cassatt, were too well known. The recording started with Freeman giving a place, time and date before he got out of his car and walked into the pub where they were meeting. Harrigan listened to the sounds of greetings, drinks being brought to the table. The background noise was a low hum broken by the occasional sound of a phone ringing somewhere.

Beck: *Your beers. My whisky. Why do we come here? It's a pig sty.*

Freeman: *No one's going to be watching us here. There's nothing wrong with the beer.*

Cassatt: *This is what I got to show you, Jerry. It looks like nothing but it fucking got me inside.*

Freeman: *Is that a key? Looks like a little metal badge. What's the logo?*

Beck: *LPS. Life Patent Strategies. I thought your mate here might want to expand his horizons. That's a key to a locked door, Mike. You keep it in your wallet. You'll need it next time you go back.*

Cassatt: *There won't be a next time. That place gave me the fucking creeps. It's a fucking prison. Getting out of the can is a piece of piss compared to getting out of there. And it was in the* middle of fucking nowhere. It's a long way out to Campbelltown that time of night.

Beck: *It doesn't matter when you go, that place never stops. It's real money. Another world. You don't walk away from chances like that, you take them. I'm getting another whisky.*

Freeman: *You got through that one quickly enough, mate. Jesus, he gives me the shits sometimes. What was he doing taking you to that place?*

Cassatt: *What he's always doing. Fucking jerking himself off. Another world. Crap! I don't need it if it is.*

Freeman: *You going to keep that little badge thing?*

Cassatt: *Yeah, think I will. Might be handy if I'm dealing with old Jerome one day. You never know. Might be a problem for him that he gave it to me. Did you see the news last night?*

Freeman: *No, mate. I don't bother with all that shit.*

Cassatt: *I turn on the TV and it's fucking Paulie talking about something or other. I thought, yeah, you cunt, where's Ambro? The way the fucking press talk about him, it's like he's Christ on skates. They should talk to me. I'll tell them how I fucking near knocked his front teeth out —*

Freeman: *Mate —*

Cassatt: *No, he says, I won't shoot him. You fucking cunt, Paulie. If I tell you to shoot Eddie, you fucking shoot him. He's there on the carpet at your feet. Do it!*

Freeman: *Matey, keep your mouth shut. You're fucking on tape. Beck's back.*

Beck: *You should listen to me. You can manufacture there, you can experiment there. You can turn out something new. You can do a good business out of that place.*

Freeman: *I thought we came here to talk about sparklers.*

Cassatt: *No one's going to let us into that place. Everyone wears a white coat.*

Beck: *If you pay the rent, why not? It's what everybody else does.*

Cassatt: *We don't need a setup like that for the shit we sell. Who was that joker you met in the corridor? The one with no fucking hair or ears, like he came out of some horror movie. He knew who you* were, mate, and you knew him. It looked to me like the last thing you two wanted was to see each other.

Beck: *He's nobody.*

Cassatt: *He wasn't acting like that. He acted like you were the nobody and he didn't know what the fuck you were doing there. What were you trying to prove? The guards fucking near spat in our eyes when you walked in. They don't like you there. They let you in because they had to. No, mate. You don't have that to offer.*

Beck: *You don't know who I am. I do have that to offer. But those guards, they're like you. They won't see the realities. I'm the side of the business they don't like to think about. I'm just reminding God's daughter who I am and who she really is. She won't insult me again. If she doesn't like it, too bad.*

Cassatt: *Who the fuck is God's daughter?*

Beck: (laughter)

Freeman: *Something tickle your funny bone, mate? Must be a pretty funny joke.*

Beck: *It is, believe me.*

Freeman: *How come you can get into a place like that?*

Beck: *Because I know where the money comes from. I know how it gets spent. That building is the biggest washing machine in the world.*

Cassatt: *Where does that much money come from?*

Beck: *From the old man. God the Father. The Alpha and the Omega. That's how he sees himself.*

Freeman: *That tells us a lot.*

Beck: *Then don't ask questions. You said we were here to talk diamonds. Okay, we will. I want to get another shipment over here. The same arrangement as last time. Can we do it?*

Cassatt: *Just where do you get your rocks from, mate?*

Beck: *Why?*

Cassatt: *I'm curious.*

Beck: *From a place called Kisangani. I've got people there.*

Freeman: *Kisangani? Sounds like kiss my arse.*

Beck: *It's a town in the Congo, a diamond market. The last time I was there, four years ago, it was a war zone. You wouldn't have lasted five minutes.*

Cassatt: *What were you doing there then?*

Beck: *We went there because we were hiding something.*

Freeman: *What do you hide in a place like that?*

Beck: *There's a civil war on, mate. Dead people. What else?*

Cassatt: *Keep your voice down. Do you want to tell the whole fucking room?*

Beck: *Who's here? Some bitch at the bar doing her business. We went there for Jean, God the father, for his daughter. She didn't know, she said. No? She must be stupid. Their names aren't on the papers but they knew what we were doing there. Jean told me to my face, you go there and you do this. You come back and you tell me what happens. And they think they're better than me.'*

Cassatt: *What are you talking about, mate?*

Beck: *This place is shit. Why do you want to drink in this pig sty? Because it suits you?*

Freeman: *If that's how you feel, I might fuck off, mate. I don't know about you but I've got better things to do.*

A second conversation followed almost immediately afterwards, again beginning with Freeman's voice giving the date and time. It was just a few days after the previous meeting. They were at someone else's house this time, neutral ground. Beck wasn't there. Baby Tooth was. Arrogantly alive, he gave Harrigan his catch-all almost straight off. There were sounds of him arriving, the offer of a drink, and then the Ice Cream Man talking.

Cassatt: *I found her, mate. I found where Paulie's stashed Ambro. It's so fucking obvious, I should have thought of it myself. I'm on my way out there as soon as I can get away.*

Baby Tooth: *I'm glad to hear it. I was pushing my luck getting that address out of my old man. I didn't want to do it for nothing.*

Freeman: *Didn't he ask you why you wanted to know, mate?*

Baby Tooth: (laughter) *You're joking, aren't you? What you don't know can't hurt you. He just called in a favour from his mate, old Roger, and gave me the address on a piece of paper. He didn't say a word. Didn't even look me in the eye. Far as he's concerned it never happened.*

Freeman: *What are you going to do about Ambro's kids, mate?*

Cassatt: *I'll work that out when I get there. Why?*

Freeman: *Because if she ends up dead, and maybe her kids too, is Sean's dad going to start asking questions?*

Baby Tooth: *You're not going to shoot the kids, are you?*

Cassatt: *I'm not planning on it, but I don't know what'll happen.*

Baby Tooth: *It'd be one way of making sure Dad never asks any questions.*

Cassatt: *Whatever. She's going to be fucking sorry, that's for sure.*

The tape finished. Harrigan hit the Stop button with relief. He debated whether to copy the tape then decided against it. Somewhere out there an unknown person had Cassatt's original tape of Eddie Lee's murder in their possession. Harrigan didn't want to create a second one that corroborated the first. He had already downloaded the CD onto his computer. That would be enough for the moment.

Freeman had been surprisingly methodical, labelling the tape with a series of numbers. When Harrigan loaded the CD onto his computer, he saw that the numbers matched the photographs of the meetings. Freeman had put together his own sound and light show. The pictures were as sordid as the tape had been. No one could have described the Ice Cream Man and his friends as eye candy. At least they showed why Beck hadn't turned up on Harrigan's radar despite several months of association with the Ice Cream Man and Freeman. They had been very careful about where they met in public, usually in out-of-the-way hotels or multi-storey car parks. Interspersed with these pictures were encounters between various sex workers and members of the syndicate, including Baby Tooth. Curiously Beck didn't feature in any of these photographs. Maybe he had no taste for that kind of group activity.

Harrigan slowed when he reached the sequences attached to the single tape he had. The Ice Cream Man and Beck sat at the table together with half-empty glasses in front of them. The camera had taken in the rest of the room behind them, which held only a few scattered drinkers. A woman sat at the bar, supposedly having a drink and reading a newspaper but in fact looking towards the men at the table. *The bitch at the bar doing her business.* Harrigan recognised Sam Jonas. She couldn't have known she was on camera. A very professional, skilled agent. Professional enough to get on to Beck's connection to Freeman and Cassatt when none of his people had managed to. It wasn't an observation that made him happy.

Harrigan reached over and picked up the LPS brochure, reading Elena Calvo's biography once again. *Daughter of renowned industrialist Jean Calvo*. Elena was God's daughter; Calvo was God, or at least according to Beck's estimation of how he saw himself. Jonas was tracking Beck, presumably keeping an eye on him for Elena Calvo and her father. Given what had happened with the Ice Cream Man, it had been a shrewd move.

Harrigan googled the Democratic Republic of the Congo. The information confirmed much of what he already knew. It was a country riven by years of civil war and invasions, with UN reports of war crimes in the east of the country, specifically in Kisangani, which was also a well-known illegal diamond market. The capital was Kinshasa, which could also be a centre of conflict. A place where someone could hide any illegal activity, including murder.

Harrigan went back to Freeman's photographs and looked again at the picture of Beck sitting at the table with Sam watching him. Had he made things too dangerous for Sam's boss? Proved to be too much of a wild card? What could be more provocative than taking the Ice Cream Man on a tour of her premises? Did Sam kill him and the others? Harrigan decided no. If Elena Calvo was behind the Pittwater murders, she wouldn't have used as her killer someone who then introduced herself as her employee to the police officer in charge of the investigation. But it would explain why Sam had offered him a bribe. If she was behind these killings, Elena Calvo had a lot to conceal. Apart from any other consideration, such as gaol, if the minister made a connection between her and his son's death, her company would be finished here.

Harrigan was deep in these thoughts when his landline phone rang. He glanced at the number on the display but didn't recognise it.

'Paul,' a familiar voice said. 'It's Marvin here. How are you tonight?'

Of course Marvin could get his home telephone number. He had access to everyone's personnel records, paper or automated.

'I'm fine, Marvin. To what do I owe the pleasure?'

'It's business. You were at Jerry Freeman's house today. You and your companion, as I believe she's called. Freeman's murder will affect the entire Pittwater investigation. I'll have to give the commissioner an updated budgetary figure as soon as possible. I need an estimate from you of the operational impact of today's events.'

'I don't think I can give you one just like that,' Harrigan said. 'I'll have to work it out with Trevor. There's no point me giving you a figure that's inaccurate.'

'Surely you can give me a ballpark.' Marvin spoke sharply. 'For example, did you find any evidence in Freeman's house that could affect the progress of this investigation? Something Freeman may possibly have given your companion. Just knowing that would be enough for me to make an estimate.'

'Any new evidence,' Harrigan repeated. 'What sort of evidence would that be, mate?'

'Anything relating to Freeman's murder, obviously. The kind of information a man like him would collect. Tapes, photographs.'

'All that will be logged.'

'There may be something you haven't recorded yet.'

Grace's information was in Harrigan's mind while Marvin was speaking. *Today's gunman is the person who turned over Freeman's house and killed the Ice Cream Man. He didn't find the tape but he did find copies of the photos on the CD.* He glanced at the photograph on his desk that Freeman had given Grace on Bondi beach that morning: Baby Tooth at dinner with the Ice Cream Man, pills on the table. He flicked through the images on his computer screen, stopping when he found another picture of Baby Tooth, this time athletically entwined with a willing sex worker.

'Paul, are you there?'

'I don't think you've ever rung me at home before, Marvin,' Harrigan said. 'There's never been an emergency that's made you pick up the phone.'

'I'm sorry to intrude but it's urgent. The commissioner needs to know.'

'Does he?'

'That's what I said.'

Again a pause.

'How's your boy, mate?'

'What?'

'Your boy. Sean. Didn't he just go over to Perth with his wife and kids? He upped and left overnight. Surprised everyone.'

'Sean's doing very well over there, as you'd expect. Marie and the children are happy. Why are you asking?'

'I just wondered why he felt like a change of scene so quickly.'

Harrigan listened to the silence. Marvin didn't even seem to be breathing.

'What's your point?' he finally asked.

'You spent some time this morning giving my inspector grief. You tried to get the both of us dumped from this investigation. You keep pushing your nose in where no one wants it. I don't think you should try any of that again if you know what's good for you and your boy. I think you should take a very hands-off attitude from now on. Because if you don't,' Harrigan twisted the knife, 'maybe you won't ever get to be commissioner. Because maybe you and your boy will be looking for new jobs together.'

Again, silence.

'What are you talking about?' Marvin said eventually.

'What fell into my hands today from Freeman. He had it in for you, mate. Even more than he did for me. He wanted to get you and your boy and he thought I might help.'

'Tell me what you're talking about.'

'A tape and a bunch of photographs. Your boy doing business with some people very well known to Jerry Freeman and having a good time with some very lithe sex workers. You'd better hope his wife doesn't see those pictures, because if she does she'll be packing her bags.'

'Does your companion know anything about what's on the tape or those photographs?' Marvin asked.

'She knows nothing, mate. Freeman gave them to her to give to me and she knew better than to look at them or ask him any questions. I've told her to keep her mouth shut. And before you ask, no, I don't have them here. I'm not that stupid.'

'Have you listened to the tape?'

'I haven't had time yet.'

When Marvin spoke again, there was a new edge to his voice. He sounded like a man who felt in control of events.

131

'Why haven't you given these things to your people, Harrigan?' he said. 'Surely they'd be relevant in some way. Is there a reason why you can't? Is there something there that incriminates you. If Freeman was involved, it would be the right people. There've been enough rumours.'

'You're forgetting something, Marvin. I'm not the one in the pictures. From what I've seen, they'd make the commissioner's last few hairs stand on end.'

'What do you want?'

'I want you to leave my people alone. You try anything like you tried this morning and you're fucking gone, mate. And something else. Maybe one day I do want to climb the ladder to the commissioner's office. If I do, then you'd better not get in my way. Do we understand each other?'

'We do. Good night, Harrigan. I expect I'll see you at the next budgetary meeting.'

I am my own stalking horse, Harrigan thought, replacing the handset in the cradle. Someone was running Marvin. Harrigan was certain of it. Someone had waved the photographs under his nose and said, 'Do what you're told.' Even now Marvin would be on the phone to his handler, telling him exactly what Harrigan had just said. Whoever the gunman was, he wouldn't go after Grace; he would come after him.

In the silence the phone rang again. This time Harrigan did recognise the number. Harold.

'Harry. What can I do for you?' he asked.

'Maybe you can help me out, mate,' Harold said reluctantly. 'I've got a problem.'

'Do you want to tell me what it is?'

There was a short silence.

'I have to say it, mate. I'm frightened. Frightened what might happen down here. I didn't think I'd ever say that. I wanted to ask if you could get down here.'

'Probably I can. Can you tell me a bit more first?'

'It's Stewie. He's put this construction on the property. I call it the Cage. The people who got shot up at Pittwater — they were out here not much more than a week ago. Sitting with Stewie in my living room. They're growing something out in that Cage. Not what you'd expect it to be from the looks of it. Whatever it is, it's dangerous.'

'Is this a personal invitation from you, Harry?'

'If you want to put it that way. Why?'

'Do you need your brother's permission to have guests on the farm?'

'Of course I don't. What are you talking about?'

'Because one day you might have to say that in a court of law. I'm making sure old Stewie can't play any legal tricks if you do. I'll be there sometime tomorrow. I'll make the arrangements and I'll be in touch. You stay by your phone tomorrow morning.'

'I might not be able to do anything else,' Harold said.

'What do you mean? What's happened?'

'I'll tell you when you get here. It's nothing special. Thanks, mate. I appreciate this.'

'Before you go, how's Ambro?' Harrigan asked.

'She's got something on her mind and she's not telling me what. You might want to talk to her as well.'

'Tell her I'll be there tomorrow.'

Harrigan hung up and sat in the silence of his house. By now it was dark and he realised how tired he was. The weight of the day's actions, the dangerous place he'd put himself in tonight, made him wonder if he still carried the death wish that had made him go after the Ice Cream Man all those years ago. Was he inviting the gunshot Mike had never fired? Marvin's runner would have no reason not to pull the trigger.

Harrigan needed company, but it was getting late and there was still no sign of Grace. Maybe one day she would make up her mind if she was staying or going.

He went into his bedroom where he made the bed and tidied up a little. There was a hint of her perfume still in the air. Otherwise, it was hot and airless. He opened the doors onto the veranda and stepped forward, almost as if he was stepping into the firing line, daring fate. Outside, it was only peaceful. He looked at the empty street, wondering if her car would appear. Then he remembered that it was in the police garage. How could he forget their public argument? No taxi appeared. Finally he turned back inside. It was a drab room to entertain a woman in, he thought. Tonight, it wouldn't matter. Grace would not visit him. Tonight he had gambled and lost.

He went back into his study where he looked at Goya's prints on his walls. He remembered the first time he'd encountered Goya's work. It had been a few years after his near murder, while he was on secondment to the Australian Federal Police and stationed in London. Everyone went to Spain for their holidays; he'd tagged along and found himself in the Prado in Madrid for no other reason than that it was in the tourist guide.

He remembered walking into a room lit with a pale light where Goya's Black Paintings were on display. It had been like walking into a room full of nightmares. He'd read the story of how these paintings were made, of the aged and sick artist nursed back from death by his doctor. Out of this sickness, Goya had turned his gifts to painting these works directly onto the walls of his own house, *Quinta del Sordo*, the House of the Deaf Man, then just outside of Madrid. Violent, shadowy mobs following each other in the dark. A dog with just its head visible in the empty landscape, staring in strange appeal at the sky. Two men sunk in mud, flailing at each other uselessly. Most terrible of all, Saturn devouring his own child. When he saw this painting, Harrigan had thought: yes, this is what we do to each other. We are like that, we eat each other.

Daily in his work, Harrigan watched the deterioration of people into strange madness, cleaned up after them when they had finished doing what they did to each other. Almost two hundred years after they had been painted, these hallucinatory works spoke to his demons and gave material form to his own nightmares. Nightmare, as he knew from his own experience, was as real in people's waking lives as in their sleep.

He took down from the shelf his facsimile edition of Goya's *Los Desastres de la Guerra* and opened it to print number 69, a print Goya had etched out of the futility of war. He studied the image of a corpse that was lying partially out of its grave, its head turned to the side, its mouth open in death. Its bony fingers held a pen. On a sheet of paper it had scrawled a single word: *Nada*. Other shadowy etched figures, one holding the scales of justice, surrounded the corpse, staring at the message. The caption Goya had originally written was: *Nothing*.

That's what it says. The publishers of the 1863 edition had changed it to: *Nothing. We shall see.* The artist's version had been too bleak for his first publishers.

More usually, Harrigan had seen himself as the figure holding the scales of justice, as useless as he knew this to be. It was still an ideal he held on to in his mind. Tonight he questioned it. He thought of the young boy, Julian Edwards, dead at the scene in Pittwater with Cassatt's grinning corpse beside him. What did he, Harrigan, achieve? Exactly what was written on the paper: *Nothing. Nada.* Tonight he became the corpse in the picture looking back at himself. His heart was dead. Even the emotional pain he felt was curiously dry, as if this too had no life force.

He was deep in these thoughts when he felt two hands pressing gently on his shoulders. He knew that touch and looked up. Grace was standing behind him. He leaned back against her. Her body was warm through her singlet T-shirt.

'Didn't you hear me come in? I called out.'

'I was lost in my head. I wasn't expecting you to be here.'

She looked down at the image on his desk. 'So you were sitting here looking at pictures from the end of nowhere instead,' she said.

'It helps to pass the time. Where were you?'

She sat down in the spare chair, dropping her shoulder bag onto the floor. Her hair was loose on her nearly bare shoulders. He closed the book.

'At the laundromat,' she said. 'I would have got here sooner but the dryer broke down.'

'You were doing your washing? Why?'

'I always do when I get depressed and I want to think things through. Have you ever sat in a half-empty laundromat on a week night when it's getting dark? It's a sad place. You can see things clearly in a place like that.'

'You decided you'd rather be here with me than there?' He had to grin. 'I'm flattered. What does this mean? You don't want to say goodbye after all? Or is this just a temporary reprieve for us?'

'I don't want us to think about that right now. All I want us to do is be in the here and now. When this is all over with, we can work out where we're going. If you can live with that arrangement.'

'You decided that sitting in a laundromat?'

'Is it any worse than sitting here looking at pictures from the grave?'

Harrigan laughed. She smiled and rolled her shoulders the way she did when she was relaxing. The more she relaxed, the longer she stayed, the better the chance of persuading her to keep staying. Or so he hoped.

'I've got to tell you something that will probably make you want to walk right out of here again,' he said. 'I've got to go to Coolemon tomorrow. Whatever Stewie and his mates were up to, it's happening on his and his brother's property.'

To his relief, she laughed. 'I should have known there'd be something like that. How long will you be away?'

'A couple of days. We've still got a little time now.'

Grace was about to speak when the phone on his desk rang. Again he didn't recognise the number.

'Harrigan,' he said.

'Commander Paul Harrigan?' a female voice asked.

'That's right.'

'I'm Dr Elena Calvo. Please forgive me for ringing you so late. I believe you've heard of me. We have a mutual acquaintance in Senator Edwards.'

Harrigan switched on the speakerphone.

'Yes, we do,' he said cordially. 'The minister mentioned you to me in very positive terms. It's not so very late, Dr Calvo. What can I do for you?'

'Please, call me Elena. I know from our mailing lists and also from Allan that at one stage you were interested in investing in my corporation, Life Patent Strategies. I wondered if you still wanted to pursue that.'

'Do you think it would be a good thing for me to do?'

'I think it would be very worth your while, yes.'

'In that case, I had thought seriously about it.'

'Good. I always think it's important to look after individual investors as well as the large institutional ones. Would you like to come and visit our research facility? I think you'll find it very impressive.'

'I can be there as soon as tomorrow morning if you like,' Harrigan replied. 'I'll have a few spare hours if that suits you.'

'That would suit me perfectly. I should warn you it's quite a drive. We're out at Campbelltown.'

'That's fine.'

'Then we'll expect you.' She gave him directions for what would normally have been a journey to the end of the city. Tomorrow it would be a small diversion from his preordained route. 'I have you down for our launch tomorrow night as well. I think you'll find a visit to Campbelltown will be a very useful background to that occasion.'

'As it happens, Dr Calvo, I have to be somewhere else tomorrow night,' Harrigan said. 'Can I send someone along in my place?'

He looked at Grace who nodded.

'Certainly. Who would this person be?'

'A friend of mine. Grace Riordan.'

'Yes, of course.' There was a faint edge of disappointment in her voice. 'Are you sure you can't be there yourself?'

'I'm afraid it's impossible.'

'I'll put her name down in that case. She will be able to understand what this is about?'

'I don't think she'll have any trouble.'

'Then we'll expect her in your place tomorrow night and we'll see you tomorrow morning. Good night.'

The room went silent.

'Do you mind going to the launch?' Harrigan asked Grace.

'No, it'll give me a chance to get frocked up. If you're down at Coolemon, I can do something up here. How did she get your number?'

'Legitimately. I would have put all those details down when I first applied for her company's prospectus. She's been thorough.'

'She's been digging into your life. She knew about me,' Grace said.

'*Yes, of course.* That was a slip. See if she doesn't try and take your meeting down to a personal level in some way.'

'Why do you say that?'

'Just the way she talked to you. It was a little too intimate for someone she's never met. And why should she be unhappy if I'm going to be at the launch instead of you?'

Harrigan decided to avoid the question.

'That's her problem, not ours,' he said. 'You said Sam Jonas was at Freeman's house today.'

'Yes. Why?'

Harrigan turned on his computer and displayed the photograph of Sam watching Beck and the Ice Cream Man in a run-down pub.

'This is from Freeman's CD. Jonas has been undercover, keeping an eye on Beck and his associates for her boss for months by the look of it. Until today, Freeman was the last of them left.'

'She didn't talk like she was planning on killing either of us. But she knew something was going to happen and she wasn't going to interfere,' Grace said. 'She knew I had a gun. According to her, the question was whether I'd use it.'

'She didn't try to offer you a bribe or threaten you? Try to get this tape out of Freeman in any way?'

He passed it to Grace who looked it over.

'No, she was completely hands off. She said that was how she did things. Why?'

'I'm trying to work out her motivation,' Harrigan said. 'My guess is that tomorrow Elena Calvo is going to offer me a good sum of money for that tape. You'd think if Jonas was working for her, she'd have tried to get her hands on it as a matter of urgency.'

'That kind of dirty work may not be Sam's job. She might just handle the intelligence side of things. Have you listened to this? What's on it?'

'Information that seriously implicates both Calvo and her father in whatever Beck was up to and links LPS to money laundering.'

'How would Calvo know you've got it?'

'Marvin rang tonight. He wanted to know if there was any evidence at Freeman's house that might affect the investigation. Specifically, did Freeman give you anything like a tape or photographs?'

'Are you sure he wasn't just being Marvin?'

'No, there's nothing in this for him. Everything he does is worked out to take him one step closer to the commissioner's office. Today, he made a fool of himself in front of a federal government minister and put God's nose out of joint, not once but twice, trying to get control of this investigation. I told him I had the tape and the CD, but I didn't have them here and I hadn't listened to the tape.'

'Paul, that was a really dangerous thing to do. What if Marvin blows the whistle on you?'

'He won't. If these pictures ever get out, maybe he won't lose his job but he'll never get to be police commissioner. By his own admission, your gunman today has these pictures and I'm very sure he's pulling Marvin's strings. Half an hour after I tell him what I've got, Elena Calvo rings with a friendly invitation to morning tea. Marvin's told his handler, his handler's told the boss. My guess is there'll be plenty of inducements offered tomorrow.'

'Are you going to turn them down?'

'What do you think? Why are you asking me that?'

'Because when you say no, you'll have made yourself a target. If today's gunman was prepared to put three bullets into either me or Freeman to get hold of that tape, then he won't care if he does the same thing to you. From what Freeman told me, he's the one who worked the Ice Cream Man over. What if he does that to you?'

'Grace, I'm not having him coming after you.'

'I don't want to see you end up looking the way the Ice Cream Man does now. Don't do this to me,' she said.

He was about to say it was exactly what she had done to him earlier on today, then changed his mind.

'I'm big enough and ugly enough to deal with him. I'm expecting him. Mike wasn't.'

'Do I get to listen to this?' she asked, handing the tape back.

'It's more dangerous information.'

'It's a bit late to worry about that now.'

'You need to be armed,' he said. 'I'd feel better if you were. I do have a gun you can have. I keep it down in my cellar. It's illegal but it'll protect you.'

He didn't tell her that it was a significant gun in his life and nothing other than the present circumstances would have made him offer it to her.

'No, leave it,' she said. 'I can fix up a gun through work.'

'Won't they ask questions as to why you want it?'

'I can handle that.'

'I didn't mean to insult you today,' he said. 'I do respect your judgement. You're brave and this information is very important. But you put yourself in danger when you didn't have to. You do that deliberately sometimes.'

She looked at him with that glint in her eye again. Maybe she was thinking: and what have you just done? He would have replied that he'd had a better reason than she did.

'Let's not go back over the argument. Let's just forget it,' she said.

Harrigan put Goya's *Los Desastres de la Guerra* back on the shelf. Until the morning, his time was his own.

'Then we're both off duty,' he said.

She smiled. 'For a little while anyway.'

At least making love was easy. For a space of time, neither of them had to think about anything else except each other, their mutual warmth, the ease with which they did this. It felt so uncomplicated; it always had between them. How can you walk out when it's like this, he thought. Later, he was to consider that sitting with her own thoughts in a late-night laundromat had been a more powerful persuader than anything he had said to her or indeed any fear that she might be in danger herself. At that moment, there were no such thoughts in his head. They slept deeply and dreamlessly. There might have been no evil in the world.

14

Elena Calvo's directions brought Harrigan to Campbelltown on the far southern edge of greater Sydney, a landscape of new and half-built suburbs merging into the countryside. He drove to the far end of an industrial estate surrounded by bare fields burnt in the drought. The isolated remnants of bushland were visible on the hillsides in the distance. On the way to the estate, the traffic was light; once there, the roads were mainly empty. No one was following him.

The road led him in a circle around the Life Patent Strategies building. It stood on a broad acreage surrounded by a high fence with powerful lights spaced at intervals along the perimeter. At night, the ground would be brightly lit. The building itself was startling. It appeared to be diamond-shaped with its four points extending into the grounds. The external walls were covered with a blue steel mesh constructed from large and interlocking triangular units. Two storeys of tinted windows reflected a skewed sunlight through the mesh. At the far end, smokestacks glittered in the clear air.

Harrigan drove up to a gatehouse at the sole point of entry. A security guard signalled for him to stop. Boom gates stood between him and another set of high steel gates giving entry to the grounds. His ID was checked, an e-tag attached to his car and the boom gate raised. The steel gates opened for him automatically as he approached; he drove in and they closed behind him.

A newly built access road took him across grounds that showed the signs of recent and extensive landscaping. Wide areas were beginning to green. The guard's direction led him to the eastern apex of the building, where the access road met a driveway leading to a blank wall made up of a high, wide metal door. Sam Jonas was waiting for him on the corner, a tall figure in a cream pants suit. Her slim form was a white shadow against the building's grey and blue bulk. She had her hands on her hips and was balanced lightly on pale court shoes. He'd been told to expect her. He stopped. She went to the passenger side of the car and opened the door.

'Good morning,' she said. 'I've been sent to escort you in.'

'I need an escort, do I?'

'You do. Mind if I get in?'

'Go ahead.'

She slid into the passenger seat. Her face had a light touching of make-up. Her black hair was plaited up at the back of her head, the way it had been the first time he'd met her.

'We meet again,' he said. 'This time you're all dressed up.'

'Elena has very particular standards of dress for the office. Leathers are okay out on the road but not at LPS. Another thing you'll find out about Elena.' Sam looked at him sideways. 'She's very good at not letting the right hand know what the left hand is doing. When you're talking to her, it's a good idea to keep to the information she wants from you. Otherwise, she'll shut you down.'

'Elena's the boss, is she?'

'Oh yes.'

'Don't worry, I don't want to embarrass anyone. I'll keep our chat confidential. Where to now?'

'Before we move, are you armed?'

'No. What about you?'

For an answer, she opened out her jacket to reveal a white silk shirt but no weapon.

'A personal bodyguard with no side arm. Why not?'

'Elena doesn't allow firearms into the building.'

'Not even for her bodyguards?'

'Not for anyone. I don't know if that includes her. If you're not carrying, let's go. You're looking at the entrance to the building's garage. Drive straight ahead. The door will recognise your e-tag and open for you.'

He started his engine and moved slowly forward. The metal door slid open and then, when he had driven down a short slope into an underground car park, closed silently behind them. The car park was lit by overhead lights; its bays were full. Sam directed him towards a visitor spot at the far end, near a set of bronze-coloured glass doors.

'Fort Knox,' he said.

'This is just the beginning. I assume you're carrying a mobile phone or a beeper?'

'Both, as it happens.'

'I'm sorry but you're going to have to hand them in at the desk. We don't allow any means of private communication into the building. Not even Senator Edwards got to take his mobile phone inside. Don't worry, the storage is secure. The way it's set up, you're the only one with the key.'

Harrigan could have argued. Of all people, he had to stay contactable.

'Anything to oblige.'

'That's a good way to start where Elena's concerned. Being obliging.'

'How long have you worked for her?'

'About a year. She pays well. Everyone here's very well paid. It makes them loyal.'

'Does money make you loyal?' he asked.

'It depends on what you think loyalty is. For a lot of people, loyalty is money.'

'I asked about you.'

'Money's not an issue for me. Yes, I am loyal if you want to put it that way, but my loyalty is something you have to earn. If you're worth it, then I give it. Otherwise, forget it. Come on. Let's go inside.'

They got out of the car. The bronze-coloured glass doors slid open for them. They walked into a sparely furnished foyer where one security guard stood beside an internal door and another behind a counter. Despite what Sam had just told him, both were armed. They had the shaved heads and humourless expressions of ex-prison guards. The wall behind the counter was covered by a bank of video screens.

'We need a visitor's badge with executive level clearance for Commander Harrigan and a locker for his mobile phone and beeper,' Sam said. 'Dr Calvo should have sent the request through.'

The guard placed a small metal box on the counter. 'Please open that,' he said.

Harrigan took out a compact if thick gold badge, almost like a large and heavy gold cufflink, decorated with the initials *LPS* in an ornate design.

'You can use that as a key to open locker number eight,' the guard said. 'You'll be able to store your devices in there. Then if you could keep that badge on you at all times, it will allow you access throughout the building. It doesn't need to be visible but it does need to be on your person.'

At the impress of the badge, the locker opened. Harrigan put his mobile and beeper inside.

'Nothing can open that door now but that badge,' Sam said. 'You get to take it with you when you leave. A gift. That's one of Elena's ideas. She likes people to have souvenirs of their visits here. Once you've left the building, it'll be deactivated.'

'Can it be reactivated?'

'For that to happen, you'd have to come in here and have it done at the desk. You really have to be invited all over again.'

'Is it really made of gold?'

'Gold-plated.' She smiled sarcastically. 'Only top-level guests get one of those. Everyone else gets the basic metal.'

Harrigan dropped the badge into his shirt pocket. He thought of the Ice Cream Man being ushered in here by Jerome Beck late one night. He glanced around. There were cameras watching his every move.

'How long do you keep your CCTV tapes?' he asked.

'We archive them for at least twelve months.'

'In the building?'

'Oh yes. Very securely. I don't go anywhere near them. If I don't need something for my work, it's off limits.'

The internal door slid open to reveal a small antechamber where there was a lift. Sam activated it with a key.

'Is this your only entrance?' Harrigan asked.

'This is the main external entrance. There's a delivery dock to the north where the smokestacks are. There's a third entry via the roof near Elena's office, which is on the other side of building. That's locked with a door built to withstand an atomic blast, I think.'

'I thought you said no firearms. Those guards were armed,' Harrigan said.

'They're just there to mind the gate. Their access is limited to that area and they can't bring those weapons into the building proper. You should know that my access throughout this building is limited as well. I can't take you into any of the labs, for example. I'd only have access to a lab on specific orders from Elena.'

'Where can I go on my pass?'

'Wherever Elena thinks you ought to be able to go.'

'She has all the keys, does she?' he asked.

'All the keys, the combinations, passwords and overrides. Who else?'

The lift arrived and they stepped inside. The building had three levels: Basement, First, Second. Sam pressed Second. Quickly they were there. The lift opened.

'Welcome to Elena's kingdom,' Sam said.

They stepped out onto a mezzanine above an atrium that soared to the height of the building. A glass wall stretched from floor to roof in front of them. A broad set of stairs led from the mezzanine to a paved area below, where doors in the glass wall opened onto a garden in the centre of the building. It was planted with well-grown tree ferns, flowering shrubbery and rich green vines. It had a cool look. A pathway led from the glass doors to the centre where Harrigan could see an ornamental pool set round with tables and chairs. The garden was covered by a glass roof, turning the whole space into a climate-controlled greenhouse.

'Very impressive,' he said.

'It is, isn't it? It's the organisation summed up for you. They make it very hard for you to get in, but once you're here, they make you very comfy. This corporation consumes what it needs to operate. It's how it works. Like some blind organism. On the basis of need, nothing else.'

Harrigan had some difficulty identifying in Sam's tone of voice what he would have called loyalty either to Elena or to her corporation. For a personal security officer, as she called herself, she seemed very free, almost unguarded, in the way she spoke about her boss. Throughout there had been an edge in her voice, almost of contempt. In her last statement, it was something deeper, more negative. By her own admission Sam was well paid. Also by her own admission, money would not buy her loyalty. Something had to make her give it of her own accord and it could be withdrawn at will. Harrigan's observation was that in this case she hadn't given it. So why was she here? If loyalty wasn't her first object, where did that leave her offer of a bribe? If her motives were questionable, why be unguarded like this? Why not hide herself? All he could conclude was that she didn't care what she did. She followed orders and collected her money because she had nothing else to do.

People passed them while they stood there. Voices echoed in the high spaces of the atrium. There was constant traffic and a sense of activity about the place. Sam leaned forward on the railing.

'The building is built on two axes, one from north to south, the other east to west, with an apex at each point of the compass,' she said. 'On each storey there are four main corridors that run from apex to apex. There are four sectors, each of which can be locked down independently of the other three. There are also independent backup systems in place for each sector. The air conditioning is a good example. It services the whole building but each individual sector has its own backup system in case of an emergency. Individual laboratories can also be sealed off, if need be. Below is the public area. You can meet for lunch, there's a gym, that sort of thing. But otherwise it's possible to avoid almost anyone in this building if you want to. It's organised so people's paths don't have to cross.'

'How many people work here?'

'A lot. But they're not actually employed by Life Patent Strategies. Elena will probably tell you about that. This way. I'll take you on the tour.'

They walked along the echoing corridor towards the northern end of the building. Harrigan watched his escort. She walked with swift, flowing steps, her spine straight.

'Have you been in this business all your working life?' he asked.

'I have. I like it.'

'You strike me as very professional.'

'I am,' she said. 'And very focused.'

'How did you get into the business?'

There was a faint pause.

'If you really want to know, I'll tell you. When I was at uni there was a fad going on — study martial arts; know how to protect yourself. Most people got bored and dropped out after a while. Not me. I decided I was going to do it properly. I liked being strong and quick. I liked the control. I got into security work from there. I like the fact that I can go out there and control a situation. Other people don't set my parameters for me. I do that myself. I say what happens. Look, if you want to know about me, why don't you ask Elena for a copy of my résumé?'

'You're Australian.'

'So?'

'You've worked in England for a long time. You can tell by the way you talk.'

'Top of the class,' she replied with a touch of irritation.

'Did you come home to be with your family?'

She laughed sarcastically. 'No,' she replied.

'Do you have one?'

'No, I came out of a test tube. My mother's a Petri dish. Have you ever thought about minding your own business?'

'You dug into my life, Sam. You told me that when you met me up at Pittwater. I can dig into yours.'

'Go right ahead.'

'What will I find if I do?'

'Someone who's very sure about what they're doing and what they're going to achieve. Happy now? Let's move on.'

They reached a junction at the far end of the corridor that marked the northern apex of the building: a wide area that served as an antechamber. As well as a lift, there was a flight of stairs in front of them leading downwards. To their right was a closed door.

'What's in there?' Harrigan asked.

'A corridor leading into the second storey of the north-western sector. That door's always locked. I don't know anyone who can get in there. Elena's office is on the floor beneath it. You might have noticed that at each junction there are lockable doors at the end of all the corridors,' she said. 'If there was a lockdown, they'd all shut and lock automatically. That would isolate all the sectors and everybody in them.'

'Why is all this security necessary?'

'Some of it's because of fire regulations. Elena will tell you about the rest.'

They went downstairs to another open area, also a junction of corridors. In front of them was a set of double doors, at that moment open onto an entry point staffed with security guards and watched by video cameras. Behind this was the delivery dock, also open. Harrigan saw a delivery van and, behind it, a flash of blue sky.

'This is the most vulnerable entrance,' Sam said. 'On week days, it stays open to the outside world for varying lengths of time. On weekends, it's usually closed up and unstaffed. But if there were any attempts to break in through here, these internal doors would shut and lock immediately, isolating any intruders.'

'What about breaking out?' Harrigan asked.

Sam laughed. 'No chance. Once you're in here, you can't get out without all the right passwords.'

A short corridor immediately behind them continued in a curve towards an unknown destination.

'What's down there?' Harrigan asked.

'That leads past the door to the main air conditioning unit to the animal house,' Sam said. 'We can't go in there either, it's quarantined. But I have been in once. That was an experience. It was vile, smelt of piss and fear. Everything in there is as good as dead. Their end point is to disappear up the smokestacks as environmentally friendly waste.

'You know a funny thing about those monkeys in there?'

'What?'

'When I saw them, they were completely passive. They didn't move. They just sat there waiting. They know what's going to happen to them. So they deal with it by going dead. There's nothing else they can do.'

'You wouldn't be like that, surely?' he asked.

'No way. You should always go down fighting whoever you're up against. But you've got to think like that if you're in this business.'

It was an argument Harrigan had heard often enough in his job: the police were the thin blue line keeping back the forces of darkness. Often, it didn't matter how you did it.

'I've always seen it more in terms of protecting people,' he said.

'Isn't it the same thing? I bet it's not for you, is it? You haven't had your mind changed about that point of view yet. But you must get pretty bleak about your work at times. Who do you protect, really?'

'As many people as I can.'

'Bullshit! People like you never protect anyone.' She spoke with sudden, unhidden and, it seemed, uncontrollable contempt.

'You want me to tell your boss you just talked to me like that?'

She drew a breath and stepped back. From the expression on her face she knew she'd gone too far. 'I get carried away sometimes. Sorry.'

It was a brush-off apology. Harrigan debated whether to push it a little more or let it go. On reflection, he had bigger fish to fry just now than resentful bodyguards.

'Let's move on,' he said.

They continued down another corridor. 'There are no windows here,' he said.

'No. There's no source of external light in this sector except in Elena's office.' Sam stopped outside another set of doors.

'You're about to meet her. Best behaviour now.'

She led him into a large, well-equipped laboratory. At one of the benches in the centre of the wide white room, a slender woman in a red suit was standing talking to a man with a ruined face. Another taller and more strongly built man stood directly behind her. Numbers of people were busy working throughout the room. There was a hum of activity. When Harrigan walked up with Sam, the woman in red turned to smile at him.

'Commander Paul Harrigan, Elena,' Sam said. 'I've just taken him on a tour of the building. We went through the security features like you asked.' Then she stepped out of the way, quietly withdrawing herself.

'Commander Harrigan. I'm very pleased to meet you. I'm Dr Elena Calvo.'

They shook hands. Her touch was firm, her skin cool. She appeared younger than her photographs and spoke with a faint accent,

149

attractive to hear. Her face was handsome, her hair cut into a soft, curled style.

'Pleased to meet you too, Dr Calvo,' he replied. 'I've heard a lot about you. I'm pleased to put a face to the name.'

'Call me Elena. We prefer informality here, I like people to feel at ease. Let me introduce you to a very good friend of mine and the head of our signature project here at LPS. Everything you see around you in this laboratory is dedicated to burns research, and the success of this work is attributable to its director. Dr Daniel Brinsmead.'

Calling on a career of meeting the atrocious without betraying a thought, Harrigan extended his hand. He didn't recall seeing a face more badly scarred than Daniel Brinsmead's. His features were slashed across with broad scarlet and pallid markings. He had no hair or eyebrows, his ears were stubs, and the skin on his neck was as damaged as his face. Sharp blue eyes like chips of shining porcelain looked directly at Harrigan. His right hand grip was strong. His left hand, its fingers reduced to stubs, was encased in a fingerless glove. Under his lab coat he wore a light white suit. Harrigan saw a badge, gold-plated like his own, pinned to Brinsmead's lapel.

'How do you do,' the man said. His voice was strange, damaged, almost a whisper. 'You see in front of you the motivation for this research. I hope you don't find it too shocking.'

'I see a lot in my work, Dr Brinsmead. It's not a problem.'

'Good.'

In his mask-like face, his sharp eyes were sizing Harrigan up, much as he might have examined cells through a microscope.

'I've asked Daniel to explain to you what he's doing here,' Elena said. 'It will help you understand why I've worked so hard to establish this place.'

'You're here, Commander, because of my face and body,' Brinsmead said. 'My skin is my project. I'm looking to see if the human body can be regenerated after burns of even greater magnitude than I have.'

'I wouldn't have said yours were trivial,' Harrigan replied.

'There are people worse off than I am. After my face, it's mostly the left side of my body and my torso that's been affected, and I've been repaired to some degree by skin grafts. Other people need virtually new skins. There are other effects which aren't always immediately apparent. Nerve damage, constant pain and, paradoxically, loss of sensitivity as well. Let me take you through what we do in this big room.'

If Harrigan hadn't had so much on his mind, the details of Brinsmead's explanation would have fascinated him. One thing he did notice: from the way Brinsmead spoke and the response of the people working for him, he was a driving force here regardless of his injuries. He led them to a computer where he displayed a detailed transparency on the monitor.

'Let me introduce myself to you again. I'm here in more than one way. This is a piece of my burnt body magnified. It's been taken from the dermis, the under layer of skin, which doesn't regenerate after severe burns. In this laboratory my researchers dissect me, even if they do it by biopsy. I've set this project up so I don't have to be here for it to work. They have bits of me to use in my place. They've charted my skin, my injuries, my DNA.'

'You may not be aware, Commander,' Elena said, 'that everything Daniel is achieving here is in the public domain. Millions of people stand to benefit from his work. I'm very proud we have it under our aegis.'

Glancing past Brinsmead, Harrigan saw Sam Jonas two steps behind, watching them closely, taking in every word, every nuance. Between her and Elena, he saw Elena's second bodyguard, a man in his mid-thirties who had not been introduced. Why in a building as secure as this should Elena feel the need for two bodyguards? All of them seemed to be positioned as if they were taking their places for some obscure dance, the outcome of which he could not foresee.

'You're interested in investing in LPS, Commander?' Brinsmead was asking him.

'I've been considering it,' he replied.

'I'm sure Elena will give you a very thorough introduction as to what you're putting your money into. Are you expecting good returns?'

'I'd call that putting the cart before the horse.'

'No one invests without a hope of return. You must have thought about it.'

'I'd consider everything here to be a long-term investment,' Harrigan replied.

'This project certainly is,' Brinsmead said in his whispered voice. 'I've set it up so that anyone properly qualified could take it over if something happened to me. It could even be shifted to a new laboratory if need be.'

'No one else would have your driving force,' Elena said. 'What would make you leave something you've put so much work into, at such a personal cost?'

'Something none of us could foresee, Elena. Call it an attempt at insurance against unexpected blows of fate.'

Harrigan couldn't work out if this was sarcastic or a warning. He felt there was a barb in the words and assumed Elena had as well. Given the way he looked, Brinsmead must have had some knowledge of unexpected blows of fate.

'Why don't we take the commander up to the roof? He can see what he's buying into,' Brinsmead said.

'I had planned to do that. Now seems to be a good time.'

'I'll get rid of my coat,' Brinsmead said.

Harrigan watched him walk into his glassed-in office near the main door and hang up his lab coat. His actions were slow and awkward, the movements of someone who dealt with pain as a matter of course. His office, on display to the room, was painstakingly ordered and plain without any hint of personal decoration. Outlined in the glass with the lights on him, his marked face seemed stripped to its essentials. There was nothing to cushion the impress of the bone beneath his damaged skin; everything had been burnt away. Harrigan was suddenly aware of Elena, standing close by. She was also watching Brinsmead, her face expressionless, almost cold. Throughout the tour of the laboratory, there had seemed no warmth or rapport between them.

She turned to see Harrigan watching her. 'Shall we go?' she said with an immediate smile.

She led them out of the laboratory into a roomy elevator, where she pressed the button marked Roof. When the doors opened, they stepped out onto a wide viewing platform. Harrigan could see the rest of the industrial estate shimmering in the mid-morning heat. The huge metal sheds and cheap brick buildings appeared like toys in the distance.

'This is the best way to see the building,' Elena said. 'As a whole, not disconnected parts. I love this building. I see it as a crystal snake biting its tail. I've watched over it ever since it was on the drawing board. Years of hard work have gone into this.'

Seen from the viewing platform, the building resembled a slice taken from a multifaceted diamond where each facet connected into the next. The garden at the centre was a startling mix of live greens while the interlocking panes of its glass roof formed an arched pattern against the grey walls.

'Everything inside those walls is cutting edge,' Elena continued. 'The waste-disposal systems, sewerage, the air conditioning, water recycling, energy efficiency, everything. Here, we're researching the regeneration of nerves and skin, the restoration of motor-skill functions, the repair of brain damage. The possibilities are limitless.'

'You have a very sizeable investment here,' Harrigan said.

'You don't build anything of value without that kind of an investment.'

'It is a sizeable investment,' Brinsmead said, at the same time. 'You could say that any number of people have put their lives into this building, including myself.'

'I've put mine into it,' Elena said. 'I was happy to.'

'This building isn't just an inanimate object to Elena,' Brinsmead said to Harrigan. 'To her, it has the status of a living thing. It means more to her than most other things that are living.'

It was an offensive thing to say about someone standing next to you. Elena moved away without looking back at Brinsmead.

'It might as well be alive,' she said. 'It's a very complex structure. Its design might almost be said to have given it an intelligence. Planning it was one thing. Standing here seeing it achieved is another. It's the best thing.'

Questions were in Harrigan's mind. Attempting to bribe a senior police office might seem trivial when you had something as significant as this at stake. But why would Elena Calvo risk anything on this scale by involving herself with chancers like Stuart Morrissey, Nattie Edwards and Jerome Beck — people with histories that tainted everything they touched? If their activities did threaten hers, would she be prepared to remove them so cold-bloodedly? If her focus was the regeneration of the human body, why involve the organisation with crop research?

'Can I ask why you came to Australia?' he said. 'Aren't we out of the mainstream here?'

'Don't undervalue yourselves. The land here is cheap, the country is one of the most stable on earth, there's an educated workforce. Your government was very welcoming, which also helped. I came here because the doors were open. I feel freer here than I have anywhere else. Location isn't as important as it used to be. The world is a global village now, communication is instantaneous. We can video conference around the world with ease whenever we need to. Quite a number of people working here have come from other countries; other people will join them. I'll build this facility up until it's in the first rank anywhere in the world. Now let's go downstairs. We have business to discuss.'

Pure steel, he thought. She has a backbone of pure steel. No one runs a business like this without it.

He glanced at Sam. She was silent, watching. Behind her was Elena's second bodyguard, always in their company. Brinsmead's strange face drew his gaze in much the same way the dead had when he'd seen them seated at the table at Pittwater. You couldn't help but be drawn to stare at something so wrecked. Harrigan looked from Brinsmead to Sam to Elena. There was no way to know what their separate motives towards each other might be. For all he knew, they were three thieves forced together, each planning the other's death. He followed Elena back into the lift without speaking.

15

When they were downstairs, on their way to Elena's office, Brinsmead turned to Harrigan.

'May I sit in on your meeting with Elena today, Commander?' he asked. 'I may be able to answer questions on the scientific side in more detail than she can. If you're going to invest, I'm sure you'd like to know all sides of the operation.'

'I asked the commander for a private meeting, Daniel. I don't think he was expecting your company.'

'I don't mind if Dr Brinsmead joins us,' Harrigan replied, curious to see how this strange dance between the two of them might work out.

Elena seemed to be teetering on the edge of saying that wasn't going to happen when she changed her mind. 'Then let's go in,' she said.

They entered a spacious office with its own view of the central garden. As well as Elena's desk, there was a lounge suite in front of a coffee table looking out of the windows at the fernery. The lush growth provided privacy. Someone had placed a folder and laptop on the table.

'Please sit down,' Elena said. 'The lounge is the most comfortable place. Coffee?'

'Thanks,' Harrigan said.

'Not for me,' Brinsmead said. 'I can't taste it.' It was another barb, one so lightly spoken as to be almost delicate.

Harrigan sat in one of the lounge chairs, sinking into the leather. Brinsmead sat in one of the single chairs. Sam positioned herself near the door, the male bodyguard by the window. Both stood watching intently, silently. The silence became a dead weight. Elena poured coffee from a silver pot into fine white cups with complete calmness. In her high heels, she was taller than Grace. She had slender ankles, well-shaped legs. Harrigan observed all this coolly; she did not attract him. Photographs lined the top of a nearby cabinet. The largest was of an old man, probably in his mid-eighties.

'My father.' Elena had followed Harrigan's line of sight. 'Jean Calvo. He's still very much in charge of his own business affairs, his mind is very active. I'm sure you've noticed how much older he is than I am. He was in his fifties when he married. My mother was only in her twenties. They weren't a happy couple. She left when I was six. I hardly saw her after that.'

She handed him his coffee. Harrigan wondered why she'd want to introduce this kind of personal history into a meeting with a stranger like himself. Perhaps she thought she was softening him up.

'I've met Jean a number of times,' Brinsmead said. 'He holds on to everything he has very tightly indeed. I don't think I've met anybody with a stronger grip.'

'I have a strong one myself,' Elena said, almost offhandedly. 'My father learned his strengths the hard way. Let me tell you his story, I think it's significant. At the end of World War Two, my father was a displaced person, stateless. All I know about his war years is that he worked in a forced labour camp where most other people died. He refused to die. He survived by obliterating the first years of his life from his mind. He still won't tell me where he was born. All I know is it was somewhere in Eastern Europe. Even his name isn't his own. He took it from a list of the dead in a displaced persons camp one day. He said it would do for him. He built everything we have from nothing.'

'Very successfully,' Harrigan felt obliged to say.

'It gave me an isolated childhood, one full of threats of abduction. I've lived with bodyguards all my life. I've learnt how to deal with it.'

Harrigan looked at another picture showing Elena with a man much closer to her own age. Both were smiling.

'That's me as I used to be,' Brinsmead said. 'I met Elena at a research institute in London five years ago. She was in management, I was in research. We know each other very well.'

'We do,' she said, an indefinable edge to her voice. 'That's how I knew Daniel was the right man to run our signature project. Not because of his terrible experiences but because of his skills. He has a lot of talent to bring to bear here.'

'As soon as I heard Elena was setting up here, I asked her for the chance to be involved and she gave it to me. It was the opportunity of my lifetime.'

'I like to be generous.'

Harrigan found himself wondering if she'd had the option to say no. Brinsmead was speaking directly to Harrigan and didn't see the look Elena gave him. It was a strange mixture of emotional pain, distrust and deep anger. Old love gone bad.

In his photograph, Daniel Brinsmead was good-looking, fashionably dressed, the top few buttons of his shirt open. Around his neck he wore a square gold locket. Someone who could play the field, promise possibilities they could forget as soon as they started talking to the next woman in line. Elena Calvo could be vulnerable to someone like that. But why continue with a connection that seemed to have lost any mutual affection, even descended to a mutual antagonism? Maybe she was ruthless. If he was the best, then she wanted him regardless of what it cost her personally.

Elena had sat down and was sipping her coffee. She sat close enough to Harrigan to assume some kind of mutual purpose. She was a very attractive woman. He was glad he had no interest in her to complicate things.

'What I've shown you is only one side of what we do here,' she said. 'We have a lot to offer besides our research program. Security is very important to us. I'm always interested to meet people like yourself who are specialists in that field.'

'Why is security so important here?' Harrigan asked.

'Mainly because of industrial espionage. Our intellectual property is our most significant and valuable asset. We have to protect that investment.'

'How does your company actually work?

'You can call me a facilitator. Life Patent Strategies manages the patents on a very large body of genetic information, which my father and a number of other business people have purchased over the years, mainly in Europe and America but also here.'

'They're called the Abaris Group,' Brinsmead interrupted. 'You should tell the commander about them, Elena.'

'We don't usually discuss Abaris,' she said, without taking her eyes off Harrigan.

'Abaris are influential, Commander. They're a small and exclusive club that you have to be invited to join. The group has investors from all over the world and includes some very well-known entrepreneurs and several ex-politicians. It's very wealthy all told.'

'Are you a member?' Harrigan asked Elena.

'She will be when her father dies.' Brinsmead continued to speak for Elena. 'He was the founder of the group. She'll take over from him.'

'It's a cooperative,' she said quietly. 'I would have to be accepted by the other members.'

'Why the name?' Harrigan asked.

'In Greek mythology, Abaris was a priest of Apollo,' Brinsmead said. 'He had special powers of invisibility and flight and also the power to cure diseases. Curing diseases is what LPS is about. This corporation is an offshoot of Abaris — its child, if you like. Elena is running it for them.'

'Abaris is a financial group that has been very strategic in its purchases,' Elena said in a cool voice. 'It has focused throughout on the regenerative capacities of the human body. Buying patents is only part of the story. Patents are mainly nationally based and they expire after certain periods of time. Abaris has put considerable funds into researching the potential application of its patented gene sequences. As a consequence, it has built up a very substantial body of intellectual property. What my company does is offer other scientific research groups the opportunity to come here and develop the possibilities of that knowledge. We license access to our intellectual property while retaining ultimate ownership of any of the results of the research. Say if a vaccine were produced, we would market it and the profits would be ours. The glory and a very generous percentage of the royalties would belong to the research team.'

'So no one here actually works for you,' Harrigan said.

'I do have my own in-house scientific staff. They have their own program. Daniel's project is an example of that. But I built this facility mainly to accommodate people who aren't employed by me. These research teams are bound by contracts. These contracts specify a certain ongoing amount payable for access to our intellectual property and, of course, our facilities, which, as I've said, are state of the art. I work very hard to make sure that all facilities available here continue to be of the highest standard.'

'There's something you should know about those contracts, Commander,' Brinsmead said. 'They're a binding legal agreement on the product to be provided and contain a scientific specification of the work to be carried out. Imbedded in that information is also a record of the ownership of the genetic patent rights and the intellectual property. Every contract that Abaris has written has that ownership information. If you have the contract, then you have that information as well. It's Abaris's way of protecting its intellectual property rights and its profits. I'm the only researcher in this building who isn't bound by one of those contracts.'

Elena had been about to take a mouthful of coffee. She turned to look at Brinsmead as he spoke, blinking a little, frozen in that pose, cup in hand.

'Would you have an example of one of these contracts?' Harrigan asked Elena.

'No, I'm afraid I don't. I wouldn't see it as relevant to our discussion,' she said with a smile.

'The people you contract in do your work for you. But you don't pay them, they pay you.'

'The original investment was ours. Unless people want to wait for our patents to expire and then do our research all over again, and, of course, pay for it again, this is the best way for them to access the knowledge we've already gained. It's a legitimate enterprise. I have a waiting list of people who want to apply here. We can do a great deal of good.'

'All owned by you, except for Dr Brinsmead's project, which is in the public domain?'

'Yes, that's the exception. Daniel and I came to that agreement mainly because it was such a personal matter for him. Now,

Commander, I have a question for you. You asked for Daniel to be here to answer your questions. But our discussion is about to focus on your interests. Would you prefer him to leave or stay?'

'What can you have to say to the commander that I couldn't hear?' Brinsmead asked.

'That's his decision,' she replied.

Harrigan decided the time had come to oblige. 'I would prefer a one-on-one meeting, yes.'

Brinsmead looked from Elena to Harrigan. Snookered.

'All right.' He got to his feet. 'I'll pack up my tent and disappear into the sunset. Nice to meet you, Commander. I'm sure Elena will make you the offer of a lifetime. I'll be in the lab if anyone wants me.'

He walked out without looking back. Harrigan watched Elena watch him leave. Just as it had been earlier, her face was expressionless, unforgiving. She turned to Harrigan. Again, her smile appeared at once.

'I always keep a bodyguard with me but today I'm going to be different,' she said. 'I'm going to trust you. Sam, that will do for now. I'll call you when I need you. Thank you.'

'If that's what you want, Elena, I'm on my way,' Sam said. She glanced once at Harrigan and walked out.

'Damien, if you could wait in the inner room.'

'Sam is very professional,' Harrigan said as soon as the door had closed and they were alone.

Elena seemed surprised. 'I would hope so. All my staff are professional. Why do you say that?'

'I wondered where you found her.'

'There's no secret to that. She came from a security agency my father and I have used for many years.'

'Who are they?'

'Why do you want to know? Are you considering offering her a job?'

'Like you, I'm always on the lookout for good people, Dr Calvo.'

'Please call me Elena. Sam was a policewoman once, but that was some years ago. She came from Griffin Enterprises. I was lucky to find her. I was very much in need of someone at the time and her skills are rare. You can ask her if she wants to change jobs but I don't think your wages will match mine.'

'May I ask why you need someone with Sam's skills on your staff?'

'I've received any number of threats in my life. Threats of abduction and murder. Threats from animal rights activists. I need someone to keep a discreet eye on the people who threaten me. Better than waiting for it to happen.'

'Very wise,' Harrigan said.

Elena smiled.

'There's another matter we need to discuss now, which is actually to do with your murder inquiry. Like everyone, I've seen the photographs of the victims at Pittwater. It's a tragedy. Julian was a very troubled but gifted young man. I was ready to offer him a job. He had skills that could have been developed. I didn't have the chance.'

A little unwillingly, Harrigan had to accept that her grief seemed sincere.

'But what you really need to know,' she continued, 'is that I recognised the fourth victim, the one you haven't officially identified. His name is Jerome Beck.'

'Is there a reason you didn't ring the hotline with this information?' Harrigan asked.

'I wanted to tell you in person. Jerome used to work here. Unfortunately, he's not someone many people would choose to associate with.'

'But you knew him. How did you meet him?'

'He was an administrator in a research facility I was managing in London a number of years ago. The same place I met Daniel. Jerome tried to harass me late one night in the car park. He was drunk. Not long after I came here, he contacted me and said he'd come to Australia as well. Could I employ him? At the time, we needed someone very badly and I hired him on a short-term contract because he had the necessary experience. I soon realised he was an alcoholic and I had to dismiss him. After that, he started to make abusive phone calls. I asked Sam to watch him. She discovered he kept company with known criminals. In fact, at one time, he attempted to have one admitted to this facility.'

'Do you know who this known criminal was?'

'One of the other victims, Michael Cassatt. At the time, we were completely unaware of who he was. It was a great shock to me.'

'We need to interview Sam if she's been tailing them.'

'I should warn you that everything she does for me is covered by a strict confidentiality agreement. All my security staff sign them. My solicitors have the information she collected. I'll ask them to contact you. They'll answer any questions you may have.'

'We'll need a formal statement from you as well,' Harrigan said.

'I'm happy to do that. Enough of this. We're both busy people. This is my card, please keep it. As I've mentioned before, there are other opportunities here besides investment. I can't offer you anything with the kudos of being the police commissioner, but I can offer you an executive position in charge of security with a very competitive remuneration package.'

'I have to say I wasn't expecting anything like that.'

'I'm not offering you the position just because of our corporate needs,' she said. 'I'm an individual woman, a single woman, and I have to be sure of my personal safety. I want someone reliable, someone who's on my side. You have a very good reputation.' She reached over and extracted a sheet of paper from the folder on the table. 'This is my offer. Please consider it.'

Harrigan's budgetary habits had been formed by watching his mother spend hours carefully choosing his clothes at the local op shop when he was a boy. He was still careful with his money. If he accepted Elena Calvo's offer, he would never have to be careful again.

'What would I have to do to earn this?' he asked.

'I'm looking for someone who will know how to remove any threats to me, internal or external, while at the same time protecting my personal reputation. You would need to be prepared to put both my own and my corporation's interests before anything else. You would have to sign a confidentiality agreement and I would expect your complete loyalty.'

'What does "remove" mean?'

'Make safe,' she replied. 'How you achieve that end is entirely up to you, but it would have to be effective. You could also expect my complete support for whatever action you undertook. I've always believed that loyalty works both ways. But I would also expect complete discretion from you regarding your actions.'

'Do you want to be a little more precise about what these threats might be?'

'Perhaps not until you've given me a firm answer to my offer,' she said. 'From what I know of you, I don't think you would encounter anything outside your experience.'

'You've checked me out,' he said.

'I always check the background of people I have an interest in employing.'

'Given what you're asking of me, can I ask you a question about Dr Brinsmead?'

'What do you want to know?'

'Dr Brinsmead and Beck worked at the same facility in London that you did. We've established that you knew both men. Did Daniel Brinsmead know Beck?'

'Yes, he did,' she replied. 'It was inevitable that he would. They would have attended the same meetings at times, that kind of thing.'

'Did you ever talk about Beck to Dr Brinsmead? Or vice versa.'

'No, of course not. Why would I? Do you have a reason for these questions?'

'I want to know what I'm dealing with. How did Dr Brinsmead get his burns?'

'In a car accident. It was very, very tragic, and since we're on the subject, let me tell you why I have his picture here. It's to remind me of who he used to be. Daniel's experience has affected him badly. It's made him resentful and misjudging of other people. I have a concern for his welfare and have done for some time. I paid his medical costs. When his recovery had reached a certain point, he made the choice that he wanted to work here. I accommodated him. He is very good at what he does. It was his wish that his work go into the public domain. I had no problem with that. But it's most correct to say I have given him everything he's asked for and have never done him any harm. Again, it comes down to loyalty and integrity. I want both qualities from my people.'

Watching her speak was like looking through a glass wall. You could see and hear her talk without any sense of what she might be feeling.

'They must have been difficult decisions to make, given his state of health,' he said.

'I've spent my life making difficult decisions, Commander. You have to if you want to succeed at anything. To get back to the point. Will you accept my offer?'

'It's very generous, Dr Calvo, but I'm not ready to give up my job. Any way I can help you in my role as commander, I'll be happy to. Otherwise, thank you for the compliment.'

'I'm disappointed to hear you say that. People speak highly of you. We can still discuss the possibility of you investing in my corporation. Now, please call me Elena. Perhaps I could call you by your first name as well?'

'I'll stay with Dr Calvo. I'd prefer to keep it businesslike. If you could do the same for me, I'd appreciate it.'

She sat upright in her seat with a slightly startled movement.

'I thought we had been talking with some degree of openness. Certainly I've answered all your questions, including those which were very personal. Perhaps you're not an easy man to connect to.'

'I'm a private man. Let's leave it at that.'

She sat completely still, staring at him. Her grey eyes had a watchful, distrusting look that reminded him strangely of the commissioner's paranoia. Whatever might have been in her mind, he could feel the possibility of any intimacy being withdrawn. She opened the folder on the coffee table.

'Whatever suits you,' she said. 'These are the details of the investment package I had in mind for you. I think you'll find it's generous. We can discuss aspects of it as you wish.'

He scanned it. Generous was the right word. 'This package is a gift from you to me,' he said.

'Are you interested?'

'Before I tell you that, are you recording this meeting?'

'No. There are no surveillance devices in here. It's one of the few parts of the building where there are none. Damien is watching us through one-way glass but he can't hear what we're saying. Which means you can tell me if you're interested.'

'If I'm not working for you, Dr Calvo, what am I doing to earn this offer?'

'As we've already discussed, you're in charge of an investigation that may affect me. I need a pair of eyes and ears in that investigation.

Please don't be concerned. It's quite innocent. It would mainly be a matter of providing me with information as I need it.'

'Why do you need that information?'

'To protect my interests. That would include knowing anything concerning Jerome Beck, for example. Or it may be that you have evidence that could be misinterpreted in a way that's detrimental to my corporation. Such evidence might not be as vital as you might think it is.'

'You want me to destroy any evidence that implicates you.'

'I didn't say that. I said, such evidence might not be as vital as you think it is. If its real value was made clear to you, you might choose to dispense with it of your own accord.'

'I need time to think about this.'

'Unfortunately, there's no time available.'

'There's always time, Dr Calvo.'

'Not on this occasion.'

She opened and turned on the laptop, shifting it to where he could see the monitor. 'I believe this is your son's website. I assumed he was the reason for your interest in my corporation in the first place. I have to say, when I first saw this, I was very impressed by his bravery.'

Toby's naked and crippled body came into view on the screen. The image dissolved into an X-ray displaying his skeleton. It was followed by the careful diagrams he'd drawn of his own frame. *This is how my body is twisted and why it can't untie itself.* The blueprint of his disability was set out for the world to see, an exposure Harrigan had forced himself to live with. He could hardly bear to look at it at any time.

'Your son writes eloquently of the pain of being disabled. His descriptions of his loneliness are very touching. *My body is my lifeline but it's my prison cell at the same time. It cramps me and it pinches me. I'm a turtle on my back.* He's a very intelligent young man, he clearly feels things deeply. You must be proud of him. We can offer him a better life. If you were to give me your son's DNA profile, I could arrange for a team to be dedicated to untying its possibilities, its relationship to his disabilities. They would work exclusively on him. Of course, their results would have a much wider application and we would own that intellectual property and any patent rights. But he would be the first beneficiary, *gratis.*'

Her speech seemed extraordinarily smooth, a business pitch. She had isolated Toby's body in the transparency of the monitor as if it were a preserved specimen in a glass jar that she was holding up to the light. Harrigan realised that in his pocket he still had the handkerchief that had been soaked in Toby's spittle the day before. Almost, he took it out and gave it to her. Instead, he reached forward and turned off the laptop. The screen went dead. Elena stared at Harrigan, more surprised than angry.

'I don't like seeing my son on the screen like that, Dr Calvo.'

'He doesn't seem to share your sensitivities.'

Her words made Harrigan cold with rage.

'How long before those promised results are available? Twenty years? Never?'

'Perhaps you should ask your son what he wants. Wouldn't it be his choice to say yes or no?'

'Even if he does make that decision, I'm the one who pays for it.'

She sat looking at him for some few seconds.

'I know a great deal about you, Commander. I know you're an ambitious man. That much seems obvious.'

She opened the folder again and slid a photograph towards him. Harrigan looked down at a police photograph of Eddie Lee lying dead on his lounge room floor, where he had been found by his cleaning lady. He looked back at Elena wordlessly.

'Do you want to throw your career away?'

'Where did you get that?'

'You can answer my question first, Commander.'

'What is potentially so damaging that it could be worth this much money and effort on your part to hide it?'

'I need a straightforward answer. Yes or no.'

'Or what? You'll release this picture? This is on the police files, it's been in the newspaper. You could have got it from anywhere.'

'Do you think this is the only piece of evidence I have relating to this incident? I have information that directly incriminates you in this man's death. I'm sure you know exactly what it is.'

'If you do, Dr Calvo, there's only one place you could have got it from. Right now we have Cassatt's body to go with it. Release any of it and you might end up being accused of murder. Do you want to risk all those negative outcomes when you're about to launch on the ASX?'

'Why should anyone trace its release back to me? Haven't you spent your working life denying the truth of this event?' She tapped the photograph with a manicured fingernail. 'All I have to do is send what I have to the press anonymously. After that, even if you did report this conversation, who would believe you? You would have been shown to be a public liar.'

Harrigan looked at the photograph. In this environmentally controlled room, he had the sense of stepping into a locked and airless space that he was going to share with Cassatt permanently.

'Give me forty-eight hours.'

She laughed. 'Why should I do that?'

'Because you're right. It's not my decision, it's my son's. I need time to talk to him about your offer. I'll ring you within two days.'

'Are you serious?' she asked, seemingly a genuine question.

'I never joke where Toby's concerned.'

'You obviously care about him a great deal. If you recall, I told you there was no time. But you sit there and ask me for forty-eight hours.'

'Can't you wait until after the launch?'

'Yes, of course I can. You're right, there is always time,' she said, suddenly relaxing. 'Does this mean your companion will still be attending?'

'I expect her to, yes.'

'Then I look forward to seeing her. Perhaps we can conclude this meeting now.'

'Yes, I think we can,' he replied, thinking gratefully of release.

Elena took her folder and laptop back to the desk where she picked up the phone. Immediately Damien stepped out of the inner room.

'Sam, would you come and show the commander out?' she said into the handset. 'Thank you.'

Elena sat down on the lounge again. They didn't speak. Shortly afterwards, there was a knock. Damien opened the door to Sam. Elena got to her feet smiling, offering her hand.

'Thank you, Commander, for a most useful discussion. I'll see you again.'

'I think you will,' Harrigan replied, even if he doubted that their expectations of that meeting were the same.

Harrigan walked with Sam in silence. She was watching him.

'Did Elena get inside your head?' she asked. 'Is that why you're so quiet?'

'It was a business meeting.'

'I don't know if Elena distinguishes between life and business. Let me tell you something. Elena will do whatever it's in her best interests to do, whatever those interests are. Don't ever expect anything else.'

At one level Elena Calvo had been playing the poor little rich girl, Harrigan thought; at another, the tough businesswoman. *I want someone to kill and possibly die for me.* Probably all her life she had been led to expect that kind of loyalty with no questions asked. As for her loyalty to him, it would be purely conditional. If he didn't do what she wanted just once, that would be the end of it. She didn't hire people; she bought them.

'Did she tell you how her father made his money?' Sam asked.

'No. We didn't talk about him after you left.'

'He's an arms dealer. He started in the black market at the end of World War Two and he's sold arms all over the world ever since, to every war you can name. Gene technology is just another line of investment for him.'

'How do you know that?' he asked.

'Check Jean Calvo on the web. It's all there. He doesn't hide what he does.'

'Does Elena ever talk to you?'

'Me? God, no. I'm the hired help. It's my job to be invisible. That suits me fine.'

Harrigan wondered if Sam realised how much antagonism she was showing. For whatever reason, her self-control was fraying at the edges, had been throughout his time here. Maybe she didn't like being bought. Maybe this strange locked-up building disturbed her. It would disturb him if he had to work here.

They had arrived back at the entry to the car park. He collected his mobile and beeper. Sam saw him out to his car.

'Your e-tag will get you out of the grounds. Once you leave, it won't get you back in again. Like your badge, it's dead as soon as you drive away from here.'

'I'll learn to live with the disappointment.'

She laughed and then her face went hard. 'You never know when someone's after you, Harrigan. Maybe you should keep an eye on your back. Bye now.'

He drove out of the car park, relieved to see the garage door slide open for him, the main gates swing back as he approached them. Out on the public road, he breathed free air. 'I know a great deal about you,' Elena Calvo had said. To Harrigan, this was an insult. She knew nothing about him. But what did he know about her?

In one way, she had told him a great deal about herself. None of it made her any easier to pin down. He could envisage much of what she had said being repeated by a lawyer in a court of law as an excuse for actions otherwise apparently incriminating. And she was a murderer: Cassatt's murderer if no one else's, and someone with the motive and the capacity to remove Beck and his cronies if only because they threatened her business. Her grief for Julian Edwards didn't mean that she wished the result undone.

The visit had only complicated matters. He put her out of his head. What he needed was solitude and space to think. Right now, he didn't have time for needy, controlling rich women and their ambitions, whatever they might be, whatever schemes they were juggling. He had a long drive ahead of him. There were other lives to protect.

16

It was well after midday, later than Harrigan had hoped it would be, by the time he was on the road to Coolemon. His first stop had been the underground car park at the Macarthur Square shopping centre at Campbelltown. While he was driving around, a parked car flashed its lights at him. He pulled into the nearest empty bay and walked over. Ralph got out of the car to meet him.

'Hi, boss. It's all ready to go.'

They swapped keys. Harrigan slid into the driver's seat of the new car. Ralph took the suicide seat. He opened the glove box and took out a shoulder holster and a gun.

'Here you go,' he said, handing them to Harrigan.

'Just call me the fashionista,' Harrigan said, covering the whole kit and caboodle with his light summer jacket.

Ralph grinned. 'Marvin knows nothing about these arrangements, boss. Trevor kept him out of the loop like you asked.'

'What about putting a guard on my son?'

'He's got that in motion. Shouldn't be a problem.'

This was more a precaution on Harrigan's part than the expectation of a real threat. He was being careful. Cotswold House was a secure environment; no one could just walk in there off the street. Harrigan's family had been threatened more than once in his career and Toby had had guards put on him before. Trevor had been obliging; doing what Harrigan had asked of him without asking too many questions.

'Tell him thanks from me. I'll be in touch as soon as I get to Yaralla.'

'How'd you go with Elena Calvo? What's she like?'

Harrigan had already spent time considering how much of his meeting he should conceal and how much reveal.

'Tough and ruthless,' he said. 'She won't be easy to deal with. She's got her own agenda. Keep her in view. Everything you can find out about her — her corporation, her father, their connections — dig it up. She's a significant player.'

'We'll handle her. Okay, boss. See you later. Good luck.'

Ralph would wait another half-hour, then leave. Harrigan drove out, the tinted glass of the car's windows providing him with some anonymity. He hit the road with a sense of freedom.

Coolemon was in the south-west of the state. Grey nomads travelling through the town were sometimes heading south-west to Adelaide and then across the Nullarbor Plain to Perth; or turning north to Broken Hill and from there, going north or west into the red heart of the continent. Their caravans trundled along the desert tracks as if they were native to the landscape.

Harrigan followed the Hume Highway south, stopping for fast food not far past Yass. Not long after, he turned off the highway onto the back roads and began heading west into the sun. The road was a single carriageway lined with old eucalyptus trees, their leaves gleaming in the hot afternoon light. Cattle trucks and local farmers were the only hazards. He drove through the old rural towns that had followed on white settlement, their main streets making up the highway: vistas of old courthouses, abandoned bank buildings and closed stores. Silent pubs stood with their doors open and their high verandas shadowing the footpath. In these towns, the war memorials stood in the main street, silent stone soldiers mourning over their guns.

As the hours passed, the road grew more straight. Flocks of grey apostle birds foraged in the red dirt either side of the bitumen. Crows, their densely black feathers glistening in the sun, settled on the roadkills. The dry, empty pastures were sapped by the drought, reduced to a scraped and pale gold marked by scattered trees and low bush-covered hills against the horizon.

The kilometres passed without incident. Despite this, he felt a sense of unease. It had been too simple, almost effortless, swapping cars and getting out on the road. But even if there was something wrong, all he could do was drive on.

Some five hours after he had left Campbelltown behind, Harrigan drove into the large, straggling town of Coolemon. He stopped at the police station. The duty sergeant had known him during his time there and was welcoming. The backup was on standby; they would be waiting for his call whenever they were needed. Harrigan accepted the sergeant's invitation to a meal and spent the occasion talking about the cricket.

By the time he left the station, it was growing dark. About a kilometre out of town, a state forest lined the roadside, the casuarinas closing in like thinned-out human figures. Eventually open pastures took their place. Harrigan opened his window to the quiet outside. Stillness stretched to the horizon. There was a full moon, scorching the surrounding paddocks to an incandescent ash. Driving in this solitary moonlit darkness, Harrigan felt a free man. In a rare moment of equilibrium, he was at ease with himself.

Eventually, he turned off the bitumen road onto dirt. Pausing at the turn, he thought he heard a car in the distance ahead of him. A farmer on his way home. He went on, his headlights illuminating the roadside scrub. Ahead, he saw the shadows of the red gums lining Naradhan Creek. He crossed the narrow bridge and drove through Yaralla's open gate, startling an owl roosting on a fencepost. It disappeared into the scrub with the slow, silent beat of its powerful wings, its pale feathers luminous in the white light.

Harrigan drove up the track and into Harold's yard. A frantic barking greeted him when he got out of the car. A light was shining brightly above the farmhouse's back door. Harold was standing on the veranda, washing his knives at an outside sink.

'Quiet!' Harold ordered the dog and she sat down. 'Don't mind Rosie. She gets excited.'

'She doesn't bother me. How are you, mate? It's good to see you.'

'Could be better. My hands are a mess. I just killed a lamb. I've had this fella in the shed for a couple of days, calming him down. I was going to share the meat with Ambro, but I thought you might want a roast dinner while you're here.'

'What's wrong with your hands, Harry?'

For an answer, Harold held them out, palms upwards. They were still covered with the transparent antiseptic dressings. Even where partly hidden by the lamb's blood, they were badly burned and blistered deep into the skin.

'How did that happen?'

'It's what Stuart's growing here. The tobacco did that to me. Come inside and I'll show you. I'll just wash the blood off and get cleaned up.'

'Can you work with those hands?'

'The doctor gave me some tablets. They help. I didn't do anything much today. I took some sleeping pills the doc gave me last night. They knocked me out till almost midday. Killing the lamb was okay. It's quick, and I've just taken some tablets. Driving's not fun.'

'Your tatts, mate.'

Harold had taken off his bloodstained shirt and was standing naked to the waist. The bright light intensified the deep colours and intricate patterns marked on his skin. Harrigan hadn't known that Ambrosine was using Harold's body as a canvas.

'Do you like them?' Harold asked.

'You could win a few awards with those. She's signed them. Ambrosine only signs her best tattoos.'

Harold put on another shirt and the tattoos disappeared. He wrapped his slaughtering and butchering knives in a leather pouch.

'She likes working on me. I don't have much bare skin left now. Come on, girl.'

He led Rosie out across the yard to her enclosure. Once inside her kennel, she settled down on her blanket.

'Do you want to put your car in the garage? Who knows? Maybe it'll rain.' Harold laughed.

'Times are bad, Harry.'

'Wait till you see the place in the daylight. It'll break your heart. Come into the kitchen once you've put your car away. Have you had anything to eat?'

'Yeah, I ate back in town.'

'We'll have a beer then.'

The farmhouse at Yaralla had the sense of time stopped. The kitchen was a large room with a window that looked out to the north-east. An ancient wood stove stood next to an electric one, now almost as much a museum piece as its companion. When Harold's mother, a woman from a family of wealthy Victorian graziers, had cooked here she had always had others to help her do it; sometimes young Aboriginal girls sent from the home at Cootamundra, sometimes white girls from other homes. They had slept in the room beside the washhouse and spent the rest of their time cleaning the house and washing basketloads of dirty laundry.

Harold put his knives away in a drawer. He opened two beers and then sat at the table without speaking. Harrigan had come to know Harold well during his years out here and he knew there was no point in rushing him. Tonight, he was tense, fatigued.

'I don't know what I'm going to do really,' he said at last. 'Every day you wake up, there's no rain. You wonder if it's ever going to end. Then something like this happens.'

He looked at his hands. Harrigan could only sidestep something so uncontainable as despair.

'What's going on out here, Harry?'

Harold's tobacco lay on the table. He picked it up, rolled a cigarette and lit it.

'Come with me. I'll show you something.'

They walked through to the front of the house. Pale incandescent lights lit the hallway. Worn carpet runners covered the floor. Harold led him to the front sitting room where he turned on the light. The furniture in this room was old and in its time had been expensive, from the years when the property had been profitable. The windows looked onto the veranda and, beyond, to the gardens that Harold's mother had once cultivated but which were now mostly dead.

'You see this room.' Harold looked around as if peopling it. 'This is my house. I've lived here all my life. A bit more than a week ago, Stuart was sitting in this room with this Jerome and that Edwards woman, drinking my whisky and treating me like I was dirt. They were going to do things with my property without even talking to me about it. Next thing I hear, they're both dead.'

He went to an old writing desk and opened it. He took out four plastic bags containing crop specimens and put them on the coffee table.

'I thought this was as good a place as any to keep them,' he said.

'Is this the one that burnt your hands?'

'I'm pretty certain it was. Be careful. I put some air holes into the bags. Make sure you don't touch it.'

Harrigan could see nothing out of ordinary about any of these four crops, among the most commonly grown food and cash crops in the world.

'Where are these being grown?' he asked.

'In this enclosure Stewie had built — I call the Cage. It's huge. It's got greenhouses, water tanks, fences around it you can't climb over. Stewie even had his own access road put in right up to the gate.'

'He didn't tell you about it?'

'He just went and did it. After that it was too late. It was built and there was nothing I could do unless I went to the law. I can't afford to do that and he knows it. He never let me in that Cage, not once. People would come and go all the time. But not me. He'd locked me out. Then the same day I hear on the news that those people are dead, this comes to me by courier.'

He handed Harrigan the small box containing the keys and note. 'That's that Jerome's keyring,' he said. 'I saw it on the table the day he was here. The people who killed him sent me this stuff, didn't they?'

'They must have done. They would have taken it off him when they killed him. Did these people know what touching that tobacco would do to your hands?'

Harold could only shrug. He rubbed out his cigarette in an ashtray already dirtied with ancient stubs.

'Come outside. I'll show you something else.'

Yaralla stood at the top of a low rise in the lightly undulating landscape. They walked through the silhouettes of what had once been ornamental trees and shrubs, then through the gate and into the house paddock. The night noises were muted, the silence all pervasive. The scattered trees in the landscape were dark shadows, the distant houses small nubs in the moonlight.

'It's quiet,' Harrigan said.

'Too quiet. It feels like everything's dead. Sometimes I think there's only me and Rosie left alive out here. And Ambro and her kids of course.'

Harrigan looked upwards. The moon was at the high arc of the sky, bright and small, the stars dimmed by its light.

'That's the Creek Lane down there,' Harold was saying. 'Standing out here, you'd say everything you could see was peaceful. About fifteen minutes before you got here, Rosie started barking. She'd heard a car. Whoever it was, they didn't come across the creek the way you did. They kept going along the Coolemon Road. Now that road crosses the creek about three miles further on from here and then goes on around the back of my place. At first, I thought it was you. Then I knew it wasn't. For one thing, they were going too fast. This is what's happening to me, mate, and I don't like it. You hear a car at night. Why shouldn't it be someone going home? People live out on that road. Why should it make me so fucking nervous just to hear a car?'

'Did it come back?'

'No. It'll be miles away by now, the way it was travelling.'

'Did you hear or see any other cars come along here this evening?'

'I saw Barry on his way home about seven. That's it.'

'It's lonely out here, mate,' Harrigan said after a pause. 'Ambro's cottage is over in that direction, isn't it?'

'Yeah. You can see her.'

Harold pointed across the moonlit darkness to the hard and dark outline of a small cottage on the Creek Road. A faint light gleamed from one of the windows.

'Did you tell her I was coming?'

Harold grinned. 'Yeah, mate. I'm not going to repeat what she said in reply. She uses a few words I don't.'

'I can guess. Harry, I don't feel right about this. I'm going down there now. I want to get Ambro and her kids back to Coolemon as soon as I can. I'll feel safer when I do.'

'Let me take you in my ute. We'll go across the paddocks. It'll be quicker. You don't want to take your car over there. It's too rough.'

'If the man in that car you heard just now is who I think it could be, he's a killer. He shot dead an ex-policeman yesterday. I ought to tell you now, I'm armed.'

'Then I'll get my shotgun. I'm sick of people walking all over my property doing what they want to do. They can pay attention to me for a change.'

176

'You can't drive with those hands. Tell me where to go and I'll drive.'

'I took a couple of tablets a little while ago. They're still working. If it gets too bad, I'll let you take over. But I'm not going to sit around. I'm not having all this turn me into something useless.'

Before they left, Harrigan rang through to local police asking for backup. He needed an escort to bring a woman and her three children into Coolemon, he said. They would be on their way as soon as possible, the duty sergeant said: half an hour to assemble and hit the road. Harrigan told them to hurry.

Outside in the yard, Harrigan stopped to look at the garage, next to Rosie's enclosure, where he had left his car. The door had a lock, but one that was so easy to break it wasn't worth securing.

'Harry, that car you heard earlier,' he said. 'Is there any other way it can get on to your property from where you think it went? What about the road Stewie put in?'

'Yeah, they could come in that way. But that'd just take you up to the Cage. You'd still have to know how to get from there to here across my paddocks.'

'What if he came back here through the main gate while we were gone?'

'We'd see him if he had his lights on. He couldn't be that close. I'd have heard him if he was. You can hear things for miles around here.'

Uneasily, Harrigan got into the ute. Rosie's disappointed barking followed them out into the night. They drove directly across Harold's pastures. The roar of the engine and the glare of the headlights must have carried for miles.

'If anyone's out there, they have to see us coming,' Harrigan said.

Harold grinned in a way that surprised him. He realised how angry the man was. 'Maybe we'll scare them off,' Harold said.

They pulled up at the back of Ambrosine's cottage. The lights had been turned off. A sense of urgency took hold of Harrigan. Without waiting, he was out of the cabin and pounding on the back door.

'Ambro? It's Paul Harrigan. Are you in there? Open the door. Open it now or I'll break it down!'

The back door was opened. Ambrosine stood there, dishevelled and sleepy-eyed. A smell of dope wafted past her.

'What the fuck are you doing out here at this time of night?'

Harrigan pushed past her into the kitchen. Harold followed him, carrying the shotgun.

'Shit,' she said. 'What are you doing with that? What's going on?'

'It's okay, mate,' Harold told her. He spoke to Harrigan. 'I'm going back outside. I'll keep a watch to see if that car comes back.'

'What fucking car?'

'Just wait,' Harrigan snapped.

Used plates, the remains of a meal, were stacked on the bench. A tiny mouse scurried down to the floor and out of sight. Harrigan looked around at the walls covered with Ambrosine's paintings. Their luminescent colours and obsessive details crowded in on him. One of them showed the cottage isolated between a vast sky and a bare red ochre foreground. Harrigan felt the sense of vulnerability powerfully. Out here, there was nothing to protect a person other than the huge distances. He should never have brought Ambrosine and her children here in the first place.

'What do you want?' Ambrosine interrupted him. 'For months you don't fucking bother getting in touch with me or coming to see me. Now you turn up in the middle of the night talking about some fucking car! What is it?'

'I'm taking you all back into Coolemon now. Get your kids and let's go.'

'You don't think I'm safe here any more? Why?'

Leaving her unanswered, he walked into the hallway. The front room had its door open. He could see it was her bedroom. There was another room opposite with its door shut. He guessed this was where her children slept. He looked through into the lounge where the moonlight cut silver-white patches onto the cracked linoleum. It was empty. He went to the front door and opened it. The dark tree line of Naradhan Creek was visible on the other side of the road. He walked outside and looked along the lane but saw nothing other than the curve of the empty road, whitened to grey by the moon. He went back inside to the kitchen.

'Did the Ice Cream Man find you out here before he went missing?' he said. 'I asked you that question once before and you said no. You can tell me the truth now.'

'It's a story, mate,' she said. 'If you're in a hurry, you don't have time for it now.'

'Did anyone follow him here?'

'Why do you want to know?'

'Because right now, I think he's out there. He didn't come here for you, he came for me. I've got something he wants. But now he's here, he won't mind finishing you and your kids off as well.'

'*Fuck*!' She hit the table. Her fingers were stained with nicotine. 'I knew he'd fucking come back for us.'

She pushed past him, opened the door to the second room and switched on the light. There were the confused sounds of children crying.

'Get up, all of you. Get your shoes. We're getting out of here right now. Laurie, get your little sister. Come on, hurry. No, Little Man, don't pick that up. *Come on*!'

They tumbled out of the room, still pulling on their clothes and shoes. Laurie, a boy of eleven; Jen, a tiny girl of eight; and the youngest, Little Man, five years old and golden-haired like a cherub. They were sleepy and frightened. Most of their lives, they had been pushed from one bit of makeshift accommodation to another. Quickly, Ambrosine took them outside. Harrigan sat them all in the cabin of the ute.

'Mate,' Harold said quietly, 'I didn't hear or see a car on the Creek Lane. But I did hear something in the distance. Sounded like it was coming from the north. On the other side of the house. I thought I heard Rosie barking as well.'

'We're all getting out of here as soon as we can,' Harrigan said. 'I'll take us to Coolemon in my car. Drive straight back to your garage, Harry. Give me your shotgun. I'll ride in the back.'

He climbed onto the tray of the ute and pounded on the window for Harold to go. The ute roared across the paddocks, bouncing over the ground, forcing Harrigan to hang on for dear life. They had driven through the last open gate before the house when the ute suddenly lurched to the right, almost upending itself. It shuddered to a halt with its right front wheel snagged deep in the ground. Harrigan was rolled hard against the side of the tray. He lay against it for a few moments getting his breath, then scrambled out, the shotgun in hand. They were on the edge of the old garden beds at the front of the house.

Immediately, Harrigan went to the cabin door on the passenger side. Before he got there, it was pushed open by Laurie. The boy climbed out. Harrigan leaned the shotgun against the ute and lifted out the other two children. Little Man was bawling loudly enough to wake the dead. Jen tried to comfort him but he pushed her away. Ambrosine was next.

'You're heavy,' Harrigan said.

'I'll be heavier if I'm dead.'

Harold had got out the other side and was leaning on the vehicle for support.

'We're lucky we didn't go all the way over,' he said, one hand on his forehead. 'I cracked my head.'

'Cracked your head?' Ambrosine laughed loudly and went and grabbed him by the arm. 'Fucking Christ, Harry. Can't you drive?'

'It was my hands. They were hurting too much.'

'Keep it quiet! Get your kids in the house now.' Harrigan spoke as quietly and urgently as he could. 'Harry, take your shotgun. I'm going to get my car out of the garage. I'll drive it to the back gate and pick you all up there.'

Harold took the shotgun and went towards the front door with the others. Harrigan walked quietly to the kitchen end of the house, past a thick-trunked old sugar gum whose branches extended above the veranda over the roof. Suddenly, he heard a scuffle behind him and turned to look back. Harold was gesturing to him. Before Harrigan could work out what he meant, he laid the shotgun on the edge of the veranda and sat down abruptly as if too shaky to stand. Ambrosine began to help him to his feet. Harrigan waved at them to get into the house as soon as possible.

The night air was warm. Harrigan stepped up on the veranda, staying close to the house and moving carefully in case the wooden boards creaked. Just before the corner, he stopped and took out his gun. From here, he could see Harold's ancient rotary clothes hoist, the house fence and beyond that the garage and the yard. Everything was still. It was deeply silent. Too silent. At once, he realised what Harold had been trying to tell him. Rosie wasn't barking. She should have been barking from the time the ute had arrived at the house. It should have been the first thing they heard. Silence is death. Someone had found a way of silencing her.

In the darkness, Harrigan almost stopped breathing. He turned off his phone in case it rang in the silence. How could you find me? Standing there, tense to every sound, he became aware of a small nugget of pain near the strap of his shoulder holster. He touched it, then reached into his shirt pocket to take out the thick gold badge he had been given at Life Patent Strategies that morning. When the ute had nearly overturned, he must have rolled onto it, pressing it into his chest. Until now, he had forgotten about it. What better way of smuggling a tracking device into his car than by pinning it to his shirt? He put the badge on the window sill beside him. Thought.

Assuming it was Grace's gunman waiting for him somewhere out there, he would have found Harrigan's car in the garage, which meant Harrigan was coming back. Unless he was blind and deaf, he would have seen and heard Harold's ute coming across the fields and heard them all arrive, no trouble. He must have worked out that somehow the ute was no longer functioning.

The scenarios were these. He would either ambush Harrigan's car on its way back to Coolemon or sabotage it beforehand so that it broke down in the middle of nowhere. In the isolation, he would pick off as many of the passengers as he could. If his purpose was getting hold of the tape, then he would try and take Harrigan alive, although not necessarily in one piece. If he was winged in the shoulder, the way the Ice Cream Man had been, he would be much easier to deal with. Or he might shoot everyone here in the backyard just as soon as they walked out of the house to the car. Leave the bodies to be found by whoever, whenever. Again, disable Harrigan so he could be dealt with more easily. An experienced gunman with the right weapon could do it.

Either way, this person would be waiting where he could see Harrigan approach the garage to get his car. In the pepper trees that lined the south-western side of the house. That vantage point would give the watcher a full view of the yard and enough of the back door to see anyone going in and out.

Leaving the LPS badge behind, Harrigan turned and silently made his way down to the other end of the house. From the front veranda, the ruined gardens were ghostly in the moonlight. He moved towards the pepper trees, the bulk of the house water tank providing him with cover while he crossed to the open space. There was too much leaf litter under the thick line of trees to walk silently. Very carefully, he moved through them to the bare ground on the other side, waiting for a shot or a blow to the head, even for Death to touch his shoulder and say 'Time, please'. Nothing happened.

On the other side of the trees, he saw a white car parked where it was invisible to the house, under the grove of coral gums that had once been part of Mrs Morrissey's gardens. It was too far away for him to get its registration number.

Slowly, Harrigan moved along the line of pepper trees, keeping close in to the shadows and stooping to get a view closer to the ground. Then he saw who he was looking for. On the other side of the water tank, a man was crouching in the trees where he had a clear view of the back of the house and the yard, his firearm at the ready. It had a scope, presumably with night vision. Harrigan raised his own gun. Whoever this man was, he wanted him alive.

Very carefully, he moved forward into the pepper trees, getting closer. Suddenly there was an ear-splitting screeching, a furious scratching and scattering of the leaves. The man jumped up immediately, turning and firing in a single action. Harrigan dodged down and sideways, slipped on the litter and smacked his left shoulder against a tree, just escaping falling into the dirt. The bullet thudded instantaneously into the tree trunk on his right, barely missing his shoulder. It was a soft sound, a quiet gun. Harrigan fired back, a loud crack in the night. The bullet scored across the man's lower left arm. He dropped his gun with a curse. Immediately Harrigan was there, kicking it across the dirt.

The man was on Harrigan before he could fire again, gripping his right wrist. The grip was painful, tight as a vice, relentlessly digging into a nerve. He was trying to numb Harrigan's hand and make him drop his gun and at the same time crash him backwards against the nearest tree. With his other hand, he punched Harrigan hard in the stomach, smacking into the soft tissue over and over. Harrigan gasped, tried to yank his right hand away but couldn't shake off the grip. He'd always had a strong left as a boxer. With his bare fist, he cracked his left hard on the man's upper arm, then smacked him in the face and neck repeatedly. They grappled silently. His right hand was growing numb, the gun slipping from his grip.

Harrigan levered himself forward, overbalancing them both, pushing the man to the ground between the trees and the house, landing on him heavily and winding him. The force of the fall knocked the gun from Harrigan's nerveless hand. The man tried to grab at it but it was on the wrong side for him and Harrigan managed to twist and skitter it out of reach with his foot. Still the man did not let go of his wrist. He had a powerful supple strength, it was like wrestling with an angry tomcat. Gripping his hand in Harrigan's hair, he tried to force Harrigan over onto his left side. Harrigan knocked the man's head hard onto the ground. The man punched his face and tried to gouge his eyes. Then Harrigan's hand was released. It was numb. The man pushed away from Harrigan with all his strength, kicking at him and rolling back out of his grip, tearing his shirt. He staggered to his feet and ran for his gun. Harrigan rolled back and went for his own gun with his left hand. Then in the night there was the roar of a shotgun.

'You fucking mongrel!' Harold shouted.

The blast had propelled Harrigan's assailant sideways. The man tried to scrabble for his firearm again, only to be driven back by another shotgun blast. He got to his feet and sprinted away, followed by a third blast. Harrigan got to his feet after him. His right hand was useless. He snatched up his gun with his left hand and ran in pursuit. The man was heading for his car. 'Police! I've got backup coming,' Harrigan shouted.

By the time he reached the far corner of the house, the man had gone into the coral gums at the end of the garden. Harrigan went after him. He heard a car starting and then roaring away. Running forward, he saw a white BMW disappearing down the track towards Harold's main gate. It didn't cross the bridge but turned right onto the Creek Road, driving away at high speed. Harrigan sheathed his gun in his holster and ran through the gardens into the house paddock. Harold joined him.

'I couldn't shoot straight, mate. My hands were hurting too much. I was worried I was going to get you.'

'Don't worry about it. You don't know what you saved us all from. If I remember rightly, he can get out onto the highway that way, can't he?'

'He can, but he must have been here before. That road's not on the maps. You'd have to know about it.'

183

Suddenly the car stopped. There was a gap in time. Then Ambrosine's cottage blossomed in flames into the night. They heard the car drive on. It hadn't turned on its headlights.

'You fucking bastard,' Harold said. 'If that spreads to the creek, all that vegetation along there will go up.'

'I'll call the fire brigade.'

Harrigan's right hand was beginning to tingle as the nerves came back to life. He ran towards the house to be met by Ambrosine running out of it.

'My house. Every fucking thing we own. Everything fucking thing the kids had. All my tattooing gear, my books, my machine, my photographs. Jesus, fucking everything.'

The flames from the cottage flared higher, visible for miles. Her children had followed her out. They stood in a straggling line behind her. Harrigan saw a look of deep anger on the older boy's face.

'Mum, something's coming,' Jen said.

'It's the backup I asked for,' Harrigan said.

Three cars were crossing the bridge in convoy. He saw one turn onto the Creek Lane and speed in the direction of Ambrosine's cottage. They would take care of the fire one way or another, including calling out the rural fire service. The other cars continued to the farmhouse.

'Whoop-de-bloody-do,' Ambrosine said. 'Too fucking late now. Come on, kids. Inside. Let's get you out of the way. We'll think about what we're going to do next tomorrow. We've got nothing now. Just a rust-bucket car and that's it.'

'Mum, Harry said that man must have shot Rosie. Why did he do that?' Jen asked.

'Not now, sweetheart.'

'But why?'

'Baby, I don't know. It's too hard for me right now. Because he's a cunt. Come on.' She took Little Man by the hand and they disappeared inside the house.

'Can you take my shotgun, mate?' Harold said. 'I'm going to have a look at Rosie.'

'No worries.'

Harold turned and walked quickly to the end of the house. Harrigan followed. At Rosie's enclosure, Harold unhooked the gate and squatted down in front of her kennel. She lay on her blanket, shot once through the head.

'At least it was quick,' he said.

After this, he did not speak. Then Ambrosine was there at the gate.

'Do you want a cigarette, mate?' she said to Harold. 'I rolled you one in case you did.'

'Yeah, thanks.'

She lit two cigarettes together, one for her and one for him, then turned and went back to the house.

'I've got to get rid of the carcass. I can't leave her here till tomorrow.'

'I'll give you a hand,' Harrigan said.

'No, I'll do it myself. Your mates are here. You'd better go talk to them.'

Shotgun in hand, Harrigan went to meet the arriving police. Looking back, he saw Harold lodge the cigarette in the corner of his mouth and drag Rosie's body from out of her kennel on her blanket. He carried her away behind the brokendown poultry sheds. Against the dark, the old struts and chicken wire were as fragile as torn cobwebs. Harrigan watched him disappear, wondering how much it had hurt him to pick her up, how heavy she was in his arms. He checked his watch. It was after midnight and the night had hardly begun. As usual, he had work to do.

17

I am a machine, Harrigan thought. He ticked off the details as if feeling and thought were dead. Mercilessly he rang Trevor, dragging him out of bed, giving him lists of directions for what he wanted to happen, people to be flown down to Yaralla first thing tomorrow, including Trevor's own people and a forensic team.

'Well, boss,' Trevor said when Harrigan had stopped talking, 'I'm glad to hear you're still alive.'

'That's nice to know. Thanks, mate,' Harrigan said, for once a little thrown.

The local police had retrieved the shooter's gun. Bagged for examination, it was slender and deadly in its cheap plastic dress. It would go back to Coolemon with one of the police cars. The gold badge would not. Harrigan had collected it from the window sill, planning to oversee its fate himself.

Out in the night, Ambrosine's cottage had subsided to a smouldering heap. The fire hadn't spread to the trees along the creek. There was no wind and both the bare soil surrounding the cottage and the dusty lane had acted as a fire break. First thing in the morning, it would be cordoned off as a crime scene. The shooter was almost certainly well on his way to Sydney by now. Even so, Harrigan wasn't going to send anyone out into the dark. He decided Ambrosine and her children would be as safe here for the night rather than making the trip to Coolemon. He told the uniformed officers to wait while he went to talk to her. Right now, he wanted information.

She was in the kitchen sitting at the table. Sheets of paper, a small array of pencils and a pencil sharpener were scattered around her. She was drawing; quick constant lines crossed the page. A bottle of whisky stood on the table with a partially drunk glass of it next to her cigarettes.

'Fucking hell, mate,' she said when he walked into the room. 'I didn't look at you properly before. You can tell you've been in fight. What does that other bloke look like?'

'Worse, I hope.'

'Do you want a drink? Harry won't mind.'

He did need a drink. Now that he had time to think about them, his bruises were beginning to hurt. He poured himself a whisky and sat down. There was a sense of late-night exhaustion in the room.

'Where'd you get the stationery?' he asked.

'Out of the drawer over there.'

'Where are the kids?'

'I got them into bed. They're asleep. They already have nightmares, poor buggers. It'll get worse now. Want a cigarette?'

'No, I don't smoke any more. You know that.'

'Yeah, you gave them up, didn't you? You used to smoke like a fucking chimney. How'd you do it?'

Brutally, during a long, scorchingly hot drive to Sydney in a car without air conditioning, the day he'd left Coolemon for good. He had woken in the morning sodden and seedy from the previous night's celebrations, melancholy with post-alcohol blues, his throat sore from too many cigarettes. Somehow he'd got through the farewell ceremonies. The senior sergeant replacing him, the mayor and the local state school principal had all come to shake his hand. On his way out of town, he'd seen by the roadside a rusting 44-gallon drum with a sign painted on it in bright yellow letters: *Plese put yr rubish in here. Thank u.* On impulse he stopped, threw his cigarettes and lighter into it, and drove on. For the next six or so hours, air at 42°C had blasted in through his windows. By the time he reached Sydney, he felt he'd sweated every lingering trace of nicotine out of his body, along with the alcohol from the night before. His shirt was drenched yellow. He hadn't had a cigarette since.

'Never mind that,' he said. 'You can tell me the truth now. Did the Ice Cream Man find you out here?'

Ambrosine was lighting her own cigarette.

'Fags will follow me to my grave. That was pretty fucking close tonight,' she said. 'Yeah, Mike came and saw me. He died out here too. How did he know I was here? Did you fucking tell anyone?'

'No, mate. It's your arms.'

She looked down at them, bare to her shoulders. They were marked with tattoos and psoriatic lesions.

'He paid someone in the health department for a list of all the chemists who were dispensing the ointment you use under the Pharmaceutical Benefits System. That list had to say Coolemon Chemist. He knew I'd spent time out here; he as good as sent me here. He just joined the dots.'

'Jesus. I never thought of that. I hardly ever go into town, just when I have to do my shopping. He must have followed me and the kids home.'

'When was this?'

'End of September.' Ambrosine put down her cigarette and started to sketch again. 'We hadn't been back from town that long. I'm unpacking things in the kitchen. Little Man was looking out the back door. He says, "Man, man." It was Mike. He was getting out of his car.' She stopped and took a drink. 'When you live like we do, you expect it to happen. We had a plan. If Mike turns up, the kids go out the back window and they head for the creek bed. I try and get to the car. If I get away, I pick them up. If I don't, they keep going till they get to a farmhouse somewhere.

'They got out but I didn't even make it to the front door. Mike got me. He was sitting on my back with his gun at my head. "Hi, Ambro. Long time, no see." Arsehole. He wanted to play games. I'm lying there, crying. Then there's a shot outside and another. Mike's off me and he's heading for the front door. It opens and someone I've never seen before walks in. Just like that, he cracks Mike one in the shoulder. It breaks the bone, I can hear it. Mike drops his gun, he's down. This guy smacks him one on the head and he's out for the count. I run for the back door but the man gets me from behind and pushes me against the wall. His gun's on my head and he says, "Are those your kids, man? They ran down into the creek. You call them back or you're dead meat."'

'What did he sound like?' Harrigan interrupted.

'He was South African. You know how they talk. I said, "Fuck you. No way." I was just waiting. Water's coming out of my body anywhere it can, I'm pissing myself. He turns me around, wants to know my name. "This man wanted to kill you. You don't care what happens to him, do you?" I said, "I don't give a shit and I know how to keep my mouth shut." He takes out his wallet and it's thick. Puts ten hundred-dollar notes in my hand. "Get your brats, get your car and get out. Don't come back until you've spent every cent of that money." I didn't look back. I was out the door.'

'What kind of car did he have?'

'It turned out he'd been at the house waiting for us and Mike before we got back. He'd put it in the shed so we didn't see it. The kids did though, when they were running away. It was some big, black four-wheel-drive. My kids heard me driving along the creek. They came out and we drove away as fast as I could. I told Laurie to keep watching just to see if that black thing was behind us. But he didn't come after us. But that's not the end of it.' She stopped and poured herself more whisky. 'About three weeks later, one night out of the dark, the guy walks in the door again with a gun in his hand. We're dead. Laurie goes for him and he hits him so I call him a fucking bastard. He laughs and he grabs me. "You don't want to die. You don't want your shitty little kids to die. You just keep your mouth shut. Because I can watch you. I've got my own dirty copper. If you tell anyone about this, you're all dead." Then he lets me go and walks out the door. We can hear him driving away. My poor kids. They were so afraid, they were all twisted up. You know why he didn't kill us? It was just too messy. If he had, one way or the other you and your mob would come crawling all over this place and who knows what you'd have turned up. But he was going to come back for us one day, I knew it.'

'Why didn't you tell me any of this before?'

'He said he had his own bent copper. How did I know it wasn't you? That guy was after Mike. I thought maybe you were getting your own back.'

'For Christ's sake,' Harrigan snapped. 'You had no reason to think that.'

'Didn't I? There's enough fucking rumours about you and him. Jesus, mate, we're talking about Mike! What the fuck did it matter if he was dead? I was so fucking paranoid, I didn't know who I could trust. Me and my kids slept in the same fucking bed for weeks afterwards. Every time we heard a noise, we freaked! I don't know how many times I've lain awake at night thinking, we'll just get in the car and go. But I knew if we did, one day we'd walk into a shotgun somewhere else. I didn't have any money anyway.'

'Did you find anything in the house when you came back?'

'My kids did. Laurie got up in the roof space one day, he was playing around. He found some ropes and a shirt with blood on them. Mike's, it had to be. Then Jen was playing outside and she found this funny-looking thing in the dirt. Some little metal stud with a logo on it.'

'Did it look like this?' Harrigan asked, showing her his own LPS badge.

'Yeah, but it was metal, not gold. Where'd you get that?'

He shook his head. 'It's a tracking device. I know Mike had one. The gunman would have tracked him here using it. What did you do with it?'

'I put it up in the roof with all the other stuff Laurie found up there. Then I told the kids to forget all about them.'

'That's why our friend burned your house down,' Harrigan said. 'He was making sure no one would find anything he'd left behind, accidentally or otherwise.'

'It's all gone now. Anyway, about a week after we got back, Jen comes running in. She says she's found something in the creek about half a kilometre away. We went down there and it was a grave, you could see it. I thought, yeah, that's Mike. After all these years, he's finally fucking dead. I told my kids, whatever you do, you don't tell anyone about this. It's just between us. It's got to stay that way.'

'Did you ever see any other cars along here?'

'Just the cars you always see, the farmers and that. Except we heard someone down here about a week ago. Really early in the morning last Thursday. It woke us up and freaked us out. I thought it was that

South African guy coming back. But whoever it was, they just drove away. I didn't see them or their car.'

'What did the South African guy look like?'

'This is him. I did this while I was waiting for you to come and talk to me. I've drawn you a couple of them.'

She pushed the pieces of paper across the table towards him. Harrigan found himself looking at the man he'd fought with tonight. An ordinary face. Square-featured, black hair, trimmed moustache. It was a good likeness. He would get it faxed to Trevor as soon as possible.

'We'll put this out in the media,' he said.

'Are you going to pay me for it?'

'No, mate. This is information received.'

'What are you going to do for me and my kids now, Harrigan?'

'I'll put you on the witness protection program as soon as possible.'

'Like last time?'

'You'll be safe this time. I'll make sure of it.'

She looked at him suspiciously and then kept drawing. He watched her work. Images filled the sheet of paper she drew on, as if it was the most natural thing in the world for her to pull them out of its whiteness. She had almost no schooling. Laurie's father, a tattooist himself, had taught her to draw when he'd taught her to tattoo. He was dead now, shot by a bikie gang when he wouldn't pay his protection money.

'What are you looking at?' she asked suddenly.

'You working. You've got a real talent.'

'You might not say that when you see this.'

It was a drawing of Harrigan at the kitchen table surrounded by a tattooist's icons of death. Old clocks, skulls on the bench with small worms crawling out of the eye sockets, flies and dying flowers on the table, an owl roosting on the window ledge. His face stared out of the paper. His hands were on the table in front of him, clasped tightly together. The gaze startled him. It was almost hungry, at once intense and detached.

'You can chuck it out if you want,' she said.

'Why would I do that? You've got a cold eye.'

'I just draw what's there.'

'Mummy.' Jen was standing in the doorway, twisting a bare foot behind her leg. 'Little Man's awake. He won't stop crying.'

'I'll come down, baby. We'll go to sleep together. How's that?'

She walked out, taking the little girl by the hand, leaving everything behind her on the table: the cigarettes, the ashtray, the sheets of paper, the empty whisky glass. More out of concern for Harold than anything, Harrigan tidied the mess away and decided it was time he got some sleep as well. He kept two constables to watch the house and sent the rest home, giving them Ambrosine's sketch of his attacker to send on to Trevor. Finally, he went to look for Harold. He found him sitting on the front step, smoking.

'Your face, mate,' Harold said when Harrigan appeared. 'You must be feeling that.'

'Are you okay?' Harrigan asked.

'Yeah, I'm all right. She was a good dog. It's a waste, that's all.'

There was silence.

'What made that racket in the trees out there?' Harrigan asked. 'Did you hear it? I thought it'd wake the dead.'

Harold almost grinned.

'One of my chickens. She got out of the chook yard a while back and she's been roosting over there ever since. There's hardly any foxes around here any more. Things are that bad.'

'I don't know about the foxes. She almost got me,' Harrigan said. He looked at his watch. It was the graveyard shift, getting on for dawn. 'Why don't you get some sleep?'

'I will in a while. I forgot to tell you — I've put you up in Dad's room. Tomorrow I'll take you out on the property and show you what I think this is all about.'

'I'll see you in the morning, mate. Try and sleep.'

Harrigan went back into the badly lit house. In Bob Morrissey's old bedroom, the dead man's clothes still hung in the wardrobe. A photograph of his two sons in their Geelong Grammar uniforms stood on the tallboy. Stuart at seventeen and Harold at fifteen, both smiling. Grit blown in through the cracks in the house covered the surface of the glass, the furniture. Stillness and dust hung in the air.

Harrigan took off his gun and shoulder holster and put them under the pillow. He put Ambrosine's sketch of him on top of the tallboy. It made him look like the death carrier, the person you least wanted to see knocking on your door. He didn't remember choosing the role willingly. He lay on the bed fully dressed and slept almost immediately. Everything else could wait until the morning.

18

Out on the harbour, a dark blue sky arched in a massive curve over the bridge. A strong easterly wind had whipped the water into white tops and brought some relief from the heat. Ferries dipped in the swell. The sails of the Opera House gleamed like cracked eggshells in the late sun. Over Port Jackson, the seagulls screamed and shat on the old prison, Pinchgut, a hard nub of angular sandstone in the water. The sky was alive with the bright clarity of the Australian light; light cut with the transparency of pure glass, hard as ineffaceable emotion and with just as much edge.

On the Quay, crowds of tourists watched the buskers against the backdrop of the ferry wharves. Grace, dressed in ultramarine blue, her dark hair curled on her bare shoulders, her stilettos clicking on the steps, made her way up to the entrance of the Museum of Contemporary Art. At the door, her name was checked and found to be acceptable. With a smile, the penguin-suited doorman ushered her in. 'Nice to see you here,' he said in his smoothly professional tones.

Inside, lights illuminated the terrazzo floor and the pale green and white marble pillars of the function room. A large area had been taken up by an array of seating facing a podium. An ornately worked acronym of the corporation's name, LPS, was displayed on a large screen, dominating both the podium and the room. Some people were already seated, others crowded around the buffet. The murmur of voices was loud. A string quartet played light classical; waiters offered trays of drinks and finger food.

The party from LPS stood waiting to welcome people as they arrived. Elena Calvo, immaculately dressed and smiling, handed out glossy named and numbered prospectuses. Beside her was Senator Edwards in black tie, his face pale, shaking hands mechanically. A third man was with them, tall in a white suit with a ruined, almost shocking face. At the sight of him, Grace stopped herself from drawing too sharp a breath. What kind of injuries would have caused that scarring? Others were less circumspect in hiding their reactions. When corporations put themselves on public display, almost everything was sanitised. On perhaps her most important night, Elena Calvo's welcoming committee included a man whose face would unsettle if not shock almost everyone he greeted.

Behind all three were two well-built men whom Grace guessed were bodyguards and, also in white, Sam Jonas. She saw Grace walking towards the group and smiled in a strange way.

'Yes, Grace Riordan.' Elena straightened a little when Grace appeared in front of her. 'Commander Harrigan's companion. We're pleased to have you here. Is it true you're in the same line of work?'

'Perhaps not any more. I am a trained police officer but I work in another line of business now.'

'Did you do it for the excitement?'

'No, it was to see if I could make a difference.'

'That's my motivation,' Elena said. 'I want to make a difference. Let me introduce you to my chief scientist, Dr Daniel Brinsmead. He is the head of our signature project, which is into burns research. He gave Commander Harrigan a tour of his project this morning.'

'Pleased to meet you,' Grace said, shaking hands while at the same noticing the fingerless left hand, the bulk of medical dressings beneath Dr Brinsmead's clothes. He was taller than her by a head. Once he must have been a good-looking man, fit and strong. Seen so close, the texture of his skin was like some reworked foreign material, almost unnatural. She fought the urge to look away.

'Are you pleased to meet me?' he replied.

'Yes.'

'I'll take you at your word. Not everybody is, as I've noticed tonight. Yes, I met Harrigan out at Campbelltown today. Have you spoken to him since?'

'No,' Grace said, feeling it.

'So he won't have had the chance to tell you what happened. You can see from my face why my project is to do with burns,' Brinsmead said. 'I'm speaking later on tonight. That's why I'm here at the door. I want everyone to see me now instead of being shocked when I step out into the light.'

'As soon as people hear what you have to say, I'm sure you'll have their complete interest. They won't be thinking about anything else.'

'I told Daniel that same thing myself,' Elena said. 'Grace, this is Senator Edwards. Grace Riordan. She's standing in for Commander Harrigan.'

'I'm pleased to meet you. You look very charming.'

The senator's eyes were bloodshot, his hands trembling slightly. There was a scent of mouthwash about him. Grace, who had once started drinking as soon as she woke up in the morning, recognised the symptoms. The first thing you did was look for ways to hide your breath.

'Harrigan's working, is he?' the senator said.

'Yes, he has to be somewhere else.'

'He must trust you if he's asked you to stand in for him.'

'I hope so.'

'I'm sure he does,' Elena interrupted. 'Grace, this is one of my security people, Sam Jonas. I've asked her to look after you tonight. If there's anything you want, just ask her for it. We'll talk to you later.'

Grace smiled and walked away. Sam followed. Grace stepped to the side, out of the way of the moving crowd where she could talk to Sam with some small privacy.

'Where would you like to sit?' Sam asked with a grin. 'You can consider me your personal servant. Do you want a glass of champagne? It's good quality.'

'No, thanks,' Grace said. 'I can find my own seat. You don't have to look after me. You can tell Dr Calvo I asked you not to bother.'

'We can still talk to each other. You and I are in the same business.'

'Are we?'

196

'Aren't you in the security game one way or another? You used to be a police officer.'

'Not any more.'

'Are you telling me you left all that behind just like that? From what I read in the newspapers, you were handy enough to walk away from a very nasty situation at Jerry Freeman's house the other day. They left your name out of the press release but you must have been there.'

'That was mainly down to him,' Grace said.

'It didn't read that way in the papers. He's the one who took three bullets, and one intrepid journalist reported there was a fourth shot through the door. Was that aimed at you? But you managed to get the door shut just in time. Now that's dancing with death.'

'Why do you want to know?'

'I told you. It's my job to keep an eye on things for Elena.'

'Why were you there?'

Sam smiled. 'To quote you, if you won't answer my question, I'm not going to answer yours.'

'You knew what was going to happen. You walked away and left me and him to get shot.'

'No. I warned you loud and clear if you were listening. After that, it was up to you to look after yourself.'

'Did you know who was going to be there?' Grace asked sharply. 'Or why they'd be coming after Freeman?'

'Why should I know any of those things? A man like Freeman must have had plenty of people who wanted to get their own back on him, even if it was at the last minute.'

'You didn't care,' Grace said. 'It didn't matter to you that two people might end up dead.'

'Am I supposed to care? Why? No one else does.'

'Maybe I care if I get shot,' Grace said, turning to walk away.

'You're standing in for Harrigan,' Sam said. 'That means you're here to observe and report back. He thinks you can do that for him usefully. So whatever you say, I'm very sure we're in the same business. Which is something I wanted to ask you. Is it good or bad having a lover in the same line of work?'

Grace turned back. Sam was watching her with a distant look, one that reduced her to a cipher.

'Why ask me?'

'I just wondered what you think. Do you go to bed at night worrying what's happened to Harrigan? Does he wonder what's happened to you? Do you gnaw at your fingernails hoping you'll both be okay?'

'Why are you trying to be offensive? You talk to people this way for fun?'

'I'm just interested in you. There's a saying that love is as strong as death. Do you think it is?'

'Do you?'

'I do as it happens, but I'm more interested right now in what you think. Maybe you'll get to find out if it's true.'

'What do you mean by that?' Grace asked.

'Nothing in particular. If you don't want me to look after you, better take a seat. There's a good turnout.'

'Who's here?'

'Financial institutions, research institutes, university bigwigs, politicians, punters, thieves, rip-off merchants. And you. The innocent bystander.'

'You are just so in your face,' Grace heard herself saying. 'You just hit people with it, don't you? Does anything frighten you? Keep you in line?'

'No,' Sam said with a broad smile. 'I can say with complete honesty that I'm not frightened of anything.'

'You just do and say what you want.'

'Try reaching the point where you can, Grace. It's very liberating.'

Grace took a seat, glancing back in time to see Sam rejoin Elena's entourage. Sam spoke a few words to Elena who nodded. Scarcely a debrief. Presumably if Sam was going to report their conversation to her boss, they would go somewhere more private.

Grace looked around at the crowd. Among an otherwise staid group, she saw those people that anyone who lived and worked in this city knew about: dealers in influence and connection. Entrepreneurs who blurred the line between the business and criminal worlds but could still open doors in the big end of town or the government. Shock jocks who spruiked these occasions on air the way they might bet on an untried filly at the track, for a flutter. The women accompanying these men were mostly young, they glittered in the light. Those who were older had held on to the same style of dress, their clothes revealing bodies carrying a little too much age, a cumulative weight hidden by tans and dyed hair. Stuart Morrissey was sitting in the middle rows, one of these old-young blonde women with him.

The room was darkening, a spotlight centring on the podium. In the light, Elena took her seat with half a dozen other people, including Edwards and Daniel Brinsmead.

'Will you please make welcome Senator Allan Edwards,' said an invisible announcer, 'the federal Minister for Science and Technology.'

There was applause. As he stepped up to the microphone, the minister's face was pale although composed.

'Well, ladies and gentlemen, as the song goes, tonight is no ordinary night. Tonight we are launching a vision I believe in so strongly that nothing could prevent me from being here. I come in the hope that I may take something positive out of the darkness that has surrounded my life lately.' A more intense silence greeted this statement. The awareness of recent, violent death seemed tangible in the atmosphere. 'I urge you to have the same belief, to help us build life out of death, hope out of despair. Let me introduce Dr Elena Calvo, the CEO of Life Patent Strategies International and one of the most impressive people I have ever met. Please make her most welcome.'

He stepped back. The audience applauded. Resplendent in the light, Elena stood up and began to speak.

'Thank you, Senator Edwards. Before anything else, I want to say that without Senator Edwards' foresight and dedication, tonight would not have been possible. I will always be deeply grateful for his support. Please, if we could show our appreciation.'

The applause was generous. Edwards nodded his thanks but appeared ill at ease, his face tense with exhaustion.

'Thank you too, ladies and gentlemen, for being here tonight. To sum up our business enterprise, we open the doors to vast possibility. Tonight we offer you the opportunity to be a part of that enterprise.'

The LPS logo on the screen had spun in on itself while she spoke. In its place, a double helix appeared in closeup, coiling across the screen: a thickish, ribbed, twisted rope made up of a darker red exterior enclosing a paler interior, its parts meshed together like teeth in a zipper.

'This is a single strand of DNA,' Elena continued. 'What you see magnified on this screen behind me is in reality only fifty-trillionths of an inch wide. This very narrow thread supports the varieties of life. At Life Patent Strategies, we experiment with this thread, we mine its unlimited potential. Genes are our latest industrial raw material, the most inexhaustible, self-generating resource humans have ever tapped into. If you own the knowledge of what this tiny strand can do, then you own the commercial power to exploit its vast capacities. With the right expertise, you can trade in its infinite possibilities across the world's marketplaces.

'We own the knowledge. We have the expertise. We offer you the chance to be a part of this new world. To make your investment in a resource that has unending potential. Tonight, at this very moment, I am going to demonstrate exactly the kind of injury that our research will one day cure. I ask you to remain seated while I invite to the microphone someone who is a very dear friend of mine. Please do not be startled by his appearance. Let me introduce Dr Daniel Brinsmead, the head of our signature research project into the regeneration of the human body following major burns.'

Like the ghost at the feast, Daniel Brinsmead stepped forward. His ruined face stood out as a strange mask, both illuminated and shaded by the fall of the light, staring back at the crowd. There was a stir throughout the audience.

'Good evening,' he said, a disembodied voice through the microphone. 'For those of you who haven't seen me before, don't be disturbed by how I look. Let me tell you where I fit in here. I'm a geneticist. You can find my résumé on the website or in your prospectus. Tonight I'm representing myself not only as the researcher but as the subject. The work that LPS does is contentious. Most biotechnology is contentious. But as a scientist, I have no doubt whatsoever that in the field of biotechnology, there are enormously positive gains to be made. Cures for crippling and painful diseases. Food crops that rely on less environmentally destructive methods of farming, with yields that promise independence for their farmers. But will we do this? Will we enhance life or produce wastelands? Or will

200

the sources of life become something owned only by a very few people for their commercial benefit alone? Out of the source of life, will we create death?'

The word carried through the high-ceilinged room with a curious resonance. The audience shivered despite the warm summer night. Brinsmead touched his face with both hands.

'That's the question I want to ask you tonight, all of you who want to invest in this corporation. Because I am the embodiment of all that LPS has to offer you. My face and this organisation are one and the same. I want you to look at my face, to remember it. To know that this is what burns do to people. Because this face is what you will be investing in. In the decisions that led to it happening and the pain that made it look the way it does now; and, paradoxically, the possibility that one day this injury may be repaired, this skin remade and the past expunged. Something that most of us would wish for at least once in our lives.' He paused. 'The questions for you as investors are: do you know what the cost of this face really is; and are you prepared to pay it? Make sure you find the right answer. That you do choose limitless possibility and not the end of life. I'll now return you to Elena.' He sat down.

'What Daniel has said is correct,' Elena Calvo said in a clear, ringing voice. 'Our research program goes to the heart of life. We will be working towards renewing the human body, regenerating the mind, the nerves, the spinal cord. Now let me take you through the projects that are already in progress.'

The curling DNA on the screen spun in on itself. A video played in its place. The audience was given a virtual tour of the building at Campbelltown. In the laboratories, the scientific personnel in charge of the individual projects spoke to the cameras. From the podium, Elena introduced her chief business officer, then her chief financial officer — individuals known and respected, with impressive résumés, all printed in the prospectus. The listeners became absorbed, a number taking notes in the half-light. Elena began to talk money: projected returns for dollars invested. The figures were impressive. She then took questions from the floor. The questioning was enthusiastic; she answered with ease.

'If there are no more questions,' she eventually said, 'I would like to invite you all to stay and enjoy the rest of the buffet. Please don't hesitate to come and speak to me or any of my colleagues. Thank you for your attention.'

She and her colleagues left the podium to considerable applause. The lights came on. People got up from their seats talking with energy. A crowd gathered around the buffet; there was the sound of champagne corks popping. The string quartet began to play again. The staff moved forward quickly, folding up the vacated seats and moving them out of the way, then shifting the podium to the side. People spilled over into the open space, talking; the noise filled the room. Only the video screen remained, again displaying its strand of DNA coiling above their heads.

Grace accepted a soda water from a passing waiter and looked around. Daniel Brinsmead was walking towards her. His movements were awkward, slow.

'Grace. I hope you don't mind if I come and talk to you. We haven't been introduced properly. This is my card.'

'This is mine,' Grace said with a smile, making the decision that this might be a useful connection.

'I'm supposed to be earning my keep by talking to the investors. But there's no reason why I can't have some time out, as they say,' Brinsmead said. 'Your card doesn't say what you do. Do you have the pleasure of not working?'

'I'm a public servant. It's very boring. Your work is much more interesting.'

'I find it hard to believe that someone like you could be in a dull job. How did you like the presentation?'

'That was quite a speech you gave. I wasn't sure if you wanted people to invest or to go away. It was almost as if you were warning them off.'

'I meant every word I said,' he replied. 'I really do believe that much of the negative press against genetic modification is misguided. It can be made to work positively to very great benefit. But, as usual, it's a question of how we do it. When have we ever only developed the positives out of any technology? We seem to have the capacity to turn almost anything into a weapon.'

'Aren't you in a position to make sure that it's only used positively in this case?'

'No, I have no power to achieve that outcome. I wish I did,' Brinsmead said. 'I run one small project. Hopefully, what I'm doing now means that in the future people won't feel the kind of pain I've felt in the past and now live with. That sounds self-pitying but it's a fact.'

'You haven't let any of that stop you from achieving something very important.'

'It's true I've never been more motivated. It's the way you feel when you know that a goal is almost in sight. It's a pity you haven't had the chance to speak to Commander Harrigan since he was out at LPS. He could have told you something about the building. As it happens, he and Elena had a very long and private conversation. She can be very charming, and today she'd taken a great deal of care with her appearance.'

Grace shouldn't have felt this but she did.

'I understood it was a business meeting.'

'I'm sure it was. It's just that Elena has a habit of appropriating what she wants sometimes. Did you pick up on the comment I made in my speech about expunging the past?' Brinsmead asked.

'Yes, I did. I don't think that's possible. What happens in the past is part of you. It's with you forever.'

'With new medical treatments, maybe that won't always be so,' he said. 'Maybe one day we'll be able to remake ourselves so completely that memory won't be necessary. Any injury you suffer will disappear, and with it the experience and the knowledge.'

'You'd still remember the shock even if you were repaired. It would be like having a phantom limb. Even though it's not there, it would still hurt you.'

'My opinion is, if past injuries could be so effectively expunged, there'd be no need to have a conscience. Whatever you did to someone, it would be repaired. You could do what you liked and not have to feel bad about it. At one level, it's an ultimate injustice.'

'Unless you'd killed them. In my experience, people who damage other people usually have no trouble arguing that it wasn't their fault. Either that, or it didn't really happen, or it was the victim's fault all along. People don't really need any help doing that.'

'That's true,' Brinsmead said.

At that moment, Elena appeared out of the crowd with her entourage. 'Daniel, here you are. The head of the Medical Research Institute is fascinated by your project. She wants to talk to you about it. Apparently, you've already had some conversations on the subject.'

'Yes, she's very interested in my work. I'll go and speak to her. I'm sure I can enthral her even more.'

Elena turned to Grace. 'How did you like the presentation?' she asked. 'Did you understand it?'

'Yes, I did, thank you,' Grace replied, flashing her most professional smile.

'What are you going to advise your companion to do?'

'I'll tell him what I saw and heard and he'll make up his own mind.'

'Yes, I'm sure he will. I'm sure he'll give it his closest attention,' Elena replied in a glacial tone. 'Sam, would you like to show Grace out? I'm sure she's seen and heard as much as she wants to.'

'I was leaving anyway, Dr Calvo. I'll see myself out, thanks.'

Grace walked away, stopping to give her empty glass to a passing waiter. Senator Edwards appeared, walking towards her. He was alone.

'Ms Riordan,' he said, 'I can see you're leaving but do you have time to talk to me? Don't worry. I'm not going to harass you in any way.'

'What do you want to talk about?'

'Could I ask you to come outside? I'll explain myself.'

They walked out of the side entrance that led to First Fleet Park, where they stood on the grass. Across Sydney Cove, the lights drew the famous sight of the Opera House out of the night. The water was an oily black, the air had a thick and close humidity. Edwards reached into his inside pocket and took out a hip flask.

'I hope you're not going to tell me it's illegal to drink in a public place.'

'I'm not with the New South Wales police any more,' Grace replied.

He smiled and took a mouthful.

'I haven't stopped drinking since I found my son dead, and I'm not ashamed to say it. It's the only way I can keep going. I don't feel the alcohol any more.'

'That's honest.'

'I wanted to talk to Harrigan. But maybe you'd be prepared to talk to me in his place? I need to talk to someone. Better a woman than a man usually, and it's clear he feels he can rely on you. Do you object?'

'No. Go ahead.'

'How much do you know about this investigation? My guess is you'd know the name Jerome Beck.'

'Yes, I do.'

'Do you know what I mean when I say "dossier"?'

'No.'

Edwards smiled in a tight way. 'Do you know the sort of man we're talking about?'

'The company he kept would give you a good idea of who he was.'

'Do you know the name Abaris?'

'No, I've never heard it before.'

'They're a financial group with a specific interest in gene technology. They're very secretive about who they are, but they're very influential. You'll never find them at the forefront of any deal. You have to trace back through the financial and legal trail before you start finding evidence of their involvement. I happen to know more about them than most people.'

'Why is that important?'

'Because Abaris is funding LPS,' he replied. 'That information is commercial-in-confidence but, quite frankly, I don't care. Just about everything is meaningless to me right now.' He took another mouthful from his hip flask. 'Usually I'm very careful with money. Elena was impressive, but she had to prove to me she had the finance behind her before I was prepared to argue for the concessions she wanted. There was no arguing with that source of money. Abaris has very deep pockets.'

'If they're secretive, Minister, how do you know about them?'

'They actually approached me on Elena's behalf quite early in her negotiations. I can only assume she asked them to. But I'd heard of them and dealt with them before. This isn't the first time they've done business in this part of the world. One of their members is an Australian entrepreneur. He's approached me on their behalf before and I've assisted them in my role as a government minister before. He's the one I mainly dealt with in establishing LPS here. I've met other members of Abaris in London, including Elena's father. He's a frightening man, to be honest. Very protective of Elena. Obsessively so. She must have been very determined in her efforts to break away from him and come here.'

He stopped, taking another drink. Grace waited. Down on the Quay, laughing groups of partygoers were heading for the train station, the buses. She glanced back at the entrance to the function room. Sam Jonas was standing there watching them. At the sight of Grace turning to look at her, she walked inside.

'Why does any of this matter, you're probably asking,' Edwards said. 'The answer is this. Beck was part of Elena's financial package. I was told by Abaris that if he wasn't given entry to the country, there'd be no funding for LPS.'

'Did you question that?'

'I was paid not to.'

'I'm sorry?'

'I was paid not to question it. Don't look so shocked. It wasn't anything so crude as money in a brown envelope. I wasn't approached by the entrepreneur about Beck until after the project had been given the go ahead. They pulled a fast one in other words. I was told that if Beck was unable to gain entry to the country, then the money would be withdrawn and the project stopped. By then we'd already announced it with great fanfare. So if it was cancelled, it would be embarrassing to everyone. Apart from that, I wanted the facility onshore. It would offer work that might keep some of our best and brightest here, rather than having them go overseas the way they do now. But I was also offered a consideration: a combination of shares and royalties in other ventures this entrepreneur is involved with. It wasn't exactly a gift. It was an investment opportunity at a very generously discounted rate, worked out through his network of associates. I thought, what harm can there be in letting a single individual into the country? I said yes.'

'Who is this entrepreneur?'

'I'm not going to tell you that. The request was that Beck receive a visa. The understanding was that later on he would also receive a passport.'

'Was Dr Calvo involved in this?'

'She wasn't involved in any of the discussions. What she knew about Beck beforehand or what connection they have, I really don't know. She's a very smart woman. She knows how to think ahead of people — I've seen her do it. I doubt we'll ever find out what her real understanding was.'

'Beck still had to get a visa,' Grace said. 'How was that arranged?'

'It was more subtle than I'm making it appear. In fairness to everyone, including me, the full extent of Beck's criminality wasn't known, nowhere near it. In fact, it was very effectively hidden. My entrepreneur put Beck forward as a man reformed.' He laughed a little too loudly. People leaving the function glanced in his direction. 'I didn't sponsor him myself, of course. I organised for someone else to do that — obviously a well-respected individual in the community. But I spoke to the then Minister for Immigration on his behalf myself. She was a long-standing acquaintance of mine; she took me at my word. I told her a very significant development was at risk. Which means the only person who can be blamed for Beck being here is me. You can see what it's cost me.'

'What about the entrepreneur?'

'He can deny everything, but my involvement is on file at the Department of Immigration. The fact that I received the inducements I did is also recorded in my financial affairs. There's nothing in those purchases that implicates the giver. It's only me. Recently, before my son's death, there had been intimations that I might be asked to provide more assistance to Beck in the future. How could I say no when I was already compromised? My son came to warn me that Beck wanted my help. He didn't believe I could possibly be corrupted.'

'Why are you telling me this, Senator? Have you received threats?' Grace asked.

'Threats? No. Should I have? I'm telling you this for the same reason that I've done everything since I found Julian. I want everything out in the open.'

He stopped speaking. His eyes were bright and focused on some unknown point in the distance.

'When I received that dossier on Beck at my electoral office, I can't tell you what I went through. I thought, I brought this man into the country and my ex-wife has brought him into my son's life. The day I went to see her, that day I found them all, I was going to take Julian out of that house no matter what. My only comfort was, he was somewhere in Tasmania where no one could get to him. Except he wasn't. He'd come home. Whatever happened in my ex-wife's house in Pittwater that evening, I set that situation up. That's what I can't live with.'

'You have to make a full statement, Senator. My advice is that you should also be very careful about your own safety, even if it's only as a precaution. Have you spoken to Dr Calvo about any of this?'

He smiled. 'I spoke to Elena about it just before the launch.'

As he said this, Grace saw one of Elena's bodyguards appear in the doorway to the function room. He saw her talking to Senator Edwards and went back inside.

'Are you sure you should have done that?' she asked.

He laughed again, more softly. 'I hope so. I hope I can rely on her. I asked her what she knew. Her reaction was strange. She said she'd come here because she had hoped it would be the new world. A long way from the many things she'd wanted to leave behind. But they'd followed her. I think she was trying to tell me that Beck had been foisted on her, possibly by her father. I almost asked her, did she have a choice? But I couldn't. She was too distressed. It's the first time I've seen her come close to losing her self-control.'

'She seems to have regained it since,' Grace said.

'She does, doesn't she? In there, she was more like the Elena I know. I don't want to think about the implications of her relationship with Beck, whatever it was, if she even had one. I can't bring myself to believe she could be implicated in my son's death in any way. But I do intend to make a full statement; in fact, I plan to sign an affidavit. Most of it's already written. I'll make sure Commander Harrigan gets it as soon as possible.'

'In the meantime, Senator, I think you need personal protection.'

'Allan. I've been looking for you everywhere.' Elena had appeared, her two bodyguards either side of her. 'Can I interrupt you? I need to introduce you to someone before they leave.'

'Of course, Elena. I was just passing the time of day here with Ms Riordan.'

'You were deep in discussion. What were you talking about?'

'Julian. She was kind enough to listen to me.'

Elena looked at Grace but didn't speak directly to her. 'I thought Ms Riordan had left some time ago. I seem to find her in conversation with people wherever I look.'

'I'm on my way now,' Grace said.

'Yes, you are.' There was a faint pause. 'The next time you see Commander Harrigan, please give him my regards. Presumably, whenever he gets back safely from wherever he is now and makes up his mind how he will invest.'

'When do you think that will be, Dr Calvo?'

'Why ask me that? Don't you know? I could have no idea. Good night.'

Elena's voice held a finely elegant malice, seeming to spell out the opposite of what was said. It implied expectation of harm, not good wishes. Already, she was on her way back to the function room, Edwards with her. Grace walked away into the night without looking back.

Harrigan had said before he left that he wouldn't call her; he would be focused on what he was doing. No news was good news; she wasn't to worry. He hadn't said, don't ring him. As soon she was home, she called and got his voicemail.

'It's me,' she said. 'I'm back from the launch. Edwards gave me some important information. He's confirmed the connection between Beck and LPS and identified it with another organisation called Abaris. You need to talk to him as soon as you can and make it clear that he needs protection. Just ring me. I need to know that you're okay,' she finished abruptly.

She sat down at the table. There was something badly wrong wherever he was, she felt it powerfully. If anything did happen to Harrigan, would they tell her? Would she hear it on the radio first? Her tiny flat closed in on her. She couldn't breathe. Most times like this, she would have called her friends, met them somewhere and gone dancing. Instead, without changing her clothes, she found paper and a pen and began to write up what had happened tonight.

Almost, she set down as the opening words: *I'm waiting to hear if you're dead.* But no such words from the heart appeared on the page. Her usual disciplined report filled the blank space. She wrote in detail. Anything to fill in the time until she heard that Harrigan was alive, or if anyone called to let her know otherwise.

19

Voices at a distance woke Harrigan. He opened his eyes to the sensation that he didn't know where he was. Time was dislocated; fleetingly, the room was an unknown precinct. Then he heard a shout: 'Watch out!' It was Harold's voice. Events slipped back into place. He thought, I have work to do. Pulling himself up off the bed, he put on his gun. Then he went outside to see what all the fuss was about.

The parched landscape brought Harold's words back. *Wait till you see it. It'll break your heart.* Clear and overarching, the blue sky offered no possibility of rain. Harrigan saw Harold and the two constables at the edge of the old garden beds, standing near the snagged ute. With one back wheel hanging just above the ground, it looked like some bizarre dead bug. Harrigan went to join them.

'Morning,' Harold said. 'Do you want to give us a hand? I can't help out too much because of my hands. This is why I almost overturned us last night. I got too close to the paving.'

The garden's ornamental paving stones had subsided over time and last night they had given way under the weight of the ute. The ground beneath had collapsed into a series of deep cracks, revealing an extensive network of ants' nests. With its right wheel caught in one of these cracks, the ute had overbalanced on its side, then become lodged. In the hot morning sun, ants were swarming out of their nests and over the ground, climbing up on the ute's body in an angry mass.

Using the police car, one of the constables towed the ute out of the crack while Harrigan and his colleague righted it from the back. It hit the ground with a thud. Even more agitated and angry, the ants flowed into the cabin and onto the tray. The constable towed the vehicle away from the nests to open ground where Harold ruthlessly sprayed the ants with what looked like homemade insecticide.

'Have you had any breakfast?' he asked Harrigan. 'We can go out to the Cage whenever you're ready.'

'In this?' Harrigan watched ants falling to the ground in dead clusters while others disappeared into the ute's bodywork. 'I don't think so. I'll get us a car. I'll drive and give your hands a break.'

He couldn't take his own car; it had to be examined by the forensic team to see if it had been tampered with. Still, there had to be some advantages to being the boss, including asking for another car to be made available for him as soon as possible. He went back inside to shower, to sustain the body. On his way to the bathroom, he looked in on Ambrosine and her children. They slept in what had once been Stuart's and Harold's bedroom: Ambrosine with her smallest son on one bed, her other two children side by side on the second. Harrigan closed the door on them quietly. Peace. Order. It was a wild ambition he had. As rare out here in the remote countryside as in the heart of the city.

A replacement car arrived later in the morning with the senior sergeant from Coolemon. He drove into the yard followed by a contingent of uniformed police drawn from other towns around the district. Harrigan sent them down to secure the remains of Ambrosine's cottage, then search along the creek bed for a makeshift grave. The other two constables, relieved from their night shift, went home.

Following Harold's directions, Harrigan drove out across the property in the opposite direction. Their drive took them along a pathway of open gates and, in some places, gaps in Harold's fences where the gunman had simply cut his way through the wire on his way to the farmhouse.

'He did come in on Stewie's private road,' Harrigan said, when they'd stopped to look at another hole in a fence.

'But how did he know what direction to take across my fields?'

Harrigan reached into his pocket and took out his LPS badge.

'This,' he said. 'It's a tracking device.'

'That thing? Is it working now?'

'Maybe. I don't know. But I don't think our gunman will be anywhere near here given the number of police around. And I'm still armed. I was given this yesterday. I was played for a fool.'

'We still got the better of him when it mattered, mate.'

Harrigan drove on until in the near distance they saw the glint of steel fences. He drove past piles of dead trees and pulled up outside an open gate. Harold was out of the car even before Harrigan had stopped.

'Jesus,' he said. 'All that water. What a waste.'

It was a scene of devastation. A wide gap had been punched in the high steel fence. Every structure inside the enclosure had been demolished. The tanks against the far fence had been torn open and their tens of thousands of litres of water had poured out, turning the ground just outside the fence into a swamp.

'Is this what you wanted to show me?' Harrigan asked.

'It wasn't like this the last time I saw it. I don't know when this happened.'

They walked past heaps of debris. Broken glass sparkled in the sun.

'I'll never be able to use this piece of land again,' Harold said.

'Take it back to the beginning, Harry. What used to be here?'

'Before? Seven months ago, this whole area was covered with grey box. Those are the trees lying outside the fence. If you mean what Stuart put here, there were three greenhouses in a line, right there. Big ones.'

Harrigan saw the indentations in the ground, now filled with smashed glass and twisted steel, where the structures had stood.

'Over there,' Harold turned and pointed to a bare area behind them, scraped clean, 'that was a small field of wheat, the kind I used to grow myself. Everything's gone. They've even taken the soil. Over there is the access road they put in. The road was fenced off from my paddocks and there was a locked gate where it met the Coolemon Road. That fence is gone now, and my guess is the gate has too.'

Harrigan looked along the broken fence line that had once marked the dirt road. Deep serrations were scored in the ground where the bulldozers had come in.

'When were you last here?' he asked.

'Two days ago. It must have happened the night after I burned my hands. I knocked myself out that night. I wouldn't have heard a thing.'

'It's a fair distance over to here from your place.'

'They would have had their lights on. With that and the racket they'd have made, I would have noticed something.'

'Lucky you didn't,' Harrigan said grimly. 'Otherwise, you might have ended up face down in the dirt.'

He looked around. Torn and twisted pieces of irrigation equipment lay broken into the ground. Near the fence, he saw the generator that had once driven the system smashed to pieces.

'Did you ever see people come out here?' he asked Harold.

'All the time. People would come in from the Coolemon Road. I never spoke to them, never really saw them close up. There was a place to sleep in one of the greenhouses so they must have spent time out here.'

'This must have cost a fortune to build. Whoever did this put a bulldozer through it without thinking about it.'

In the debris, Harrigan saw the carcasses of small animals and birds.

'Have you told anyone you took those specimens or that you've still got them?' he asked.

'No one but you, mate.'

'I think we should keep it that way for the time being. My officers are going to take your statement sometime today. Bring them out here and show them this. Give them the keys. Tell them everything you've told me since I got here. But don't tell them that one small detail.'

'What do I tell them about my hands?'

'That you went in there, you looked it over, you handled what you found,' Harrigan said.

'Can't you trust your people, mate?'

'Some I can and some I can't. I'm not sure which is which at the moment.'

'You're joking, aren't you?'

'No, I'm not. I don't want any more people dead, including you or me. Let's go and see where they came in.'

They followed the indentations in the ground until they reached the Coolemon Road. The gate that had once secured the private road from intruders was smashed and lay half across the road, while a gap had been torn in Harold's fence. Working together, they managed to drag the gate out of the path of any traffic. Harrigan stopped to look down the empty road. In the distance, he heard the sound of a crow.

'The gunman had to know there was an entry point here. Otherwise, it'd just be any other gate,' he said.

'How was this planned?' Harold asked. 'Did they know you were coming here yesterday?'

'They couldn't have known beforehand. Once I left the city, they had the means to track exactly where I was going.' Harrigan grinned. 'He wasn't following me, he was in front of me. I wasn't looking for him there. But that means they organised this demolition separately to me coming here. They must have put this in motion as soon as they heard those people at Pittwater were dead.'

'How am I going to get all this fixed? I don't have that kind of money.'

'Can you borrow it?' Harrigan asked.

'I don't dare do that, mate. Stewie's been trying to get me to raise a mortgage on Yaralla ever since Dad died. We both have to agree to it. I won't do it. Because I know as soon as I do, he'll take the money and run and I'll never see a cent of it again. I haven't been able to do any improvements for years because I can't trust him enough. I could lose everything. I used to think having the property was better than nothing. That was before the drought.'

They drove back to the farmhouse in silence. About halfway, Harold asked Harrigan to stop.

'What is it?'

'Just about here, I'd stop and let Rosie off the ute. She'd race me back to the house. She was quick.'

'Did you get her buried?'

'I had to burn her. I've got a pit where I put my carcasses. I did it there.'

'I'm sorry about what's happened, Harry.'

Harold shrugged. 'It's not your fault. Do you want to get going now?'

Harrigan glanced at his passenger but there was no sign of emotion in Harold's face. He drove on.

*   *   *

At the farmhouse, more people were waiting for Harrigan. Members of the task force and the forensic team who had just arrived on the early plane from Sydney; the local police who wanted to know what they were expected to do next.

'I'll leave you to it,' Harold said. 'I've got to organise for someone to come up here and feed my stock.'

He walked back inside the house. Surrounded by demanding people, Harrigan watched him disappear almost with envy.

Harrigan most wanted to see what his people had found in Naradhan Creek. As soon as he'd given his orders, he asked to be driven down to the Creek Lane. Several kilometres along the dirt road, he stopped to look over the remains of Ambrosine's cottage. Surreal in the sunlight, a bathtub with a shower attached and the kitchen stove stood upright in the ash and ruins. Next to them, an old shed was also a pile of ash and burned boards. They drove about half a kilometre further on. After climbing down a steep incline into the creek bed, he was shown a shallow and narrow grave dug into sand.

Harrigan looked into the open trench and then at the cracked and eroded banks around him, which exposed a tangle of tree roots to the air. In the creek bed itself were young trees and scrub, stressed in the drought. In the early afternoon heat, he heard the sound of insects, the occasional bird call. Otherwise, it was deeply quiet. He imagined a human scream falling into a silence much deeper and more intensely still than this one. If the gunman had got the better of him last night, this could have been his grave and his scream falling into silence. This time, that wasn't his fate.

Harrigan went back to the farmhouse. He wanted to talk to Ambro about what to do with her and her children. When he arrived, the kids were playing through the house while she was in the kitchen, peeling potatoes.

'What are you doing?' he asked.

'Fucking cooking tea. What does it look like?'

'I didn't know you did that sort of thing.'

'Everyone's got to eat, mate. Talking of which, help yourself to what's on the table. That was brought in for your mob.'

She was referring to a spread of food set out on the kitchen table. Famished, Harrigan sat down and took a sandwich.

'We've got to talk about your safety,' he said.

'What? You're going to put me and my kids back on the witness program. Forget it.'

'You can't stay here.'

'Why not? You think that guy is coming back again? What the fuck for? He must have worked out by now that everything I know, you know. Didn't you send my drawing out? He's got to know he can't hide any more. No, we're staying here. Harry's said we can, and I'm going to give him something out of my pension for our keep. We've got nothing now, so if we do go somewhere else, what's going to be there for us? Like he said, there's plenty of room. Laurie and Jen can have their own rooms. They've never had that before. The kids like Harry. He said he's going to teach Laurie to ride.'

'Do you want to stay here?' Harrigan asked.

'Oh, you know. I get fucking lonely out here sometimes, even with Harry. But the kids like it. They like the school. They fit there a bit better. They've made friends, you know. I don't want to shift them again. Maybe now we can stay in one place for a while. There's something else as well. Harry's not showing it but he's on the edge. He fucking needs someone to talk to, mate. We're going to stay and keep him company. Because I don't know what he might do if he's left alone. I don't want to hear he's blown his head off.'

'And what about if someone comes looking for you here? It's going to get out now that this is where you are. It has to, with all these people crawling over the place. What if Little Joe turns up here with a shotgun? Is he going to take Harry out as well as you?'

Ambrosine was frowning, staring at the pile of potato peelings. 'I'm going to find out if that's going to happen,' she said. 'You never know. Things might have changed because of what's gone on this last week.'

'How are you going to do that?'

'I've got my own contacts. I know who I can ring safely. If we have to go, we'll go. I'm not putting Harry in danger. But until I know that, we're staying.'

'Okay, you make your contact. You find out what's going on and you tell me what happens. All right?'

'Yeah, yeah.' She shrugged him off. 'Are you going to stay for tea? Harry's got this leg of lamb.'

'No, I've got to get back to the city. Where is he?'

'Out the front.'

He found Harold sitting on the edge of the veranda, drinking tea and smoking.

'Come and sit down,' he said. 'Want a cuppa?'

'Thanks,' Harrigan replied, although he rarely drank tea. He accepted a cup of the powerfully tannic liquid. Tattoos of Naradhan Creek were curled around Harold's muscular arms, much the same way as the dry creek twisted its way through the landscape.

'You're the tattooed man, mate,' Harrigan said.

Harold glanced at his forearm. 'She's a good tattooist. She and the kids are staying on here. They'll be company.'

Harrigan looked out at the blasted landscape. The only line of green was Naradhan Creek.

'Sorry we're marching all over your property like this, mate,' he said.

Harry shrugged. 'That started with old Stewie. It hasn't stopped.'

'Harry, there's something you've got a right to know. The same man who tried to kill us last night killed another man in Ambro's cottage back in September. He buried him down in the creek but the body's not there any more. It was dug up and transported back to Sydney about a week ago. It was one of the bodies found at Pittwater. You'll know the name. He was an ex-policeman called the Ice Cream Man. I've got a forensic team down there now checking out the gravesite.'

Harold looked at the line of trees and scrub bordering the creek.

'I had my first fuck down there,' he said. 'I was fifteen. She came out here one year with her father, he was working on the property as a fencer. He was a bastard to her. He used to say he was stuck with her because no one else wanted her. She asked me to meet her down there one night, then she turned up with a blanket. After that, I saw her every night until they went away. I guess she wanted a bit of comfort. I liked her, she was nice. I still think about her sometimes. Hope she's okay.'

Harrigan sipped the bitter drink Harold had given him and said nothing.

'You see the way the creek winds?' Harold continued. 'It's like a snake. A dry snake. When it rains, that creek will fill up and it'll flood the roads. That water will get channelled through this country for miles. It's a stupid place to bury someone because one day they'll get washed away. If it ever rains again.'

'It will,' Harrigan said.

'I don't believe that. Not any more. You see the red gums down there? They're big trees, they've been here for a long time. They're dying now, there's so little water.' He put down his mug. 'I guess you're not staying for dinner. Ambro's cooking.'

'I've got to be back in the city tonight.'

There was silence.

'Are you going to be okay out here?' Harrigan said.

Harold sat for a few moments, smoking.

'Yeah, I think I will now. Ambro's here with her kids. That'll make a difference. This is where I live. I don't want to be anywhere else, even when it's like this.'

'I owe you for last night, Harry. If it hadn't been for you, everyone here would be dead and I could have ended up using the same grave as the man in the creek. If you ever need any help, you call me.'

'Call it even, mate. How are you travelling?'

'I'm getting the afternoon plane from Wagga. My lift should be here soon.'

Harold looked at his watch. 'You'd better hurry, mate. It's an hour's drive.'

'Boss.' One of Trevor's people sent down from the city appeared in the doorway, his mobile in his hand. 'I've got an urgent call here from Trevor. Can you take it now?'

'Why didn't he ring me on my phone?'

'I was already talking to him.'

Harrigan took the phone and walked to the end of the veranda.

'Trev. What is it?' he asked.

'Boss, I've got some bad news for you.'

'Has something happened to Grace?'

'No, she's fine as far as I know. In fact, she rang me a while ago. Wanted to know how you were. I told her you'd had a brush with death but you were okay.'

Fuck, Harrigan thought, remembering that he hadn't returned her call.

'It's something else. Your son. I've got a report here of a kidnapping from Cotswold House, forty-five minutes ago.'

'I told you to put a guard on that place!'

'I did, mate,' Trevor said. 'Hear me out. I've got details of Susie Pavic and Tim Masson suffering from concussion and bruising. They were both knocked out, locked in an office, and your son was snatched. They're on their way to RPA, if they're not already there. Masson is serious but none of the injuries are life-threatening. I'm putting a task force into action now. We're pulling out all the stops.'

'Why wasn't there a guard on Cotswold?'

'There was until eleven o'clock today, boss. Marvin found out I'd organised it behind his back. He rescinded the order and didn't tell me. When I found out, I rang him and asked what he was up to. He ripped into me like you wouldn't believe and hauled me in front of the commissioner who told me off for insubordination.'

'Why the fuck didn't they ring me? Why didn't you?'

'Marvin told God that you were hypersensitive about your son and the best thing to do was not to run it past you because you'd just be unreasonable. Meanwhile, there was no need to waste resources. I just got out of that meeting, boss. My ears are still ringing. I was about to call you when Colin rang me instead.'

Harrigan's mind was so filled with white fury he couldn't speak.

'I'm on my way back,' he said at last. 'I'm leaving now.'

He cut the connection and handed the phone back.

'Are you okay, boss?'

'Is my lift ready? I've got to go now.'

'I'll check.'

'What's up?' Harold asked.

'It's my son. He's the latest collateral damage. He's not dead, someone's got him. I've got to leave.'

'Mate, come with me. Whatever's happened, you have to take these with you.'

In the living room, Harold handed Harrigan a soft package, carefully wrapped. 'It's the crop specimens. Someone has to test them out.'

'Okay, Harry, I'll take them. I've got to leave now. I'll see you.'

His car was waiting for him at the back gate. He told the driver to get him to the airport in time for the afternoon flight, no matter what. They sped down the track, leaving a trail of red dust. The terrain out here was as wide as the sea. You either connected to its huge, open distances or the loneliness crushed you.

I have my own tattoos, Harrigan thought. Unlike Harry, his were on the inside. Experience had cut scars into his mind, into the underside of his skin. Marks as permanent as the colours Ambro had fixed onto his old friend's body. Harrigan's invisible markings made up who he was; Harold's showed him to be a part of this stretch of red ground forever. Implicitly, they understood this about each other. It was why they could trust each other. The way Harrigan trusted Grace. The way he hoped she trusted him.

Whatever trust there was between them, they would need it all. He wouldn't have the time to see her when he got back. He wouldn't even be able to tell her when he might have the time. The only question on his mind was where was Toby? The world had changed these last twenty-four hours. He had a murderer and an abductor to go after, even if she'd never pulled a trigger in her life, even if she hired other people to do her dirty work for her. *I have been threatened with abduction and murder all my life*, Elena Calvo had told him, fishing for his sympathy and loyalty. She'd had no qualms about inflicting these fates on other people. There was no way she would walk away from this. The thought gave him no relief. They drove on through the dry landscape.

20

A car was waiting for Harrigan at Sydney airport and he drove straight to police headquarters. Arriving at the incident room, he found it closed up and apparently empty. He tried the door but it was locked.

'Boss.' Frankie appeared in the corridor behind him. 'I heard you were in the building. We were told not to call you.'

'What's happening?'

'Marvin told us to stop what we were doing and get out of there. Then he locked the door. We might be being replaced, every one of us.'

'Why?'

'The contract's been stolen from the evidence room. We had a forensic scientist coming in tomorrow to have a look at it. When I went to check it, it was gone. Someone's stolen it, they must have done. When Trev reported it to Marvin, he came down and stuck the knife into him and then locked us out.'

'Where's Trev now?'

'He's in the commissioner's office with Marvin, probably being sacked.'

'Where's the rest of the team?'

'We're all in the tea room. We were thinking about going to the pub,' Frankie said. 'We've got nothing else to do.'

'Like fuck you don't. You can get back inside this room and get back to work right now.'

'We don't have the key. It's in Marvin's pocket.'

'Then use your initiative. Don't you have some manpower? Break the door down if you have to.'

Frankie laughed. 'Okay, boss. Whatever you say.'

Without another word, Harrigan headed for the commissioner's office.

He startled Chloe at her desk. It was a fitting name for a woman who was always as chillingly stylish as a spun-steel mannequin.

'I understand the commissioner is interviewing Inspector Gabriel at this moment. Given that he's my officer, I'd like to be present.'

'Both Inspector Gabriel and the special assistant commissioner are in there with the commissioner now. I don't know if they want to be disturbed.' She hesitated. 'I'll buzz them.'

Immediately she had, Marvin came outside, blocking the door to the commissioner's office. Harrigan looked past him. The commissioner stood behind his desk, Trevor in front of it, both confronting each other, both clearly angry. Marvin shut the door quickly. Harrigan saw him take in the marks on his face.

'There's no need for you to be here,' he said. 'This is under control.'

Harrigan looked at Chloe. She got to her feet and walked out of the room. Harrigan was still carrying the small photograph Freeman had given Grace on Bondi beach. The second Chloe was gone, he took it out of his wallet and pushed it under Marvin's nose. Marvin looked but didn't touch it. His face went blank. Harrigan spoke softly.

'How's your boy? Is he still this photogenic? Want me to show this to the commissioner now and to hell with the consequences?' There was silence. 'You're inviting me in. When I'm in there, mate, you will back off.'

'Put that picture away first,' Marvin replied in an oddly detached tone.

Harrigan did. Marvin opened the door. Harrigan brushed past him and walked in first.

'Commander Harrigan wants to join us. I agreed it was the best course of action,' Marvin called after him.

'Why? What does he have to say that I need to hear?' The commissioner's voice was sharp and loud with anger. 'I want to know why within days of Senator Edwards telling me we have corrupt police

222

on my watch, there's a security breach of this order. Is your inspector trustworthy? Is any member of his team trustworthy? The answer appears to be no.'

'Commissioner, would you listen to me?' Trevor was barely controlling himself. 'I'm not responsible for the loss of that contract. I will vouch that no member of my team is responsible. We have no knowledge of how it was stolen. You shouldn't be accusing us like this. We should be starting an inquiry.'

'*Quiet!*' the commissioner roared.

There was silence. Harrigan could feel Marvin breathing down his neck. The commissioner sat down.

'As Marvin has said to me on more than one occasion, even if your word is reliable, it's unlikely to carry any weight in the media. The nature of your private life would ensure that.'

'What did you say?'

'Marvin?'

'I'm only speaking realistically.' Marvin's voice was smooth, the way it usually was. 'I've heard it said repeatedly that Inspector Gabriel's personal lifestyle has the potential to embarrass the image of the service. Not because anyone here necessarily disapproves of who he lives with, but because of how it will be perceived by the general public. If there are compromised officers in this service who were linked to Cassatt, and if that fact comes out in the media, then the press will focus on the weakest link we have, and in this case that means Inspector Gabriel. We may think we don't have an issue to be concerned with, but the media won't agree with us. Talkback radio certainly won't. As regrettable as it is, the general prejudice is still against him. We'll be slaughtered in the court of public opinion.'

'I don't believe this,' Trevor said, almost softly. 'I just don't believe it. It's crap.'

'Unfortunately it's not,' the commissioner said angrily. 'Whatever you choose to say, there are still many people in the general public who view your lifestyle with aversion and may question why we put you in charge of an investigation of this significance, particularly if it proves to be compromised. There will be the suggestion that you were susceptible to blackmail.'

'Commissioner, that's garbage.'

'It's a matter of perception. We cannot afford the perception,' the commissioner as good as yelled. 'I don't intend to be hounded out of this job by shock jocks.'

Harrigan could almost admire Marvin's strategy. There was no better way to sool the commissioner onto someone than by appealing to that all too easily aroused paranoia. He moved forward.

'There are two things I want to say, Commissioner. While we're standing here gasbagging, the investigation is at a standstill and my son could be dead or dying somewhere.'

'Putting that search in place was Inspector Gabriel's responsibility,' Marvin countered.

'He can't do it while he's here, can he?' Harrigan snapped, not bothering to hide his anger. 'Commissioner, you're just about to put your head in the noose. Do you really want to do that?'

'I am in control here!'

'The public won't think so once you go through with this. Neither will our political masters. You're about to remove a team of people the minister has expressed confidence in. When he finds out you've sacked the whole team, he'll want to know why. Whatever we tell him, he'll raise all hell and he won't be shy about going to the media. He'll talk about his dead son and there'll be a huge response. Then you'll have to face explaining why you did this. What are you going to tell our own minister in the state government? You sacked the whole team because the New South Wales Police Service doesn't have a secure evidence room? How do you think that will play in the media? What if we have another security breach? Who do we blame then? Do we replace the next group of people? People will say we're running around like chickens with their heads cut off. They'll laugh at you.'

The commissioner was rocked by this. His face was a mixture of fury and fear. They waited for him to speak. He rubbed his mouth.

'The minister could do that,' he said bitterly. 'He could raise all hell. It could seem that we're out of control.' Suddenly he snapped at Marvin. 'I'm surprised you didn't think of these ramifications. That's what you're supposed to do. Why did this have to happen? This whole thing is a can of worms.'

'Commissioner, we need the continuity.' Harrigan pressed on, hiding desperation. 'It's the best way to keep this whole incident under control.'

'But if it wasn't a member of the team, who was it? Who else had access?' the commissioner asked furiously.

'If you want to start at the top, what about Marvin here. You have access, don't you, Marvin?'

Marvin laughed sourly. 'I had nothing to do with this.'

'Don't you want to play fair, mate? Isn't everyone under suspicion? Why shouldn't that include you? Maybe while we're here, we should be asking questions about the special assistant commissioner's competence. I direct Trevor to put a guard on my son. Marvin rescinds the order without notice and look at the result! Does that look like good policing? How many extra resources do we have to expend now because of his actions?'

Marvin jerked backwards, his face red. 'That's a complete distortion —'

'Could we have quiet, please?' the commissioner ordered. 'The commander has made his point. Inspector Gabriel and his team will remain in control of the investigation for the time being. I will instigate an Internal Affairs investigation. Everyone on the team will cooperate with them.'

'There's no need, Commissioner,' Marvin said. 'I can liaise with IA for you.'

'No, Marvin. I want to control this directly. This meeting is finished.'

Trevor interrupted them. 'Since you've all been talking about me, am I allowed to say something?'

In the silence, the commissioner signalled for him to go ahead. Harrigan held his breath.

'I've been a copper for twenty-one years. I've received commendations and a bravery medal. You will not find one single fact about me anywhere that could embarrass anyone or that's remotely bent.'

The commissioner stared at him, his thoughts unreadable.

'I've already said we are maintaining arrangements as they are,' he replied, apparently unmoved. 'Now everyone can get back to work.'

Trevor walked out of the office immediately.

'Commissioner,' Marvin said, 'if I could just have a word in private.'

'I don't have time now, Marvin. Why don't you make an appointment with Chloe? Before you go, Paul. I hope you left a few marks of your own on that other man's face.'

'I did my best, Commissioner.'

'You can also tell me why you think this kidnapping has happened.'

'It's either a matter of revenge because of what happened at Yaralla, or this individual wants to put pressure on the investigation in some way.'

'We don't know, in other words,' the Commissioner said.

'At this stage, anything we decide on is only supposition.'

'Then Marvin isn't completely at fault for not seeing a risk and acting as he did. That's all. Thank you.'

Stung, Harrigan turned away. They walked out in silence. Marvin glared angrily at Chloe but she made a point of not seeing him. He didn't stop to arrange another meeting. Outside, the corridor was empty. Trevor had already disappeared, presumably down the fire stairs.

'Come into my office,' Marvin said quietly, almost in Harrigan's ear. 'There's something I want you to listen to.'

Marvin's office was just along the hallway. Like the commissioner's, it had a view. They walked past Marvin's personal assistant, a loyal, middle-aged woman called Sharon, without speaking to her. She watched them with a puzzled expression on her face. Inside, Marvin sat down without speaking. Harrigan pulled up a chair without being asked. Marvin put a cassette player on his desk and hit the Play button.

'*Paul. It's Marvin here. How are you tonight?*'

'*I'm fine, Marvin. To what do I owe the pleasure?*'

'*It's business. You were at Jerry Freeman's house today. You and your companion, as I believe she's called. Freeman's murder will affect the entire Pittwater investigation.*'

Marvin hit the Stop button.

'I have that whole conversation recorded, including where you say you have a tape and photographs. Do you think you're the only person who thinks things through, Harrigan? I didn't get to where I am today in this organisation without knowing how to protect myself. If you take me or my son down, you're coming with us.'

Harrigan stared at Marvin. Any number of possible rejoinders were in his head. Haven't you already taken my son down by collaborating in his abduction? You stole that contract on orders, didn't you? You'll never be the police commissioner. Perhaps his stare and the silence were more disturbing than he realised. Marvin was forced to look away. Harrigan got to his feet and leaned across Marvin's desk, face to face. He spoke with an anger all the more powerful for being controlled.

'What can you tell me about the whereabouts of my son?'

'That had nothing to do with me!'

'What can you tell me?'

'Nothing! I have no information at all! None! You can believe that!' Marvin was shouting now.

'If you step out of line again the way you did today, we'll both be clearing our desks. If my son isn't found in one piece, then you are going to pay for it with your skin. I fucking mean that, mate.'

'You have no business threatening me, Harrigan.'

'You just remember what I said. If my son doesn't come home in one piece, you pay. You pay in spades.'

He walked to the door. For some reason, he stopped and looked back. Marvin was staring after him, his expression a mixture of calculation and a curious blank-eyed look. Harrigan walked out, shutting the door behind him with a sharp click. His back felt the imprint of an invisible knife.

The main door to the incident room was propped against the wall and the door frame was splintered. There was a buzz of subdued busyness; people were settling back to their desks. Trevor was in his office, just hanging up from a phone call. Harrigan walked in to be met by a furious glare.

'How are you?' he asked.

'How am I? I'm just fucking fine. I've just had the special assistant commissioner tell me I'm an embarrassment to the service while the rest of you stand around and fucking patronise me like I'm not there. And that fucking includes you, thank you very much, boss!'

Trevor leaned across his desk, stabbing a finger at Harrigan while he shouted. Outside, silence fell like a guillotine. Harrigan shut the door immediately.

'Do you know what colour your face is right now?' he said. 'Do you want to take a pill?'

'Jesus!' Trevor said softly.

He poured himself a glass of water and with shaking hands took a tablet.

'You know what you're doing?' Harrigan went on. 'Exactly what Marvin wants. If you let him get to you, you'll be taken out of here on a stretcher. Don't let him do it to you.'

'I'm one of those boofheads who's honest,' Trevor said, when he was calmer. 'It means fuck all to God.'

'God's paranoid. Spook him and he won't care who he walks over to protect his backside. At the moment, his paranoia is working for us. We've got to keep it that way. Now forget all that crap. What are you doing about Toby?'

'Give God his due, as soon as he heard, he said forget the money. Just get the personnel out there. I've got a team at Cotswold, we're canvassing and searching the district, and I've sent out a state-wide alert. We're checking all stolen vehicles for a possible lead. As soon we've got something to guide us, we'll hone the search in that direction. Why do you reckon this man is the kidnapper?' Trevor passed Ambrosine's sketch of the gunman across his desk to Harrigan.

'My guess is he's the same man who shot Freeman,' Harrigan said. 'He's a South African. Grace said the gunman had a South African accent. He's a small man as well.'

'We've sent his picture out everywhere as a person of interest. If anyone sees him, we'll hear. But why has he got your boy, boss?'

'I think it's to do with this.' Harrigan put his LPS badge on Trevor's desk. 'I was given that when I saw Elena Calvo. It gives you access to the building at Campbelltown. I think they tracked me to Yaralla using that. I want you to get it checked out.'

'No worries. She's a player, you say.'

'Up to her neck. We need to talk to the minister again. Grace went to the LPS launch for me. Edwards spoke to her there and established a connection between LPS and Beck. We need to interview him about it.'

'He's been on to us, boss. His adviser rang the commissioner this morning requesting a meeting,' Trevor replied. 'That's just been confirmed as happening tomorrow afternoon around four if you're available.'

'I'll be there. Who's invited?'

'I know you and me are supposed to be there, but I haven't been told who else is coming. Apparently, Edwards has beefed up his personal security since the launch. I think Gracie must have told him to do that. All well and good. She's a professional. But why snatch your boy? You still haven't told me that.'

'I think the gunman's working for Calvo and this is her way of putting pressure on the police investigation.'

Trevor glanced at the door.

'Did she offer you something the other day, mate?' he asked.

'Money and a job. I said no. She's playing for keeps. Whatever Beck was up to, she's implicated in it.'

'Are you saying we have a working scenario?' Trevor asked. 'Calvo has Beck removed to protect herself, then tries to get you onside to cruel the investigation. It's a possible fit. Do you want to make a statement?'

'It's my word against hers. It'd be difficult to sustain in a courtroom. Which brings us to the contract. What happened to it?'

'Fucked if I know,' Trevor said. 'Frankie went to check it and it wasn't there. I don't even know how long it's been gone. That's one line of inquiry stone dead. Assuming I ever get to run this investigation properly with all these fucking firefights.'

Harrigan thought of taking Freeman's photograph out of his wallet and sharing the story with Trevor. He chose not to.

'Calvo's reached in here to get her hands on it,' he said. 'She's bought someone.'

'Would she know who to ask?'

'Beck knew the right people. If he and Calvo are connected in some way, why shouldn't that information have made it back to her, or at least to her dirty tricks man? But if she did have Beck killed to hide what he was doing, why leave the contract behind? Why publicise the killings on the net? Unless she wanted to scare other people off.'

'Maybe leaving the contract behind was an oversight,' Trevor said. 'The killer could have been rushing to finish. Maybe he thought he had both contracts and then realised he only had one.'

'I'm not convinced by that. It was too much of a setup. But either way, Elena Calvo is still a player in this. Right now I need to see the scene where Toby was snatched.'

'I'll ring the sergeant in charge and tell him you're on your way. As soon as we hear anything, I'll be on the phone to you. What do you think he'll want?'

'I can't know that till he contacts me,' Harrigan said. 'Maybe he doesn't want anything. Maybe he just wants to put me through hell.'

'It's a lot of trouble to go to just for that, boss. We need to organise taps on your phones and a watch on your internet connections. If anyone does contact you, we'll be listening.'

'Leave my personal mobile alone,' Harrigan said. 'He can't know that number. He'll ring on my work phone. Watch that.'

'If that's what you want. Do I post people to sit with you while you wait?'

'No,' Harrigan said. 'I don't know when he'll call. Have people standing by. We can make arrangements quickly enough if they're ready to go.'

'Boss, I haven't thanked you for what you did up there in the commissioner's office. I know I shouted at you but I appreciate you putting your neck out and I owe you. But I've got a question to ask you. Gracie at Freeman's house the other day. What was that really about?'

'Mate, I'm going to have to ask you to trust me,' Harrigan said.

'Then tell me something. What does it mean for this investigation? Is it compromised? Is the shit going to hit the fan and take us with it?'

'No. This investigation's on track and it's going to stay there.'

'Are you playing me for a fool?' Trevor asked quietly.

The only fool in this is me, Harrigan thought. Fool and liar.

'That's the last thing I'd do,' he said. 'In this case, the buck stops with me.'

'I'll take you at your word. There's one more thing you should know. Gracie. I know Toby's on your mind more than anything, but if you get the chance, I'd pick up the phone if I were you. I rang to tell her about Toby and she didn't sound too happy. I think she's waiting for you to tell her you want to talk to her. I don't know if you want to be a single man again. You might want to think about it.'

Grace and Trevor had been old friends; a friendship that had slipped a little since she had been seeing Harrigan. Trevor would have picked up the vibe.

'I'll call her.'

Before Harrigan could get to his feet, there was a knock on the door. Chloe stood there, Harrigan's briefcase in her hand.

'I've brought this down for you,' she said. 'You left it upstairs.'

Harrigan realised with a shock that he had forgotten about and then almost lost one of the keys to the investigation. The crop specimens Harold had packed for him were in his briefcase.

'Thanks, Chloe. Where was it?'

'Next to my desk. Don't worry,' she said, giving him sharp look, 'no one's touched it but me.'

She was gone.

'You had things on your mind, boss,' Trevor said.

'We all did. I'll see you, mate.'

Down in his car, Harrigan spun the combination on his briefcase and opened it. The parcel hadn't been touched. He locked the briefcase again and sat there weighing the options. With Marvin still in place, it was too dangerous to give these to Trevor. The evidence room wasn't secure; that had already been proved. But if he kept them, the chain of evidence was compromised. Better for them to go where they could be accounted for. Harrigan had dealt with any number of forensic laboratories in his career. The name of one, Millennium Forensic Technologies, discreet and professional, was already in his mind. Tomorrow he would see them and start to find out what the fuss was about. First, he had his son to think about.

21

Harrigan arrived at the familiar grounds of Cotswold House at a time when the residents were usually asleep. Tonight, all the lights were on. The sergeant was there to meet him and take him through what had happened. A white van had arrived in the car park during the mid-afternoon. The driver had been wearing a hat and sunglasses. No one had got a clear view of his face. A little later, one of the residents had seen Tim wheeling Toby through to the car park. There had been a smallish man with Tim, walking very close to him. Toby's head was slumped forward but he sometimes did sit that way in his chair. The resident had thought that Toby was going on an excursion and Tim was wheeling him out to the house van.

Harrigan looked into Susie's office. The chairs were knocked over, Susie's loved pot plants had been upended on the floor and the phone torn out.

Toby's rooms were empty. All they had to offer was his absence. Harrigan walked into a space he'd visited as often as he could these last ten years or so. It was the carefully designed cradle that had kept Toby functioning and allowed his mind the chance to work effectively. Cramped in his body and in this room, working through his computer and his imagination, Toby's mind had ranged over infinite space. But he was fragile. His body did not withstand extremes of temperature; he had difficulty eating and drinking and he needed medications. Had he been left in a locked van in the sun all day? Was he even still alive? How could Harrigan know?

He brought these thoughts to a stop purely for self-preservation. As soon as he'd finished at Cotswold House, he went to Royal Prince Alfred Hospital. Tim was still unconscious, his face pale. Although not life-threatening, his injury was serious. Susie was sedated. Her face was badly bruised, her eye black and her lip cut. Harrigan walked away. Out in his car, he rang Trevor.

'Anything to guide us yet?' he asked.

'No, boss. You'll be the first to hear. Maybe you should get some sleep.'

How was he going to sleep? He drove home to his empty house. By now, it was late. He had half-hoped Grace would be there but why should she be? He hadn't called her and she didn't know where he was or what he was doing. Why would she wait for him in an empty house?

On the way home, he checked his post office box where there was nothing but the usual collections of official and junk mail. At his house, he checked his mailbox. A small parcel was inside. Once in the house, he opened it to find a mobile phone.

The house had a cool, silent emptiness, which for a few seconds felt almost comforting, a feeling that dissipated almost as quickly. Harrigan had no appetite and poured himself a whisky. In his study, he saw on his desk an envelope addressed to him in Grace's handwriting. His heart dipped but it was no 'Dear John' letter, instead a report on the launch which, on reading, proved to be as good, if not better, than any he could have received from his own people. Her writing was clear, easy to read. He thought of her in the dead hours smoking endless cigarettes and making these notes and then later waiting for a phone call that never came. I was busy. I was exhausted. I told you that if you didn't hear anything, that was good. Points of view which were mutually exclusive. Maybe for her it had been the final straw.

He opened his briefcase and took out the drawing Ambrosine had made of him. I'm not as cold as that. I feel everything. It wasn't what was inside but how others saw you. Few people got under that skin of his. Those who did, he often drove away. He picked up his personal mobile and rang Grace. When she answered, he heard loud music and laughter in the background.

'It's me,' he said. 'Where are you?'

There was a pause.

'I'm out with the girls,' she said, a catch in her voice. 'We're at a party.'

Grace's female friends were lawyers, high-flyers with astronomical incomes. In certain circles they were famous for their hard partying; gossip he had never enquired into too deeply in case he heard something about Grace he didn't want to know.

'Can you talk?' he asked.

'Sure.' The background became quieter. 'What is it?'

There was a touch of distance in her voice.

'I'm sorry I didn't call you. I got what you wrote and it's been acted on. We're talking to Edwards tomorrow.'

She didn't reply.

'Are you there?'

'I'm still here. Where are you?'

'At home. I'm waiting for a call to tell me what they want in exchange for Toby.'

'Do you think it's the same man who shot at me and tried to kill you?'

'I'm sure of it. He's Elena Calvo's dirty tricks man.'

'At the launch, she said to me the next time I saw you I should give you her regards. All the time she seemed to be really saying, you'll never see him again.'

'I didn't ring you. I was weighed down. I'm sorry.'

'That's how you live. You're always weighed down. You take everything on.'

He almost said: who else is going to?

'You don't have to do that. There's no need for you to be responsible for everything and everyone,' she went on, as if she had heard his thoughts.

'I'd ask if you wanted to come around, but I'm in one of those places you say doesn't have any light or air,' he said. 'I wouldn't be able to talk to you and it's not a good place for anyone else to be. I just wanted to say I was thinking about you.'

There was a pause. She didn't ask what he was going to do when someone did call. She was too discreet for that, and she knew the answer already.

'When do we see each other?'

'Soon,' he said. 'Trust me.'

'You always ask people to trust you. I'll see you.'

When he reached Birchgrove, his exhaustion was so profound he was able to sleep. Very late in the morning, he woke and went to check his email and his answering machine. There was nothing. The day stretched forward like an empty space. He realised he was frozen at the heart, in the grip of the black dog that prevented him from speaking to people outside of the necessities. He couldn't even pick up the phone to call Grace; he didn't know how to frame the words. If he tried to speak to her, he wouldn't be able to breathe.

Later on that day, he drove to Millennium Forensic Laboratories where he asked to speak confidentially to the head scientist who was also the owner: a man in his forties who had grown tired of waiting for promotion in the forensic laboratories of the police force.

In the quiet sterility of the laboratory, the scientist, his hands gloved, laid out on the benchtop the crop specimens Harrigan had given him. They became hothouse plants, espaliered on a device stretching out their facets for display.

'Do I really need gloves to handle these?' the scientist asked.

'For the tobacco you do,' Harrigan replied. 'A friend of mine sustained a significant injury handling that tobacco.'

'They look so ordinary. These must be among the most widely grown crops in the world.'

Harrigan considered what these pieces of plant matter were worth, one way or another: the Pittwater killings, Freeman's and Cassatt's murders, his son's abduction, the cost of bulldozing into the ground what had once been a huge investment of money.

'My information is they're anything but ordinary. What I want you to tell me is what's different about them,' he said.

'Can you tell me the source of the specimens?'

'I can't give you that information, I'm sorry,' Harrigan said.

'Have they been genetically modified?'

'Almost certainly.'

'Is there any specification, any research information, about these crops available from any source?'

'I'm afraid not. That's one reason I want a full analysis of their properties.'

'Are these the only specimens available?'

Ever cautious, Harrigan had kept back a portion of each of the plants.

'Yes,' he said.

'If we destroy them, then they're gone.'

'I don't want you to destroy them,' Harrigan said. 'I need to know enough about them to possibly track the owners of the intellectual property and the patents.'

'That is possible, I suppose, although it's a very complex job. An analysis like that won't be quick.'

The sound of the traffic outside was muted through the tinted, double-glazed windows. Millennium Forensic Technologies was in Alexandria, in a plain, grey-green building that had once been a factory for manufacturing cardboard boxes. The scientist was tapping his pen on a notepad on the bench. He knew Harrigan well; had done work for him often enough before.

'Are we going to be in danger doing this work?' he asked.

'You will be if it's known you have these specimens.'

'Who's going to be paying for this?'

'The police service. I want you to send the invoices directly to me. I guarantee you'll be paid.'

'And contact you personally when the results are in?'

'Yes.'

'All right,' the scientist said after some moments. 'I'll take control of this job myself. Is there any backup in case someone does come knocking on my door?'

Harrigan handed over his card. 'I'm contactable day and night if there are any issues, problems, anything.'

'If there are, I'll call.'

Harrigan left to go to his meeting with the minister, pleased that he had something else to occupy his mind. Otherwise caught on this rack, he would have gone mad. Mechanical speech and everyday actions were all that was possible. Everything else was closed down. Like Edwards, he thought, briefly caught with the irony of it all.

22

When, in the morning, the phone rang next to Grace's bed, she hoped it was Harrigan. Instead, the whispered voice was one she had first heard only a few days ago.

'Grace,' Daniel Brinsmead said. 'I hope I'm not disturbing you.'

'No,' she said, sitting up in bed and glancing at the clock. It was 11 a.m. 'How are you?'

'I wondered if you had any spare time this afternoon. I wanted to talk to you about something.'

'What?'

'The police have released a sketch to the media, someone who's implicated in kidnapping the commander's son. I'm ringing you because I know him.'

'You should call the police and talk to them,' Grace said. 'If you know where to find him, you have to tell them that immediately.'

'I haven't seen him for a number of years. I have a history relating to him. He's responsible for the way I look now. This is more about my past than your companion's son.'

'You should still talk to the police.'

'I would talk to the commander, but he must have other things on his mind right now and I wondered if you might be prepared to be a bridge between us. This is a personal story. Would you be prepared to come and see me? I don't usually go out except to go to work so that means coming to where I live. It's close to the city. I promise you, you'll be completely safe. I'm not in a position to hurt a fly.'

When the phone rang, Grace had been lying in bed thinking that what she most wanted was for Harrigan to be here with her and for them to make love. The way things were, maybe they never would again. She thought of the gun in her bottom drawer and then tried to think why Daniel Brinsmead might mean her harm. What reason could he have? She was in a mood to walk out on that tightrope once again. It would make her feel better.

'If it's important, I can come and talk to you.'

'I think it is,' he said. 'I should warn you, I'm not much of a housekeeper. But I can make us some coffee.'

'It'll be fine. We can just talk. When?'

'Early afternoon. I'll give you the address.'

Grace's taxi dropped her outside an older-style apartment building up on the hill overlooking Rushcutters Bay Park. The entrance was a wooden-framed double glass door next to a bank of mailboxes. She buzzed the intercom and waited.

'Grace?'

'Yes, I'm downstairs.'

'I'm in the penthouse. I'll buzz you in.'

An old lift hauled her up slowly to the roof. On stepping out of the iron cage, the view was spectacular. The penthouse took up the western side of the top floor and looked across the harbour in the direction of the heads. Grace stopped to look over the railings at the park below. Crowds of tiny people covered the grass on the summer's day. Around them, the city was spread out as an interwoven and chaotic pattern. To the west and the north, high-rises studded the foreshore. The harbour glittered, the Rushcutters Bay marina was packed with pleasure craft.

Close by was a rooftop swimming pool, emptied out by the city's water restrictions in the continuing drought. Dead pot plants lined the pool's fence and the gate was locked with a closed sign hung on it. She walked past it to reach the penthouse's front door. Despite the spectacular view and the bright sunlight, all its curtains were drawn. It was some moments after she had rung the bell that Daniel

Brinsmead opened the door. The sight of his face still had the power to shock.

'Hi,' she said.

'Grace. Thanks for coming. I'm afraid the place is a mess and it's dark as well. I have difficulty with the light. Believe me, I'm not trying to frighten you.'

'You're not.'

Even if he had, her gun was within reach in her shoulder bag. Dressed as he was in a white shirt and trousers, there seemed to be no place where he could have concealed a weapon. Through the light fabric she could see that his torso and the full length of his left arm were covered in dressings. At the hem of his trousers, the bandages from another dressing on his left leg were also visible.

She walked inside. He shut the front door behind her but left it on the latch; she could walk out any time she wanted to. His feet were covered with white ankle socks, which also had a medical look, and he moved awkwardly. A short entranceway took them through to a spacious lounge room that was partially lit by a standard lamp casting a soft light. A high bar stood between this room and a kitchen where the blinds were also drawn and a dull overhead light was on. No one had cleaned up from the last meal and the dishes were piled beside the sink despite there being a dishwasher. To her left, the lounge opened onto a hallway, again partially dark. She saw a row of three closed doors, with a fourth at the end of the hall facing towards the lounge. The apartment was silent. The air was cool, almost chill.

'I keep the air conditioning up very high, I find it more comfortable that way,' he said. 'I hope it's not too cold. Please sit down. Would you like a drink? Tea? A soft drink?'

'No, I'm fine, thanks.'

She sat in a damask armchair, taking it for its proximity to the entranceway and the front door. The penthouse had the look of a place that was no one's home. Sometime ago it had been furnished for hire with an expensive if impersonal veneer, now grubby with use. Used cups and old newspapers had been left lying on any spare surface, including the floor. On the sofa was a pile of car magazines. A stained and empty wine glass and a mobile phone stood on the coffee table. An unfinished game of two-pack patience was laid out on a nearby table. Brinsmead sat on the sofa beside the car magazines, pushing them out of his way.

'This must look bad,' he said. 'I seem to have reached a point in my life where nothing that's external to me matters. I have a carer who comes in and dresses my left side. She does that in the bathroom and makes sure it's clean. But outside of that, I don't seem to care. Unfortunately I'm in pain a lot of the time. The question is whether it's bearable or not.'

'It's very impressive that you should be running the LPS signature project under those circumstances.'

'Running that project doesn't weigh me down as you might think it could. The opposite: it helps. I have to occupy my mind.'

'I read in your résumé you were in the army once. So was my father. He was a professional soldier. A brigadier.'

'I was at Sandhurst. I didn't last that long. I was very young and realised I wasn't cut out for it. I had the idea that I was going to save the world. The army wasn't the right place for that, I found out. Also I was very bad at taking orders. I went back to science. I have a doctorate from Durham University. I've worked in research institutes most of my working life, mainly in London.'

'Very successfully,' Grace said. 'You said you knew the man who may have abducted Toby Harrigan. What can you tell me about him?'

'Andreas du Plessis. Yes, I do know him.'

'If you know his name, you should call the police.'

'He won't be using that name here. He'll be using false papers. I don't know what his present name will be or where he can be found. If I did, I would have called the police straightaway. It's more likely they'll find him using the drawing they have. It's a very good likeness.'

'How do you know him?'

Brinsmead seemed to smile in that ruined face. 'I'm going to have to destroy all the good impressions you have of me,' he said. 'I'm not a good man. I'm a very flawed man. But before I do, do you want to tell me something about yourself? What you do, for example?'

She laughed a little. 'There isn't much to tell. I have a dull job.'

'I find that hard to believe.'

'I'm a public servant with the Attorney-General's Department. I collate reports for the minister. It's not very interesting.'

This description, as far as it went, was true. The reports were classified as top secret and dealt with issues of terrorism, gun running and terrorist financing but they were still reports. Grace worked mainly in intelligence analysis but also occasionally in the field on surveillance. It was nothing she could talk about, not even to Harrigan. If she had been asked why she did this work, she would have said it was to protect people.

'You went from policing to something that was completely a desk job?' Brinsmead said.

'A lot of policing is paperwork. I have a background in law and criminology. I worked for the police because I wanted to have some practical experience.'

'You make it sound very staid. But you don't look staid.'

'It's just work. I was a singer once, in another life,' she said. 'I can sing but I wasn't cut out to be a performer.'

'Why not?'

'You have to put yourself right out there when you perform and it's always in front of strangers. I didn't like doing that so I stopped.'

It was another simple sentence behind which lay a history of heartbreak and alcoholism and a worse memory: her old lover who, until recently, had stalked her; the man who had once raped her and given her the scar on her neck. She never spoke of these things, not even with her father and her brother, who were the only ones who knew the full story. She had hinted at the details with Harrigan but could go no further than that. She knew he had put at least some of the story together but had never tried to ask her any questions about it; she liked it that he hadn't.

'You wouldn't be prepared to sing a few bars for me, just so I have an idea what your voice is like?' Brinsmead said.

She laughed. 'No, I don't do that. Sorry.'

'Another time maybe. I should get on with why I asked you here. There's a fact we need to start with. I'm a gambler. It's a fundamental aspect of who I am. I still gamble, although I don't do it at the roulette table any more.'

'Why is it fundamental to you?'

'It's how I see the world working. In the end, all life comes down to whether or not you're holding the right cards. That's true even for

243

genetics. Someone has the gene for muscular dystrophy or Huntington's chorea. Do they deserve to? No, of course they don't, and who could make the judgement that they did? For each of us, it's pure chance. If that chance goes against you, you can live badly and die violently. I've seen the world this way ever since I was thirteen and nothing has changed my mind. I've always had to play the odds. Mainly because a few years ago, I didn't play the odds particularly well. I got involved with Jerome Beck and du Plessis. Or DP as he's known to his friends, so called.'

'How?'

'About five years ago, I was working in London at a science research facility. I met Jerome Beck there. He was a financial manager. I recognised him when I saw his picture on the net after he was murdered.'

'But you didn't tell the police,' Grace said.

'No, I didn't and you'll know why when I've finished this story. I found out Jerome liked to gamble as well. We started going to casinos together. He knew I was badly in debt and getting deeper. He said he could help me. He was involved in a business venture of some kind, building infrastructure in the Democratic Republic of the Congo. If I was interested, I could use my ex-army skills to manage the project and I'd be very well paid. I would only need to be away for a matter of weeks, it was a fly-in and fly-out affair. I think we both accepted implicitly that his offer was a cover for something else and I always assumed it would be criminal in some way. But, as always, I went to the DRC as a gamble. I decided to do that even after I'd researched the country and discovered how dangerous it was. I thought, if this is where the possibilities are, I'll follow them and see where we end up. God knows, I needed the money badly enough. What are you thinking?'

'I was wondering why you'd be so open about yourself with me,' Grace said. 'I can understand you telling this story to the police but not to someone you've only met once.'

'You used to be a police officer and you're well known for your connection to another senior police officer.'

'You've checked me out on the web.'

'Yes,' Brinsmead said. 'You see, I'm not talking to you as a complete stranger. I've tried to find out something about you. We spoke for a little while at the launch as well. What you've said today hasn't changed my impression of you. I think you listen to people and that you're reliable. You understand what people are saying to you.'

'I like to think my training has made it possible for me to do that,' she replied carefully.

Brinsmead leaned towards her. 'It's something you do naturally,' he said. 'At one level, I don't care who knows this story. To be honest, everything except the essentials has been burnt out of me. I can't see any reason why I shouldn't talk with complete honesty about almost anything, including myself. Do you know anything about the DRC?'

'I know it's in a state of civil war and there have been terrible atrocities there. I'm sure it's full of people who'd like to live ordinary lives but aren't given the chance,' she said. 'What was it like for you to be there?'

'Unimaginable. Not long after I got there, I realised I was involved with illegal diamond trading. I thought I could deal with that. Then I discovered I was the fall guy. I had no criminal history so I was going to be the mule. My problem was, there was no way out for me. The parts of the DRC we were in were very dangerous. The people I was with might have been vile but they were my protection. DP was one of them, he was the boss. *Baass*, the African mercenaries called him. It sounded almost like an insult. At one time, he and his mercenaries raped and killed a woman in front of my eyes. She was probably only twenty. Jerome didn't involve himself but he didn't care either. He laughed. "Let DP have his fun," he said.' Brinsmead stopped and closed his eyes. 'I shouldn't have told you that. I don't want to bring it back.'

Grace waited.

'The trouble is, there's no way I can bring this to the law,' he said eventually. 'I have no evidence against them other than my word. At the time I was a debt-ridden gambler. I have no real names for most of them — we didn't exchange email addresses and telephone numbers. DP was South African, you could tell that by his accent. He may have been in the army once. From the way they spoke to each other, he and Jerome were long-time partners. That's all I know about any of them.'

'How long were you there?'

'I was with them for eighteen days. A lifetime. I learned there are events so serious, the only people who know what they really mean are the dead. The ones in the mass graves. If I say to you, you can't know, that's not an insult to you. You're lucky you can't know. Every day in my mind I replay what I witnessed there. It's like being in hell.'

'You don't have to tell me any of this,' she said.

'Don't you want to hear it? I'm sorry. I've imposed on you very badly.'

'I can listen to what you're saying because that's what I'm trained to do,' Grace said. 'I've had to go in and deal with situations where people have been murdered. I can listen to you. But you have to live with bringing it back like this and then with knowing that you've told me that story. You may tell me something you wish you hadn't.'

'That last point is the least of my concerns. Our so-called expedition had a number of trucks. On the nineteenth day, I stole one and made a run for it. But the truck broke down and my colleagues caught up with me. I tried to take refuge in a building but they burned it to the ground around me. There were other people inside at the time. Somehow, I survived. I was the one who brought that death on those people and I was the only one who survived. A group of villagers found me barely alive. They took me to a local aid hospital, then to Kinshasa. Finally I was flown home to London.'

'That's a terrible story,' Grace said.

'What I can't get out of my mind is that I didn't die. There were other people who did die around me. I think about those people every day. I know some of their names and I repeat them every morning when I wake up. I tell them I haven't forgotten them. Yet, somehow, here I am with a new debt-free life and a first-class research project. What did I do to deserve that?'

'How did you get debt free?'

'I can thank Elena for that.'

'Elena Calvo?'

'Yes. She worked at the same institute in London as myself and Beck. I knew her quite well; we went out for a little while. She's a rich man's daughter. She picked me up, paid my medical costs, paid my debts and offered me this project as part of my rehabilitation.'

'That was very generous of her.'

'I think she was horrified by the way I looked. She'd never seen anything like that before.'

Brinsmead was silent, lost in his thoughts. He had spoken bitterly. Then, suddenly, he laughed. 'You see, in a number of ways I'm really already dead. I just keep breathing for some reason. What keeps me going is my work. Usually I don't focus on anything outside of that. Today has been different. Talking to you has made the difference. It's the first time in years I've felt a sense of being alive.'

'Should you rely on a chance encounter to feel something like that?'

'I'll take whatever's available,' he said.

Grace was about to ask another question when she became aware of a faint underlying odour in the chill of the room, a decayed animal smell. Once noticed, it was impossible to ignore. The light had sketched out the structure of Brinsmead's face. The covering of his features seemed thin, the bones too close to the surface. She suppressed a shiver. He was watching her.

'Am I frightening you? Either because of my face or anything I've said?' he asked.

'Maybe,' she replied.

'Don't be frightened. I can't imagine anyone I'd least like to hurt or see hurt than you.'

Bizarrely, this also had a chilling ring to it. From the kitchen came the sound of an alarm.

'That's a reminder for me to take some medication,' he said. 'Usually I don't need reminding. Excuse me.'

'Go ahead.'

In the kitchen, he poured himself a glass of water and swallowed tablets. Sitting down again, he leaned back, his eyes closed. He was in crippling pain, it was impossible for him to hide it.

'Is there anything I can do?' Grace asked.

'Yes,' he said. 'These tablets aren't going to be strong enough. I need an injection. Could you look in the fridge? There are some ampoules there and some syringes. If you could get one for me.'

She found them on the second shelf down, wrapped in thick, protective plastic.

'You'll need scissors to cut the package open,' he called. 'There's a junk drawer in the high bar, the top drawer. Look in there.'

Grace looked among the envelopes, twine and bills to find a pair of scissors and a key on a plastic keyring marked 'P'. A set of keys was already on the bench: Brinsmead's, she guessed. She took the key out of the drawer and dropped it in her pocket, then took out the scissors.

'I've found them,' she said.

'If you give everything to me, I'll put it together,' he said.

'I can do it for you. I know how to. I'm good at first aid.'

'I can inject myself.'

'I'll do it. You're in pain. Where do you usually have it?'

'Right arm,' Brinsmead said. 'Where did you learn first aid?'

'My father made me and my brother learn when we were young. He thought we should know. Then when I was with the police, I did a refresher course.'

She pushed up his sleeve. His undamaged arm had pale European skin, the blue veins close to the surface. He didn't seem to react when she touched him. Part way through administering the medication, she glanced up. He was watching her with those reflective blue eyes. They were so clear, it was as if they had rolled back onto empty space.

'I'm taking your likeness,' he said.

'You don't need to do that.'

When she'd finished, he rolled back his own sleeve. After a while, she could see the medication taking effect.

'If you're okay now, it's probably time for me to go.'

'Yes, probably it is, unfortunately,' he said. 'I have to go to work as well. It's a long way from here, out at Campbelltown. I have some test results due later on today. I want to be there to review them.'

'It's a long drive out there.'

'Too far for me, I can only manage short distances these days. I used to drive a lot, quite fast. I had one or two very nice sports cars. These days, I have a hire car with a driver. I'm one of their favourite customers. I have them booked, they're due quite soon.'

'Will you be going to the police?' Grace asked.

'I'll call them. Will they come to me?'

'I'm sure they will.'

'I'll call tomorrow. I have no information that will bring the commander's son home. Also, I have Elena to think about; I should discuss it with her first. It might not go down too well that her chief scientist has this particular history. Especially since she's just launched on the ASX. That launch has been very successful so far. The share price is doing well.'

'Do you think the corporation will be a success out here?'

'I'm sure it will,' Brinsmead replied. 'With Elena driving it, it'll be very successful indeed. She'll make sure that organisation works exactly the way she wants it to. When she says that one day it will be one of the best in the world, I'm sure she's right.'

'Is that good or bad?' Grace asked.

'I don't understand.'

'The way you spoke about it just then. It seems almost as if you wish it wasn't going to be that way.'

'Does it? That's unintentional. Elena's very skilled, very sharp. She's very much her father's daughter, continuing in his footsteps. He's a strange, possessive old man whose past has crippled him at every other level of his humanity except for the one that allows him to be a businessman. A little like me. I'm only able to do the work I do now. Nothing else is left.'

'I should go,' Grace said, getting to her feet.

'It's been my pleasure, Grace. I'll see you out.'

'You don't have to if you're still in pain.'

'No, it's better now. Those injections are powerful. Thanks for coming to see me.'

Once outside, she walked to the lift and glanced back. He was standing at the door, watching her. He waved, she waved back and then she was in the slow elevator, going down. As soon as Daniel Brinsmead was out of sight, she took a deep breath, not only for the release of tension. The smell of death had grown more powerful the longer she had sat there in the penthouse. Brinsmead could have no sense of smell left and must have forgotten that other people did.

Down in the foyer, Grace was looking for ways to hide inside the building when she saw a car pulling up outside. The driver didn't get out. Grace guessed it to be Brinsmead's hire car and stepped into the fire escape. Holding it open by a crack, she waited. She could see the foyer clearly, although not the front doors or the street. After almost ten minutes, Daniel appeared, stepping out of the lift. He was still dressed in white, wearing soft loafers on his feet, and walked awkwardly. She heard him leave the building, waited some minutes longer, then stepped out of the fire escape. Both he and the car were gone.

Again, she took the lift to the top floor. Bracing herself, she rang the doorbell to the penthouse. There was no response. The key turned easily in the lock and she let herself in.

The rodent smell was even stronger than it had been earlier. All the lights had been turned off except the standard lamp in the lounge room. The mobile phone was missing from the coffee table. Grace went into the kitchen and, in the half-dark, saw that Daniel's keys were also gone. There would be enough time. It was an hour to Campbelltown and an hour back. She moved to search the rest of the penthouse.

In the hallway, one of the doors had been left open. She switched on the light and went inside. It was the master bedroom, large with a king-sized bed and a walk-in wardrobe whose doors were floor-to-ceiling glass. The bed had been slept in but not made. There was an en suite, scrupulously clean, and more pain medications on the bedside table. Daniel Brinsmead slept here with his temporary anaesthetics and his memories of the dead.

In the top drawer of the bedside table she found a small photograph album. Opening it, she saw pictures of Daniel before he had been burnt. Fit, good-looking and well dressed, he shared most of these photographs with Elena Calvo. They hadn't just gone out for a little while. They must have been lovers, deeply attached, at least on her side. There was adoration in the looks she gave Brinsmead in these pictures. His response was harder to read. Even so, the happiness in their faces was unforced. Fashion, attraction, wealth, it was all there for them. Then the photographs stopped. She checked the backs of some of the pictures but there were no dates or places given.

Turning a page, Grace found herself looking at very different picture, a black and white photograph from a time that seemed to be immediately post-World War Two. A pale-haired young man and a woman the same age were standing against the background of a ruined European city. The man was holding a baby. No one in this picture was smiling. Their faces were hollowed out, exhausted and hungry; their clothing dark and ragged. Grace slipped the picture out of its sleeve. It was a new photograph of an old image and showed the original's creases and tears. Stamped on the back in blue ink were two words: *Kinshasa Photographique.* She put the photograph back and returned the album to the bedside table. Then she left the room, switching off the light behind her.

She checked the other rooms but they were unused. At the end of the hallway, she went to the fourth door and opened it. Immediately, the animal smell filled the air. She had found the main bathroom, a large room with a spa bath. The blinds were drawn here as elsewhere, but the overhead lights, artificially bright, had been left on, illuminating the white tiles. The bathroom didn't seem to have been used for some time; it was completely dry and the spiders had woven their webs in the corners of the room.

Someone had built a makeshift set of shelves against one wall. They held a dozen cages. She heard a soft rustling. Small animals were in some of these cages; she saw the occasional dull glint of a tiny eye. She walked closer to them. In about three of the cages, white mice sniffed at the air through a strong, closely woven steel mesh or were huddled together in corners, motionless. In all the rest they lay dead beside their feeding and watering trays, all of which were filled with pieces of grain. Each of the cages was locked. Next to the shelves, there was a large steel cabinet. She tried to open it but it was also locked.

It was time to leave; she had seen all she could. She shut the bathroom door behind her and was about to walk into the lounge room when she heard the front door being opened. Quickly she went into the master bedroom and stepped inside the walk-in wardrobe.

'Danny?' a woman called in a clear voice. 'Are you here? Have I missed you?'

It was Sam Jonas. Grace took out her gun. In the silence, she heard quick footsteps that stopped at the bedroom doorway for a few seconds before continuing along the hallway. There was the sound of another door opening.

'How are you poor little critters today?' she heard Sam say. 'It's the end of the road, boys. I'm taking you to our safe house, all of you, dead or alive. It's time for you to fulfil your destiny. Lucky you.'

Sam could only be in the bathroom. While Grace listened, she made a number of trips up and down the hallway and in and out of the penthouse, evidently moving the cages out. Finally, there was the sound of the metal cabinet being opened; then another sound; the front door opening again. Grace heard Brinsmead's voice.

'Sam? Careful with them. Don't disturb them any more than you have to.'

'I am being careful. Anyway, I'm almost finished. What are you doing here? Shouldn't you be on your way to the bunker?'

'I realised I'd forgotten my dog tag. It's the painkillers, they're addling my mind.'

'You've got to hang in there for a while yet. We're not finished by a long chalk. Where did you leave your tag?'

'In the bedroom.'

The light was switched on and Grace heard the footsteps of two people entering the room.

'Is it in the wardrobe? Maybe you left it pinned to one of your jackets.'

'No, the last time I took it off, I put it on the chest of drawers. But it's not there now.'

There was a creaking sound, as if he'd sat on the bed.

'Are you okay, Danny? Are you in pain? Do you want a shot?'

'I've had one already. Riordan gave it to me.'

'You let her touch you.'

'She offered and I didn't say no. She was being kind to me, I was in some bad pain. She had a gentle touch and lovely hands. Don't worry. It's just a fantasy on my part.'

'Enjoy it while it lasts,' Sam said. 'Did you tell her the story?'

'In full gruesome detail. It almost got too much for me. She was a good listener.'

'As long as it eases your mind, I don't care. Did she notice the smell in here?'

'If she did, she was too polite to say so. I want her to understand. Almost as soon as I started talking to her at the launch, I wanted her to know. Then today when I was talking to her, I kept thinking she made me feel almost human. The world had some colour in it for once. If I was the man I used to be, I would have asked her to have dinner with me.'

Sam laughed. 'You're in love. You can't let it distract you.'

'It's a passing dream. It's not going to turn into anything else. Look at me. How can it? It's something a little different for me to say good night on. It means I can pass out of consciousness in a better place in my head.'

'One thing we know for sure now,' Sam said. 'Harrigan isn't Elena's little running dog. DP wouldn't have snatched his son if he was onside. He must have said no the other day. She wouldn't have liked that.'

'She must be getting frustrated,' Brinsmead said. 'This isn't proving as straightforward as she thought it would be. What do you think she wants from Harrigan? You say she already has a stooge in the police. So why put pressure on Harrigan?'

'She does have a stooge. Marvin Tooth. He and DP were having a very intense conversation that morning in that car park. Harrigan must have something she wants. Freeman gave Riordan something the other day — he must have done. Something to do with Jerome's grubby mates. Why else would his place have been turned over like that? She's passed it on to Harrigan. Whatever it is, it's enough to spook Elena and get her running around like a blue-arsed fly. She takes her eye off the ball, it makes it easier for us.'

'You still let DP walk away. You shouldn't have done that.'

'I was only ever there on the off chance that Elena would send him after Freeman. Whatever DP did to you, Danny, he's still just a foot soldier. His picture's out there everywhere now. It's only a matter of time before his name joins it. I'm going to tip off Interpol myself in the next twenty-four hours. Someone will get him. He'll pay.'

'Do you think he'll return Harrigan's son?'

'I doubt it. It would be DP's idea of a good joke not to. For all we know, the kid's dead already.'

'If we could find out where he was, we could let Harrigan know,' Brinsmead said.

'How are we going to do that? DP probably hasn't even told Elena. She wouldn't want him to. The last thing she wants is the details of what he's doing.'

'Couldn't you work it out? You know his MO better than anyone.'

Sam was silent for a while. 'He's got to be very careful where he goes,' she said eventually. 'His picture's all over the place. There's a car park not far from Redfern station — Prestige Car Parking, long and short stay. You can leave your car there for months if you want to. I'd look there. DP used to park his van there when he was doing Elena's dirty work. I tracked him there just before he gave me the slip. He could leave his van there for days and no one would look at it. Until the smell got too bad.'

'Wouldn't he use a stolen vehicle?'

'No. That'd give the police a lead. He's got a white Toyota HiAce under the name of Robert Woods. He's probably used that.'

'Do you know the registration number?' Brinsmead asked.

Sam recited the letters and digits then seemed to regret it. 'Danny, whatever else you do, you can't ring Riordan with that information. However much you want to.' Her voice was urgent.

'How could it hurt to do that?'

'Because it'll bring the police here. They won't stop asking questions until they know exactly where you got that information from. Then my cover could be blown. If Elena gets wind of any suspicion that I'm not who I say I am, we're both gone. Listen to me. I'm the professional officer here. You're the civilian operative. It's my call. We have an operation to finish. We came here to find out what LPS is really up to and we've pretty well done that. If we don't finish and report back, we've failed. Then more people stand to die than Harrigan's son. You have to make these kinds of nasty decisions in this business. It's what you signed up for.'

'Why don't we go and get the kid out ourselves?' Brinsmead asked, his tone confrontational.

'Because we'll be picked up on the CCTV.'

'Make an anonymous call. You've done that before today.'

'No. As soon as that boy's found, it'll be all over the news. DP almost saw me that day in the car park with Marvin Tooth. It was enough for him to know he was being followed. He'll join the dots and he'll tell Elena. She's already pretty suss about you as it is. You've been putting the wind up her lately. You shouldn't do that, it's unprofessional. We can't risk it. There's too much at stake.'

'He's an innocent —'

'No!'

There was silence.

'Sam, why are you so sure about all this?'

254

'I've told you why. This is the only way I can make a difference. One thing I said I would do in my life is make a difference. I've made my decision and nothing's happened to make me change my mind. Now I've got to get going. I've got things to do. Hang on. I've just seen your dog tag. It's on the floor. There you go.'

Again there was the sound of the bed creaking.

'I should get going as well. The car's waiting downstairs,' Brinsmead said. 'Did you finish cleaning out the pool?'

'Yeah, that's done. I'll leave first.'

There was a brief pause.

'Bye, Sophia,' Brinsmead said quietly.

'Don't call me that. Sophia's dead. I said goodbye to all that when I signed up with you. I'll get the last of that stuff out of the bathroom and I'll go.' There was another silence. 'Are you okay?'

'I'm just going to lie here for a little while longer. That wasn't a good combination, the tablets and the shot.'

'You wanted her to touch you.'

'I don't want to live like this.'

'Stay the course, Danny. We'll get you there. I promise.'

There was the sound of Sam going into the bathroom and then walking back down the hallway. 'See you,' she called, and the front door slammed shut. After a little while, Grace heard Brinsmead open a drawer in his bedside cabinet. She looked at her watch. The minutes ticked by and still there was no sound of him leaving, although once he went into the bathroom for a glass of water. Eventually half an hour had passed. Her feet were beginning to ache. She thought of Harrigan and Toby and decided she would walk out of the wardrobe regardless of the outcome. Then there was the sound of the downstairs buzzer. Brinsmead got up, and after some minutes more there was the sound of the doorbell. The voices were distant. Grace stepped out of the wardrobe to hear them.

'— waiting for you for over an hour, Dr Brinsmead. Do you still want the car?'

'My painkillers immobilised me. I couldn't move very easily. I'll meet the cost. I just have to get something. Please wait, I'll be down soon. Leave the door open.'

He came back to the bedroom. It was still almost another ten minutes before he left the penthouse. Finally, there was the sound of the front door being shut.

Grace waited for a few minutes more before leaving the wardrobe. The small photograph album she had seen in the drawer was lying face down on the bed. She picked it up. It wasn't open at any of the pictures of Brinsmead and Elena Calvo but at the black and white photograph at the end, of the couple and their child in the ruined city.

The apartment was silent and empty, the bathroom door left open and the lights turned off. All the cages were gone and whatever had been inside the steel cabinet had been emptied out.

Grace took out her mobile phone and rang Harrigan. She didn't even get his voicemail, only a message saying the caller wasn't answering. She tried Trevor. No response there either. She thought of who else she might ring but decided it would be too hard to explain to anyone else. If they were going to find Toby alive, she couldn't waste time convincing people that her information was reliable. She rang for a taxi as an emergency and headed for the door.

It hadn't been deadlocked. Maybe Brinsmead's mind was so clouded he'd forgotten to do it. She returned the key to the drawer before leaving. Outside, she quickly checked the swimming pool, climbing over the low fence to get inside the enclosure. Looking down into its blue-painted expanse, she saw empty plant trays, both wide and deep, covering the pool floor. Nothing remained of what might have been growing in them except for scraps of dirt and a scattering of unidentifiable plant matter. She climbed back over the fence.

Suddenly, she needed a cigarette badly. The smell of those tiny, dead animals was still with her. Anything to wipe that stink away. On the street, she smoked while she waited for the taxi to arrive. It was getting on to peak hour. Finally it was there.

'Are you the lady who ran for a taxi to police headquarters?' the driver said. 'I can't take you there, the streets are closed off. There's been a disturbance of some kind.'

'What do you mean?'

'I can't tell you. It's just happened. It's complete mayhem up there. Now's the time to rob a bank. They're all looking the other way.'

'This is urgent and official business. Get me as close as you can.'

'I'm telling you, you can't get in there. All the streets are blocked off.'

'Do you know a long-stay car park not far from Redfern station called Prestige Car Parking?' Grace asked.

'Yeah, I know that.'

'Get me there then, as soon as you can.'

They were away, jerking in and out of the traffic. Grace called Harrigan again but there was still no answer. Were the phones out? Was he preoccupied? Or was he some kind of a casualty?

As they approached the city, the taxi driver avoided the area near police headquarters. The traffic was heavy. Grace saw fire engines racing through the cross streets but put any speculation of what might have happened out of her thoughts. One step at a time, she told herself, her mind on Toby.

23

Leaving Millennium, the traffic was bad. Harrigan barely made it to police headquarters in time for his meeting. When he walked into the commissioner's office, he found the commissioner, Marvin and Trevor sitting in a strained silence, not looking at each other. His arrival punctured the tension noticeably. It was a relief to know the minister had also not yet arrived. He and Marvin looked at each other but neither spoke.

'Paul. Good afternoon,' the commissioner said. 'I understand you've had no calls.'

'No, no one's contacted me.'

'I want you to know I've authorised all resources in the search for Toby. We'll do everything we can to find your son.'

It was a rare expression of concern from the commissioner.

'Thank you,' Harrigan replied.

'Information for you, boss,' Trevor said, passing over a photograph. 'We found it on page 228 of the dossier. Recognise him? We've put a copy up on the board and added a few bruises just for you.'

'That's the man who wanted to rearrange my face. Who is he?'

'Andreas du Plessis. Born in Johannesburg thirty-nine years ago. Ex-South African army. He worked for their special forces under apartheid. The South African government's Truth and Reconciliation Commission want to talk to him about the torture and death of

258

detainees in his custody but so far they haven't been able to get hold of him. He's been on the books of a private military services company called Griffin Enterprises for a number of years. They provide security for corporations operating in dangerous environments such as theatres of war. He's had a long association with Beck. We've got a face and now a name. We'll get him.'

Before anyone could speak, Chloe knocked on the door.

'The minister rang to say he'll be at the front entrance in about five minutes. Who do you want to escort him up?'

'Harrigan will want to do that,' Marvin said.

'Yeah, I'll go,' Harrigan replied. 'Why is he coming in that way? He'd have been safer coming in through the car park.'

'Marvin made the arrangements for today's meeting,' the commissioner said.

'I don't see how anyone can be in danger coming in through our front door,' Marvin replied heatedly. 'Why don't you take your inspector with you as well, Harrigan? Bolster the party.'

'Jesus,' Trevor said softly.

'This is a business meeting, Marvin. Behave yourself,' the commissioner snapped.

Harrigan was too tense to be troubled by Marvin's ego. 'There's no point in the two of us going down. I'll go and meet him.'

He walked out. He'd just got out of the lift on the ground floor and was walking through to the foyer when he heard high heels clattering behind him.

'Commander,' a woman called. 'I heard you were here. Then Chloe said you'd gone down in the lift. Could you wait, please? I have to get your signature.'

Harrigan turned to see Mandy, a tiny, black-haired spark of a woman from finance whose height was increased in inches by her shoes. She ran towards him dressed in a tight leather skirt and bright gold shirt. He held up his hands to protect himself.

'Mandy, I don't have the time. I have to meet a government minister. I'll ring you when I'm finished.'

He walked on into the wide foyer, towards the security checkpoints. She came after him, her needle-point heels clicking on the floor. She overtook him and brought him to a sudden stop.

'Adam says I have to get your signature. It's about the door.'

Adam was her boss, an old-school manager well known for getting a kick out of making her life as miserable as possible.

'What door?'

'Your people broke down a door. They said you told them to. Adam says he won't pay for a new one unless you sign the authorisation yourself. Could you just sign it and I promise I'll go away?'

Through the glass entranceway, Harrigan saw the minister's car pull up outside. The front door opened and his adviser stepped out, carrying a thick folder and a laptop. Harrigan had the awful vision of escorting the minister through the building with Mandy's heels rattling along behind them.

'Where do I sign?'

'Just there.'

Harrigan took the document, a financial form, and scrawled his name across it. He saw the minister get out of the back seat and join his adviser. They were sharing a brief conversation. He should already have been with them.

'Tell your arsehole of a boss I'm going to come and talk to him just as soon as I get the time.'

'I'd love someone to do that,' Mandy said, as an all-engulfing roar smashed forwards into the glass front doors. Harrigan saw flames encompass the two figures standing beside the minister's car and then the car itself. Instantaneously, the power of the explosion tore through the security guards' stations, knocking them and the guards down and throwing everyone else in the foyer, Harrigan and Mandy included, to the floor. The noise roared in their ears and dust, broken glass and debris filled the air, creating an artificial darkness. The building alarms began to shriek piercingly and the sprinklers came on. Water bucketed down, soaking everyone. Mandy curled up on the floor, screaming. Other cries could be heard, including from people who had been injured. The foyer seemed to have filled with shouting, panicking people.

Harrigan scrambled to his feet. What had once been whole lay in ruins around them. Outside, the car was burning. The dead were not so much dead as destroyed. Harrigan's mechanical side took over, the way it always did under this kind of pressure. He became what he was often accused of being: unfeeling, driven. A machine with that original ghost inside who watched his movements while he organised everything as calmly as if they were only retrieving stolen plasma screens or laptops. He took out his phone and rang Trevor.

'Boss, what's going on? The alarms have started ringing.'

'Tell God we've just had a political assassination. I think something the minister's adviser was carrying has just blown up. Edwards and his adviser are dead and possibly other people as well. The security guards here are injured, and the minister's car is burning. Where's Marvin?'

'In his office. He walked out after you did, he said he'd forgotten something. Why?'

'Brief the commissioner. Tell him I'll find him when I've sorted something out.'

The building's own emergency fire-control team had appeared, racing for the burning car. Harrigan heard sirens outside on the street. He left Mandy to the care of whoever found her first and ran. Sirens were screeching throughout the building, signalling the evacuation of all staff. All lifts would stop on the next floor they came to and immobilise as soon as the doors were opened. He ran up the fire stairs, dripping water, passing people coming down who stared at him. He ran into Marvin's office. Sharon gaped at him. She was collecting her bags to leave.

'Where's Marvin?'

'He's packing to go now, with everyone else. What is it? What's going on?'

Without replying, Harrigan walked towards Marvin's office. The door opened and Marvin appeared, about to leave. He saw Harrigan and stopped.

'No, mate. I wasn't there when the bomb went off,' Harrigan said. 'You might have wanted me dead but it hasn't happened. You're not going anywhere. Let's talk.'

Marvin pushed past him. 'I'm leaving.'

'Don't you fucking walk out, not unless you want to see your boy on the net fucking pros along with the Ice Cream Man. Think of the number of hits that'll get!'

Marvin stopped. Behind him, Harrigan could see Chloe. She had just appeared in the corridor outside.

'I'm the fire warden for this floor,' she said, white-faced. 'Everyone has to leave.'

'We're having a talk,' Harrigan said. 'The building's not going to burn down. Leave it!'

She walked away immediately. Marvin's assistant, Sharon, sat down heavily in her chair. Her mouth was open in shock.

'There's a general evacuation on, Harrigan,' Marvin said in a shaking voice.

'Get back in your fucking office!'

Without a word, Marvin walked inside.

'Keep everyone out,' Harrigan said to Sharon. 'He'll thank you for it one day.'

Marvin was standing behind his desk, staring out at the view. 'What do you want, Harrigan? Don't we have a deal? Have you forgotten my tape?'

'No, we don't have a deal. It went up in flames with Edwards' car. You can tell me what I want to know. Who's running you? How did they contact you?'

'No one's running me!' Marvin shouted. 'What are you talking about? I told you. If I go down, you come with me.'

'Then we go together. With what I've got to say about you, I can wreck your life. You'll lose your pension. You start talking to me! I know you're being run. It's du Plessis, the man in the photo Trevor just showed me. The same man who tried to kill me and snatched my son. I know he's shoved those pictures under your nose and said "Dance". Now tell me where to find him!'

Harrigan saw Marvin break apart before his eyes. His mouth went slack; his expression was like a beaten dog's. Harrigan looked away. Desperation like that was ugly. Marvin slumped down into his chair.

'I don't know where to find him. He contacts me. For Christ's sake, Harrigan, I don't know where your boy is. I can understand how —'

Harrigan sat opposite. 'Talk. When did it start?'

'Just before you upgraded Cassatt's disappearance to murder. I got a CD in the mail and a note to ring a mobile telephone number. Otherwise what was on the CD would end up on the net. I looked at it and I felt sick.'

'Give me that number.'

Marvin wrote it down on a piece of paper and passed it across the desk. It was the same number Harrigan had been given the previous night.

'I couldn't believe Sean was mixing with people like Freeman and Cassatt. *You* might —'

'Careful what you say, mate!'

'I called. He wanted to meet me. It was this du Plessis. I saw his picture in the dossier while Edwards was sitting in the commissioner's office that first day. I felt the floor had opened underneath me.'

'You knew who he was back then. Why didn't you tell us? You must have known he was the man who almost killed Grace.'

'How could I know that?'

'It had to be. His voice, the accent —'

'No!' Marvin shouted back. 'She didn't see him. There was no way of knowing. You can't hang that one on me.'

The door opened. Sharon stood there, shaking visibly. 'I can hear the both of you out here,' she said, and shut the door again.

'Where'd you meet him?' Harrigan asked, controlling himself.

'Always somewhere different. He liked car parks. We always met in a different one, very early in the morning.'

'What did he want?'

'The first time, he wanted me to keep an eye on the investigation into Cassatt's death. He said to tell him if any witnesses came forward.'

'Did he mention any names?'

Marvin shook his head.

'You're lying. He said that if a woman called Ambrosine gave a statement, you were to tell him. Am I right?'

Suddenly, something like the old Marvin returned. 'Something you should realise, Harrigan. I'm the one who tipped you off about her safe house in the first place.'

'You're the one who fucking leaked the information!'

'I didn't know why Sean —'

'Yes, you did. Your son was involved in a conspiracy to murder!'

'No, I didn't know.' Marvin leaned across the table. 'I was asked a question, I answered it. Why shouldn't I trust my son? How could I know?'

'What happened with du Plessis after that?' Harrigan asked abruptly.

'He said it would be a good idea if Sean and Marie didn't stay in Sydney. I had to send him to the other side of the continent. You wouldn't understand, Harrigan. I've had to keep on with my job with all this weighing on me. It hasn't been easy.'

'I'm sure it's been really tough. What happened after Pittwater? He told you to get control of the job as soon as you could.'

'He wouldn't believe I couldn't do that. He rang before the bodies were discovered. I didn't know what he was talking about. I said we'd had no notifications. Then he told me that, if a call did come through, I was to take control. I couldn't. I was in a meeting with the regional commanders when it happened. I didn't know about it for another two hours. Your people cut me out of the loop. They always do.'

'He knew beforehand? Didn't it ever occur to you he was probably responsible?'

'No, he wasn't. He wasn't responsible,' Marvin snapped back. 'He said, *if* this happens, you take control. He said there should be two copies of a contract in the house. I was to get hold of them no matter what. It took me a couple of days but I did it.'

'What did du Plessis say when there was only one copy?'

'He went spare. I thought he was going to attack me. He's a vicious little man.'

'You told du Plessis that if he wanted the tape, he should come after me.'

'That tape. There must be something on it you don't want anyone else to hear, Harrigan. I'd love to know what it is.' Marvin leaned forward across the desk. 'There's no need for us to talk like this. I'm in a position to assist your career. I have the commissioner's ear. The top job could be yours one day. Will be, if I have anything to do with it. You can take the chair after me — I'll retire long before you will. The two of us, we can deal with du Plessis. We'll bamboozle him. He won't know what's going on.'

Marvin had regained his equilibrium; he had the look of a man about to engage in a deal he believed would be to his advantage.

'For Christ's sake, Marvin,' Harrigan said. 'There could be any number of dead people at the front door right now and you want to make a deal.'

'I didn't know that was going to happen.'

'Didn't you? Isn't that why you wanted me to take Trev along with me? You told du Plessis Edwards was going to be here today. You told him when he was arriving and at what entrance. You did, didn't you?'

'I couldn't know what he was going to do. He didn't tell me anything like that.'

'You could guess.'

'No. No, I couldn't. I've told you everything you wanted to know! Stop stalling me. It's *quid pro quo* time. Where do we go from here?'

'You write your letter of resignation,' Harrigan said.

Marvin shook his head 'No. I'm not going to resign.'

'Yes, you are, you and your son together, but you're going first. You're going to be out of this job in an hour. You've been playing with fire, Marvin. You know what I'm advising you to do? Go to the commissioner. Tell him everything you've just told me. Get him to put you in a safe house. Because once your cover is blown, or even when he doesn't need you any more, du Plessis is going to kill you.'

'What about my reputation? I could be charged. I'm not going to gaol.'

Marvin got to his feet. He picked up his briefcase and walked to the door.

'Where are you going?'

'You can't stop me, Harrigan. I'm leaving the building with everyone else. It's going-home time anyway. Good afternoon.'

He walked quickly past Sharon who was still sitting at her desk. Harrigan went after him. She picked up her bag and followed them both. The corridor was deserted. Marvin was heading for the fire escape.

'Your reputation is more important than your life?' Harrigan called after him.

'You're talking rubbish. I'm not in any danger.'

He opened the fire door and began to walk down the fire stairs at speed. Harrigan followed.

'I'll do it myself,' he called. 'I'm not having you on my conscience.'

'You will not!'

'Watch me. I'm going to talk to the commissioner as soon as I can. I'll tell him everything you told me, everything I said to you. And I mean everything.'

Marvin had reached the landing of the next floor down. Harrigan pushed behind him to get past and be in front of him. When he did, Marvin charged him, ramming him into the corner of the stairwell, smacking his shoulder against the concrete wall. They wrestled, almost tumbling down the stairs, forcing each other to a standstill. Harrigan's feet gripped the floor as he swayed dangerously.

'For God's sake, stop it!' White-faced, Sharon stood a step above them. 'People will see, people will hear.'

Marvin let Harrigan go and drew back. 'I am not going to the commissioner. Nothing will make me do that.'

'Go away,' Harrigan said to Sharon, who ran past them down the stairs. Then to Marvin: 'You don't know what you're saying.'

'Yes, I do. If you tell the commissioner, then it'll be on your head. I'll deny everything. I'll tell them you're a liar. I'll say I've never seen any of those pictures before, I've never spoken to du Plessis, I've never heard of him before today. It's your word against mine. You can't prove anything.'

'Sharon was outside the door the whole time.'

'She won't support you over me.'

'Marvin, you'll be dead. As soon as he thinks you're a danger to him, you'll be dead.'

Marvin had turned to go down the stairs. He spun round. Harrigan couldn't have described the intensity of emotion in his eyes at that moment.

'I'd rather *be* dead!'

He ran down the stairs. Harrigan went after him.

'You're going to have to lie, Marvin,' he shouted. 'I'm still going to the commissioner.'

'You can find me at home. Then you can die in hell!'

They had reached the ground floor. Marvin moved with quick, long strides towards the emergency evacuation point. Fire wardens gestured for them both to hurry. Harrigan followed Marvin outside, through the crowds that were hurrying across the street to get clear of the building. Marvin continued to walk quickly, turning a corner of the building and heading down a side street, towards the nearest railway station. He began to cross the road.

'Marvin, stop,' Harrigan shouted, going after him.

Marvin turned, standing halfway across the street. They were at a distance from the crowd. The expression on his face brought Harrigan to a halt. It was the look of a man you've hurt so badly he'll never be able to forgive you.

'For God's sake, Harrigan, what do you want from me? You've forced me out. What can I do for you now? I can't tell you anything that will pin du Plessis down. I don't know where to find him.'

'You can sting him for us. That could be a way back for you.'

'He won't meet with me after today. Not with his name and photo out there everywhere. Now leave me alone! You can wait to get my resignation.'

Suddenly Marvin's head was punched sideways and he staggered forward. Simultaneously dark, wet red lines poured down his face and neck. 'Marvin!' Harrigan shouted. Marvin's body jerked and he crumpled to the ground, his briefcase still clutched in his hand. Another bullet cracked on the pavement beside Harrigan. Instantaneously, he hit the road behind a parked car. He stayed rigidly still but there was silence. The shooting had stopped.

He found himself staring under the car into Marvin's vacant eyes. There was no expression, just the terrible emptiness of death. There was silence in his own head, before he was engulfed by the shock, the high whine of sirens at a distance, and then of other people screaming and shouting for help.

24

Grace's taxi pulled up outside the parking station, a converted warehouse several streets away from Redfern station.

'Do you want me to wait?' the driver asked.

'No,' she said.

It was peak hour, the traffic was busy. She was standing on the footpath sizing up the building and the parking station's operations when her phone rang.

'Grace,' Brinsmead said. 'Can you talk to me?'

'What is it?'

'I have some information on the Commander's son but I can only give it to you if you give me your word that you won't tell the police where you got it.'

'I can do my best,' she replied. 'But that isn't going to be easy.'

'You have to give me your word or I'll have to hang up. If I do, that'll be the end of it.'

'All right. You've got my word.'

'It's vital you keep it. Check a car park called Prestige Car Parking near Redfern station for a white Toyota HiAce with this registration number.' Daniel read out a New South Wales plate number. 'Do you have that?'

'Yes, I do.'

He cut the call immediately.

Grace had thought through everything she'd overheard that

afternoon and had decided that Sam Jonas and Daniel Brinsmead were very possibly deep-cover operatives working for a secret service agency. Sam's attitude, her professionalism, together with the setup — one career agent and one civilian cover with the advantage of an army background — was a situation Grace had come across in the past. If, as it seemed, Sam was the controlling agent in the duo, then Brinsmead had gone against her direct orders.

The sign on the parking station entrance said *24-hour Parking, Cash Only*. Secure weekly and monthly parking was also available. All payments for long stay in advance, drivers granted individual keycard access. At this time of day, the station was at its busiest with cars queuing to pay for their day's parking and get out onto Elizabeth Street.

Grace thought about the warrant card she used for her work. It carried the legal power to get her into almost anywhere; a piece of plastic that gave her more powers of entry than the police had. If she used it here for a purpose unrelated to her work, she would be in serious breach of her organisation's regulations. She went inside the parking station.

'Where do you keep your long-stay vehicles?' she asked the attendant.

'Top floor.'

'All of them?'

'Top floor!'

He was busy giving change to a driver. Grace was standing on a dangerously narrow walkway. The driver honked his horn at her when he drove out. She looked around at the inside of the parking station. It was a wide area, separated into sections by pillars. She would waste time searching for a white van in that broad space.

'Is it full?'

'Jesus!' the attendant said, and tapped into a computer. 'You shouldn't be standing there, it's dangerous. No. There are eleven spaces left. If you want to leave your car in long stay, you've got pay cash upfront.'

'I need to find a white Toyota HiAce with this registration number,' she said.

'Why?'

269

He was a young man, no more than eighteen, nervous and overweight with a pencil-thin beard. Quickly, she flashed her warrant card.

'Police,' she said. 'This may be a lead in a kidnapping. We're looking for a white van and we have a tipoff that it may be here on a long-stay rental.'

Another vehicle pulled up. The driver handed in his ticket. Confused, the attendant fluffed the change, then after a sharp reprimand from the driver gave the correct money.

'Yeah, I heard about that on TV. I don't know if I should. I'll get Ray. He's the boss.'

'Check my warrant card again and give me the information.'

'It doesn't say police.'

'This card comes with powers of entry. If you don't believe me, ring the number on it.'

He grew more flustered. 'Okay,' he said and keyed the number into the computer. 'Top floor. Bay 25. A white Toyota HiAce. Paid a month's rental. Mr Robert Woods from Coolangatta. He's a regular. He can't be who you're looking for.'

'Do you have a key to that van? I need to open it.'

'No, we don't do that. You leave it at your own risk. I couldn't give it to you anyway.'

Grace thought of what she might have in her bag.

'I'm going to check it out,' she said. 'In the meantime, call the police and tell them it's an emergency.'

'I thought you said you were the police.'

'Just do what I say. Call the police now!'

She took the lift to the top floor. Bay 25 was at the back in the corner. The van had been parked with its back doors against the wall, making it impossible to open them without moving the vehicle. There were cars either side of it, hemming it in. There were no side windows on the body of the van and both the windscreen and the windows in the doors were covered with blinds. Grace looked at her watch. It was well after six. If Toby was inside, he would have been there for over twenty-four hours. There was no one around. She took out her illegal gun and used it to smash the windscreen, put it away quickly, and then tore out the blinds, using them to clear away the remains of the smashed safety glass. The smell of human waste hit her powerfully.

'What the fuck have you done? Shit!'

It wasn't the attendant but whoever was in charge, a tall, thin and bearded man in his mid-thirties; Ray, she supposed. He had been running towards her but the smell brought him to a stop.

'There's someone in there,' she said. 'It's a kidnap victim and he's been left here to die. I'm going to ring for an ambulance. Can you get this van out of there and get the back doors open? And is there anywhere I can get some water around here?'

'Hang on. I've got to check this out,' he replied and levered himself into the van through the gap where the windscreen had been. He called out, 'There is someone here. Yeah, it's that crippled kid. But I don't know if he's alive.'

Grace was ringing for an ambulance. 'Can you just get that van out of there so we can open the doors?' she repeated.

She had barely hung up when the van came to life and moved forward, swinging around into the lane. Then shortly afterwards, the side door was opened and Ray got out.

'You know how to do that,' Grace said, with a relieved grin.

'Years of practice,' he replied, grinning back. 'You wanted water, you said.'

'And a clean cloth if you've got one.'

He was gone; she scrambled inside. Toby was dressed and on his side on a blanket. He had been tied with rough ropes and couldn't move from the centre of the van. It looked as if a rag had been pushed into his mouth but somehow he'd spat it out. His mouth was open, as if he'd tried to speak or even shout before he'd passed out. His body was rigid. The blanket was wet with urine and Toby was dirtied but he was breathing. Grace checked his pulse. It was regular if weak.

Ray had come back. He handed her a bottle of water and a clean handkerchief. She soaked the handkerchief in water and put it into Toby's mouth. Instinctively, he began to suck it.

'You need to call the police,' Grace said to Ray.

'I already did that.' He laughed. 'I was asking them to come and get you. But there's been some kind of explosion at the police building. There's three people dead, one of them's a government minister. Lucky I've got a mate over here at Redfern. They're on their way.'

Was Harrigan one of the dead? She stopped and stared at Ray then shook off the question as quickly as she could. Everything in her rejected the possibility. And there was no point in trying to call him to find out what had happened. All she could usefully do now was focus on Toby and see him to hospital alive.

'Do you have CCTV?' she asked.

'Yeah, we do.'

'You need to give the police footage of the man who left this van here and anything else you have about him.'

'I'll do that.'

The ambulance arrived before the police. The paramedics cut the ropes with a fine disregard for forensic niceties. Grace went with Toby to Royal Prince Alfred Hospital, where he was washed and cleaned, then put on a drip and connected to the various monitors that read his body. The doctor told her he was badly dehydrated and in pain but it was most likely no lasting damage had been done.

By now it was growing dark. She tried to ring Harrigan again and again got his voicemail. It was too late to be messing around. She rang the commissioner's assistant, a number she had been given in case of dire emergency.

'I'm trying to get hold of Commander Harrigan,' she said. 'It's very, very urgent and he's not answering his phone.'

'The commander can't be disturbed. There's been a significant incident here, as you may have heard, and he's in a meeting with representatives from ASIO and the Australian Federal Police at this moment. I can take a message.'

As usual, Chloe's voice dripped with frost. Grace took a few moments to draw breath over the fact that at least Harrigan was alive.

'It's to do with his son. He's been found and he's in Royal Prince Alfred Hospital right now. The commander may want to see him. You can tell him Toby's going to survive but he's badly dehydrated.'

She hung up. Harrigan could call her back if he wanted to. Instead, he arrived in person not long afterwards, hurrying down the corridor. She felt that odd, sharp shock of seeing someone you care about too much after they've been absent from your life for a while. The sight of the marks on his face made her heart tighten even though Trevor had already told her he'd been in a fight. He walked up to her and touched her face but didn't speak, just looked at her. Then he went into the glassed-in room where Toby was asleep and touched his son's hand. After some moments, he walked outside.

'I didn't believe it at first,' he said. 'I thought it must be a joke.'

'I'd never joke about something like this.'

'I didn't mean you. I meant fate.'

'He's your other half,' she said. 'His mind reflects yours.'

'His mind is clear. Mine's clouded with too much past.'

He hugged her then, unexpectedly and tightly, almost too tightly, and they kissed. They held on to each other in stillness in the centre of the busy corridor. Time stopped and acquired depth in place of movement. Whether people were watching neither of them thought. For that short space of time, everything between them was in balance, all questions were resolved.

'Thanks,' he said. 'I'll say it again. Thanks. I'll never be able to thank you enough. Is he unconscious or asleep?'

'He's sedated,' she said. 'They're trying to relax him and stabilise his body temperature. He's very weak at the moment.'

Harrigan glanced around to see who was within hearing distance.

'I've stabbed all my people in the back, Grace, and flushed everything I believe in down the toilet on a false promise. He left him there to die, didn't he?'

'Yes.'

'Bastard,' Harrigan said softly, shaking his head.

'Don't talk about it here. Let's go into Toby's room.'

Harrigan sat beside the bed. Toby's skin was pale against the crisp white sheets, his eyelids dark. It was the same steel cot that had cosseted him all his life.

'Is it true Edwards is dead?' she asked.

'He was blown sky high, him and his adviser. The blast killed one of the officers on duty at the front desk as well. There's something else. Marvin's dead. He was shot by a sniper. Assassinated. I'm asking myself when this is going to stop.'

'Do you have any idea who?'

'Possibly.' He looked at Toby again. 'How did you find out where he was? Someone must have told you.'

'I gave my word that I wouldn't say who it was.'

'You have to tell me more than that,' Harrigan said. 'There's a lot of dead people out there. We've got to bring this to an end.'

'I can tell you how I got this information, but there's also a question of secrecy and I think that secrecy is important.'

'Before we go any further, let me ask you this. Did your information come via Sam Jonas in any way?'

'Why do you think that?'

'Because in my judgement, there's no else in this who's enough of a wild card and who knows more about what's going on than she does. I know the name of our gunman now. Du Plessis. My guess is Sam knows him. Maybe she's been on his tail or they're mates.'

'I don't think they're mates,' Grace said.

'It was her. What do you know?'

'It's complicated. There's a connection between Sam Jonas and Brinsmead.'

'Are you sure?'

'Just take it from me: they're a team and they're targeting Elena Calvo and LPS in some way. They may be operatives from a secret service agency, possibly a British one. She's the professional, he's the civilian cover, probably chosen because he has a personal connection to Calvo and he's in the right profession. He's also ex-army. That counts.'

'What are these people doing here in Sydney if that is who they are?'

'Finding out what LPS is really up to. But if they are operatives, I would have expected someone at senior federal government level to know they're here and to have given them the go ahead. The problem is whether they really are legitimate. If they are, and this information becomes known, we could jeopardise their operation. If we do that, more people could end up dead. At best, we could abort what they're doing.'

'Wouldn't Edwards have known about them?'

'Not necessarily,' she said. 'Their minders might have thought his connection to Elena Calvo made it too dangerous to tell him.'

'Grace, at the moment we have representatives from every federal agency connected to intelligence in the police building. ASIO, the AFP, your people as well,' he said, referring to the Orion task force she worked for. 'I was in a meeting with them all when I got your message. Wouldn't Orion know if people like this were here?'

'I would have expected Orion to know, but there's no reason why I would have been told. ASIO should have been.'

'If ASIO or Orion do know about these people,' Harrigan said, 'and if what they're doing is legitimate, then I'd expect to have been told by now given what's happened.'

'Sam talked like she was the controlling operative,' Grace said. 'If she is, she wouldn't be briefing anyone in those agencies on what they're doing day to day. Her minders wouldn't necessarily give any details on the nature of the operation to other than a very few people. You've identified a connection between your murder investigation and LPS but that connection isn't known outside of your squad. And for all we know, their presence here is clandestine and the government hasn't been told. If Sam and Brinsmead are working for an anti-terrorist cell that has unorthodox methods, then the rules for those cells have changed in the last few years.'

'I can't prove the connections,' Harrigan said. 'I gave the evidence away.'

'You didn't have a choice.'

'You found him anyway, Grace.'

'That was pure luck. There's something else that's important. Brinsmead has a connection with Beck and this du Plessis. He was in the Congo with them — that's where he got his burns. They were involved in diamond smuggling. Also, Sam Jonas isn't her real name. It's Sophia something. Whatever they're doing, it's serious.'

'Do you think they're legitimate?'

'From the sounds of it, yes. Legitimate and ruthless.'

'Ruthless enough to shoot dead a senior policeman?' Harrigan asked.

'Marvin? Why?'

'If their target is Elena Calvo, then he was her ears and eyes in the police. It makes operational sense.'

'They couldn't do that. If he was an obstacle, they'd organise for someone to tap him discreetly on the shoulder. But that does mean somebody in authority would have to know they were here.'

'We do have some intelligence that an agency like the one you describe has been on Beck's tail in the past. Who knows about this?'

'You and me.'

'Grace, how did you get this kind of information?' he asked. 'Don't take this the wrong way, but how do I know it's reliable?'

Toby stirred. A nurse arrived.

'I have to check on him,' she said.

They stepped outside into the corridor.

'What did you do?' Harrigan asked.

'You'd call it illegal entry. Brinsmead wanted to see me at his flat. He wanted to talk about his burns, how he got them. He said he wanted me to understand him.'

'He took a shine to you.'

Grace shrugged. 'It was all harmless enough. While I was there, I got hold of a key. After he left to go to LPS, I went back in. I was snooping when Sam Jonas turned up and he came back. Brinsmead was conducting some kind of experiment in his flat and she'd come to clean it up. I think that experiment was to find out what Beck was really doing. I hid in a wardrobe and heard everything they said to each other. They talked about their operation, the instructions they had, how they had to report back. Sam came over as a professional, focused agent. She's the type; I've met people like her before. It's why she's so in your face when she talks to you. Everything she does is undercover. That world's not normal. It's got very strange reference points. There's almost no law to control you and nothing's what it seems. It's very easy to lose perspective.'

'Then what would she have done if she'd found you? Grace, you were putting yourself in danger again. When are you going to stop doing that? One day it's going to backfire on you.'

'If I hadn't done it, Toby would still be in that parking station.'

He was stopped. He looked from her to Toby and back to her. This was no place to argue.

'You're the fault lines in my life, the two of you,' he said quietly. 'You don't know the things you put me through.'

'What does that mean? You wish we weren't? You wish I hadn't done what I did?'

'No, it doesn't mean that. It means the opposite.'

Before Harrigan could say anything more, his phone rang.

'Yes, as soon as I can. You can tell the commissioner that Toby's going to be okay. Thanks.' He put the phone away. 'I've got to go. I've got work to do.'

'You always do,' she said.

He looked in at Toby through the glass before he answered her. The nurse came out.

'He's comfortable,' she said.

Harrigan nodded to her and went back inside to look at Toby one last time. Gently, he moved some of his son's hair that had fallen across his forehead. Then he walked back to Grace.

'He's very attached to you,' he said.

'I like him. He knows what it means to be attached to you.'

'Is it really that bad?'

'Sometimes. When do we see each other again?'

'I've got a briefing with the AFP first thing tomorrow morning on where the case is. The assassination of federal government ministers is their responsibility,' he said dryly. 'I've still managed to convince everyone the best way to solve this is by keeping the Pittwater investigation on track. After that, as soon as I can get some time I want to see you. I'll call you.'

'Why can't we see each other tonight when you're finished?'

'Now that you've given me this information, I've got to think about how it fits in. I have to act on it. I need some head space to work that out. But I will call you.'

They held on to each other again. He didn't seem to want to let her go and then did. Then he was gone.

'I guess you will,' Grace said to herself, watching him disappear down the corridor.

Very shortly afterwards, two uniformed police appeared, heading towards her. Time to be economical with the truth, she thought, preparing to meet them.

25

It was late by the time Harrigan got back to Birchgrove for the night, and later still when he went to bed having spent some time thinking the case through over a glass of whisky. When he woke in the morning, it was early. He felt unexpectedly refreshed from a short sleep. He took a little time to prepare for the day. There was a phone call he had to make; a course of action he had agreed on with Trevor the previous night. He dialled the number, certain there would be an answer even at this early hour.

'Elena Calvo.'

'Good morning, Dr Calvo. I didn't think you'd mind me ringing you so early. You struck me as the type to be at your desk first thing. How are you today?'

'Are you making this call in an official capacity?'

'No, I'd see this as a personal call. A very personal and confidential call.'

'I can think of no reason why you would have anything personal or confidential to discuss with me.'

'I thought you'd like to know we've found my son and he's alive.'

'I'm very pleased to hear it on your behalf, but it has nothing to do with me.'

'I think it does. I'll get straight to the point. I think you should make some time to see me, Dr Calvo. Because how long do you think it's going to take us to find du Plessis?'

'I have no idea what you're talking about,' she said.

'Whatever you do, whatever strings you pull, whatever money you throw at it, we're going to get to him sooner or later,' Harrigan continued. 'Do you want to know how many people are out there looking for him right now? He can't leave the country. All the exits are blocked. Do you think he's going to keep his mouth shut when we do get him? We can send him back to South Africa any time we want to. He's looking at a lifetime in gaol over there. He's probably got a lot of enemies waiting to get their hands on him back home. I don't think they'll be very gentle when they do get hold of him. Those are prospects that might make him very talkative.'

'I don't understand why you're saying such things to me,' she replied. 'I asked you a number of days ago if you wanted us to undertake scientific research into your son's physical condition. You said you needed time to make up your mind. I can see you in relation to that. That would make sense to me.'

'Then let's get together. I'm busy most of the day. I can see you later on this afternoon. You can come to me this time.'

'We can compromise,' she said, almost with sarcasm. 'We have a city office in the Australia Square building. I'll be here until this evening. You can find the address in the phone book. Come to the entrance to the car park. Someone will meet you.'

They hung up on each other almost simultaneously. Harrigan felt detached; it was a relief. Revenge was not part of the strategy he and Trevor had put together last night but it was still in his mind. He had never had so much desire to exact it as he did now.

When Harrigan drove into the police headquarters car park for his meeting, Chloe was waiting for him.

'Does the commissioner want to see me?' he asked.

'No, no,' she said. 'I've got something for you.'

She handed him a cassette tape. He looked it over.

'Sharon gave that to me yesterday evening. Apparently, the special assistant commissioner requested it go to the commissioner in the event of anything happening to him. It's a recording of a recent phone conversation between the two of you.'

'Did she listen to it?' he asked.

'She says no. I haven't listened to it either. I'm not quite sure why the commissioner would need to be concerned with it. I thought you'd be the best person to decide whether he does or not.'

'Thanks,' Harrigan said.

'You're welcome. They're waiting for you upstairs,' she said, raising her carefully waxed eyebrows at him before walking away.

Harrigan locked the tape in his briefcase and made his way to the briefing room feeling like a liar and a thief. He accepted people's congratulations for his son's safety like the hypocrite he was, barely able to thank them in return. His people put his mood down to relief and exhaustion. They were generous; it galled him.

Officers from the federal police arrived. Two men and a woman, dressed in what seemed almost identical grey suits. They sat together at the back of the room. Their boss, Kevin Parkin, was a thin-faced man in his early fifties, his hair slicked forward to hide a bald spot. They carried nothing other than their notepads and, in the hand of the woman, an audio recording device. Supposedly they were part of a cooperative investigation, but even in his meeting with them last night, Harrigan had felt them drawing a fence around themselves.

The second guest was an inspector from the task force set up to investigate Marvin's assassination. Meredith O'Connor arrived in what looked like full dress uniform, her hair and make-up immaculate. Approaching retirement, she'd been around for more than thirty years, a biography that suggested impressive survival skills. Experience had taught Harrigan she was a dogged worker and a rigid thinker.

Trevor did the introductions to a group of weary people in a room that smelt of takeaway food and coffee. Harrigan stood to the side, leaving it to his 2IC to run the show.

'Meredith doesn't have a great deal of time,' Trevor said. 'I'm going to ask her to quickly go through what we know about Marvin's shooting and then let her go. But before we start, some news.'

There was a laptop computer on the table. Trevor hit a key and the first page of the dossier appeared on the screen behind him.

'This hit the net at seven this morning. It's Edwards' copy of the dossier. He left instructions that if anything happened to him, this was to be posted on the net as soon as possible. His staff did just that and there's no taking it back. Anyone can download it whenever they want to and I'm sure they already have. I'm waiting for the agency who owns it to come pounding on our door. At least Edwards was responsible: his staff blacked out any names that might identify any innocent parties.'

'There wasn't much information of that nature in there, Trev,' Ralph called. 'There were no agents' names.'

'He also had this put online,' Trevor went on. 'Most of you have read it already. It's a digital copy of an affidavit he swore that says he was bribed to get Beck into the country. He accuses one person in particular, a very well-known entrepreneur. If we weren't all so cynical to start with, the name might surprise us. Apparently there are already enraged denials out there in cyberspace. Lucky you can't sue the dead. Now, Meredith. Can you tell us what you know about Marvin's shooting?'

'I'd like to ask the commander a question about Marvin Tooth first,' Parkin called from the back of the room. 'You've stated that he called you back to confess to you that he had been under duress to sabotage this investigation. He did this because he was shocked by the deaths caused by yesterday's bombings and now wanted to help identify who was responsible. Is that correct?'

'So he said,' Harrigan replied.

'That's quite a confession given what had just happened. Implicating himself in the murders of a government minister and his adviser is no small thing.'

'I don't believe that was his motive at all, whatever he may have told the commander here.' Meredith interrupted with her usual brusqueness. 'My own judgement is that he realised his position was becoming untenable. He must have known it was only a matter of time and was seeking to justify himself.'

Thank you, Meredith, Harrigan thought. She had moved forward, taking over the laptop and projecting a map of the streets surrounding police headquarters onto the screen.

'The initial findings are that the special assistant commissioner was shot by a high-powered rifle from vacant office space on the fourth floor of this building here, on the eastern side of the street that our building backs on to,' she said. 'We have no sightings of the killer and obviously no descriptions.'

'How could they know their target was going to be there?' Parkin asked.

'They couldn't. Our consensus is, this was an opportunistic shooting. That building has a public gymnasium on the top floor. Anyone in a tracksuit, either in the elevator or on the fire stairs, carrying a sports bag perhaps, would attract no attention at all. One of our team has argued, convincingly, I think, that the special assistant commissioner was possibly being cased for assassination. His controllers may have considered he was becoming a danger to them, as indeed he was. That building overlooks the entrance to our building's garage where his entrance and exit could be watched. There's also a line of coffee shops at street level that everyone here uses. But then, all of a sudden yesterday, the special assistant commissioner is out there on the street and he's the perfect target. They took their chance when they could.'

'Bye, bye, Fang,' Ralph muttered.

'I think this also solves the question of how vital evidence — a contract, I believe — was stolen from the evidence room,' Meredith said. 'It seems almost certain that the special assistant commissioner was responsible.'

'Can you tell us anything about how they blackmailed him?' Trevor asked.

'We won't be able to answer that question until we've finished searching his office and house. Those searches are happening now. If that's all you need me for, I'll leave it there in case some information does come through.'

'That's fine, Meredith. Thanks for being here.'

She left the room. There was a stir among those remaining. A sense of distaste and betrayal was written on people's faces. Harrigan wondered what they would think of him if they knew that he'd handed over evidence in a way no different from Marvin. They'd see its uselessness; he could have said no to Toby's kidnapper and still got his son back. Either way he would lose their respect.

'Kevin,' Trevor was saying. 'What can you tell us about the minister's death?'

Parkin got to his feet but didn't walk to the front of the room, forcing those present to turn and look at him. 'We know where the bomb was,' he said. 'In his adviser's laptop. It was detonated when the adviser and Edwards were talking together at the front entrance. They were both killed instantly. The driver survived but he's critical. As we all know, the blast also killed one of the guards at the door.'

'When was the bomb planted?' Harrigan asked.

'We haven't narrowed down any times as yet. According to Edwards' PA, the senator's adviser always took the laptop home with him. He rents a house in Summer Hill and he's frequently out in the evenings. Our bomber would have had the fairly simple task of breaking into a not very secure house and doing a fairly straightforward job. In my opinion, the adviser was careless. He should have kept the laptop in more secure storage.'

'In other words, Edwards could have been singled out for assassination some days ago?'

'It's possible.'

'How was the bomb detonated?'

'It was almost certainly a timing device triggered by a mobile telephone call. I would speculate that the bomber was watching Edwards and his adviser leave his electorate office, which is at Ashfield, for police headquarters. That way he could be sure they were travelling together. He would have followed them for some distance and then started the countdown. The bomb must have been intended to explode where it did. There was ample opportunity beforehand to detonate it almost anywhere else.'

'Marvin didn't want you to go down to that front door by yourself, boss,' Trevor said. 'He asked you to take me along as well.'

'Could he have known?' Parkin asked sharply.

'Of course he fucking knew!' Frankie retorted softly, looking away.

Again there was a stir of anger throughout the room. 'Pity they didn't shoot him earlier,' Harrigan heard someone mutter. 'Dog!' someone else said. With a nod to Trevor, Harrigan moved forward to shut down the mood as quickly as possible.

'Okay, let's stand back from what we know,' he said. 'In my opinion, there's no chance that having detonated a bomb at our front door, the bomber would wait around to watch what happened next. Whoever the bomber is, he didn't kill Marvin. He wouldn't have had the time. Also, Meredith's scenario means that someone was already in position, spying out the land.'

'What are you suggesting?' Parkin asked. 'Two dirty tricks men?'

'Before I make any judgements on that, I want to hear what the task force has turned over in relation to what happened at Pittwater. Okay, thanks for that, Kevin. Trevor. Where are you taking us from here?'

'Jacquie, you're on,' Trevor said. 'Dazzle us.'

Parkin sat down. Jacquie, young, new to the squad and ambitious, was proving herself. She began by projecting a photograph of the murder scene onto the screen. The dead sat at the table, waiting for nothing. Harrigan glanced quickly at his federal counterparts. They were poker-faced.

'We were asked to reconstruct the murder scene,' Jacquie said. 'Okay, so what's the key to this picture? They're at dinner. How did that meal get there? One of the neighbours told us that a van from Sweet Delights Catering at Mona Vale drove up to the gates at about 8.10 the night of the murders. No one got out so we have no descriptions. The gates are automatic. They were opened for the van, it drove in and then the gates were closed again. Our neighbour didn't see the van leave, but a man walking his dog saw it on its way down the hill just after nine. So the killings took up to fifty minutes maximum.'

'Could this man see into the van?' Harrigan asked.

'No. The windscreen was reflective. He could see his own face but not who was inside. He didn't look at the number plate. We went to Sweet Delights. It turns out that someone claiming to be Natalie Edwards' private secretary — she does have one —'

'Was it a woman or man?' Harrigan asked.

'A woman.'

'What did her voice sound like? Any accents, anything unusual?'

'Nothing they noticed. She rang and cancelled the arrangements Natalie Edwards had made two hours before they were due to deliver the meal. They did what they always do when that happens: they put the charge through on her credit card. The van the neighbour saw arrived exactly when it was supposed to. She'd asked for an evening supper. Our murderers not only knew about Natalie Edwards' arrangements; they impersonated the caterers to get into the house and went to some trouble to do it. But taking you back to this picture. What's on the table? A meal. The killer, or killers, whichever, must

284

have brought this food with them. Our murderers catered a meal they knew their victims were never going to eat. Why?'

'Were they shot at the table?' Harrigan asked.

'I think it worked like this. The killer walks in, maybe Natalie Edwards meets him —'

'Him.' Harrigan interrupted again. 'But the person who rang the caterers was a woman.'

'And she could have been the killer, no mistaking that. Whoever they were, they made everyone lie down on the lounge room floor and they restrained them. Everyone had restraint marks. Because of where the blood was, we know the meal must have been set out beforehand, presumably by the killer. Then I think they took the victims out to the patio one by one.'

'All of them?'

'All of them, including Julian Edwards.' Her voice broke a little over this. 'Then they unloaded the Ice Cream Man, took this photograph and went home. Then they released it on the net under the subject line: *They gather for the feast.* It's the food that's important here. That's the imagery they're projecting.'

Briefly, people were silent.

'Why kill the boy?' Parkin asked. 'Could he identify them?'

'That's a motive. But there's also a question of leverage,' Harrigan said. 'Shooting that boy was a terrible crime. His father was a government minister. We know they made sure Edwards saw his son dead because they sent him the combination to the gate by SMS. That combination of circumstances means there was no way this investigation was going to be swept under the carpet. They wanted us to dig.'

'That is so cold-blooded,' Ralph said.

'Does that assume they knew Edwards?' Frankie asked.

'Maybe they did,' Harrigan replied.

'They wanted us to dig, you said, Commander.' Parkin got to his feet. 'That seems to assume they wanted this murder solved. That is, we have the means to catch them. I've never come across that scenario before in this type of context. It's true that people who do this kind of thing often want to claim responsibility and give a motive. But there's been no statement put out to that effect. Am I right?'

'Not so far,' Harrigan said. 'But it hasn't been that long.'

'Long enough, unless they're planning something else. Also, while people like this may want to draw attention to what they've done, they don't want to be apprehended. If your theory is going to fly, you need to give us a reason for it.'

'I didn't say they wanted to be apprehended. I said they wanted us to dig,' Harrigan replied in his detached voice. 'My theory does fit with one undeniable point: the possibility that the killer or killers were expecting resistance to this investigation. That's proven to be true. Someone has gone to great lengths to sabotage it.'

'Again you're implying we have two parties involved,' Parkin said. 'Do you have any evidence for that?'

'It's like I said before. We work through what we know, then we make a judgement. Jackie, is that it?'

'There's more. It's to do with Beck.'

'Let's hear it,' Harrigan said.

Parkin sat down again.

'We checked his movements and telephone records. We know he got to Pittwater about ten to eight. Just before he arrived, he made a call on his mobile. He spoke for about fifty seconds. I think he probably left a message. It was the last call he ever made. At about 1 a.m. he got a call back from that same number but obviously he didn't answer it. It went through to his voicemail where the call was disconnected without anyone leaving a message. That number called Beck another three times over the next eleven hours and then stopped.'

'Someone was checking up on him,' Ralph said.

'I'd guess they wanted to know whether the contract had been signed,' Harrigan said. 'Could you trace the number?'

'We rang but the number was discontinued. We're tracing its history now.'

'Anything else?'

'One final thing. When we checked Beck's wallet, we found this.'

Another image appeared on the screen, a black and white photograph showing a man with a woman carrying a baby, both standing in the midst of a ruined city.

'It was the original and it wasn't in good condition. On the back, it says in pencil *Dresden 1946*. We know that's when Beck was born. I think that's him with his mother and father. But if that is his father, then he either walked out on them or he died, because the dossier says father unknown. There was only his mother and she died in 1997.'

'Do we have any names?' Harrigan asked.

'None for the father. His mother was married during her life but not until after Beck had left East Germany. There were no children from that marriage and the husband is still alive. There's no record of any earlier marriage.'

'If she knew who her son's father was — and from this picture it looks like she did — she would have told her son, surely. When she died, if not earlier,' Harrigan said. 'Beck had that picture on him when he died.'

'Yes. I think it meant something to him,' Jacquie said. 'That's it.'

'Good work.'

She smiled and sat down.

'All right,' Harrigan said. 'It's time to talk about Beck. Trev?'

'First off, we searched his house. Frankie. Do you want to take us through what you found?'

'The first thing is that someone got there before us,' Frankie said. 'Whatever they were looking for, they found it in a drawer in the lounge room because they didn't even bother to close the drawer. They stopped right there and left.'

'Did you find an LPS badge?' Harrigan asked.

'Not a whisker. Maybe that was what they took away.'

'What do you mean, LPS badge?' Parkin asked. 'We know the minister was involved with that corporation. Was Beck?'

'According to the CEO, Dr Calvo, he was briefly employed by them earlier this year,' Harrigan replied. 'The badges are security passes that get you in and out of their facility at Campbelltown. I was given one when I visited there a few days ago. It's a sophisticated tracking device. You get to keep it as a memento, but once you leave it's deactivated. If Beck was an employee, he would have had one. We know from other sources that he was, so what happened to his?'

'Couldn't he have lost it easily enough?' Parkin asked.

'Not if it was his key to the door. I think we should question whether he really was sacked as Elena Calvo says he was. Frankie, anything else?'

'No, boss, we found zip,' Frankie said. 'Beck had a nice house with a lovely view of the harbour but there was nothing personal in there. We did find out a few things about him. He suffered from high blood pressure and liver disease, he had the meds to prove it. He liked the best. The clothes, the booze — there was a lot of booze, he obviously drank very heavily — it was all nothing but the best. There was money in the house and a lot of money in his various bank accounts as well. We're tracking his financials now. There was a lot more information about him in the dossier.'

'Ralph, do you want to talk to that?' Trevor said.

'Yeah, the dossier.' Ralph moved to the head of the table. The image of the dossier's front page reappeared on the screen. 'We don't know the name of the agency that owns this document, but now it's out there in cyberspace, I'm sure they'll find us soon enough.'

'Stop there, Ralph,' Harrigan said.

'What is it, boss?'

'What you just said. Now it's out there in cyberspace, its owners will find us. Given what's been put out on the net already, why wasn't this document online as well?'

'I'll tell you,' Parkin called. 'Because it could identify them.'

'That's right. I think this will signal to someone out there who these people are. Okay, Ralph. What can you tell us?'

'Mainly that this is a very long-standing document. It incorporates information from the various agencies who've been watching Beck since 1970. He had a long career as an illegal arms dealer dating from the late 1960s right through to the 1990s. He's involved himself in theatres of war from South East Asia to Africa. He met du Plessis in the 1980s when he was working for the South African apartheid government. In 1990 he went back to Europe. The apartheid regime was on its last legs and he'd made too many enemies over there. By now the Berlin Wall is down. He became involved with the Russian mafia, wisely not for too long. His mother died in Berlin in 1997 and, like a dutiful son, he was there with her.'

'You're breaking my heart,' Frankie murmured.

Ralph grinned. 'That's just one side of the story. In fact, Beck was a double agent, a very useful source of intelligence for the agencies who were watching him. He did business for himself and provided information to the British government at the same time. In exchange for which they left him alone and paid him. It's a common enough arrangement. After his mother died, he went to London. And here the first part of the dossier is ruled off. The final note is: *Minister's direction is discontinue and hands off.* It was a thirty-year connection. They closed it down without a murmur. There's no indication they even debriefed Beck.'

'No reasons given? Nothing?' Harrigan asked.

'Nothing that's on this file,' Ralph said.

'Why would it go to the minister? Was Beck that important?'

'He wouldn't be,' Parkin said. 'Ministers don't deal directly with operatives at that level. Somehow he must have drawn attention to himself.'

'There's no indication on file as to what he might have done,' Ralph said. 'Then five years ago, the dossier was reopened. Not because of Beck but because of du Plessis. Du Plessis was in London. At the time, he was wanted for murder in South Africa but the government there agreed to the agency keeping him under surveillance rather than arresting him. That warrant is still out against him. At the time, he was known to be involved in illegal diamond trading. The agency's main concern was with the kind of activities financed by that trade, such as illegal arms dealing. The surveillance operation caught du Plessis meeting with Beck. It was the first time Beck had been on the radar for years. They met often enough for the agency to conclude they were in business together and they needed to watch Beck as well as du Plessis.

'After this, they traced Beck to a scientific research facility in north London. At the time he'd been employed there for several years. The investigation identifies him as a manager of some kind. From this point on, the agency put an operative into that research facility to watch him. This operative is referred to by a number only. This is where Elena Calvo turns up, boss. You said she was a player. She was the CEO there, and while she was there, she had an encounter with Beck. That brings us to this series of photographs. The time and date stamp says 22:38 one night in June four-and-a-half years ago. They must have both been working late.'

Up on the screen, there flashed in succession pictures of Elena Calvo standing beside her car in an underground car park, talking to

Jerome Beck. The body language made it clear there was a fierce argument going on. Towards the end he was pushing his wallet at her. She refused to look at it. The last photographs in the series showed her slamming her car door and driving away.

'That argument went on for eighteen minutes,' Ralph continued. 'Pity we can't know what was being said. Or shouted.'

'That's where Beck kept his photograph,' Jacquie said. 'It was in his wallet like that. At the front, behind a window.'

'Did he have it with him then?' Ralph asked.

'If he got it from his dying mother, why not?' Harrigan said. 'What do we know about this research institute?'

'So far we've only checked its website. There's nothing to indicate it's anything but legitimate. There is one significant fact. Although this is hidden behind various companies, it's owned by Jean Calvo. The dossier traces that ownership in detail.'

'Did Senator Edwards see those photographs of Beck arguing with Calvo? Did he know they had this previous connection?' Harrigan asked.

'He must have done,' Ralph said. 'I spoke with his adviser any number of times this last week. He told me they'd both been through the dossier in detail. Now the poor bastards are dead.'

'Did the minister mention this to her?' Parkin asked. 'Did she know this dossier existed?'

'She's the only one who can answer those questions now,' Trevor said. 'Edwards told us no one besides his staff knew about it and he could trust his staff. We've also kept its existence confidential. Maybe the boss can add something to this. He's spoken to Calvo.'

'Why did you do that?'

'Her connections to the minister make her significant in this. She told me about this same incident while I was there,' Harrigan said. 'She was explaining it away. Beck was a drunken bum who harassed her. She hired him over here because she needed someone, then fired him almost immediately because he was a drunk. He started making abusive phone calls and she got one of her security people to watch him for her. I don't think she would have told me any of that unless she expected me to know it from another source.'

'Why couldn't she be being truthful?' Parkin asked.

'She's not someone who tells you things unless it's in her interests. In my opinion, the connections here are too close to ignore. Also, Marvin had his own copy of this dossier. Which means he would have told du Plessis about its existence. Did Calvo know about it because du Plessis was working for her and he told her this information was out there? Maybe she even got her own copy that way. That's another line of possible communication we can't ignore.'

'Something else for you to prove, Commander,' Parkin replied.

'I think it's something anyone involved in this job has to consider,' Harrigan said.

There was a brief silence.

'Why would you waste eighteen minutes talking to a drunken bum late one night in a car park?' Frankie asked, spiking the tension. 'If he harassed you, why would you go ahead and hire him again? Only if you had to.'

'What happened after those pictures were taken?' Harrigan asked.

'They kept a watching operation on Beck,' Ralph said. 'We get a series of weekly reports from their operative. Whoever this person was, they weren't able to gain access to the research projects Beck was involved in. Access to the laboratories was tightly controlled and there was no public information available concerning the projects themselves. Instead the operative formed a personal connection to Beck, close enough to get a good view of his lifestyle. Whatever Beck was doing, it paid well. He liked to gamble; not always successfully, but he never seemed to have any trouble paying his debts.'

'Just Beck?' Harrigan asked. 'There's no indication this operative's assignment extended to Elena Calvo?'

'If they did, boss, it was extracurricular. There's no information about it here.'

'What happens then?' he asked.

'There's a note on file that says the operative's last report was removed because it had been requested by the under-secretary to the Ministry of Defence for use at a briefing. That report never made it back to the file. After that, there's no more information from the operative. The reports stop.'

'Is that the end of the information?'

'No. As well the operative's reports, the surveillance team's reports are also in the dossier. Now according to them, Beck was still meeting du Plessis regularly. Their reports record that their operative was at the last two meetings these men had. Usually there are photographs of the meetings, but on this occasion those photographs have been removed.'

'By who?' Harrigan asked sharply.

'By the agency. There's a note to say they can be found on another file. After the final meeting, du Plessis left the country, flying to Kinshasa in the Democratic Republic of the Congo. That's the last piece of information on file. The last page is stamped: *Operation terminated: Archive.* After that, there's no indication it did anything but go back into the filing cabinet.'

'What was the date of du Plessis's departure?'

'November four years ago,' Ralph said.

'Do we know what Beck was doing between then and now?' Harrigan asked. 'Do we know if he joined his mate over there?'

'We do, and we can thank Edwards for that,' Trevor said. 'He fast-tracked the information out of the Department of Immigration. It hit our desks by courier yesterday morning. Otherwise, we'd still be scratching our bums for it six months from now. Beck left for Africa two weeks after du Plessis. He said he didn't go to Kinshasa, he went to Nairobi.'

'Do we know what either of them was doing over there?' Harrigan asked.

'We've got no information on du Plessis. But according to the information immigration had from Beck himself, he went to Africa as part of a religious educational aid project.'

Even the federal police contingent laughed.

'Would I lie to people?' Trevor said. 'The project was based in Nairobi. It was called Christian Educational Initiatives, providing education at village level. Supposedly, Beck was their financial manager. Probably he spent most of his time sitting around playing pocket billiards.'

'Does this charity really exist?' Harrigan asked.

'Apparently. There was correspondence between its head office in the UK and the Department of Immigration. The High Commission sent people out to have a look at its Nairobi office. Obviously, anyone can hang out a shingle and ask a few mates to hang around some rented rooms for a day or two. But you can see the department being able to justify what it did. Beck spends a number of years supposedly as an administrator in a respectable scientific research facility, then goes back to a country he's had a long association with to work in an aid program. If that's all the information you've got, on paper it doesn't look so implausible. He came here from Nairobi via Johannesburg a year ago. His visa was handled through the Australian High Commission in Kenya.'

'Then why pay Edwards to get him into the country?' Frankie asked.

'The department did have enough information about Beck's real past to make them think twice,' Trevor said. 'It's a fraction of what he was involved in but it does make his application questionable. The way he was presented, with testimonials that he was a changed man, he was being whitewashed from the start. Someone really wanted him over here.'

'Also, paying Edwards implicates him from the start,' Parkin said. 'It ties him in to whoever's paying him. Call it a guarantee. Someone wanted to make sure he was onside.'

'Is there anything to connect Beck to the Democratic Republic of the Congo?' Harrigan asked.

'Nothing in the files,' Trevor said.

There would have been a means to make the connection if the tape that Harrigan had given du Plessis still existed. Like Marvin, Harrigan had covered Elena Calvo's tracks for her. But there was still Grace's information from Brinsmead if he could find some other facts to substantiate what she had told him.

'Find out where Beck was really going when he left London four years ago,' he said. 'If you can, get hold of the manifest for his flight. I'd like to know who else was on that plane.' Harrigan was tapping the table with his fingertips. 'What do we know about World Food and Crop Providers, the organisation that was supposedly receiving seed stocks from this International Agricultural Research Consortium, so called?'

'Frankie's people have been looking at it. Frankie?' Trevor said.

'The contract gave us their contact details in Johannesburg. Lucky we recorded those details before it got stolen,' she said. 'They don't have a website or an email address. We rang the contact number and it was disconnected. We contacted the local police and asked them to check out the offices for us. According to them, the address we gave them is just vacant rooms. Whatever this company was supposed to be, they've wiped themselves out of existence.'

'You say Tooth said this du Plessis was his handler,' Parkin said. 'Is there any information how he got into the country?'

'Not as yet,' Trevor said. 'Immigration are still checking him for us. He'll be using false papers.'

'Where does all this information lead us?' Parkin went on. 'I can't see that you've actually analysed any of it yet.'

There was a whiteboard beside the screen. Harrigan went over to it and began to write.

'Possible scenario,' he said. 'A connection exists between Beck and Calvo at the north London facility where they both worked. Whatever there is between them, it doesn't make her happy. Our secret service agency sends an undercover operative in to watch Beck and they discover this connection. What they made of it, we don't know. Whatever Beck is up to, this operative goes with him to Africa. Who that operative was, what happened over there, all that information has been expunged from the file. Why? Maybe because it all went badly pear-shaped. Four years later, Calvo comes here, establishes the dream of her life. Beck turns up on the scene out here at the same time, doing something much more undercover. His arrival here is organised by the same people funding Elena Calvo. One way or the other, he goes to work for her. Question: did Calvo have no choice but to take him on?

'Whatever the answer, everything bumps along the way it's supposed to for a while. Then three people get shot up at Pittwater. What's the immediate outcome of these murders? The International Agricultural Research Consortium was due to harvest whatever they were growing. That seed stock was supposed to be sent to the World Food and Crop Providers company for testing somewhere in Africa. None of that happens because all the principals of the IAR Consortium except one have been murdered, and the last man standing is so shit scared, he goes to ground. Next point: whoever the killers are, they splash a photograph of the murder scene all over the web. Jacquie, you told us the main point of that picture. A meal they couldn't eat. What was the IAR Consortium growing? Food crops mainly. My judgement is, that scene was a comment on exactly what the IAR was growing and the killers threw in their own death figure, the Ice Cream Man, as a final touch. I think we were looking at genetically modified crops that don't do what they're supposed to do.'

'As far as I know, all those crops were destroyed,' Parkin said. 'How do we prove this?'

'Harold Morrissey was badly injured handling the tobacco. We have documented proof of that.'

'If it was the tobacco that caused those injuries and not a farming accident. What happens next in this scenario of yours?'

Harrigan almost announced that crop samples did exist, then changed his mind. It was information he would share later with Trevor.

'Whoever shot those people, after they're dead the shit hits the fan,' he replied. 'Calvo goes into survival mode. She wipes the IAR Consortium off the face of the earth. She tries to shut down this investigation and stop anyone from implicating her and her company in whatever Beck was doing. Which means that whatever Beck was up to, it was dynamite.'

'Hold it right there,' Parkin said. 'You're telling us she's behind this sabotage. She hired the man who blew a government minister, his adviser and a police guard to eternity. We know that Elena Calvo was a good friend of Edwards. She's also the CEO of a cutting-edge scientific institution he helped bring here. Besides which, the senator doesn't refer to her in his affidavit. Also, he makes no connection between Beck and LPS. Given who he has accused, surely he would have voiced any suspicions he might have had about her? Especially since he knew from the dossier that she did have this connection with Beck.'

'Given the senator's friendship with Calvo, he may not have wanted to face up to the possibility that she was implicated in these events,' Harrigan said. 'Secondly, he may not have wanted to bring down a company he'd worked so hard to establish here. That affidavit is almost entirely a personal attack on the man he accuses of bribing him, so much so it undermines what he has to say. I'd like to know what his state of mind was when he wrote it. If we'd had the chance to go through it with him, it might have been a different story.'

'That can't happen now.'

'That's the point.'

'This is all conjecture. Do you have any real evidence to back this scenario other than these assertions?' Parkin asked. 'Because let me tell you, Commander, even if this was true, you'd have the devil's own job proving it.'

'Proof is what we're looking for,' Harrigan said. 'Trev. I asked you to look into Sam Jonas. What did you find out about her?'

'She's on the books of the same security firm as du Plessis,' Trevor said. 'Griffin Enterprises. She gave their name and number as a reference on her résumé. When we rang, they confirmed that, but as soon as we said who we were they put the phone down and now they won't take our calls.'

'Who is this person?' Parkin asked.

'One of Elena Calvo's security people,' Harrigan said. 'She's a wild card. I think it's worth finding out who she really is.'

'Do you have any reason to believe she's involved in any of this?'

'We've just heard she shares an agency with du Plessis. My information is, she was tailing Beck for months before his death. Yes, I think she'll have something to tell us.'

'Then we'll wait to find out what she has to say. But all these things you've put forward need proof,' Parkin said.

'If we get du Plessis, we have a good chance of getting some of the information we need. This is where your people and mine could cooperate.'

'Commander, we all know that du Plessis supposedly abducted your son. Are you sure you're not letting any personal feelings get in the way of your judgement?'

'I never do. If you knew anything about the way I work, you'd know that was true.'

'So you say.' Parkin stood up. 'In my eyes, we're already cooperating. Every law enforcement agency in the country is out there searching for this man. But if this scenario is where your antenna is fixed right now, I prefer to follow my own investigation. Is that the full body of information you have for us so far?'

'Pretty much,' Trevor said.

'Then thank you again.' Parkin's two colleagues got to their feet as well. 'We'll get to work. We'll certainly be in touch with what we find, and we expect to hear from you too. In the meantime, Commander, if you get any proof of that scenario, you bring it to us. I'm happy to hear facts but I've never been interested in fantasies.'

Harrigan didn't reply. They walked out.

'Arseholes,' Frankie muttered.

There was silence.

'Where do we go from here, boss?' Trevor asked.

'Where you're going now,' Harrigan replied. 'Keep looking into Calvo's background. Check out Sam Jonas. Sit down and work through the information again. In my opinion, you're on the right track. Meantime, I think everyone here needs a break. Get some fresh air. Trev, your office now.'

At his desk, a change came over Trevor. The public face had gone; he seemed to have trouble looking Harrigan in the eye.

'I got your wire, boss. I'm guessing that's why you wanted to talk to me.' He passed the paraphernalia over to Harrigan. 'Are you sure you just want to record? You don't want us to listen in?'

'No, what you've given me is fine.'

'Boss, your son being snatched like that. What was it really about?'

'What do you think it's about?' Harrigan said.

'He wanted something from you, didn't he?' Trevor asked quietly.

Harrigan shook his head.

'Come on, boss. Was it what Freeman gave Gracie, maybe? Did you give it to this du Plessis? He didn't even tell you where your boy was. Gracie found him, thank Christ.'

'Grace got some information for us,' Harrigan said, changing the subject. 'She gave it to me last night. She says there's a connection between Jonas and Brinsmead.'

'How can she know that?'

'To put it simply, she found it out talking to Brinsmead. He'd met her at the LPS launch. He wanted to tell her how he got his burns. He's got a connection to the DRC with du Plessis and Beck. According to him, all three of them were there together.'

'Are you telling me Brinsmead is our anonymous operative in the dossier?' Trevor asked.

'He'd have all the right qualifications,' Harrigan said.

'You didn't say that to the boys and girls out there.'

'Grace thinks Brinsmead and Jonas might be legitimate operatives from a secret service agency and their brief is to find out what Beck and LPS are up to. Now that scenario makes sense, but we have to find out whether it's actually true. If we advertise this information, we could be sabotaging their investigation. But if they're rogue, then they're right in the picture for this. They're an obvious source for the dossier, for example.' Harrigan spoke more quietly. 'I'd also be looking at Sam Jonas for Marvin's shooting.'

'What makes you think that?'

'Gut. And the fact that it couldn't have been du Plessis.'

'What are you going to do, boss?'

'See the commissioner as soon as I leave this office. Ask him to take the question to ASIO. If Brinsmead and Jonas are legitimate, then they're the ones who should be able to find that fact out for us. Until we know that, I don't want this information going anywhere. It's between you and me. That's why I've waited until now to discuss it with you. I wanted to think it through first.'

'What about getting a statement from Gracie?'

'We do need to do that. I'll talk to her about it. In the meantime, add Brinsmead to your list of people to check out. There's something else you need to know. There are crop specimens in existence. Harold Morrissey took some and gave them to me to bring back. They're at the Millennium lab right now being tested.'

'You didn't enlighten our federal friends about that.'

'Right now I want this information kept confidential until we know who Jonas and Brinsmead are.'

'Why didn't you tell me you had those specimens before, boss? Was it because of Marvin. You knew he was being run, didn't you?' Trevor said.

'I guessed.'

'Look, as far as I'm concerned you're still the boss. I haven't forgotten what you did for me in the commissioner's office the other day. But Jesus, mate, if you had an idea about Marvin you could have told me. Maybe we could have worked something out. We've lost enough evidence as it is.'

'I warned you, mate, if you remember. I spent a lot of time and effort keeping him at bay. It's why I'm going after Calvo now. I want her to incriminate herself.'

'Isn't she too smart for that?'

'It depends on how desperate she is.'

'All right, we'll go with it.'

'There are no secrets from now on, mate,' Harrigan said.

'You've got nothing left to hide, boss. Is that what you mean?'

'I mean you can trust me.'

'I always have, mate. Believe it or not, I still do.'

The commissioner made time for Harrigan as soon as he heard his request and then listened to what he had to say intently. Once Harrigan had finished, it took him some minutes to reply

'That's one way of getting information,' he said. 'But I know Ms Riordan was a police officer and my understanding is she still works in the field in some way. Her reputation says her word is reliable. She was also able to find Toby.'

'Our investigation can't move forward until we get the status of these two individuals cleared up.'

'I've found your judgement dependable, Paul. Leave it with me. I'll ask ASIO the question. We can't be assured of an immediate response but we'll see what they have to say. If they tell us hands off, we'll know where we stand.'

When Harrigan finally left the building, he was wired for sound. He had Elena Calvo to see; it wasn't a prospect that made him happy. Later this evening he wanted to see Grace if he could, badly. Someone to make him feel human, to get him out of his head. At the moment, the idea had the appeal of a very welcome change.

26

The city offices of Life Patent Strategies were on the thirty-third floor of Australia Square. As promised, a man was waiting to meet Harrigan at the entrance to the underground car park. He didn't introduce himself, but politely showed Harrigan where to park and then led him into the elevator. It deposited them near a glass door decorated with the LPS insignia. Elena's bodyguard Damien was waiting to let them into a reception area furnished with soft chairs. A padded silence absorbed sound. The first bodyguard stationed himself by the door while Damien showed Harrigan to Elena's office.

It was a large and uncluttered room with a minimal amount of furniture. Clearly, she liked space around her. It stretched from the door to her desk and on either side of her. She had been waiting for him in silence; a visitor's chair was already in place. Briefly, he looked past her at the view. Against a perfect sky, the glass towers at North Sydney showed a strangely insubstantial outline. She turned to look as well.

'It's breathtaking, isn't it?' she said. 'I'm never tired of that view, it makes me feel free. I've very rarely felt that in my life. Please sit down, Commander. I'm going to trust you once again. That's all, Damien. I'll call you.'

Both waited until the door had closed behind the bodyguard. Harrigan watched her take in the sight of his damaged face.

'You can trust me, Dr Calvo,' he said. 'In fact, you can rely on me.'

'Why do I need to rely on you? My understanding of this meeting is that we're here to discuss your son. Does this mean you've changed your mind since the last time I saw you? If I recall, at that time I offered you a number of things and you refused them all. Are you now prepared to accept them?'

'Like you said that first time we met, Dr Calvo, assuming we go ahead with those arrangements, you'd have expectations of me. There are a few matters in relation to those expectations I'd like to discuss. If you really do want my services, that is.'

He stopped. She gestured for him to go on.

'My guess is, you know more about what's going on right now than just about anybody else. I think you have a very good idea of why those people were shot up at Pittwater even if you don't necessarily know who did it.'

'We're not here to talk about me, Commander.' She shut him down with one of the iciest stares he had seen. 'You've changed the subject. We're here to talk about your son. Are you prepared to enter into an agreement with me concerning his future wellbeing?'

'That depends. Andreas du Plessis kidnapped my son and put me through hell. Worse, he left my son to die of thirst in a long-stay car park. The deal was that my son came home alive. I want an answer from you. Whose idea was it to renege on the deal?'

'I know nothing about those events and I don't see what this has to do with me,' she said. 'But I will say that in business, you will almost certainly fail, and fail very badly, if you don't keep your word once you've given it. If I give an undertaking, I always stand by it without exception.'

'In other words, you're washing your hands of your dirty tricks man.'

'Why are you saying that to me? Are you recording this? This smells of entrapment, Commander. I have two bodyguards waiting outside. Should I call them in here? I know a great deal about you. It's unwise for you to put me offside.'

'I know quite a lot about you too, Dr Calvo. Have a look at this.'

From his wallet, he took a copy of the photograph of the couple and their child in a ruined city in 1946. She glanced down at it on the desk and then back at him. She said nothing and didn't touch it.

'My squad found this picture in Jerome Beck's wallet when we found his body. You said that at the end of World War Two, your father was a displaced person. Was he ever in Dresden? It's a long way from your childhood, isn't it? Something for Beck to resent mightily. Is that what you were arguing about in the car park that night in June four-and-a-half years ago? You deal in DNA, Dr Calvo. We have Beck's DNA. Would you like to do a match?'

Elena rested her elbows on her desk, her chin on her hands, looking at him. She was very still. Harrigan put the photograph back in his wallet.

'My guess is, when Beck found out from his mother who his father really was, he went looking for him. Your father gave him a job. Everything I've heard about your father tells me he's not the sentimental type. He must have found something for his long lost son to do. Something useful to the family firm. Whatever it was, it paid very well. That probably means it was something no one else was prepared to do. I think he went to the Democratic Republic of the Congo with du Plessis. They were working for your father. Whatever Beck was doing here, he was doing it for your father as well. That's the key, isn't it? Whatever program Beck was running at that research facility in north London, it was for your father. In this country, it was genetically modified crops that harm people in some way and the research was being done out at Campbelltown. Now, that's not good publicity.'

She leant forward to speak.

'In business, it's never a good idea to use guesswork as a basis for a decision. It's much better to work from factual information. I don't think you have any means of backing up these bizarre theories.'

'The contract would have given us that information if we still had it. What did Daniel tell me the morning I visited you? Every contract Abaris draws up records in detail who owns the patent rights and the intellectual property. That's one of the reasons you wanted to get hold of it so badly, isn't it? Except someone was thinking ahead of you. There's still another copy out there somewhere. The killers have got it. You've got no leverage where they're concerned.'

'Are you telling me you do?' she asked. 'You don't know who they are. I don't think you have any way of finding out.'

'Do you have a way of finding out? Do you have something to guide you that we don't? A suspicion that you can't quite shake off as impossible? Do you think they're going to come after you? Is that why you have two bodyguards in a building as secure as the facility at Campbelltown? You do need me.'

'If you don't know who these killers are, what can you do for me? A bodyguard is more useful.'

'In business,' Harrigan said, 'it's a good idea to trust people who can offer you something no one else can. You just accused me of entrapment. There are two things you can do. You can trust me and give me what I want. Or I can walk out of here and run this investigation the way it should be run, the way I would usually run it. I can do that now Marvin Tooth is a dead man. Then one day, sooner rather than later, we'll find your dirty tricks man and come knocking on your door. Then everything you've worked for will be on the line. You know that. You've moved heaven and earth to protect yourself already.'

'What do you want?'

'I want du Plessis. No one does that to my son and gets away with it. I want him to pay personally for what he did to Toby. Organise that for me, Dr Calvo, and we both get what we want. Wouldn't you call that a win-win situation?'

'And after that?' she said.

'One step at a time,' Harrigan replied.

'How can I arrange to give you something I don't have?'

'I said I wanted you to trust me. You set it up, Dr Calvo. You set up a meeting and you give me the details.'

'For any deal, there's always a cooling-off period. I need twenty-four hours.'

'The last time I spoke to you, you told me there was no time.'

'I gave you time anyway, if you recall. You can do the same for me,' she replied. She glanced at her watch and then at him. The intensity of her stare made him want to look away. 'I'll call you tomorrow morning first thing. Can we say this meeting is finished?'

'If you call me tomorrow morning, what do we do? Do we meet here?'

'Most probably, yes. I'm usually here on a Saturday.' She pressed a button on her intercom. 'Damien, would you come in, please?'

Almost immediately, Damien appeared.

'Good afternoon,' Elena said to Harrigan with a polite smile. 'Damien, see the commander gets to his car. Make sure he gets there safely.'

Harrigan decided it was better to say nothing.

Damien didn't leave until he had watched him drive out of the car park. At the next set of red lights, Harrigan turned off the wire. There was more space left on the tape. He would wear it again tomorrow. One step at a time. She was more desperate than he'd thought. Now he just had to wait and see if throwing the berley would work.

Harrigan didn't go home. He drove to the Bondi Junction shopping mall where he went to the gents and took off the wire, locking it in his briefcase. The florist was about to close. He was just in time to buy Grace a dozen long-stemmed red roses before driving over to see her unannounced. He didn't want to risk calling her first and have her tell him she didn't want to see him. To his relief, she answered the buzzer.

'Hi, Abbie, you didn't have to come and get me. I'm not ready yet. I'll buzz you in.'

Abbie was Abigail, Grace's closest friend and a criminal lawyer with a fierce reputation.

'It's not Abbie,' Harrigan said. 'It's me. Do you want to see me?'

There was the briefest of pauses.

'Okay.'

When he reached her floor, he found that her front door was ajar for him. Inside, she was standing in front of the full-length mirror on her wardrobe applying the last of her make-up. Her dress shimmered in the glass. He shut the door behind him.

'You're going out,' he said. 'Where are you going?'

'To dinner with the girls. Then we're going to a party at Noah's.'

She put her lipstick down on her dressing table and looked at herself. There was silence.

'You look lovely,' he said. 'I've brought you some flowers.'

She took them from him, awkwardly, without looking at him. 'Thanks. They're beautiful. I'll put them in water.'

She didn't sound as if she meant it. In her tiny kitchen, she filled the sink with water and left them there, not looking for a vase. Suddenly, she opened the drawer where she kept her bills and then shut it. Immediately, he knew what she was doing: searching for her cigarettes. It was one of her strategies, so called, for dealing with her addiction. She refused to buy cartons, only single packets of twenties, and sometimes found herself late at night without a cigarette. On these occasions, she tried to hang on. In her flat, she kept a spare packet salted away for those emergencies when her stamina gave out and she had to light up. Sometimes, when she hadn't used it for a while, she forgot where this packet was hidden.

'You'll have some in your bag,' he said.

'It doesn't matter.'

'Where are you going for dinner?'

She had knelt down and was looking in the cupboard under the sink.

'Claude's,' she said. 'I didn't ask you because I didn't think there was any chance you'd have the time.'

He had never liked going to expensive restaurants; he always thought of it as a waste of money. It was another difference between them. To Grace, money was something you spent. She shut the cupboard door and stood in front of the sink with her hands on her hips, not looking at him.

'What do you want?' she asked.

'I wanted to see you. I have time. Maybe we could go somewhere. If you want to go out, why don't you let me take you out? Just you and me. You choose. Wherever you like.'

'Maybe we could go somewhere. Why don't I let you take me out?' she repeated and then pulled open another kitchen drawer. She stood there looking down at it. 'I wanted to see you last night and you didn't have the time. Now you've got a couple of hours to spare for me and you just breeze in here like this and say that. The roses are supposed to make it all okay. That's one way you can get your sex, I suppose.'

Harrigan was genuinely insulted. 'Grace, I've never treated you like that. I think you should take it easy with what you say. I've been under a lot of pressure lately.'

'You always are. You always will be. You'll always have a really good reason why you can't be here. Fine. I'm not going to ask you for one. The other night I thought, I can't put myself through this again. Let's just finish with it.'

'I thought we were going to see it through until I had this investigation under control.'

'That was before you didn't ring me when I asked you to and before you gave me all this time to think about it. Nothing's going to change. We might as well face up to that now.'

She pushed the kitchen drawer shut. A bag the same colour as her dress was on the table. He picked it up.

'You'll have some cigarettes in here. I'll get them for you.'

'No, don't do that!'

It was too late. He took out not her cigarettes but a small old handgun. He put her bag back on the table and turned the gun over in his hand.

'Do you carry this around with you all the time? Are you taking this to your party tonight?'

'I've got a place in my car where I hide it,' she said. 'Give it back.'

'You don't have your car with you right now. Is this legal?'

'What do you think?'

'No wonder you didn't want a gun when I offered you one the other day. You already had one. Why do you need this?'

'You're the one who said I needed protection. Anyway, aren't you armed?'

'Not at the moment. Don't change the subject. You didn't get this in the last few days. Why do you need it? Why do you need to have it in your car?'

'It's none of your business,' she said, her voice growing angry. 'Give it back.'

'Not until you tell me why you've got it. Have you had this all the time we've been together? Because you thought you needed the protection. From me? Or from someone else? Do you think I wouldn't protect you?'

'How could you? You don't have enough time to do that.'

This hurt him.

'You tell me what this is about, Grace. I'm not leaving until you do.'

'Don't talk to me like that. You're so used to telling people what to do. Give that back to me. It's got nothing to do with you. I'm going out now and I need it.' Moving suddenly and quickly, she reached to snatch the gun out of his hand.

'Don't do that! I am not going to fight with you over a gun!'

He felt himself losing control at some deeper level. He spun away from her, turning his back. He broke the gun down instinctively, shaking out the bullets, then with all the strength he had, he smashed it down on the floor tiles in her small kitchen alcove. It cracked with a noise that made him think it must have accidentally fired. It couldn't have fired, he'd broken it down. It would be unusable now, the barrel cracked or damaged in some way, making it too dangerous to fire. Ammunition lay scattered where it had fallen. Her tiles were cracked and splintered. He turned to her. She was gaping at him.

'Why did you do that?'

'You get shot fighting over guns. Do you think I want to see you with a bullet wound in your head? One I put there? If that did happen, I'd probably feel like putting one in my own head!'

They stared at each other in silence. Then she took her cigarettes out of her bag and lit one.

'No,' she said. 'That isn't the reason, not for you to act like that. Why did you do that? Tell me.'

He looked down at the shattered tiles and then at her.

'When I was eighteen, my father shot my mother. It was Cassatt's gun, I've got it in my cellar. He'd had a run-in with a dealer on the docks and he'd shot him. He gave my father the gun to hide. My mother did what you just tried to do, take it out of his hands. He shot her in the face. Cassatt handled the investigation, he got my father off. When we were leaving the law courts, he turned me and said "Your father loved your mother, mate. You ought to realise that." I hit him so hard, I knocked out one of his front teeth. I saw what my mother looked like when she died. I'm not going to live with another memory like that.'

She put her cigarette in an ashtray on the table and sat down with her face in her hands. 'That's why you went after him. I didn't know. I'm so sorry.'

'You don't have to say any more than that. This is as much as we'll ever need to say about this ever again.' He sat down opposite her. 'Your turn, Grace. Tell me why you've got that gun.'

She picked up her cigarette and smoked with her eyes closed, shaking from head to foot. He had never seen her like this. He thought it was better that he didn't try to touch her. She opened her eyes.

'Someone used to stalk me once. He was sort of a boyfriend for a while. We broke up over ten years ago but he kept coming back. I got that gun —' She stopped. 'I got that gun after I came home from a party one night and he was waiting for me in the car park. He threw petrol all over me.'

Harrigan was silent. It was one of the few occasions in his life when he could truthfully say he was shocked.

'I heard him say, "My lighter's not working." Something like that. I turned and ran. I wondered later if it was a joke but I don't think it was. I locked myself in my flat and I sat under the shower fully dressed for hours just soaking myself with water. The next day I moved out of that flat and into this one. Then I got hold of that gun. That's why I have it, in case he comes back.'

Harrigan was drumming his fingers softly on the table top.

'Who is this person? What's his name?'

She shook her head.

'No, what's his name?'

'Chris Newell,' she said after a while.

He took out his notebook and wrote it down.

'Where is he now?'

'Silverwater. He got seven years for armed robbery about a year ago. I kept my gun just in case he got out again somehow. It's a security blanket. I don't feel safe without it now.'

Harrigan jotted down these small details without asking how she'd got involved with someone like that in the first place.

'What are you going to do?' she asked.

'Keep an eye on him. Maybe a little more. He sounds like he deserves some attention. Why didn't you tell me? I would have warned him off for you. I would have made sure he never came back.'

She lit another cigarette from the end of the one she was smoking without answering him.

'Is he the one who gave you your scar?'

'It was a long time ago. I was only nineteen. It was when I was still singing with my band. He was supposed to be our manager. Then we found out he was dealing on the side. I'd already decided I didn't want to sing any more. When I told him it was all over between us, he beat me up and told me I wasn't going anywhere. When he wasn't looking, I walked out. I took my car and I drove and I didn't stop. Then I heard he was in gaol, he'd walked into a sting. He thought I'd dobbed him in but I hadn't. When he got out, he came after me.' She put her second cigarette in the ashtray and drew a deep breath. 'I thought I knew everything back then. I was so green. It's all over now. I'm a different person.'

'You never reported him.'

'I was drinking back then. I don't know what kind of a witness I would have made. I didn't want to put myself through that. I was too frightened of him. That's the truth.'

'If he ever comes near you again, it'll be the last time he ever does. That's a promise.'

He raped you, he understood, watching her ash, then scrub out her cigarette. He raped you and he left you with that scar. Because men who give women scars like you have almost always do that. Seventeen years on the job had taught him this as a fact of experience. She would never tell him that directly to his face; it would always be unspoken.

She had stopped shaking. Her face was drawn, her eye make-up smudged.

'You matter to me,' he said. 'You must know that. You must know how much.'

'Then why are you never here? It's the work you do. It crushes everything else out of your life except Toby, and that's only because he's the other half of you.'

'You want me to change.'

'You don't have to work the hours you work. You don't have to be everyone's saviour. I know an addiction when I see one. It fills a gap for you. Can't you imagine having something else in your life as well?'

'What do you want me to do?'

'I'm not going to live with things the way they are now. I don't want to break up. I don't want to put myself through that. But I don't want to live like this either. You have to make a choice as to what you really want. You're the only one who can do that. I have to wash my face.'

When she came back out of the bathroom, he was clearing away the broken gun into a plastic bag.

'I'll get rid of this,' he said. 'I'll get your tiles fixed. I know someone who owes me a favour. He'll do a good job.'

She smiled. 'I'd be surprised if you didn't.'

The phone rang. Grace let it go through to the answering machine.

'Hi, Gracie, it's Abbie. We're all at Claude's wondering where you are but I guess you've found something better to do. Hope so anyway. Maybe we'll see you at Noah's. We just hope you're not with Harrigan. Give us a call tomorrow, will you? See you.'

'Don't they approve of me?' he asked.

'Of course they don't. They think you're a Neanderthal. But then they think the same thing about me for doing what I do. According to Abbie's latest boyfriend, I'm the original fascist.'

He laughed.

'You look beautiful. We don't have to sit here all night. Let's go out.'

'Not just like that. What happens tomorrow?'

'After twenty-four hours, I may have all the time you want me to have with you.'

'What do you mean?'

'I'm fishing for Elena Calvo. I've already seen her to get it started. I'm waiting to see if she's going to bite and if she's going to give me du Plessis as well as herself. If she does, that could be the end of my career.'

'You gave him the tape. She knows that.'

'It's not just that. Du Plessis has the contents of Mike's safety deposit box. If I take Elena Calvo down, I'm sure she'll take me with her.'

'This could cost you a lot more than your job,' she said. 'What are you setting up?'

'A sting. There's no way back from it now. You say I work too much. Let me stop working for now. Let's go out and enjoy ourselves.'

'You didn't answer my question. What happens tomorrow?'

'Let's wait for the sun to come up on Sunday morning first. When it does, if it does, I work out what I want. I do want you in my life. If you want to be there.'

'I'm here now. If that's how things are, then I think we should go out. Have fun. We may not get another chance. Wait till I put my make-up on again.'

She had other places to go besides Claude's. A smaller restaurant she'd just discovered; a nightclub where the band was the best she'd heard all year. 'The singer has a magic voice,' she told him. He didn't drink much; tomorrow he needed a clear head.

'What happens now?' she asked, much later when they were lying in her bed. 'How do you know when you've caught your fish?'

'Whatever Calvo's going to do, she'll move quickly. Probably she'll want to see me sometime tomorrow. She'll have the meeting set up already. When I go to it, du Plessis will either be there waiting for me or he'll be following me. If Calvo wants him to get rid of me, my bet is that everything Cassatt had on me will be left behind with my body. That'll take care of my credibility forever. But if Calvo wants me to remove du Plessis for her, then he won't be expecting me. The difficulty I have is getting her to incriminate herself on tape. She's very cagey about what she says. But she's frightened. That'll work for me.'

'That strategy is so dangerous.'

'I'll get through it. I've got Trevor onside and my backup in place. Let's sleep now. We need to.'

They did sleep. For now, the morning could take care of itself.

27

When Harrigan's phone woke him, it was still dark. When he sat up, he felt Grace stir beside him.

'Harrigan.'

'Sorry to wake you, boss. It's Jacquie here. I'm on the night shift. Do you have access to a computer? You should have an email in your inbox now. You need to see it.'

'Can you tell me what I'll be looking at?'

'A video that's been posted on the Pittwater website. I'd say it was shot clandestinely. It's got the same file reference number as the dossier. It must have been made as part of that whole operation. Also, the dossier and the senator's affidavit have been put up on the Pittwater site as well. Whoever's behind this is making sure everyone can join the dots.'

'I'll look at it now.'

Grace came and sat beside him while he turned her computer on. This time, a single email had been posted to his mailbox. The subject line read: *This is real.* In the body of the email was a URL. Harrigan hit it.

He found himself watching a video. A reference number with a time and date stamp were visible in a header. It was December four years ago. From a camera's eye view, there appeared on the monitor the sight of raggedly dressed, armed African men climbing onto the back of a truck. The angle looked down at the troops; the photographer must have been standing against the back of the cabin. Another truck was following the first. They drove out of a city affected by war, through local markets, hurrying crowds, buildings marked by decay and painted with slogans. The name Kinshasa appeared in the header. Then the photographer sat down like the others on the floor of the tray.

There was a jump in the sequence. The photographer must have been sitting in the cabin. The truck was driving along a forested road. In front was a group of civilians with their belongings in bundles on their heads and backs, their children hurrying with them. They ran into the forest at the sight of the truck. A skeleton lay in thick vines on the side of the road, still fully dressed, its death's head looking out at the watcher.

The trucks came to a stop in a deserted village. The photographer got out and went to meet the driver, who was also getting out of the truck. Harrigan recognised Jerome Beck. He grinned and spoke but there was no sound. The other driver appeared from the second truck: du Plessis, also talking and grinning soundlessly.

The next image showed the village turned into an encampment with two tents set up in the centre. Two of the soldiers were dragging a terrified young girl towards one of the tents. Again the video jumped. The eye was now inside one of the tents. It watched one figure hold the young girl in a chair while another injected her with something. Both wore protective clothing. Then the eye followed her running out of the tent and through the encampment, while the soldiers watched her from a distance, laughing. She made her escape along a dirt road through a partially forested landscape. The camera turned back to the entrance to the tent. The people in protective clothing were seen walking outside. They washed their gloved hands in some solution, then poured it over their heads. Then they took off their headgear. Harrigan again found himself looking at Beck and du Plessis.

Next, Beck, without protective clothing, was walking through a village where a number of people lay either dead or dying on the ground outside their houses. He stopped to look down at them, his hands on his hips. Then he went inside a house. The young girl from the earlier video, recognisable by the dress she had been wearing, lay curled up on a mat, her face to the wall. Beck was joined by du Plessis.

The angle was from behind them, looking between them. They stood looking at the girl, talking, then walked away.

The watcher and the two men moved from house to house. Other people were shown inside, most of them dead. Some were still alive but sick, lying in their beds, turning their faces away from the intruders.

Then the eye went back outside. It showed the armed men standing on the periphery of the small village, apparently refusing to come any closer. Du Plessis went up to them; some backed away. He talked angrily to them, gesturing to them to come closer. Reluctantly, they began to move forward. Then, with du Plessis, they moved through the village, shooting whoever had been left alive. Meanwhile, Beck was talking to one of the men. The man was gesturing down the road; the inference was that some of the villagers had fled.

The eye swung around quickly. It was heading towards one of the trucks on the edge of the village. The truck door was pulled open, the photographer was climbing inside the cabin. Then his hands were on the wheel and he was driving away at speed. A distance down the road, he stopped to collect a small group of villagers, one of whom was carrying a child. A man climbed in the front and spoke to the driver. He was directing him. Presumably the others had climbed into the back.

The truck moved on down the dirt road. Eventually it came to another, larger village that seemed equally deserted. They were passing a large white building when the truck stopped suddenly. It had broken down.

Next, the driver and the villagers were inside what must have once been a schoolhouse. The eye looked out of the window. The other truck carrying the soldiers had stopped outside. In the open space in front of the school, Beck and du Plessis got out of the cabin; the armed men spilled out of the back. They surrounded the building. Through a window, Beck could be seen standing and shouting at whoever was inside the school.

Then Beck gestured to three of the men. The eye watched them return from the truck carrying jerry cans. Then it followed them from window to window as they threw what could only be petrol against the walls of the building. One of them tossed a lighted rag onto the petrol, which burst into flames. The woman with the child ran out of one of the doors. What happened to her the camera did not show and there was no sound. In its eye view, the walls and roof had begun to burn fiercely. Flames rained down around the camera. It saw people burning. Then it was pushed through a door into another room, a storage area with a window on one side. At floor level there was a long metal grille. The ceiling came down in curtains of flame. The eye was propelled towards the dirt floor against the grille. Then there was nothing.

When the video was over, Harrigan and Grace sat in silence for some moments. Then she got to her feet and went to the kitchen where she began to make coffee.

'Now we know how Brinsmead got his burns,' Harrigan said. 'He was an agent in an undercover operation that went wrong.'

'Yes,' Grace said shortly, her back to him.

He went to her. She was crying. He put his arms around her and comforted her, pleased that he had this to do. Anything to occupy his thoughts while he tried to find some meaningful way to deal with what he had just seen.

'That's why I do the job I do,' she said. 'Knowing that people can do that kind of thing to other people. I hate it, and if I can stop them or get them, I will.'

The coffee was ready. She poured them a mug each and lit a cigarette.

'Go after them,' she said. 'Go after the people behind that massacre with everything you've got. Get du Plessis. Take him to trial.'

'I'm doing my best. But someone with the authority to do it shut down that original operation.'

'Had they seen that video? They could have prosecuted Beck and du Plessis on the strength of that.'

'But they didn't. We don't know why and I don't think anyone's going to tell us.'

'Daniel Brinsmead will know,' she said. 'Somehow he got out of there and was still alive enough to be flown back to London. He must have had that video on him then.'

'You want my opinion? He's involved in the shooting up at Pittwater. Him and Jonas together. For all I know, they're our murderers. I can't feel for him.'

315

'We don't know that for sure.'

'Calvo didn't have the motive to kill those people and then advertise it. That video gives Brinsmead all the motive he needs to kill Beck.'

'He and Sam didn't talk that way when I was listening to them the other day. They talked like professional agents. If they are, they can't be your murderers. Did you find out if they were legitimate?'

'I've asked the question. I don't know when I'll get an answer or even if I'll be told.'

'That video is as much motive for Calvo as it is for Daniel Brinsmead,' Grace said. 'It's what she has to cover up. She is a murderer. A murderer just like the people behind the killings we saw on that video just now. Someone who gets other people to do it for them. They don't even have the guts to do it for themselves. They're worse than the people who actually pull the triggers.'

'She's definitely one of them. Grace, you need to calm down. We can only deal with this calmly. That's the only thing we can do for those people now.'

Grace moved away, restlessly. 'I want to know the whys and the wherefores,' she said. 'Who's behind what. Calvo would know.'

Harrigan's phone rang.

'Paul,' the commissioner said. 'Can you come to a meeting in my office immediately? We have a significant development in the Pittwater investigation.'

'Are you referring to the video that's on the net, Commissioner?'

'It's connected to that. We'll see you as soon as you can get here.'

'I'm on my way.'

'You have to go again,' Grace said.

'I don't know when I'll be back but I'll call you. I'll let you know what's going on. That's a promise this time.'

'I'll wait,' she said, wiping her eyes. 'What else can I do but sit here and be useless?'

'Just stay safe.'

It wasn't yet five when Harrigan hit the road. The traffic was sparse in the early summer Saturday morning. There was a fragile sense of the dawn's coolness soon to disappear in the heat of the day. When he reached the commissioner's office, Chloe was waiting for him. She ushered him in immediately. Another man was there for the meeting. Harrigan didn't recognise him.

'Paul, let me introduce you,' the commissioner said. 'This is Stephen Grey; he's a first assistant commissioner with ASIO. Stephen, this is Commander Paul Harrigan. With the special assistant commissioner's demise, he's the executive officer in charge of the Pittwater task force.'

They shook hands.

'Thank you for coming in at this hour, Commander,' Grey said. 'I'll get to the heart of the matter. I'm here to advise you that at about 3 a.m. today, we attempted to execute arrest warrants on two individuals who, the commissioner tells me, are persons of interest to your investigation: Dr Daniel Brinsmead and Sam Jonas.'

'Do you have them in custody?'

'We do not. They'd flown the coop. At present, their whereabouts are unknown. Let me give you the background. The photograph of the dead associated with your investigation showed a Jerome Beck. Shortly after that photograph was published on the net, he was recognised by a certain agency in Britain with the code name Falcon, a highly secret anti-terrorist organisation. They contacted us and asked us to place a watching brief on your investigation. They sent us photographs of two individuals they were interested in, the two I've just identified to you. Both are former agents of Falcon. Both were the primary operatives for the operation recorded in that dossier and also in the video that was posted on the net this morning. Their operation was shut down in December four years ago. It was ruled a failure that almost resulted in Brinsmead's death. These two individuals have stolen and now illegally published secret information. Both have turned rogue, in other words. Jonas was at one time a highly respected career agent named Sophia Ricks. At present, she's impersonating a dead woman.'

'I should tell you, Paul, I was aware that this watching brief was in place,' the commissioner said. 'When you spoke to me yesterday, I rang ASIO to take advice on what information your squad should receive. It's impressive that you found these two individuals out through your own investigations.'

'It's also the reason we're having this meeting,' Grey said. 'Secrecy is of the utmost importance at the present. It was necessary for you to be made aware of the gravity of the situation before that information was passed on.'

Harrigan thought how much easier life would have been if he had been told sooner.

'Do we know what made these people turn rogue?' he asked. 'Because that operation had gone bad and was shut down?'

'I think that's a question you should ask them,' Grey said. 'They may have felt it was an act of betrayal. From the information I have, my opinion is that Brinsmead was a poor choice for an operation of this nature. I'm advised he was a close, long-term friend of Ricks — not a good situation to begin with — and was chosen on her recommendation for his scientific skills and his previous experience in the army. By all accounts, he didn't have the temperament for undercover work.'

'You are aware that both individuals were in the employ of or were connected to a Dr Elena Calvo?'

'We do know that. It's clear she's been imposed upon. We will be speaking to Dr Calvo in due course. At present, we don't consider it the right time for an interview. We're uncertain about her allegiances to Dr Brinsmead. She was previously involved with him, and since his return from the DRC she's given him a great deal of support. We don't want her warning him.'

'I think it will be the other way around,' Harrigan said. 'I think you should warn her.'

'I'm sorry but that can't happen. It could jeopardise the operation. I understand she has very professional security of her own. We'll rely on that.'

'Did the parent agency in Britain know these two people were working for her?'

'They were aware of Brinsmead. We found Ricks for them. As part of our watching brief, we sent an agent to Dr Calvo's launch. She identified her as Calvo's personal bodyguard.'

Harrigan decided there was no future in advising either Grey or the commissioner that he had known about Sam from the beginning and could have identified her from whatever picture they happened to have.

'I've advised Stephen that both they and an individual who appeared in this morning's video, Andreas du Plessis, are persons of interest to us,' the commissioner said. 'Could you tell us where we are with that?'

'It's very early days. The case we have against them is in its infancy,' Harrigan replied. 'It's more a matter of circumstance than evidence, but in my judgement Brinsmead and Jonas are responsible for the killings at Pittwater and also the special assistant commissioner's shooting. Again in my judgement, du Plessis was the agent responsible for the murder of Senator Edwards and his adviser. Obviously we're still acquiring evidence.'

'Do you have any idea who du Plessis was an agent for?' Grey asked.

'Elena Calvo,' Harrigan said after a pause.

'Are you sure?' the commissioner asked.

'She's the one with the motive. She's got a lot to protect.'

'The senator was a friend of hers. Is she a danger to the community?'

Harrigan considered it was fair enough to say Elena Calvo had taken care of all eventualities and probably didn't mean anyone else any harm. Why else might she be prepared to give him the opportunity to remove the one person who could incriminate her: du Plessis?

'No,' he said.

'Do you have any proof?' Grey asked.

'We're in the process of acquiring it. Circumstances indicate there is a connection between Elena Calvo and Beck and also between LPS and Beck's activities with the International Agricultural Research Consortium. At this stage, I can't afford to rule her out as a possibility.'

'Whatever Beck was doing has been shut down, hasn't it?' Grey said. 'In which case, Commissioner, we will leave that part of the investigation to you and your people. It's not our responsibility. That's a case you'll have to prove yourself.'

'The issue we have to deal with now is where this leaves our entire investigation,' the commissioner said. 'The Minister for Police spoke to me late last night, Paul. The federal government has requested we direct our manpower to support ASIO in their hunt for these two individuals. Obviously, we'll comply with that.'

'You should know that the British government intends to extradite both Brinsmead and Jonas for stealing and publishing top secret government information,' Grey said. 'Those extradition warrants will be ready to be executed very soon.'

'Be that as it may, we still have a significant murder inquiry to pursue,' the Commissioner said.

'As I've said,' Grey replied, 'for the British government this is a matter of national security. Falcon is an extremely important agency. Its operations cannot be compromised. If there is a murder trial for these two individuals here in Australia, then there is certain evidence they cannot be allowed to present in an open court. If a prosecution is to proceed, it will need a narrow focus. Specifically, any information relating to the operation in which Brinsmead received his burns will need to be excluded.'

'We can try to do that,' Harrigan said, 'but there's so much information out on the net, it's impossible that any kind of suppression orders will be effective. Everything on their website has been posted all over the world.'

'Then we have to move into damage control. From here on in we must maintain secrecy and let that publicity die.'

It would be a useless exercise. Harrigan left this unsaid.

'Do we know why Falcon didn't pursue Beck and du Plessis for murder four years ago?' he asked instead. 'There was enough evidence.'

'I have no information on that,' Grey said. 'Our primary role in this is to arrest two individuals who have contravened British national security laws.'

'Where does that leave du Plessis? If we apprehend him, is there any intention he be charged for the massacre we just saw on the net?'

'Before anything, Falcon will want to interview him and determine what he does and doesn't know. He may also need to be extradited. If his evidence in any way revealed knowledge of Falcon's operations or its operatives, then that information would have to be prevented from entering the public domain. I understand he's wanted for murder in South Africa. That may have to be sufficient retribution.'

'There's a question of how much access we'll be allowed to any of these individuals once they are apprehended,' the commissioner said. 'If they're to be returned to Britain for questioning almost immediately, when do we get to interview them?'

'You will be given access in due time. But the individuals in question will need to be debriefed first and made to understand what they can and cannot say. Please be assured that we have the political authority of the federal and state governments behind us. It's their intention we cooperate with the British secret service.'

'How long will these debriefings take?' the commissioner asked. 'How will we be advised when these people are available to us?'

'You will be informed at the right time. You have my word on that. Meanwhile, we'll continue with the manhunt. Does that cover everything?'

'Paul. Do you have any questions or comments?'

'These two people have already been driven to act in extreme ways,' Harrigan said. 'I wouldn't underestimate them, particularly now. You may not find them easy to track down, particularly Jonas.'

'This is where you come in, Paul,' the commissioner said. 'I'm making the information you've collected so far available to ASIO. With your and your squad's assistance, they will analyse it here. That process will begin first thing this morning.'

'We'll cooperate in every way.'

'Thank you,' Grey said. 'I think that's all for the time being. Our agents will be here soon. I understand your people are on their way in, those that aren't here already. Good morning.'

'Is Elena Calvo really your choice for the individual du Plessis is working for?' the commissioner asked as soon as Grey had left the room.

'The evidence is circumstantial. But she's the one with the motive and the means.'

'If that's the brief you're going to present to me, it will need to be based on something stronger than circumstantial evidence. Now, regarding this turn of events. Realistically, we have no choice, Paul. The Minister for Police made it very clear to me last night that we are to cooperate. I advised him we'll do what's asked of us.'

'Commissioner, if I could say this. You didn't advise me that this watching brief was in place. We might have been able to assist you with it.'

'I advised no one,' the commissioner said. 'At that stage, I didn't know who I could trust and that's a fact. Given the events of this last week, I think that judgement has been well and truly borne out. But the situation has changed. There's another matter I wanted to discuss with you. Are you happy in your present job?'

'It's challenging. I find it satisfying,' Harrigan replied, taken by surprise.

'Now that the special assistant commissioner is no longer with us, I intend to reorganise the executive ranks. I will be advertising several senior positions quite soon. My advice to you is that you apply for one. I can't promise you a position, of course, but I can promise you your application will receive very careful consideration.'

'Thank you, Commissioner. I'll think very carefully about it.'

'Good. Now, this morning's liaison meeting between ASIO and your squad's senior people — I want you to chair it. I've scheduled it to start at seven thirty. In the meantime, would you like to get some breakfast? Chloe's arranged a buffet in the executive meeting room.'

'Commissioner,' Harrigan said, 'the video that was on the net this morning. What action are we taking about it?'

The commissioner pushed his papers to the side irritably.

'It's not in our jurisdiction. Leave it to the International Criminal Court. Realistically, we have no power to act. You must know that.'

The executive meeting room had a view. If Harrigan's application was successful, he would get an office like the one Marvin used to have, with a similar outlook. Better than the villagers he'd seen on the net this morning, whose only view was the dirt on the sides of their makeshift graves. He ate from Chloe's generous buffet with a bitter taste in his mouth. If he applied for a senior executive position, where would that leave him with Grace? Nowhere, most likely. It would demand even more of his time. Life had snookered him by giving him what he most wanted while making it taste sour at the same time. His phone rang. He was relieved to have his thoughts broken.

'Commander. It's Elena Calvo. If you have the time, can you see me at my office in Australia Square right away? I've decided I do need your help. There are some matters I would like to discuss with you privately.'

Harrigan decided the job could spare him between now and seven thirty.

'I don't have much time, but I can be there.'

'My bodyguard will meet you at the entrance to the car park.'

'I'll see you shortly.'

She was more frightened than he had realised. He went to his office where he put on his wire and checked his firearm. He didn't ring Grace; he would do that later. Everything would happen later.

28

Grace's mobile rang while she was finishing dressing. She wondered if it could be Harrigan. When she answered, it was Daniel Brinsmead.

'Will you come and talk to me?' he asked. 'I'm sitting in a visitor's parking spot outside your building in a white Toyota sedan. Will you come down?'

If her mind hadn't been so troubled by what she'd just seen on the net, she would have said no.

'Okay.'

She had no gun; Harrigan had taken care of that. Armed with only her mobile phone, she went downstairs. A white Toyota sedan was parked in the spot closest to the ramp. The driver's door was open; Brinsmead was sitting in the passenger seat. Through the open door, she saw his burns, the shock of his scarring.

'Will you get in?' he said.

'Are you armed?'

'Me? No. What for? Look.' He spread his arms as far as he could in the car, then opened the glove box. 'Check wherever you want. I don't have a gun.'

They sat beside each other in the car. Grace had already turned off her mobile. She wanted no interruptions, no questions from Harrigan about what she was doing.

'What do you want?' she asked.

'I want to talk to you. Have you turned on your computer this morning?' he asked.

'Yes. I saw what you posted there. You did post that video, didn't you? That's how you got your scars. Those were the people who died when you didn't. You know their names, and you repeat them every morning when you wake up and tell them you haven't forgotten them.'

'We introduced ourselves inside the school. I couldn't speak the local language, but one of the villagers spoke a little English, the man who rode in the front with me. Before they all died in the flames. The ones who didn't run outside and were shot.'

'Is that what you wanted to talk to me about?'

'I wanted to ask you if you'd drive me to Campbelltown and back. I won't make the distance out there driving myself. I only just made it here.'

'Why don't you call your hire car firm?'

'LPS pays for my hire car and driver,' he said. 'It's part of the arrangement that they always let Elena know when I'm on my way out there. I don't want her knowing I'm going out there today. That's why I have a different car. I hired this one myself.'

'Why don't you call a taxi? I'm sure the driver would be happy to take you there and back.'

'I want to speak to you. I'm looking for a witness, someone who'll report back once this whole set of affairs is finished with. You know half the story already. I want to tell you the other half. I want you to be my witness. You're a reliable listener. You'll be one other person who knows what actually happened, and then when this is over you can tell other people.'

'I want you to answer a question first. Did you kill those people at Pittwater?'

'No.'

'Who did?' Grace asked.

'I'm guessing in some way or another that Elena was behind it and DP was her killer. Jerome was unreliable. He was an alcoholic; apparently, he was approaching the point where there was nothing left in his life but the drink. Sometime or another, he was going to do something that would bring the whole thing tumbling down, including LPS. I think Elena would have felt she had no choice but to act.'

Why should I believe you? Grace asked herself. And then considered that whether he was lying or not, and whatever type of man he was, he had information. By his own admission, he wanted her to pass that information on to other people. Right now she needed to hear what he had to say. It was better than sitting useless, waiting for Harrigan to call. She could sift the truth from the lies later when she had enough facts to know which was which.

'How did Elena know she was in danger?' she asked.

'Because she was having Jerome watched. She knew everything he was doing. She's a smart woman. She was protecting her back.'

'How do you know?'

'Because the individual watching him is a colleague of mine. I'm here, Grace, for the same reason that I called you and told you where you could find the commander's son. I'm not what I seem. In fact, I've undertaken a job I'm not cut out for, least of all now that I'm damaged the way I am.'

'What job is that?'

'I was recruited by a secret security agency to act as a mole and get as close as I could to some of the scientific programs LPS is involved in. They picked me because I was ex-army. They had evidence indicating that the organisation backing Elena, Abaris, was involved in a wide-ranging experimental program developing biological weapons and they were using LPS facilities for research. Before he was shot, Jerome had been growing experimental crops at a property near the Riverina as part of that program. My colleague was able to get hold of some seed stock so I could test the wheat they'd developed. It gives no nourishment. You eat it and you starve. Can you imagine that? It's almost beyond comprehension. But that's what they were doing. There's no better way to undermine a country than to target its food supply, particularly a Third World country. Abaris was also behind what you just saw on the video. They produced a very short-lived but virulent virus, not unlike bird flu, and tested it in Africa. That was done in a research facility I used to work in in north London.'

'You were there when they tested it,' Grace said.

'I was, and I took on this second task because I thought that having seen them do that, I had to get the evidence that would allow us to shut them down. They're not running a government-sponsored program. What they produce is for sale to the highest bidder. It could easily be a government, of course, but it could be anybody else as well. Either way, it's a crime against humanity. But I shouldn't have taken on this second task. I don't have the physical stamina for it.'

'Who's your colleague?'

'I can't tell you that. In fact, if that person even knew I was here talking to you, they'd be very angry. I'll tell you why I want to go to LPS. I'm not going to last much longer after today. I've reached the end of my endurance. But I do have comprehensive access to the LPS building. I'm the only one after Elena who does, including access to her office. I'm very certain that Elena has the contracts covering Jerome's last venture. They're in her office, just sitting innocently in a drawer. I want to get hold of them and send them back to our handlers. Those contracts will provide a proof of ownership of the biotechnology. I'll be able to demonstrate once and for all who's behind this program. Even if no one goes to gaol, at least it will bring the whole process to a stop.'

'Why aren't you asking your colleague to drive you?'

'Once I've done this, I've blown my cover with Elena. There's no CCTV in her office, but the building cameras will still show me going in and out. She has to put it together. My colleague doesn't think we're finished. You see, those contracts aren't going anywhere until Elena safe-hands them to her father the next time she goes to London. That won't be for another three weeks. My colleague wants to keep our options open until then.'

'Why?'

'They believe Elena was behind the murders at Pittwater and they want to prove it. You saw the net. In their opinion, that photograph was sent out as a warning to anyone who wants to mess with Abaris. This will happen to you if you push too hard. My colleague has no intention of taking that lying down. They want whoever killed those people and that boy.'

'Why not leave it to the police?'

'They have no faith in the police force, let me tell you that now. I'm different, I'd be happy to. But my colleague is more professional than me. They can make hard decisions I can't. If I keep on with this undercover, I'm going to let them down so badly they could end up dead. I don't want that to happen.'

'Does anyone know the two of you are here?' Grace asked.

'No. It's a breach of protocol, but the organisation we work for often works like that.'

'Tell me its name.'

'I can't do that,' Brinsmead said.

'Then I'm not going to drive you,' Grace replied.

'What could the name possibly mean to you? You won't have heard of it.'

'Just tell me.'

'Falcon.'

Grace had heard of them and their methods. They operated as Brinsmead had described: undercover, dangerously, and usually past the edge of legality. Their modus operandi fitted with Sam's traits: always on the edge and aggressive.

Brinsmead was still talking. 'What I'm doing is calling our operation to a halt. If I can get possession of those contracts, then I think we'll have achieved a good outcome. But I'm not just bailing out. What I'm really doing is blowing the whole rotten business sky high. This is a nasty business, Grace, where innocent bystanders can end up dead. That's why I posted that video on the net. It can go with everything else that's already out there, including the material Edwards put out. People can make their own judgements. All I want to achieve is to get hold of those contracts and protect the identity of my colleague. Then that'll be the end of it.'

'Why should I believe anything you've said?' she asked.

'There's no reason whatsoever, Grace. You can get out of the car and walk away now.'

The video was powerful in Grace's mind. She was thinking of the dead, of some kind of redress. A hope that the people who were responsible might be found out and stopped, even if they were never prosecuted.

'I'll drive you out there and then back to the city,' she said, 'but only if you answer some questions for me about who you are.'

'Before you do, I have to ring Elena. If she's going to be out there today, then I can't do this.'

'Why didn't you make sure of that beforehand?'

'What Elena does from day to day is up to her. There was no point in asking her if I wasn't going to be able to get there.'

He called and held the phone where Grace could hear what was being said. It was answered.

'Elena. It's Daniel. Yes, I know it's early. Sorry. I can't get out to Campbelltown today. I'm not well enough. Are you going to be there? If you are, could you check with my staff? Their latest test results should be through this morning.'

'*No, I won't be out there today. I'm too busy here,*' she replied. '*I won't be able to help with that, I'm sorry. Goodbye.*'

'She was very formal,' Grace said.

'She always is with me now. She's changed these last few years. She's closed up like her father. Go via the M5. Once we get to Campbelltown, I'll direct you.'

At this time on a Saturday morning, most people were still in bed. The traffic was light. Brinsmead leaned back in his seat and closed his eyes. 'A bit of pain,' he said. He wasn't acting; it was all too obviously real. They drove in silence until they reached the motorway. The air conditioning in the car was set to high. Finally he opened his eyes.

'What do you want to know?' he asked.

'You're an agent for Falcon. You were with Beck and du Plessis on an undercover operation. They were your targets.'

'That's right. Falcon was interested in DP because they had evidence he was involved in a diamond-smuggling racket. That business was financing arms trading to various radical insurgent groups in Africa. DP led them to Beck. They wanted to know what that connection involved. I was drafted in because I had the scientific skills they needed. My brief was to get close enough to Jerome to find out what he was up to. What I told you before was true. I'd gamble with him. That's how I got my invitation to Africa. I kept losing. I said I needed money, I didn't care how I got it. He told me he knew a way I could make some very easy money and a lot of it. Then one night, just days before we were leaving, I had to take him out of a casino before he got thrown out. He was drunk as usual. I took him home, he was so angry. He started to rant. Didn't they know who he was? He

329

was Jean Calvo's son. Calvo was the man and he was his son, somebody important, while everybody else at that casino was shit. He didn't just work for some cheap nobody. He was working for Calvo right now. He knew things about Calvo no one else did. He went on and on. The interesting thing is, I reported all that back to Falcon. But when I was looking over Edwards' dossier on the net this morning, I found that the particular report with that information in it was gone. It'd been pulled from the file, probably shredded. I wish I knew who did that and why.'

'Don't you trust your agency?' Grace asked.

'I trust Falcon. I don't necessarily trust the politicians it answers to. Jean Calvo has a lot of clout in government circles. But I wasn't the best agent Falcon could have had either. For one thing, I was involved with Elena. I shouldn't have been, but at the time I really cared for her.'

'Your minders should have known that,' Grace said after a pause. 'They should have pulled you out.'

'I kept it from them. I'm not a professional — I've been told that before in no uncertain terms. I didn't want to believe Elena could know what Jerome was doing. But she did. She knew it all.'

'How did Beck react to seeing you out here?'

'It was the other way around, Grace. They worked really hard at keeping him out of my way.'

'How did you take that video?'

'I always used to wear a gold locket. It was part of my look. Falcon converted it into a camera.'

'How did you survive the fire?' Grace asked.

'I can thank the villager who spoke English. He pushed me into that storeroom, threw us both against that grille and covered me with his body. I could breathe through the grille but I still almost died of smoke inhalation. I think my heart just kept beating. No one bothered to check the dead. Once Jerome and his mercenaries were gone, some of the local people came and found me. The wall beside me had collapsed and I'd dragged myself away from the remains of the building. I don't remember that at all. They took me to a local aid hospital, where the people took me to Kinshasa. I was conscious enough to give the doctor the emergency phone number Falcon gave to all its agents. The embassy flew me back to London; they chartered a flight to get me out.' He laughed. 'They didn't realise the doctor had taken my locket off me. The chain melted in the fire but I was holding it in my right hand. I'd fallen on that side and it didn't burn like my left. The doctor had to prise my hand open. She kept the locket for me; she was worried it would get stolen. Then a year later, she tracked me down in London. She'd finished her tour of duty and she wanted to give me back my locket and see how I was. By that time, Falcon had closed down the operation and pensioned me off.'

'Didn't you show them that video once you got it back?'

'I did. It was on that basis they reopened the operation. We viewed the video together and then they asked me if I was prepared to put myself on the line again. I said I was. I overestimated myself. Something I haven't told you. I'd been rumbled by Jerome before I left for Africa. I didn't realise that until I was there. I overheard DP and Jerome talking one night. It was what the old man and his daughter wanted, they said. Elena had thought I was using her. I wasn't. Then I had to realise she knew as much about what was going on as her father did. Everything seemed to implode at once. To be completely honest, it's another reason I ran when I did.'

'Did Falcon debrief you?'

'In depth. For them, the operation had been a complete failure. There was no firm evidence they could use and they were worried their secrecy had been compromised. It wasn't until I got the video back that we had the key we needed and they were prepared to move forward. I was still suspicious enough to take a copy. I'm glad I did now.'

'What's Elena doing out here?'

'Trying to shake off her father. It was supposed to be a new start after the African debacle. He didn't let her get away completely. He insisted she take Jerome on whether she liked it or not.'

'Why should she agree to taking you on after what happened in Africa? She must have known you knew about her.'

'Guilt, pure and simple. That's why she put my project in the public domain. I didn't want Abaris to own it. It's her way of assuaging her conscience.'

'Are you sure you didn't blackmail her with that video?' Grace asked.

'I know too much, Grace. It was as simple as that. I knew too much and I was still alive. She couldn't lock me out.'

'If she and her father are the sort of people you say they are, why didn't they have you killed?'

He smiled.

'I often wonder how they reacted when they heard I was back in London, still alive if barely. There must have been panic. We had no real proof at the time that would stand up in court, but there was enough information to bring pressure to bear on Jean. I'm pretty sure Falcon would have made it clear to him they didn't want one of their ex-agents being executed. He knew not to push his credit too far.'

'Did they also ask him to shut down the biological weapons program?' she asked.

'I don't know. That would have depended on who his clients were. That was something we never found out. What he did was move it offshore.'

They sped down the motorway in silence. Brinsmead was staring at the road. Grace weighed the alternatives. In the first, Daniel Brinsmead was the murderer Harrigan said he was and this was some kind of trap, the reason for which she did not know. But why would he want to harm her? If he wanted a witness, she was a reliable witness. She had given him no reason to hurt her. She glanced quickly at him. He was too frail and in too much pain to threaten her physically. Harrigan had told her that no guns were allowed in the LPS building. She remembered his description of a place full of people and activity.

In the second alternative, there were the dead. The people she had seen on the net, murdered and then buried in a makeshift grave. She could see this as the kind of operation she did in her own work. Staying with the target, calling in backup when she needed it. But in this case, the man she would have called her target, Brinsmead, clearly wanted to die. Maybe that was the most merciful thing to let happen.

When she had been a singer out on the road with her ramshackle band, she had liked driving those long empty roads in the outback. The name of the town they were going to had never mattered much. She had been driven by a different compulsion. For her, the destination was always a vanishing point in the distance. That was why she was driving towards it, to find out what it was. A hunger to see what was next. She had lived all her adult life with that need; it was a way of cleaning away all that emotional dross from the past that was otherwise stuck to her. That compulsion was in her mind now, driving her to what was next.

One day your judgement has to be wrong. Harrigan's voice came back to her.

The images of the dead were more powerful than his words. She was on the trajectory; she would see this through.

29

Harrigan drove the distance from the police building to Australia Square in clear sunlight. It was a quick journey in light traffic. Yesterday's bodyguard was again waiting for him at the ramp leading down into the car park. He delivered Harrigan to the thirty-third floor, where Damien showed him into Elena Calvo's office.

'Please sit down,' she said. 'Coffee?'

'Thanks. We'll have to make this very quick.'

'We will. Damien, could you get the commander coffee, please? And some for me as well. I think we're ready to talk business.'

'I'm ready when you are, Dr Calvo,' Harrigan said as the bodyguard moved to the door. An instant later, the door was kicked open and Sam Jonas walked in, her gun in her hand outstretched to be fired. She shot Damien in the chest, her actions making up a single movement so fast that to Harrigan's eyes, paradoxically, it seemed to be in slow motion. Red markings appeared on the man's shirt. He fell to the floor. The shots had been quiet. Sam had her gun aimed directly at Elena.

'Put your hands where I can see them, the two of you, now! If you move, Harrigan, I'll do to both of you exactly what I just did to Damien. Believe me, you'll be dead before you can blink. If you don't believe it, try me.'

Elena was standing behind her desk, her mouth open in shock. Harrigan had pushed back his chair and was on his feet, but was stopped where he was. Standing at the door, Sam was too far away for heroics.

'My other bodyguard,' Elena said in a shaking voice. 'Where is he?'

'Gone to meet his maker as well,' Sam replied. 'Don't think he can help you now.'

'How could you do that?' Elena, staring at Damien where he lay, could barely get the words out. 'He had a wife and a child.'

'That's a joke coming from you. You don't get to see this sort of thing, do you? Other people do it for you.'

'You work for me,' Elena said, dumbfounded. 'Who are you? Why are you doing this? I don't understand. I pay you.'

'It's a different sort of payday now, Elena. That's all you need to know. It'll all become clear soon enough.'

'Payday for what?'

'Africa, Elena. The DRC.' Sam laughed. 'You know what that means. I can see it in your face. You know what happened there, don't you? You keep standing. Don't move a muscle, I'm watching you. Now, Harrigan. Do you have a gun? You do. Don't try anything with it. Throw it as far as you can across the room. Your phone, turn it off. Then get your wallet and your buzzer. Throw them to the other side of the office. Is there anything else? What about a wire? Let's see. Come on. Get your gear off. Don't be shy.'

Slowly Harrigan began to undress. He unbuttoned his shirt to expose the wire he was wearing. Again, Sam laughed. Harrigan saw Elena give him a single look of direct and unforgiving accusation, then she refused to meet his eyes again.

'You can't trust anyone these days, Elena. There are some people you just can't buy. Who's listening?'

'No one's listening. I'm just recording.'

'Throw it on the floor over here! Go on!'

Harrigan threw the miniature recording device to the floor. Sam smashed it to pieces with the heel of her boot.

'Put your clothes back on and then lie on the floor away from the desk, face down,' she said. 'Stay there. Remember, I've got a gun trained on Elena.'

He heard her walk to the dead bodyguard. She disarmed him, taking his gun for herself.

'All right, Elena, I want your mobile. Where is it?'

'On my desk.'

'Hands where I can see them. Wait there.'

Harrigan looked up from the floor. Sam had moved around to Elena and taken her in a grip that made her bend over. She had her gun at the back of her head.

'Face down, Harrigan. Now! Elena, wait. Someone's going to call you. You're going to tell them you're not going out to Campbelltown today. You're going to be very calm or you'll be dead.'

They waited. Harrigan heard the phone ring.

'Elena Calvo. Hello, Daniel. Why are you ringing me so early? No, I won't be out there today. I'm too busy here. I won't be able to help with that, I'm sorry. Goodbye.'

'What did he say?' Sam asked.

'He said he couldn't get out to Campbelltown today. Could I check with his staff if his test results had come through? I never involve myself with his work. Why would he ask me to do that?'

'Maybe you'll find out. Turn off your phone and give it to me. Now sit down at your desk and turn on your computer.'

'Why?'

'Just do it. Don't move, Harrigan. For your information, Elena has her own personal high-speed secure network here and at Campbelltown. It's separate to the rest of the IT out there and it's very fast. I want your log-on code and your password, Elena. You have three seconds to give it to me or you can join Damien.'

'That's a bluff.'

'No, it's not. Because if you won't do that, you're useless to me and you might as well be dead. Remember that. You only last as long as I find you useful. Take your choice. Write it down for me.'

Elena did so.

'Good. Now log on for me and prove it works. Then log out and shut down. Good girl. Now, we're ready. Where are your car keys?'

'In Damien's pocket.'

'Stand up and get them, Harrigan,' Sam said. 'We're going down to the car park. You walk in front of us out to the lift. Do anything and you'll have a dead woman on your hands. You can die a hero as well.'

'What's the point of this?' Harrigan said. 'I've got backup waiting for me. This is just going to put you in gaol for the rest of your life.'

'How much backup and where are they? How do they know when you need them?'

'Why should I tell you that?'

'Because if you don't answer my question, I'll kill you and I mean that.'

'They're at the police building. They're waiting for me to call,' Harrigan said.

'I thought so. My guess is, right now this is the last place anyone would expect to find me. Now get the keys, including the lift key.'

'How did you get in here?' Elena asked.

'I've had after-hours access to this office for months, Elena. I don't know why you're so surprised. You hired me because I can do this sort of thing. I've been watching you for a long time. That's the good thing about being undercover. No one knows what you're really up to.'

Harrigan went through the dead man's pockets. He found the keys and straightened up.

'Let's go,' Sam said. 'Keep your hands where I can see them, Harrigan.'

They walked through the empty office. The other bodyguard lay dead inside the door. They walked past him to the lift.

'You get in first and stand in one corner,' Sam said. 'Elena and I will stand in the other. Harrigan, when we stop, you get out first. Now, you can feel that gun in your ribs, can't you, Elena? If either of you does anything, it fires and keeps firing. Down we go. If anyone gets in, everyone act normal.'

'They'll pick us up on CCTV,' Elena said.

'So what? It's a Saturday. We'll be long gone before they do anything about it. Anyway, what's to see? You with your bodyguard stuck to you like glue and someone who looks like a driver. What's so different about that?'

On a Saturday morning this early, no one did get into the lift. The only sound was Elena's shallow breathing and a single, sharp comment from Sam. 'Keep it quiet, Elena. You're annoying me.'

There were few vehicles in the car park. They stopped by Elena's car, a Mercedes with tinted windows. Harrigan glanced at his own car, parked a short distance away. No one would find it here.

'Open the car, Harrigan. Elena and I are getting in the back. You're driving. We're all getting in together. Nice and cosy in the back, Elena. That's right. Drive, Harrigan. Carefully. Don't attract attention.'

'Where are we going?'

'Where do you think? Campbelltown. We've got an appointment.'

'Who are we going to meet out there?'

'Maybe we've got a date with destiny. You have, that's for sure. I wasn't expecting to see you today. You're a bonus. Otherwise, I might have had to put Elena in the boot.'

'What's happening out at Campbelltown?' Harrigan asked.

'Wait and you'll find out. Meantime, have you seen the net this morning, either of you? Bet you have, Harrigan. There should be an email waiting for you, Elena. I wanted to make you watch it but we don't have the time.'

'I haven't seen it,' Elena said.

'Yes, you have. Don't pretend you haven't. I bet Daddy rang you about it. Guess what? That video we tried so hard to suppress is out on the net. Live with it. People know who you really are now. You and your father.'

'That video has nothing to do with us and you can't prove that it does.'

'We will before we're finished,' Sam said. 'You don't know how much I know about you. I know who your brother is, for example. Your half-brother, that is. But Jerome's dead now. Did that upset Daddy at all? You wouldn't think it would given that he walked out on him. I'm curious.'

'You're a sick woman,' Elena said softly.

'Not as sick as you. I'd be careful, Elena. I don't care if you get roughed up.'

'Sam, did you kill Marvin?' Harrigan asked quickly.

'You bet I did,' Sam replied. 'It was just luck he was there. I took advantage of it.'

'Why?' he asked.

'I knew DP was running him for Elena. I wanted him out of the way in case he made trouble later. You see, Elena, I've been following DP ever since he got here. You know how I knew he was here, Harrigan? She told me to go and meet him. I had to give him all the stuff I had on Jerome and your squalid little friends. I used to have a tracking device on his car. Very handy. I was there watching the very first time he ever met Marvin Tooth. Trouble was, DP saw me as well. Not close enough to really see me, but enough to work out he was probably being followed. We lost him after that. He dumped his car and we couldn't track him any more.'

'Did you kill those people up at Pittwater?'

'Yes, they did,' Elena said, again softly.

'Did we? Why should anyone believe what you say?' Sam said. 'It was DP cleaning up for you. Jerome was getting too unreliable. You had to protect yourself. You didn't want anyone connecting his dirty little business to your organisation. You took control and did what you've always wanted to do. Get that whole side of Abaris out of your life and your business. Then you sent that piccie out just to show other people what would happen to them if they crossed you.'

'Then why leave the contract behind?' Harrigan asked.

'Because DP is careless. He goes at things like a bull at a gate. Elena will tell you that. I bet she's bitched about him to her father a million times. She probably wanted you to take over from him. Do you know how I found your old friend the Ice Cream Man's body, Harrigan? Because Elena here asked me to go and pick up DP's black beast out at Yaralla after he'd killed him. Even DP can't drive two cars. He had to torch one of them and he didn't want to do it down there. I had a good look around and I found the grave. But I'd already been out to Yaralla. I used to tail Jerome out there. I got into one of his vans once. I got hold of some seed, I made it look like the sack had burst. We knew what he was growing. Elena wants to hide all that. But we're going to tell the world.'

'I had nothing to do with Jerome's business. I had no reason to kill those people,' Elena said angrily.

'She's baiting you,' Harrigan said to Elena in his detached voice.

Sam laughed. 'No, Elena didn't kill them. Why would she want the publicity? But my take on it was plausible, wasn't it? It might convince someone who knew some of the facts but not all of them.'

For first time, Harrigan felt real terror.

'Who?' he asked.

'Does that worry you, Harrigan?'

'Who's this "we"?' he said. 'You and Brinsmead.'

'Daniel?' Elena said in surprise. 'What do you have to do with Daniel?'

'He's my very old friend, Elena. I've known him for twenty years close enough. We're probably the only true friends each of us has ever really had. I know him better than you ever will. He fucks women like you. Me, he talks to.'

In the rear-vision mirror, Harrigan saw Elena look out of the window. Her expression was a mix of anger and loathing. There were insults which were unforgivable. Sam had just made one.

'Is he your reason for doing this?' she asked with contempt.

'Yes and no. We both used to work for an organisation called Falcon. I persuaded him to offer his services; I thought he'd be good at it. But then he met you, didn't he? You corrupted his mind.'

'You're jealous.'

'No. We don't have that kind of relationship; we never have had. I didn't want anything like that messing us up. He's my soul mate and I'm his. You betrayed him to your father.'

'I did not. My father didn't know anything about him being an agent. He just found his connection to me and Jerome too convenient. He was right. Daniel was a user. But I still rescued him. If I hadn't taken care of him after he came back, he would have died.'

She had spoken with deep bitterness, saying Jerome's name with distaste. Sam answered with growing and dangerous anger.

'Your father told DP and Jerome to kill Daniel and you knew that. You knew and you didn't warn him.'

'I didn't know.'

'Do you want to understand grief? I can't describe to you what I felt when I saw Danny after he got back. If I could have, Elena, I would have got you on your knees and killed you then. Instead, Daddy called in his credit with the government. Falcon shut the whole thing down and hung us out to dry. Well, it's not over yet. Like I said, it's payday.'

'Did you kill that boy?' Harrigan asked quickly.

'Do you care?'

'Yes.'

'Well, don't. What about the people you saw on the net this morning? What about that girl they injected? Does anyone care about her?'

'Does killing that boy bother you, Sam?'

'There are times when you have to do things like that. He shouldn't have been there. Danny wanted Jerome to see him, but it meant the boy saw us as well. There was nothing we could do about it. I made sure he didn't realise what was going to happen. He was first. I didn't give either of us time to think about it.'

'You did it.'

'I had to. He didn't know. We're not like these people. We don't go after innocent civilians for the fun of it.'

'You want this whole dirty story out in the open,' Harrigan said. 'But one way or the other, it'll be swept under the carpet. You must know that. You'll have done all this for nothing.'

'No, Harrigan. That's not what we're doing. We're not that naïve. Yes, it would be nice if it all got out there on the net. We're putting out as much information as we can. There's more to come, that's why I wanted Elena's log-on. But it's not the only thing. It's not even the main thing. It's the future we're thinking about. We're doing what people like us should do. Protecting innocent people, not the backside of some rich industrialist. We're the real anti-terrorists, not the idiots who are in control.'

'What's going to happen?'

'I told you. Wait and find out.'

You're going to kill us, aren't you, Harrigan thought. Not without a fight. He concentrated on the road ahead.

'Don't drive too fast,' Sam said. 'Just on the speed limit will be fine. Don't attract attention.'

Harrigan glanced in the rear-vision mirror. Elena's face was turned aside, her chin buried in her shoulder. Her shoulders were shaking. Sam had her in a tight grip, the gun jammed painfully in her ribs. She was looking directly at the back of his head. Her expression was as detached as any he'd ever seen. He reminded himself that she was a trained killer. She wasn't someone to play games with on the off chance. He drove on. There was nothing else he could do.

30

Past Campbelltown, Daniel Brinsmead directed Grace through the industrial estate. Rising like a monolith out of the ground, the LPS building flashed a hard blue in the early morning sunlight. Grace whistled at the sight of it.

'It is impressive,' Brinsmead said. 'I'll give Elena that. Don't stop for the boom gates. Just keep driving.'

The boom lifted for her automatically, the gates swung open. The security guard watched them drive by.

'You're privileged.'

'I told you, my e-tag gives me full access rights.'

They drove into the garage. Even early on a Saturday morning, there were a number of cars in the car park.

'Scientists,' Brinsmead said. 'We all have tunnel vision. You'd think they could stay home in bed on a weekend morning. But here they are, working. Why couldn't they have taken a day off?'

The sight of the cars gave Grace confidence. She got out after Brinsmead.

'Do you want to come in?' he asked, as if surprised.

'This is too much of a cave to stay in. I'd like to see the inside of the building.'

'It may not be straightforward. I may have to persuade the security people to let you in. Do you have any kind of ID on you?'

'Yes.'

'You may have to use it. I've got my dog tag on but you'll need to be granted visitor's access rights.'

On his lapel, he was wearing a small gold badge. They went into the foyer to be met by the guards. The man behind the counter listened to Brinsmead stony-faced.

'We've been directed by Dr Calvo not to give admittance to individuals whose names haven't been cleared beforehand,' he said. 'Miss Riordan's name hasn't been cleared with me. I'll have to call Dr Calvo before I can grant her admission.'

'Please, go ahead,' Brinsmead replied.

The guard picked up the phone.

'She's not answering,' he said.

'She's probably in a meeting of some kind. The responsibility for this visit is mine. Let me point out to you that I'm the chief scientist here. I'll be the one who deals with the issue if Dr Calvo doesn't approve. But Miss Riordan is here for a specific purpose which I'm not at liberty to divulge.'

'Can I see some ID?'

Grace showed the small leather wallet that identified her as an agent for a classified government agency. Then, at the guard's request, she filled out a form identifying herself for the corporation's records. This made her feel secure. People knew she was here, it was some protection.

'All right,' the guard said, reading over the details and taking a breath. 'I'll grant you admission. If you have a mobile phone on you, could you please place it in locker number six and then you can go in.'

'We have to hurry,' Brinsmead said, once they had passed through the inner door and were in the lift. 'He's too uncertain about the situation. He'll get on to Elena soon enough.'

They stepped out of the lift on the ground floor into the atrium, where small groups of people were hurrying places. A well-dressed woman greeted Brinsmead and smiled at Grace. Nearby, a small restaurant was open and several people sat inside eating breakfast. It made Grace feel at ease. She stopped to look at the glass wall rising above her head. It was breathtaking.

'This is grand ambition, Grace,' Brinsmead said. 'You don't care what it costs. Since you're inside now, I'm going to have to ask you to wait in my lab while I go down to Elena's office. You can have a look around and meet some of my people. This way.'

He led her through corridors to the north-western side of the building, walking with more determination than speed. This part of the facility seemed empty. He stopped outside a door halfway along a corridor and punched in a combination to a lock.

'Elena's office is just along there,' he said. 'This is my laboratory. You can wait in here for me.'

'Isn't there anyone else here?' she asked.

'They should be. They may just have locked the door. After you.'

As soon as they had stepped inside, he shut the door. Grace heard the click of the automatic lock behind them and felt a chill in her backbone. Moving more quickly than usual, Brinsmead had already pushed past her and was inside a glassed-in office. She heard him lock the door and knew she couldn't get to him. Instead, she looked around the lab. There were no people here; it was silent and mostly dark. Only the night lights were on, the room fading into shadow. There was nowhere to hide where he could not find her.

She looked towards Brinsmead's office to see what he was doing. He had opened a secure filing cabinet and was taking out a thick booklet with a blue, bloodstained cover, which he put on his desk. Several sets of restraints appeared, followed by a mobile phone. Then he turned back to the filing cabinet. When he opened the door to his office and came out, he was carrying a gun. He was smiling strangely.

'Come inside my office and sit down, Grace,' he said. 'If you do, I won't have to use this.'

Suddenly everything was clear to her. The guards at the desk might know of her presence, but there was no one in the laboratory but the two of them and no way in or out. No one could hear her. *One day your judgement has to be wrong.* She should have listened to Harrigan.

The LPS building was huge in the landscape. Harrigan drove towards the gate. This time, the boom lifted for him automatically, and the gates swung open. The security guard raised a hand in greeting.

'No one stops the boss,' Sam said.

'Where are we going?' Harrigan asked. 'The car park?'

'No, the delivery dock. It's closed up on a Saturday. There'll be no one there.'

The delivery dock was at the furthest end of the building. As Sam had said, the doors were locked, the area deserted.

'Won't the guards at the front desk know this door has been opened?' Harrigan asked.

'They will, but they won't question it if it's on Elena's override. Elena, here's your phone. Turn it on. This is what we do. You use your mobile phone to key in the emergency override and open the fire door. Go on, you can do it. You're the only one who can. When we go inside, you sit straight down at the console. First thing you turn on all the lights, and then you do what I tell you to do.'

Elena turned her phone on. It rang to announce a missed call. Sam snatched the phone out of her hands.

'This is from the guards at the front desk. Why are they calling you?'

'They only call me when there's a question of access. Someone wants to be admitted who's not on the authorised list.'

'Who?' Harrigan asked.

'Who knows?' Sam said. 'Harrigan, you get out of the car first and walk in front of us. Put yourself between me and Elena and the cameras. Let's go.'

The emergency exit was a single metal door set to the side of the main entrance to the delivery dock. It swung open. As soon as it did, Sam took the phone back from Elena. Harrigan looked around for the cameras.

'Don't try anything, Harrigan,' Sam said. 'Yes, the guards are watching but it won't do them much good. I'm right here.'

They stepped inside. Sam kicked the door shut behind them. The security guard's station was lit with emergency lighting. All the internal doors were locked, turning the area into an isolated chamber.

'Harrigan, put the car keys down on the edge of the desk. Then stand over there. Don't move. All right, Elena, log on and do an emergency lockdown on all sectors.'

Elena sat at the desk. Her hands were shaking. Sam stood behind her.

'Do it now! Remember, I'm watching you and watching the screen.'

Elena began to punch in the codes; the lights came on. Suddenly her phone rang again. Sam took it out of her pocket.

'It's a message. *Despatch. 45. CPT.* Sent by S. CPT must be Campbelltown. What does the rest of it mean?'

'It means my father has sent me an encrypted email message and he wants me to reply within forty-five minutes,' Elena replied.

'Why say CPT?'

'It means it has something to do with the building here. He was unhappy I spent so much money on landscaping. Maybe it's that.'

'Why S?'

'Because it's meaningless,' Elena said angrily. 'When I send him a message back, I'm L. That way no one knows it's us.'

'Paranoia plus. You won't get to read it, will you? Anyway, it doesn't matter what it means, no one will be able to get in here. Get on with it. Quickly!'

Sam put the phone in her pocket and turned around. 'What are you looking at, Harrigan?'

Harrigan had been watching Elena's face in those few seconds. It was unguardedly calculating, almost shrewd. If asked, he would have said she'd got one past Sam.

'I'm watching what Elena's doing. What's this all about?'

'Elena is shutting everyone in, including the guards at the main desk. Even the emergency exits will be locked. Don't worry. The backup systems will kick in. They'll all have air, they can go to the toilet. They just can't get out.'

'Why do that?'

'So they won't interrupt us.'

'They can phone people,' he said. 'They can call the police.'

'They can call whoever they like. No one can get in or out. They can send email messages too. We're not monsters. We don't mind people talking to their loved ones.'

'Elena,' Harrigan said, 'this is a suicide pact. You've got nothing to lose.'

'You shut up!' Sam shouted, and shot a bullet past his head. He froze. It embedded itself in the wall behind him. 'You keep your mouth shut from now on. Yes, it's a suicide pact, which means I can kill you any time I want.'

346

'What do you want to die for?' Harrigan said. 'You're young, you're fit.'

'Yeah, and I can spend the rest of my life in gaol for breaching national security, or one day some thug Elena's father has sent after me will find me. These are my terms. I'm dictating here. This world is a dead place. I'm cleaning a little bit of the shit away before I die. Elena, what the fuck are you doing? Okay, the shutdown's just happened, I can see it on the screen. Everyone wait.'

The lights went out and then came on again almost immediately. There was the sound of the air conditioning changing.

'Good girl,' Sam said. 'We've got three hours now. That's how long the lockdown lasts without being reinstated. Now, open up the north-western sector. Open all the doors and lock them open.'

'Why?' Elena asked.

'The idea frightens you, does it? Who knows what we might find if we can go wherever we want? For your information, Harrigan, no one's in this sector today. All the admin staff are home. The IT staff are offsite and Danny's shut down his project for the weekend. Otherwise, it's only the CEO's suite and the animal house over here. That's a good combination, isn't it? Also, we shouldn't forget the air conditioning unit.'

At that moment, all the doors around them snapped open automatically and stayed open.

'Now we wait,' she said. The silence was oppressive. Elena's phone rang. Sam took it out of her pocket. 'Danny. He is here. Good.' This time, she turned the phone off before putting it back in her pocket. 'Okay, next step. Danny's lab. Wait five minutes, then lock it down and put it back on its emergency air conditioning. I want you to seal it off from the rest of the building.'

'Why?'

'Just do it! When you've done that, you can put the rest of the building back on the main air conditioning unit.'

They waited for five minutes, barely breathing.

'All right, do it. Good. Finally, we're ready. Harrigan, there's a package on the floor beside you. Open it.'

It had been addressed to Dr Brinsmead. It was large and tightly packed.

'I need a knife,' he said.

347

'Forget it. Use your hands.'

He managed it, and found himself looking at a series of canisters. He looked up at Sam.

'It's gas,' she said. 'Elena, get over there next to Harrigan. Both of you pick one up and walk. You know the way, Elena. The air conditioning unit.'

'You're not going to do that. You can't,' Elena said. 'Whatever you think of me —'

'Shut up! We're going to put this building out of action. When we're finished, it'll be so toxic it'll never be used again. Everything except for Danny's lab. When someone's able to get back in here, what's inside that lab will be okay. They can pick up his project and keep it working somewhere else. But the rest of this place is Abaris. We're stopping you now, once and forever. That's why we don't care if we die. We're taking you with us.'

Harrigan heard Elena draw in her breath with a sharp gasp. She was staring at Sam.

'How many other people are here?' he asked.

'Do you want to die now? Because if you do, keep asking questions like that. Now pick up one of those canisters and get going.'

For a few seconds, he didn't move. Then Elena bent down and picked one up.

'I'll do it,' she said. 'But they're heavy. I can't move very fast.'

'Move as fast as you can.'

Harrigan took her hint and matched his pace to hers. Just as they were about to walk out, he glanced back. He saw Sam pick up the car keys and put them in her pocket. They walked along a corridor to the air conditioning unit and set the canisters down as requested. It took three trips, there and back. Harrigan looked around at the room and then at the small deadly canisters stacked in a neat row.

'What are you going to do? Release it into the pipes? Where are we when that happens?'

'You don't have to know. Back to the delivery dock.'

He stepped outside. He was thinking. Rush her. If he did that now, all he would do was die. Look for an opportunity. He had noticed Elena had been moving more and more slowly. Maybe she was planning something that needed time.

348

'Move it!' Sam snapped.

Harrigan glanced down the corridor. Unlike the others, this corridor curved around like the edge of a sliver of moon.

'Isn't that the animal house down there?' he asked.

'We're not going in there. Hurry.'

Once back at the delivery dock, Sam did a quick check of the console.

'It's all working. Good. Elena, you see that metal box over there, the one with a handle. Pick it up.'

The box, an enclosed version of the small cages used to carry animals, was sitting against one wall.

'How did that get in here?' Elena asked.

'Danny put it there last night. He can get in everywhere. Lucky us.'

'Is he here?'

'He's waiting for us. What did you expect?'

Elena picked up the box and they walked out.

This time they went past the corridor to the air conditioning unit and the animal house and on to the foot of the staircase. Harrigan stopped and glanced back at Sam. Her expression was not so much calm as businesslike.

'What are you waiting for?' she said. 'Get up the stairs.'

He was waiting his time. Not the end-time she had decided on for him but the moment of his own choosing when he would take her on. He would have to make that opportunity happen soon. There was almost no time left.

31

Grace walked slowly into the office. Brinsmead moved to one side to let her sit in a chair.

'I'm sorry, Grace,' he said. 'I'm really not going to hurt you if I can avoid it.'

She laughed. 'Then why are you pointing a gun at me?'

'That's only if you don't cooperate. You're too nice to look at, I don't want you to be damaged. If you cooperate, you won't be. We have a little time to wait. We might as well be civil to each other.'

'How did you get that in here? I thought guns weren't allowed.'

'They're not. I brought this one in piece by piece over time and built it myself. I know how to do that. There's no perfectly secure place. Or only one. It's called a grave.'

'You're a very good liar. You weren't acting when you were talking to me. I think you convinced yourself. That's you, isn't it? You can be more than one person. Even if they act in ways completely opposite to each other. No matter what you do, it's okay just because you do it.'

'Say what you like. It won't make any difference.'

'Falcon never reopened your operation, did they?' she said. 'Not even after they saw that video.'

'They said it was a tragedy but it proved nothing. They told me I'd compromised their secrecy and if I was concerned for innocent lives, the best thing I could do was keep my mouth shut. Just to calm me down, they put me through a charade with these Ministry of Defence officials. I told them my story; they told me it would be taken seriously. Nothing happened. I realised nothing was going to happen. I told my dead companions that I'd just have to do it myself. They would have justice even if it was a rough justice.'

'What happens now?'

'I told you. We're waiting for someone.'

'Why do you want me here?'

'I told you when I first spoke to you: you made me feel human for the first time in years. This is my last morning on this planet and I want you with me when I go. I'll look at you and my head won't be full of the memories I've lived with for the last four years. The last thing I want is to die with those thoughts in my head.'

'What happens to me?'

'You won't feel anything. None of us will. No one's going to feel the kind of pain those villagers would have felt when they died. We'll just go to sleep.'

'We?'

'This building is a living thing to Elena. As long as it's here, it's going to produce the kinds of things that Jerome was producing. There's only one way to stop it and that's to kill it. We're going to poison the entire building with gas.'

'What about the people here?'

'I wish they'd stayed home this morning, Grace, but they didn't. I'm sorry but there's nothing I can do. There are more lives at stake than theirs. Life is just one long gamble and this morning all those people drew the wrong cards.'

'I don't understand how you can even think that way.'

'You should understand. I've already told you why. I've been where you can never go. I've had all my constraints burnt out of me. I know exactly why I'm doing this. I've never seen anything more clearly in my life.'

'This is premeditated. You planned how to get me here.'

'From the time you gave me that injection. I was waiting to see if Harrigan was going to leave your flat this morning. We were fairly certain he was there. We decided if he didn't leave before a certain time, I'd have to go without you. But he did leave and here we are.'

'You're no different from the people you're fighting.'

'Think about that statement. If that's the case, then it doesn't matter whose side you're on. What matters is that you leave behind a blank surface where someone else can start again with something new and clean.'

'That never happens,' Grace said.

For a brief second, all the lights went out and then came on again. At the same time, there was a sound like a catch of breath in the air conditioning. In the quick blink of darkness, Grace stood up to run.

'Don't do anything,' Brinsmead said, as soon as they could see each other again. 'You see that mobile on the desk. Press the call button. Let it ring a few times, then turn it off. It's time to go. Pick up the contract and those restraints and bring them with you.'

'Where are we going?'

'Upstairs. Walk in front of me. Turn right at the main door. If you try to do anything, I'll have to shoot you even if I don't want to. For us, it's not a matter of if. It's a matter of how and when.'

The main door to the laboratory had opened automatically and stayed open.

'Who's us?' she asked.

'Don't ask questions. Let's just walk. Quickly now.'

Grace held the contract in one hand and the restraints in the other. I'm being asked to walk to my execution, she thought. She and Brinsmead faced each other. Give me the gun and I'll shoot you. I'll put you out of your misery. Go down fighting, whatever happens.

'Walk,' he said.

They went out into the corridor. They'd gone a short distance along the corridor when the door to the laboratory slammed shut behind them.

'What's happening?' she asked.

'My lab is being sealed off. The building's security system allows you to do that. Everything inside it will be protected.'

All the doors along the corridor were open. They passed a short corridor branching off to the right.

'Elena's office is down there,' Brinsmead said. 'That's open too. Sam will need to get in there later.'

'Sam Jonas. She's here. She's your colleague.'

'She's my friend. She's the bravest woman I've ever met.'

They reached a door that opened onto the junction of the northern and southern sectors. The door leading to the south-western sector was closed.

'Why is that door closed?' Grace asked.

'The entire building except for this sector is locked down. No one can get out of where they are, including the guards at the desk. Don't worry, they have air conditioning. They can breathe. For the moment.'

'For the moment,' Grace repeated.

'Up the stairs.'

They climbed the stairs. At the top, they reached another corridor.

'Along there and in the first door,' Brinsmead said.

This corridor had no windows. They reached the door; like all the others in this sector, it was open.

'This used to be Jerome's laboratory,' he said. 'It's maximum security. This is where the science behind his program was researched. God knows where those researchers are now. Probably scattered all over the world, paid to keep their mouths shut. Look at it. It's been thoroughly cleaned out. Except for that. That's useful.'

Along one wall was a series of photographs of the most common food and cash crops in the world. Wheat, rice, barley, yams, maize, sorghum, potatoes, tobacco, cotton. They dominated one side of the room. The photographs were illuminated from behind, appearing against the backdrop of the light in silhouette. The plants seemed as if they were preserved in fluid, fixed permanently as something dead.

'Go and sit at the bench with your back to those photographs,' he said. 'Put the contract and the restraints in the middle of the bench in front of you.'

She sat down on a stool with the pictures behind her. He stood on the other side, still holding the gun on her.

'How many people are you expecting?' she asked, looking down at the plastic ties.

'Only two. But I like to be prepared. Now we wait. Don't talk. All I want is silence.'

Grace looked around at the concrete shell that enclosed them. Along one wall was a row of empty cages, and there was a faint animal odour in the air, like the one she had smelt in his penthouse. It was a smell of death.

32

They climbed up the stairs to the second floor. The last time Harrigan had been here, the door at the top of the stairs leading to the western sector had been locked. Now it was open and the door on the eastern side was locked in its place. They walked down to an empty laboratory.

'Jerome's lab,' Sam said.

'There's nothing here,' Harrigan said. 'Why bring us here?'

'Because it's your grave. And there are people waiting for us. Have a look.'

At the back of the laboratory, Harrigan saw Daniel Brinsmead, and sitting at a bench near him, Grace. She was staring at him. He saw the contract and the restraints on the table. What would happen was clear to him. They would be restrained sitting at the table with those ghostly pictures behind them. Then they would be photographed and the picture posted on the Pittwater website with the picture of the dead at Natalie Edwards' house. Sam would release the gas from the canisters into the air conditioning. She would come up here to be with them. Probably she would set it up so it would go out on the net live. Everything in him refused to let this happen.

Just behind him, Sam laughed. 'Danny's really convincing when he wants to be. Elena will tell you that.'

Grace and Harrigan were still staring at each other. In their exchange of glances there was a simple communication. They were not going down without a fight.

Brinsmead had moved to where he had his gun trained on them all.

'Harrigan,' he said. 'I'd prefer you were out there, but it hasn't worked out that way. And Elena. I've been waiting for you. How are you?'

She turned to look at the wall.

'Elena, put your carry case on the bench in front of Grace,' Sam said. 'Harrigan, you go and stand near her.'

Harrigan positioned himself at a short distance from the bench. He stood between Brinsmead and Grace. Sam was more to his left, her gun trained on Elena.

'You were right,' Grace said to him. 'He's a very good liar.'

'I wish I'd been wrong.'

'No talking! Elena, open that carry case and then move away.'

The carry case opened on all four sides to reveal an open-meshed cage. On the tray lay dead white mice, starved around a full feeding bowl.

'That's the wheat Jerome was growing out at Yaralla,' Brinsmead said. 'I've been feeding it to my mice and every single one of them has died of starvation. People can find them when they find us.'

'Meanwhile, look at this, Elena.' Sam took out a flash drive. 'I've digitised your contract. It's all on here. Our two final statements are on here as well. Now that you've given me your ID and password, I'm going to release it on the net. This time I'm going to call it *This is where the feast was prepared*. We'll join the dead at the table that you prepared, Elena. You can go out just like your half-brother, Jerome. People will be able to put it all together. Harrigan, you said this would all get swept under the carpet. Well, maybe it won't now.

'All right, I'm putting those restraints on you all. We don't have much time. I've got to get back to the air conditioning unit and set it up.'

'Is this the part where you stop all those innocent people from breathing?' Grace asked.

'We're killing the building,' Brinsmead said. 'Call it a war. These people have chosen their side.'

'No, they didn't. They just came to work this morning.'

'Stop playing for time!' Sam shouted. 'Harrigan first. Sit down next to your girlfriend.'

He didn't move.

'You said you want to die on your own terms. You're not giving us that choice,' he said.

'That's your problem.'

'No one's going to call you heroes,' Harrigan went on. 'They're going to call you mass murderers. They could close down Brinsmead's project because of this.'

'I don't think so,' Brinsmead said. 'When there's money involved, people can usually forgive just about anything. The Medical Research Institute will take it over free of charge. They won't knock that back. Now, we don't have any more time to waste.'

Before anyone could move, Elena ran forward between Harrigan and Grace and pushed the cage to the floor. It fell with a crash, scattering its contents across the floor. On a hair trigger, Sam fired at Elena. Harrigan, who had a split second to anticipate this, grabbed her and jerked her out of the line of fire. The bullet ricocheted, they all ducked. When they righted, Grace had swept the restraints to the floor and jumped up from her stool and away from the bench. The stool clattered to the floor. Elena had moved back to stand near her.

'*Don't!*' Brinsmead shouted at Sam who had her gun raised. 'I want her to talk first.'

'What do you mean?' Harrigan said. He was judging the distance between him and the scientist.

'Elena's going to talk to a camera before she dies. She's going to tell the world what Jerome was doing, what Abaris is.'

'No, I'm not.'

'Yes, you are. Sam's going to make you. Now pick up everything, the both of you,' he said to Elena and Grace.

'You like ordering women around, do you?' Grace needled.

'Do it.'

'No. You do it,' Elena said. 'You're going to kill us all. Do your own dirty work.'

Suddenly she laughed at Sam. 'Look at you. He's persuaded you to die for him because of the way he is now. He doesn't want to live so you have to go with him. Then he wants this woman here because he has some little fancy for her.'

She looked at Brinsmead. 'You're nothing.'

'Don't you talk to me or Danny like that!'

'Do it!'

Both Sam and Brinsmead had turned angrily towards the two women. Harrigan launched himself at Brinsmead, smacking him to the floor. In the same instant, the entire laboratory was plunged into blackness. Sam's shot echoed past his head.

'Did you put that in the shutdown codes?' Sam shouted. 'Elena, where are you?'

Shots illuminated the room like lightning.

'Sam, no. Keep her alive!' Brinsmead shouted as best as he could with Harrigan on top of him, pressing him down and squeezing the gun from his hand.

A line of emergency lights began to appear on the floor leading to the main door. A slender female figure flashed briefly as a darker shadow in the doorway. A shot went past her and she was gone.

'She'll be heading for her office to reverse the lockdowns. I'll get her,' Sam called. Her running footsteps were muted on the floor's soft linoleum. The emergency lighting was growing stronger.

'Alive!' Brinsmead tried to shout.

He dropped his gun. Grace, who had hit the floor during the shooting, grabbed it. Harrigan got off him and Brinsmead rolled over onto his stomach, gasping in genuine pain.

'Get me one of those restraints,' Harrigan said to Grace. He tied Brinsmead's hands behind his back and left him on the floor. He searched him quickly. 'He doesn't have another gun. Let's get out of here.'

'Are you going to leave him here?'

'There's nothing else we can do. Where's the contract? Let's go.'

'It's gone,' Grace said. 'Elena must have it. She doesn't stop thinking.'

They left Brinsmead and ran for the door. Outside, the corridor was lit only with a single line of floor lights. The length of it was otherwise in solid darkness.

'Where to?' Grace asked.

'The air conditioning unit,' Harrigan said. 'I want to see if I can shut the door, or at least keep them out. Then we head for the delivery dock. All we need is silence and a bit of darkness to get there.'

'And another gun. That wouldn't hurt.'

They reached the bottom of the stairs. The door to the eastern sectors was still closed. Beside them was the corridor that led to the animal house. Ahead, they had a clear view through to the delivery dock. The area was lit only by floor lights while the location of the emergency exit was given by a green sign. That door was shut. The surrounds, including the corridors, were in deep shadow.

'Can we open that door?' Grace asked.

'It's a fire door. There should be a way to open it from the inside. Down here first.'

They hurried along the curve of the corridor as best they could in the dark. At the air conditioning unit, Harrigan tried to pull the door closed. Suddenly it gave way and almost knocked him backwards as it slammed shut. He tried it; it had locked on closing.

'They can't poison everyone now.'

'Can they open it?' Grace asked.

'Elena can. But I think she'd let them shoot her first this time. Let's get out into the open air.'

They went back to the junction of the corridor opposite the delivery dock. They stopped, standing back from the main corridor, listening for the sounds of anyone approaching. There was silence. Before they could move forward, the fire door opened inwards. A man walked into the space of the delivery dock, leaving the door open behind him. Bright sunlight, a glimpse of the outside world, appeared. Even in silhouette, Harrigan knew the short, dark-haired man immediately. Du Plessis shut the door and the outside world was gone.

In the shadows of corridor they couldn't be seen and instead watched him. He carried a gun in one hand. In the other, he held his mobile phone. It showed a small pinprick of blue light on its display. He was tracking someone. Brinsmead, Harrigan decided. Elena Calvo must have finally had enough. He turned in their direction, apparently heading for the stairs they had just come down. Harrigan and Grace withdrew silently back into the darkness of the corridor. They waited but he didn't come to where they were.

'DP,' Grace whispered.

'Is that what you call him?'

'It's what Brinsmead calls him. What's he doing here?'

'My guess is he's after Brinsmead,' Harrigan said. 'Elena's been playing for time throughout. There was a message on her phone earlier. *Despatch. 45. CPT.* I think it was from DP saying he was on his way to get Brinsmead and where it was going to happen. She was waiting for the lights to go out, but I think she might have been waiting for him as well. It was about forty-five minutes ago.'

'Didn't Sam work it out?'

'Elena's like Brinsmead — she can lie convincingly. It was signed S. I don't know what that stands for.'

'Saviour,' Grace said sarcastically. 'He's not coming after us.'

'He might do if he gets both Sam and Brinsmead. I don't think Elena would be very sentimental about either of us ending up dead.'

'She can't just kill us. The security guards know I'm here.'

'If you end up shot in a situation like this, who knows who shot you? Come on. He's gone. Let's see if we can open that door from the inside.'

They reached the main corridor again but heard shots down the stairs. Harrigan dragged Grace to the ground as one cracked past them. There was the sound of footsteps running down the stairs towards them.

'Back this way,' Harrigan said urgently. 'Let's find a place to hide.'

They turned and ran down towards the animal house. Running into the dark. It was no way to die.

33

A small shadowed creature sat in front of them near a floor light. When it saw them it shrieked and ran back towards the animal house.

'Was that a monkey?' Grace asked.

'The cages must have been locked open as well,' Harrigan said.

They ran into a huge and cavernous room lit by pale lights spaced at intervals high up on the walls. The lower half of the room was in deep shadow. On three sides, two tiers of glass cells rose up to the ceiling. A set of ladders and walkways gave access to these enclosures. The wall lights were reflected in the glass. Faintly visible in the centre of the room was a long and wide stainless-steel bench, set crosswise. The wall lights glimmered on its surface in the dark. There were no windows; no means of external light. A strong animal smell filled the room, a stench of urine and sweet rotting fruit. All the doors to the glass enclosures were open. The monkeys had climbed down into the room. Several sat on the steel bench, darker shapes against the shadows. They scattered when Grace and Harrigan ran into the room. There was the sound of rustling, of animal movement and hissing.

'Get down behind the bench,' Harrigan whispered. 'It'll give us some cover.'

They crouched down. Very soon afterwards they heard shrieking from just outside the doorway. 'Fuck you,' a voice muttered softly, angrily, followed by more shrieking and then silence. The door was lit more strongly than the rest of the room, the lights casting a square of low yellow light around it. DP appeared, shaking his head angrily. Immediately, he crouched down in the shadows out of their sight. There was a short pause, then words echoed bizarrely around the room. 'I'm waiting. You come to me, man.' The acoustics of the room were such that any sound carried clearly to all listeners. The words were followed by a deeper silence, as if the speaker realised quiet was his only option.

Harrigan hoped DP couldn't know they were there. They stayed still and silent as the room slowly filled again with the soft sounds of animals moving, small hissings, occasional shrieks. Harrigan tapped Grace on the shoulder. He wanted the gun; she gave it to him. She didn't need to be told he was going after DP. Still crouching, he moved to the end of the bench. Seen from Harrigan's perspective, DP was somewhere to the left of the doorway. In the darkness, Harrigan saw a fine blue light that shifted slightly while he watched. DP would be intent on that tiny bit of light. Harrigan knelt and aimed at the deeper shadow.

Suddenly there were running footsteps along the corridor. Before Harrigan could fire, Elena, seen briefly in the yellow light, the contract clutched in her hand, rushed inside the room at full speed. There was shrieking as Elena fell heavily to the floor, then more shrieks. She had collided with at least one monkey. Harrigan could not fire; she was between him and DP. There was a flurry of movement as several monkeys leapt up onto the bench and then down on the other side, climbing up the ladders and walkways that led to their cages.

'Get to the back,' DP hissed.

Elena scrambled to her feet and ran behind the bench. Harrigan was already there. Elena was about to call out when Grace got her in a hold, pressing her down on the floor with a hand over her mouth.

'What's that? Who's back there?' DP called, but there was no answer from Elena who was pinned to the floor by Grace.

Harrigan was back at the end of the bench but the blue light was gone. There was a brief waiting silence, then a shot flashed across the room in their direction. It cannoned into the glass, filling the room with a shattering sound, then further clatter as the broken glass hit the floor. Elena began to wrestle hard with Grace, scrabbling to get to the end of the bench. She made enough noise to be heard.

'There is someone. I know where you are, man. I'm coming for you.'

You do that, Harrigan thought. I'm waiting for you.

Intent on DP, he then realised that another figure was entering the room at speed, disappearing into the dark. A bright flashlight raked across the darkness above his head. It caught DP in its beam. Harrigan fired from a crouching position, almost with no time to aim. There was darkness again. DP gasped. Harrigan heard a clatter. DP had dropped his gun. Brinsmead was outlined against the door, then gone.

'Fuck you, man,' DP said.

'Danny, get down!' Sam shouted.

The two voices clashed.

'We've got a fish, Danny,' Sam called out. 'One you've wanted for a while. He's your protector, Elena. We've got him. You're screwed even with a gun. I'm going to see him burn like the others.'

'Jesus, man. You're not going to do that.'

Sam laughed.

Behind the bench, Elena stopped wrestling with Grace. She lay on the floor, breathing hard. She didn't have the contract with her. When she fell, it must have dropped from her hands and been lost in the dark. A monkey landed lightly on the bench just above their heads, peering down. In the shadows, there was the gleam of its eyes. By now Harrigan's vision was accustomed to the darkness. He saw moving shadows near the door.

'Crawl,' Brinsmead's voice said.

'Come on, man.'

'*Crawl!*'

'You take it all so fucking personally. It could have been any of us in there.'

In the dark, Harrigan moved close to Grace. He didn't trust Elena to be on their side if he took out either Brinsmead or Sam.

'We need to get DP's gun,' he whispered to Grace.

'I'll get it. I can shoot,' Elena said. 'My father taught me.'

'You'll shoot us,' Grace said softly.

'No,' she said.

362

'We can hear you back there,' Sam called in a slightly sing-song voice. 'Here we all are in the dark. You can't see us and we can't see you. Isn't that fun?'

Yes, I can, Harrigan thought. Again he was moving to the end of the bench when there was a struggle near the door, then a cry of pain from Brinsmead. DP was scrambling away in the dark.

'Get him!' Brinsmead shouted.

The torchlight flashed again, followed by a shot. DP was seen rolling away but not quickly enough to dodge a bullet. Sam was in outline to the side. Harrigan saw DP's gun in the centre of the floor. He had been reaching to it when the bullet hit. His blood was highlighted blue in the light against the floor. Harrigan fired at Sam but she had hit the ground. The room plunged into darkness again.

'Dead as a door nail,' Sam said, catching her breath. 'I wanted to drag it out.'

Harrigan fired in the direction of her voice but to no effect.

'Door, Danny! Now! Keep low.'

There were quick footsteps in the dark.

'What do we do?' Grace asked. 'Rush them?'

'They're probably planning to rush us. Let's get either side of the door. All of us. No point in anyone staying back here now. Someone get DP's gun.'

They moved forward in the shadows. A sustained flurry of shots from the door cracked over the benchtop. The monkeys shrieked and ran. Harrigan heard the crack of glass above his head; it fell to the floor beside him, splintering.

Sam appeared as a tall shadow in the dark, running towards him, the flashes from her gun lighting the room into disjointed sequences. Harrigan felt the bullets whiz past his head, he hit the floor. All the lights came on in one glaring burst. At the same time, a monkey landed full on Sam's face, panicking. It clung on.

'Get it off me,' Sam yelled, dragging at it with one hand.

Elena ran past Harrigan, grabbed DP's gun and shot Sam in the chest several times. Sam crumpled to the floor, the monkey still clinging to her shoulder. It was dead too.

Blinking in the light, Harrigan looked for Grace. She lay face down on the floor behind him, blood seeping from her head.

Suddenly, Brinsmead was in front of Elena, staring at her. He walked towards her slowly. She kept the gun on him. He had his own gun but was holding it by his side. She backed away, then stopped.

'You're not going to frighten me,' she said.

Harrigan turned Grace over. Her face was intact. A cut was scored along the side of her head through her hair but she was breathing. His terror subsided.

'What are you going to do, kill me?' Brinsmead was saying. 'I don't care. You've just killed my only true friend.'

'In self-defence,' Elena said. 'She was a cold-blooded murderer.'

'So are you.'

He was very close to Elena now. Slowly she kept moving backwards.

'Brinsmead, get away from her,' Harrigan shouted. He was on his feet but he was too late.

'Watch this, Elena. Live with this. Dream it for the rest of your life. You can't hide from this.'

Brinsmead fired, not at Elena but at himself. She staggered back, screaming. His blood stained her face and her clothing. Then he was falling to the floor with the rest of the dead.

Elena threw away her gun. She scrabbled at Sam's clothing. She had the flash drive. She looked around and found the contract against the wall.

Harrigan had turned Grace on her side so she could breathe and was trying to stop the bleeding from her wound. 'Never mind that,' he shouted at Elena. 'Help me here.'

But Elena was scrabbling at du Plessis, then she was gone.

34

Harrigan had no choice: he went after Elena. He wasn't going to have her lock them in the animal house while she cleaned up around her. Outside, at the juncture of the corridors, he couldn't see which way she had gone. Then something occurred to him. He ran upstairs to the laboratory. She was there, standing in front of a wall furnace. The lights and the thermostat indicated it was on at a very high temperature. He grabbed her by the arm and pulled her away.

'You can't open it,' she said. 'It's locked and I'm not going to open it for you. It's very hot in there. If you could open it, you'd burn yourself badly.'

He looked around. Not only had she burned the contract, she had cleaned up the cage with its dead mice and pieces of grain and presumably thrown them in there as well.

'You've won,' he said. 'Even if you had to kill a string of people to do it.'

She turned on him. Her hair and clothes were still covered in blood. 'I killed one woman in self-defence because I had to. What have I supposedly won? I'm a businesswoman with assets to protect. That's all I've done.'

'When we were down in that animal house, you didn't tell us those lights were going to come on. You would have let us die in there to protect yourself.'

'I saved all our lives by removing a killer.'

'You tried to alert your own paid killer to where we were. What was du Plessis doing here?'

'Wasn't he with them? I don't know him.'

'When you got away from Sam, why didn't you reverse the lockdowns? Was it because you knew DP was coming and you wanted to give him a chance to get on with the job?'

'I had to hide in the dark. If I'd gone to my office, she would have found me.'

'How did he get past the front gate, let alone open the emergency exit from the outside? Sam said you were the only one who could do that.'

'No, Daniel could have set that up. Maybe he was trapping that man as well as us. Anyway, how do you know he got in that way?'

'I saw it happen. I bet you'd reached breaking point. When was it? The day I was here and Daniel told me loud and clear the kind of information I would find in the Pittwater contract? I bet you told DP to get after him as soon as he could. What did you do? Tell the guards at the gate that no matter what happened, they were to let him in? What did you take off DP just now? His mobile? You gave him the code to open the door. You said, get Brinsmead out of my life once and for all, I don't care what it involves. Get rid of his body. This wouldn't be the only furnace in this place. Or maybe he was supposed to make it look like suicide.'

'If you repeat what you've just said in public, I'll sue you until you have nothing left to stand up in. Now leave me alone.'

'I need a phone. I need to call an ambulance and I need backup. This place will be swarming with police and you'll have to put up with it.'

'Believe me, I'll cooperate. I always cooperate with the police. You can use my office.'

They walked in silence down to her office, each withdrawing from the other's presence. She took a mobile phone out of a drawer in her desk and threw it to him without looking at him.

'Where's your other phone?' he asked.

'Still in her pocket.'

The *her* was said with detestation.

'We'll take it in and examine it for evidence.'

'Go ahead. I don't care if you do.'

Of course she didn't. If she had received a cryptic message from her hired killer, it would be sourced to someone or something innocent.

He started to make his calls. She sat at her desk and began to work on her computer.

'What are you doing?' he asked.

'Reversing the lockdowns.'

'Leave the doors open in this sector.'

'I have to close the animal house.'

He leaned over her desk. 'Grace is in there. Leave it open. If you close that door, you'll regret it. Now, I've got people on the way, they'll need to talk to you. Just sit here. Don't worry, I won't come anywhere near you if I don't have to. Believe me.'

He walked out without looking back. Then he stopped. Nothing was happening the way it had when Sam had made Elena do the lockdowns the first time around.

'What were you really just doing?' he asked.

'Nothing.'

'You've just wiped out Brinsmead's personal files, haven't you? Just in case there's something in there that incriminates you.'

'I'm going to reverse the lockdowns now. This is my office. Get out.'

He ignored her and waited while she continued to work on her computer. This time, the lights briefly went out and came on again, the air conditioning changed. The doors stayed open. She didn't look at him. Once she'd finished, she picked up her phone to make a call. Even without washing the blood off her face, she was putting the essentials in place. Harrigan leaned forward and took the phone out of her hand.

'You owe me your life,' he said.

'You owe me yours.'

'No. I told you it was a suicide pact. I gave you the time to manipulate the lockdown. Upstairs, I dragged you out of the way of Sam's bullet. I would have saved your neck in there if you'd bothered to cooperate with us. Because you didn't, someone I care about almost got killed. You have something I want. You'll remember. You tried to use it once to blackmail me. If you have any decency at all, you'll send it to me.'

'Decency!'

'If you don't, I'll walk out of here thinking you're nothing but a piece of rubbish, Dr Calvo. I thought you told me you always fulfilled your business obligations, no matter what.'

He left without looking back.

By the time the paramedics were wheeling her out to the ambulance, Grace had woken up. She moved her head one way and then stopped.

'Don't move,' the paramedic said.

'I can't, my head hurts too much.' She looked at Harrigan. 'You're blurry. Is it really you?'

'I'm still here, believe me,' he said. 'I'll come and see you in hospital as soon as I can.'

'You have work to do,' she said to him in a soft, drifting voice.

He did have work to do. By the time the police got there, Elena had called in her lawyers. They arrived before the forensic team and were escorted in by one of the security guards from the front desk. Harrigan didn't speak to her again. He organised the crime scene, directed the allocation of jobs. Throughout this, the police left the emergency exits open, moving in and out. As a result, numbers of the monkeys made their escape out of the building. Others were dead. The forensic team marked where their carcasses lay. Harrigan watched as the human dead were taken away. This is futile, he thought. It means nothing. *Nada*.

He left the scene as soon as he could. At the main gate, the media was assembled *en masse*. He drove through the crowds, heading for Liverpool Hospital where Grace was. Several crews followed him. There were uniformed police on duty at the hospital. Harrigan told them to keep the media out whatever else they did. Grace was in Emergency. She managed faintly to raise an eyebrow at him.

'You got here,' she said. 'They're talking about scanning my brain. I told them it's probably pea-sized but they should be able to find it if they look hard enough.'

'You're alive. I didn't have to see you with a bullet in your head. I don't care about anything else.'

'Not even about the job?'

'No,' he said. 'I don't.'

He realised that for the first time in his working life, this was probably true.

35

The medical staff moved Grace to Royal North Shore Hospital and told Harrigan she would be there for several weeks while they assessed any possible damage. He visited her every day. For the rest of the time, he worked at his job with one aim in mind: setting up the investigation so it could run without his daily involvement. He spoke to ASIO, made statements, worked through the evidence with Trevor and his senior people. Any information concerning Falcon's operations was classified, they were told. It could only be presented in a closed court and now there was no one left alive to try. After consultations with all parties, the commissioner's directive was to close the Pittwater case as soon as possible and let the dead bury the dead. The investigation into the murder of Senator Edwards, his adviser and a police guard remained in the hands of the AFP and was continuing. Harrigan looked at the bald facts and knew they would not even get close to Elena Calvo.

Harrigan knew she had won most comprehensively when he received a phone call from Millennium Forensic Technologies.

'We have ASIO on the premises,' the owner said. 'They want the plant specimens you gave me and also any information I have on the subject. All my notes, all my test results, everything. Do I give it to them?'

'I don't think you have any choice,' Harrigan replied. 'I can't stop them.'

Harrigan rang Stephen Grey, the only useful contact he had in ASIO. He was almost surprised when Grey took his call.

'We're seizing those specimens and that information on behalf of our counterparts in Britain,' he said. 'It's been authorised at the highest levels in both governments. All that evidence will be sent to London.'

'Why is that necessary? We can do a very professional analysis here.'

'I haven't been made privy to the reason,' Grey replied. 'I've been told that the data attached to those specimens is classified as top secret. I can't give you any more information than that.'

'Those specimens are obviously connected to the operation around Brinsmead and Jonas. Why is it necessary to close this analysis down? On the face of it, it has nothing to do with the events in the DRC.'

'There are still issues of secrecy involved. I think you should also realise that once those specimens are gone, that will be the end of your people's involvement concerning anything to do with Brinsmead, Jonas or these plants. I have no more information than that to give you. Good morning.'

Toby was also still in hospital. Without his computer, he had to pen their one-sided conversations with his single hand.

'I want you to know that I didn't leave you to die,' Harrigan said. 'I did everything I could to get you back.'

That man wanted something for me, Dad. Something important. I heard him say so. Did you give it to him?

'Yes, but he didn't keep his word. He left you in that car park to die. Grace found you on a tipoff. There's something else I think you should know. Someone made me an offer to research you personally. To try and find a way to repair some of the things that don't work the way we'd like them to. I said no before I asked you what you wanted.'

What do they want you to do?

'That's not the point.'

Yes, it is. They wouldn't be doing something like that for nothing. They must want something from you. What is it?

'That's my side of it. I want to know what you think.'

Are they going to find a cure for me? No, they're not. Maybe twenty years from now, maybe never. I've read about these things. No one's thought about them more than me. They're asking me to hope. I'm not going to do that. I'm not having anyone getting into my head for things I might never be able to have. I'll keep wanting to be something I'm not and then I won't do anything with my life. I'll never be happy.

'You're happy now. Is that what you're telling me?'

I make my life work. Yes, I am in my own way.

'Good,' Harrigan said. 'I'm glad.'

Later, he shredded this sheet of paper down the men's toilet. His actions in trying to get his son back remained what they had always been: a matter of necessity, something unquestionable.

Harrigan had other obligations to fulfil. As soon as he could, he asked the commissioner for a recommencement of his leave. The commissioner offered him the time while reminding him that he was still waiting on his application for a senior position. Harrigan spent the evening staring at a blank computer screen before giving up and deciding to write it later.

The next day he flew to Wagga, then hired a car to drive out to Yaralla. To Harrigan's mind, Harold had a right to a visit and a personal explanation. The heat shimmered off the roads during the uneventful drive. At the junction of the Coolemon Road and Naradhan Creek Bridge, Harrigan pulled up behind a small truck that was crossing the Creek Lane in front of him and then drove up Harold's track to the farmhouse. Harrigan waited until their dust had settled before following. In the yard, he pulled up next to where they'd parked. Written on the door of the cabin in fading and scratched green paint were the words *Coolemon Fencing Contractors*. Harold was talking to the two men who had got out.

'I'll be with you as soon as I can, mate,' he called out to Harrigan. 'Ambro's inside. Go in and have a beer while you're waiting.'

Ambrosine was in the kitchen, which was no tidier or cleaner than it had been when Harold had been doing the cooking. She got him a can of Melbourne Bitter out of the fridge, then sat down and joined him, lighting up a cigarette. Harrigan could hear her children playing noisily in the hallway.

'What's all that about outside?' he asked.

'Harry's getting his fences fixed. He's just sorting out a few details.'

'How come he can afford to do that?'

She grinned at him. 'You're not the only one with contacts, mate. Let me tell you something. Little Joe's not coming after me any more. I've been talking to Mad Dog.'

'He talks to you, does he?'

'I've tattooed his whole fucking back, mate. That's not little. Yeah, he does talk to me. Little Joe's gone off to America somewhere. Maybe LA but no one's sure. He's been fucking Mad Dog's old lady. He had to leave quick smart.'

'What happened to her?' Harrigan asked.

'She went with him. They're not coming back in a hurry, not unless they want to die. You know, Mad Dog never liked Mike. He had it in for him. He wasn't too sad to hear he was dead. He said if I gave him a tattoo free — one of my good ones — I could put my head above ground. So I asked for a favour as well.'

'What sort of favour?'

Ambrosine laughed. 'I said a good friend of mine was being screwed around by old Stewie Morrissey and, to make matters worse, it was his own brother. He was hanging on to money that was really Harry's. If they could get it out of him, they could take their cut as well. So Mad Dog and his mates dropped round to say hello. I wish I could have seen Stewie's face when he opened the door and saw them there.'

'Did you get the money?'

'Oh yeah. It was nice lot of money with no strings attached. Harry's getting a lot of work done. He's feeling better than he has for a while.'

'What are you going to do? Stay here?'

'Yeah, for a bit. The kids are happy. I'm going to open a tattoo parlour in Coolemon. Harry's put some cash aside for me to do that. I can make a bit of money and I want to start teaching Laurie. He's got talent. He's like his dad.'

Hopefully he'd have a better fate, Harrigan thought.

Harold arrived and they walked out onto the veranda for a chat.

'How are your hands?' Harrigan asked.

'They're getting there.' Harold held them up to show they were healing. 'Mate, I'm not too interested in chasing after Stewie over what he was doing out there. I'm working out ways to clean up that bit of land. If I can, I'm going to plant some trees. You say that whole affair, whatever it was, is finished with now. I want to put it behind me. Things are looking up at the moment. I want it to stay that way.'

Harrigan's people had interviewed Stuart Morrissey several times since their first encounter but with limited success. It had been another stumbling block in the investigation. Few people could stonewall like old Stewie, except presumably when he was dealing with Mad Dog and his bikie mates.

'Ambro told me,' Harrigan said. 'Stewie owes you that money.'

Harold shrugged. 'It's half his property as well. If it's building the place up, he shouldn't complain. Are you staying for dinner tonight?'

'No, mate. Flying visit.'

'You're always working.'

On his way back to Wagga, Harrigan turned onto the Creek Lane. Ambrosine's cottage was still a pile of ash. Half a kilometre further along, he stopped near Cassatt's grave and got out of his car, then scrambled down into the dry creek bed. The narrow trench was still there. Its fading outlines showed the tracks of animals searching for water, while around about the ants were building their nests. The silence was intense and the mid-afternoon heat had an iron grip. Everything was stilled under the hard blue arc of the sky and the pure clarity of the Australian light. There was no sound of the gunshot he had been waiting to hear for a dozen years. It had faded into silence with the Ice Cream Man's death. Finally, the violence in his life had played itself out.

The day after he'd got back to Birchgrove, a courier delivered a parcel to him. When he opened it, he found himself in possession of the contents of the Ice Cream Man's safety deposit box. The accusation that she had failed to meet a business obligation had got under Elena Calvo's skin more than being called a murderer. He destroyed the tape and the tie immediately and cleaned the gun. Then he went down to his cellar where he took a rusted metal cash box out from behind a sandstone block.

Upstairs in his kitchen, he opened the box and took out the gun which, years ago, his father had used to shoot his mother. Until now he had kept it as his own memorial to her. He wrapped both guns in plastic and stuck it down with masking tape. After midnight, he went out, walking around Snails Bay past the oval and down Louisa Road to Long Nose Point. He stood on the old ferry wharf looking out at the river. It was deep here. Pleasure craft cruised by; he heard the laughing voices of people on board, the drifting sounds of music. Then there were no more boats, the stretch of water was empty. He threw both guns as far out across the river as he could. He heard them hit the water. They would sink without a trace and take the past with them.

In the dark, he sat on the public jetty and watched the water lap around the wooden steps. When had it ever been his own life? When had the decisions been his and his alone? Had he ever decided for himself what he wanted from his life or had all those decisions been made for him by other people?

He walked back into his house and went up into his study. He sat at his desk and looked at Goya's prints on the wall. *One can't look*, the caption said, showing villagers about to be massacred by unseen soldiers.

He reached for a sheet of paper and began to write a letter of resignation. The words came to him easily, he wrote without making a single correction. Then he typed it up as an email and sent it, aware when he pressed the Send button that there was no way back. Despite the lateness of the hour, he went out and posted the handwritten version by snail mail. It was his life. For the first time, it was his own life.

The next morning, he went back into his study, opened his safe and checked those pieces of the plant specimens he still had in his keeping. When he first put them in here, he had opened the plastic bags to let them breathe. They had dehydrated but were otherwise intact. He locked the safe again and left them where they were.

Out on the net, he surfed into the Human Rights Watch website. It had collected all the information relating to the Pittwater killings and posted its own theory of what had happened. It was a perceptive analysis that hinted at a possible involvement by the Calvos but was careful not to invite any legal threats. Their home page had a pointer to the video Daniel Brinsmead had posted on the net. *Do you have any information about this video? If so, please contact us.* Other similar websites had done the same thing and posted this same request. Harrigan hit the Contact Us button and began to write an email.

The commissioner rang, hoping the email he had received from Harrigan was a mistake. Could he be persuaded to change his mind? For Harrigan, saying no had never felt sweeter.

It was Grace's first full day out of hospital and he went to meet her for lunch. She arrived at the café on Darling Street just as he did. She had cut her hair short, which made her look even more striking. Her face was pale and finely lined after her weeks in hospital.

'You look beautiful,' he said. 'It's different but it suits you.'

'I had to cut it,' she said. 'I couldn't go around with one side short and one side long.'

They sat outside. The waiter came and took their order. As he was leaving, he picked up the ashtray.

'No,' Harrigan said, 'we'll need that.'

'No, we won't,' Grace said. 'I've stopped smoking as of today. I'm never going to have another cigarette.'

Hallelujah, Harrigan thought. 'Isn't that a bit sudden?' he asked. 'Shouldn't you get some Nicorette to deal with the cravings?'

'No, it's best to go cold turkey. I've thrown away every last cigarette together with my lighter.'

'I've got some news for you as well,' he said. 'I've resigned. I sent my resignation in last night. It was accepted with regret this morning.'

She couldn't believe it.

'It's not possible,' she said. 'You won't survive. What are you going to do?'

'I'm going into business for myself. As a consultant. I've got a lot of knowledge, I know a lot of people and I know how the system works. I can tell people how they can get things done, how to protect themselves. I've already got something moving. I'm going to be a free man for the first time in my life.'

The waiter came with their coffees. Harrigan had ordered a long black, she had asked for a decaffeinated flat white.

'That's great,' she said.

Both the expression on her face and her tone of voice said the opposite.

'What is it? Is there something you haven't told me? Are you going to recover? You said the prognosis was good.'

'No, the doctors said I was very lucky. I should be okay. They just have to keep an eye on me for a while.'

She wasn't looking at him directly.

'Grace, why aren't you smoking? And why did you order decaf? You hate it.'

She glanced around and then back at him. 'I'm pregnant,' she said.

'When did that happen?'

'The night you took out my kitchen tiles,' she said, giving him that look of hers. 'I was going to fix everything in the morning. I never got the chance.'

'What do you want to do?'

'I've binned my cigarettes, Paul, and I'm drinking this stuff. What do you want to do?'

Harrigan had always had an eye for the main chance. 'We can do this together. You could move in with me.'

'Well,' she said a little breathlessly, 'you could move in with me.'

'You, me and a baby are going to live in your little pocket handkerchief?'

'There's probably enough room for a bassinet if I move the guitar off the top of the wardrobe,' she said.

There was a pause.

'What happens if after five years we decide we hate each other?' she asked.

'Why don't we worry about that five years from now?'

They looked at each other. He thought of Toby and of a child who could walk.

'Go on, Grace,' he said. 'I've just jumped out into mid-air. You can do it too. Be brave.'

'You always tell me I'm too brave.'

'Prove me right.'

'All right. I'll be brave.'

ACKNOWLEDGMENTS

My thanks to everyone for their generous advice, interest and time. For their information, advice and demonstration of the art of tattooing: eX de Medici; the staff and research students at the Division of Pacific and Asian History at the Research School of Pacific and Asian Studies at ANU; and Deus Ex Machina of North Lyneham.

Ron and Deborah Gilchrist for their hospitality.

Dr Carol Nottenburg for her advice on patents.